An Indian Princess

Thomas Kidwell

Proudly Published in the USA

Other books by this author

Novels:

"Above The Red"© 2013 ISBN 978-1-4817-6761-3
"Loweja"© 2013 ISBN 978-1-5306-0421-0
"A Certain Superstition"© 2013 ISBN 978-1-4817-6765-1
"A Parting Of The Clouds"© 2013 978-1-62994-687-0
"The Wolves Of Calamity"© 2013 ISBN 978-1-5301-3775-6
"Beyond Absolution"© 2014 ISBN 978-1-4897-0215-9
"Lang's Paradox"© 2016 ISBN 978-1-5300-6138-9
"Forever Will - From The Ashes Of War"© 2014
ISBN 978-1-4897-0343-9
"A Thousand Miles From Here"© 2014 ISBN in production
"Running The Distance"© 2016 ISBN 978-1-5300-6474-8
"Taylorstown"© 2015 ISBN in production
"Joseph"© 2016 ISBN 978-1-5238-8841-2
"Saddletramp" © 2016 ISBN 978-1530315451
"Stonemill"© 2016 ISBN 978-1-5300-9848-4

Non-Fiction:

"Just Another Old Bowhunter"© 2009 ISBN 978-0-692-00281-0
"Another Old Bowhunter"© 2010 ISBN 978-1-4575-0977-3
"The American Feral Hog"© 2012 ISBN 978-1-4575-1405-0
"First Footsteps West"© 2013 ISBN in production

Copyright© 2011
All rights reserved

Edited by John Stockman, USMC, Ret.
Content Edited by Dr. David Landis

Although the characters, places, and events portrayed herein have been inspired by true events, and actual places, the content is intended to be conveyed as entirely fictional. Any resemblance to actual people or places is purely coincidental. The vintage stock photographs and drawings are displayed merely to remind the reader of the attire of the period, and not intended to represent any of the characters portrayed herein.

Table of Contents

Prologue 7
My Darling, Elizabeth 23
St. Louis 39
The Outpost 63
On the Trail 105
A Chance Encounter 131
A Most Unusual Cure 157
The Passage Home 193
Fort Saint Joseph 221
We are back! 247
Lectūschemă 295
Life in the Valley of Love 301
Home Again 319
The Weasel in the Henhouse 343
Visitors 391
A Valley Rendezvous 421

Prologue

The veins in the old man's hands were pronounced and leathery, appearing as dark lavender streaks below the surface of his toughened skin. He lay there on a bed in my home... a bed which we both knew to be his death bed. His eyes had become narrow slits which barely enabled him to see objects and people, but only when they were very close to him. Sitting beside his bed, I held his hand and looked down upon his yellowish fingernails and his crooked, swollen knuckles and wondered what work he had done with these hands in his life. He had obviously used these hands for many years to perform hard labor of some type, but for what other purposes had he used these hands? Had he used these hands to serve the good of his fellow man, or had he used them to practice wickedness? Had these hands ever been used to take the life of another man? Perhaps these hands had been used to save lives. Perhaps they have been used for the betterment of mankind. I did not know. I wished that I could have seen these hands when they were younger... and when I was younger. I wished that I could have known these hands when I was a child. Perhaps these hands had held me at some time when I was just an infant, yet they had never been there to comfort me in the years of my adolescence. They were not there to guide and direct me as I grew to become a man. They were not there for me to hold when I had needed them so badly.

There were scars on these old hands – scars which each bore silent witness to some event, or some part, of which collectively were the story of this man's life... Yet the scars could not speak, and as much as I yearned to know more about this man, knowledge of his life story would remain something which I was denied. The old man's hair was white and thin with age, and his face bore testimony to many years of exposure to the elements of nature. Whatever these hands had done, and whatever these eyes had seen, it was clearly evident that hard labor had been a constant presence in this man's life. He lay here, before me, on the threshold of exchanging his earthly, worn and frail body, for a spiritual journey into the unknown. His would be an ascent from his mortal hurts and pains into a place where he could hopefully find eternal heavenly comfort. I prayed for his salvation and his liberation from all the torments of life on earth. I studied the features of his face, and wondered what he must have looked like as a younger man. I speculated that he must have looked somewhat like me when he was younger, for there was a strong family resemblance. However, this was mere speculation, for I did not know this man as my father. He was but a stranger in my home. He was a person unknown to me. I imagined what it would have been like to have had him in my life. Would he have been kind and compassionate? Would he have smiled at me occasionally, patted me on the head, and said "*I love you, son*" when I needed to hear it?

    I did not know this man who lay before me, yet I loved him. He was my father. How could I *not* love him? He had produced the seed from which I came to be. Yet, I could not completely pardon him for the sins which he had committed against my mother and me, and in my heart I knew that abandonment of one's family was indeed a sin. He was not there for me as a child, during the years that I had continually longed for him to magically appear in our doorway one day. He had never been there as a husband for my mother. He was not there when my mother had breathed her last, to aid and comfort her… or me. He had always been a mysterious, abstract figure in my life. He was a person whom I had known to exist, yet could not see, and could not touch. I could not even remember his face. He had paid money over the years of his absence which had more than amply provided for mother and me, but he had denied us the satisfaction and comfort of his presence in our lives. He was naught but an anonymous benefactor, a person of unknown identity, and a curious missing element from our lives... especially mine. But he was my father, and as such, I loved him.

By my reckoning, and from what Mother had told me, he was but sixty-one or sixty-two years of age now, yet he appeared to be a much older man. Perhaps the work which he had attended during his lifetime had caused him to age prematurely. His life had always been a series of unanswered questions for me – an enigma – a phantasm. And even now, as he lay here before me, dying in my home, I still had no answers with which to satisfy all of my many questions. All that I had was the body of an old man who was clinging precariously to his final moments of life.

He had arrived at my house by coach, with a slightly younger gentleman, just two days earlier. Unable to speak, and obviously dying, the younger gentleman simply said that my father wanted to come home to die, and look upon me once again before he breathed his last. Despite my anger and frustration with the mysterious gentleman, he would offer no further information. I didn't even have the benefit of learning the stranger's name, or how to contact him. He helped me carry Father and his few belongings into my house, where we placed him on a bed, and then the strange man vanished, as quickly and as quietly as he had appeared, leaving my father's frail and sickly body in an upstairs bedchamber. I summoned a physician immediately, who only confirmed what I already knew. My father was about to die at any time. The physician assured me that there was nothing that could be done to delay his death. He said that I should expect his departure at any moment, and then he, too, left my home.

I held Father's hand in mine, awaiting his inevitable departure and expecting him to expire at any moment, when the narrow slits in his eyes widened momentarily, and his lips softly said the first words that I ever remembered hearing from my father. His voice was weak, and he was obviously putting forth a great deal of effort to speak. Between sprees of coughing, my name was the first discernable word which flowed from his lips.

"John... John?"

"Yes, Father. It is me, John, and I'm here, beside you." He looked at me for a moment, seeking to identify the face which was responsible for my voice. For a brief instant, he seemed surprised by the man which I had grown to be... as if he had expected to see a much younger and smaller man. Perhaps he had even anticipated seeing a child again... these many years later.

"I'm sorry, John... I'm sorry for the life that I had to live away from you, my son... I'm sorry for the suffering that my absence must have caused you and your mother. Please forgive me, son... please."

"I too, am sorry, yet I *do* forgive you, Father. I really do, but ultimate forgiveness is not mine to grant. Would you like for me to summon a priest, to hear your confession?"

"No, son, I have confessed my sins at Saint Michael's before I was brought here to your house."

"Is there anything that I can do for you, Father? Is there anything I can do which might bring you comfort?"

"My satchel! My God, where's my satchel?"

"Do not worry... it's over here, Father."

"Oh, thank God! Hand it to me, please, John. There's something I must show you before I die. Quickly, my son!"

I retrieved his weather-scarred leather satchel, embossed with his initials, from among the few belongings which he had, and handed it to him. Holding the satchel closely to his chest, he looked at me with weary eyes which he barely managed to keep open, and said, "When I am gone, I want you to read what's inside. You will find maps and directions to... the... fortune that... I spent my life finding. It's yours now, John. Please believe me, son... I have always loved you."

"I do believe you, Father, and even though I have never known you, I have always loved you, as well. I am compelled to ask you a question which has been at the forefront of my mind for my entire life… Why did you abandon Mother and I? I was not even two years old, Father! Why?"

"In the beginning… I was driven… by… (*coughing*) by my own selfish… greed. To make a fortune… but then I found an even greater treasure… one which… I had not expected… one which I could not bring back to Baltimore…"

"What fortune could have possibly benefited you more than being here, among those who loved you?"

"John… John… my son…"

"Father?"

"Stee…….. Sha…….. Nay………"

"What? I do not understand you, Father…"

"*Necu-ta-say-ha*, John…"

"*Necu-ta-say-ha*? What do those strange words mean, Father?"

My question was answered only by more coughing, labored breathing, and then a relaxed limpness of his hand which I held. Without answering my question, his eyes returned to narrow slits and he struggled for a final breath. My question would remain unanswered forever, for a few minutes later he expelled one final breath and was gone from this life. I sat there for a few moments staring at the lifeless body of this man who lay before me… wondering if he had found peace and comfort, and wondering where his spiritual journey was taking him now. I held his eyelids closed momentarily until they set, and remained closed. I thought of all of the unanswered questions, and although he had been absent from most of my life, I regretted his passing. Death is a permanent circumstance. As much as I wanted to hear answers to my questions, I knew there would never be answers now. My father had taken the answers with him when he passed.

After pulling a bedsheet over his face, I put his satchel back with his other belongings and walked out into the streets of Baltimore to summon the mortician, much as I had done when Mother had passed a year and a half earlier, and in that very same bed. I would have liked to have spent some more time with this man who was purportedly my father... to have learned something about the mysterious reasons which kept him apart from Mother and me. He had not provided me with any of the answers which I had so desperately craved. In fact, quite the contrary was true, as I now had more questions in my mind than I had prior to our all-to-brief conversation. And what fortune could he have been speaking of? What did he mean when he said that it was mine now? And what were those strange sounding word which he uttered at last, "*Necu-ta-say-ha?*"

I buried Father next to my mother's grave in the cemetery behind Saint Michael's Cathedral. My fiancée, Elizabeth, was in attendance for the simple burial and brief commemorative service, yet she had watched the short, cursory service from her coach, rather than stand by my side during the proceedings. Our Priest and I were the only two persons at graveside when his casket was lowered into the dark earth. The Priest had known my father in earlier years, yet he made no comment other than to say that he and Father were merely, "*casual*" acquaintances when he was in his years of young Priesthood. Two cemetery employees unconcernedly waited nearby to bury Father's coffin once we had left, and I thought; '*what poor tribute this is to a man's life, that he should be so uncelebrated and alone at the very service which was supposed to commemorate his life, as well as his inglorious passing.*'

I paused in my prayers momentarily, and gazed up at Elizabeth's coach. She appeared to be bored as she waited for me, and I asked myself, '*Am I the only person on this earth to mourn this man's passing? Perhaps not,*' I thought, '*but I certainly appear to be the only person in Baltimore.*' Before Father had arrived at my home, I knew almost nothing about him. Now, his body was in a casket and dirt was being shoveled upon him for eternity. I stood there alone, still knowing almost nothing of this man who called himself my father. He was but an enigma, a ghost who had left me to be alone with my thoughts and questions. All opportunities to obtain answers to my many questions had died with him. Perhaps the only clue to his mysterious past may lie within the soiled leather satchel which he had brought to my house and entrusted to me. Having paid my final respects, I turned from his grave and walked away.

    A full two weeks had passed after Father had died before I poured a glass of wine one evening and sat down near an oil lamp to inspect the contents of the satchel. I tried to remember the strange words which he had spoken to me just before he died, but they had escaped me. I looked into the satchel and began to retrieve some of the items inside. The contents were an odd assortment of letters, sealed envelopes, maps, and strange lists, which appeared to be supply manifests of some sort. There were a few quill pens inside, a small, sealed bottle of ink, and a blotting pad and blotting powder. I sat there with my wine, took another sip, and began to inspect the documents more closely. In the very front, there was an envelope addressed to me. The mysterious letter inside was from my father, and dated nine months earlier.

John Welch   *Third day of July, 1832*
Canterbury House
Baltimore, Maryland

John,

Please do not think poorly of me for my absence from the lives of you and your mother. It is my hope that you may one day learn the true cause of my absence.

I have discovered a far place in the Northwest Territory which contains vast riches in gold. It is my desire that you acquire as much as you wish from this place, in order that you may return to your home and live a comfortable life with the family that you will one day have. With these riches, it is my hope that you may prosper in your life without ever having to leave your family behind as I did. Be aware that there are riches in life which are far greater than gold. You may discover them some day, and I hope and pray that you do. Do not forfeit the greater treasure by surrendering yourself to the lesser.

You will find directions and instruction within this satchel which will lead you to this place. There is also sufficient money within my satchel to fund your expedition. I am the only man alive who knows the location of this fortune. If you are reading this, then I too have passed from this life. Others are aware that this fortune exists, and will therefore not hesitate to bring harm to you in order to learn of its location. Trust no one. Confide in no one. Always be aware that enemies will become your enemies once I have died, and they may be anywhere about you. God keep you safe, and may the wealth I found there bring you happiness.

William H. Welch

In the privacy of my study, a rather intriguing and inviting prospective lay manifest before me. If Father's manuscripts were to be taken quite literally, there was a possibly of acquiring great wealth, and it had been mysteriously delivered to my very doorstep by my own father. Why would an opportunity such as this be presented to me? Did Father deem me worthy of such great generosity? Was it because of Father's great love for me that he would present me with such promising prosperity? Spare me the thought! With no lingering ill thoughts directed at my father, if my father had any great love for me, at some point during his twenty year absence he would have succumbed to a desire to see me, and it doesn't seem that it would have been such a terrible inconvenience for him to have visited me once or twice over the years to inquire of my wellbeing, if nothing else. At the very least, he could have written me, in order that we might establish some token degree of familiarity in our relationship as father and son. I would have delighted in corresponding with him. But no, he had not chosen to do that. Instead, he chose to exclude me from his life; to cast me aside as if my existence was but an inconsequential triviance to him. He chose to allow me to mature into manhood without the benefit of his companionship... his guidance... his reassurance... and his love; either of which I would have much preferred to embrace than his regular annual monetary symbol of atonement. I had been abandoned by him, save for his financial ingratiation of Mother and me. It was as simple as that. Is any of the information contained within this satchel to be taken literally? These may very well be the writings of a madman, for all that I know. I knew naught of his character, save for the few things that Mother had told me. These letters and manuscripts may be the random scribblings of a frail old man, whose mind had been consumed and tormented by his guilt of twenty years. Nevertheless, because Father had thought the information worthy enough to deliver in person during his final precious moments on earth, I decided that I would blindly place my trust in both the documents and his words, without reservation or skepticism. I would fully assume that everything which he had written was the absolute truth. At which time I should encounter a situation or a circumstance which teaches me otherwise, I would dismiss all confidence in his words, cease further efforts, and attribute all of Father's writings to the mere fantasies of a dying old man. After all... despite my resentment for his abandonment of me for twenty years, he was still my father.

    I sat there in my study and evaluated my situation. Father had arranged for a generous endowment years earlier which had provided Mother and me with an unpretentious, yet comfortable lifestyle here in Baltimore. There was nothing particular which I longed for in life, or so it would seem as I studied Father's notes. Supposedly, I had arrived at a good station in life. My fiancée was from a rather wealthy and prestigious family here in Baltimore. Thanks to my Father's endowment, I had received a proper education at George Washington University, where I had met my fiancée, and was currently considering several options which could offer a possible means of self-support for my future, and the security of my future family, if there was to be one. More than anything, I believed that I was hopelessly restless and too unsettled to seek a permanent vocation at that time. My mind seemed to wander about on random occasions, as if my inner being was in search of a meaningful purpose for my existence... something to justify my being here on earth. I lacked a feeling of security, and the reassuring confidence which drives an individual toward an ultimate goal in life. I had achieved many great things academically in college, yet in my life outside of the university I had achieved nothing meaningful at all. Early in life I had felt cheated, because I did not have a father like the other children. I was often teased by other boys in crass manners, knowing that they would never have to reckon with my father's defense or retribution. I toughened myself soon in life, however, and fought back... viciously. I found pleasure in taking my young frustrations out on those who would attempt to anger me. Soon, my classmates came to realize that if they wanted to taunt me, and tease me, there would be painful consequences. I often emerged the loser in these boyish brawls, but my opponents never walked away unscathed. Nay, they paid a price for their misconduct. In older childhood, the teasing ceased, and I became well known as an individual who was eager to embrace the fight... an adversary to be wary of. I suppose that it was my way of seeking a small measure of recompense from the world at large.

  My life continued to lack fulfillment and direction as I eventually grew into a young man... a stigma which I carried with me into young adulthood. Here before me now, it seemed, was an opportunity to obtain several things which had always been absent in my life. There was a possibility for me to achieve sustained wealth, if there really was any truth to Father's claim, and an opportunity for some adventure of sorts, and the opportunity to satisfy my father's dream by completing his mysterious mission in life. To escape the doldrums of Baltimore in quest of an ambiguous future only served to intrigue me. The idea of doing so within the passion of some sort of adventurous journey intrigued me even more. Perhaps I could find what my inner self seemed to be searching for. I had always entertained a passion for challenges, and to embark on a mission such as this would certainly present the epitome of all challenges, I thought. I had no family about me who relied on my immediate presence for their wellbeing. In fact, I had no surviving family at all. I had no obligations that would prevent my participating in a mission such as this, save for my recent betrothal to the daughter of a socially prominent shipping magnate here in Baltimore. I would give this venture its due consideration, for I found myself fascinated by the allure of seeing this great wilderness area which everyone called the *Northwest Territories*. Tales of this wondrous place had been an active topic on everyone's lips since the "*Corps of Discovery Expedition*."

I firmly decided that I would discuss the issue of a prolonged absence with my fiancée, Elizabeth, and arrive at a decision in a timely manner. It now being late February, I knew that a journey such as this would be out of the question once Elizabeth and I had wed, so the only possible time which would accommodate an endeavor such as this, would be if I were to leave Baltimore rather hastily, in order that I should return by the date of our October wedding. On the evening of the third morrow, I was obligated to dine with my fiancée and her father. We would discuss the issue then, and I would make a final decision.

I had never traveled to the west any farther than

Morgantown. Aside from what I had read in the newspapers and the library, I had little idea of what to expect or prepare for. While the idea intrigued me, I had obtained sufficient wisdom in my twenty-two years of life to know that a journey of this nature would require a great deal of knowledge on the subject of wilderness travel, and a great deal of preparation as well. I visited an old family friend, *Marcus Attenborough*, who had at one time been in the employment of the American Fur Company in the Northwest Territory as a '*Procurer of furs.*' Having been a longtime personal friend of both *William Clark* and *Meriwether Lewis*, he was the perfect consultant. He told me that William Clark was in St. Louis, and was the Superintendent of Indian Affairs, for all Indians west of the Mississippi. We talked for more than six hours at his home in North Baltimore during our initial meeting. Without telling him my true reasons for wanting to mount such an expedition into the Northwest Territories, I persisted to inquire of him for any information which would be helpful to my mission. In exchange for my persistence, I obtained a wealth of knowledge from him. He enthusiastically endowed me with pertinent information which had taken him years to acquire. He advised me of the dangers, such as Indian encounters, how best to deal with those encounters, what kind of weather to expect, and warned me profoundly of the devilish nature of some of the French trappers and merchants in the region. He also told me many stories of huge bears and packs of ravenous wolves.

    I clung to every word which he shared, and despite his repeated forewarnings, my interest in this mysterious mission only augmented and intensified. He advised me of the cautions which were necessary during unexpected encounters with grizzly bears and packs of wolves, and the steps to be taken to avoid these dangerous encounters. I produced three maps from my father's satchel and he obligingly studied over them with me, paying compliments to their accuracy. He pointed to an area on the map in which I could expect to meet semi-friendly Indians from a tribe called, Arikara, and advised me that I could purchase horses from them. He warned me stalwartly regarding the infestation of venereal diseases within some tribes of Indians; a shameful European legacy of earlier French and English explorers and trappers. He said that copulation with women of the more remote tribes was relatively safe, but that venereal diseases were rampant among the tribes which were accessed more easily by river travel. He advised me to take liberal amounts of mercury and a penis syringe if I wished to fornicate with the Indians. He told me that Meriwether Lewis himself, had suffered greatly from syphilis upon his return from the Northwest Territories, and that this disease had contributed greatly to his mental depression. I personally, entertained no such belief, and held Captain Lewis in the highest esteem. As far as the idea of coupling with a savage woman was concerned, I would do no such thing, and therefore it was not necessary for me to take along any such horrible remedies or the hideous devices which were used to administer them. Men of conscience would entertain no such depraved and immoral behavior.

Marcus Attenborough told me that there was a French outpost near the Arikara village as well, where I could purchase any horses that I could not obtain through bartering directly with the Arikara, but he warned me of the objectionable character of the trading post's owner. He advised me to purchase only those horses from the French which could not be obtained from the Arikara. He pointed to a region where it was likely to encounter Indians of the *Pawnee* Nation. He warned me explicitly of their fierce nature and their intolerance of trespassers. We studied over the maps for a long period of time, and when the hour grew quite late, I returned the maps to the satchel and thanked Mr. Attenborough for his valuable information. Before leaving, I arranged to have a subsequent visit with him as my preparations advanced, and as new questions materialized. With my carriage bouncing and wheels sparking along the cobblestones of the Baltimore streets, my passion to embrace the mission grew stronger and stronger. The words, and even the cautions, of Mr. Attenborough had served only to invigorate and entice me. I was exhilarated with the prospects of a campaign such as this. My enthusiasm was piqued, indeed, but became depressingly mitigated somewhat when I returned home.

Upon my arrival home from Marcus Attenborough's house, I was astonished to find that my entire house had been ransacked during my eight-hour absence. A rear window had been broken open, whereby the thief or thieves had gained entrance, and every drawer, every cabinet, and every wardrobe had been rifled and searched. My normally clean and spotless home was in utter disarray and shambles. Even the kitchen cabinets had been pilfered, and broken glassware lay about on the floors. My study had been terribly ravaged, and every page of every book in my library had been searched and tossed aside. All of this devilment had taken place without arousing the attention of my neighbors. Stark realization of the potential value of the satchel's contents began to fully register with me. This attempted robbery dramatically added to the credibility of Father's claim... that there was great wealth to be obtained from this mission. Having ownership of the manuscripts and maps which detailed the location of the inferred prosperity, put me at a greater risk of having to deal with similar incidents in the future. I immediately summoned a constable, but could find no objects about the house that were missing. It was obvious to me that the sole objective of the search had been, in fact, the satchel which I had taken with me. I vowed to keep the satchel and its contents with me at all times after that. I would prime and load my *'gentleman's'* pistol and keep it with me at all times.

The attempted theft had also further strengthened my resolve to embark on this mission. I grew more and more eager to engage this new adventure. In an odd sort of way, the challenge of matching wits with an unknown adversary only seemed to heighten the allure of the mission. I had firmly decided that I would in fact make this journey, even if I were to meet with stout disapproval from my fiancée, Elizabeth. I would advise her of my intended plans at dinner on the evening of the morrow.

The following morning, I enlisted the service of a carpenter to repair the broken window on the rear of my house, and two maids were hired to assist me in cleaning and reorganizing the contents of my home. I also took advantage of the opportunity to gather pieces of clothing from my closets which I felt would be suitable and necessary for a journey into the Northwest Territories. I retrieved a pair of fowling boots from a closet and oiled them until the leather was soft and supple, and gathered various other sundries which I felt would benefit me. From a drawer in my parlor, I recovered a fine compass which had once been owned by my father, and cleaned the leather and brass parts well. The four of us worked diligently all day restoring the inside of my home, finishing the job shortly before I was due to leave to attend Elizabeth's dinner party.

I had given serious consideration to sending my fondest regrets to Elizabeth, and telling her that due to the attempted theft at my home, I would not be able to attend her dinner party. However, because I intended to use the opportunity to discuss my impending departure to the Northwest Territories, I relegated myself to comply with the commitment that I had made to her. Besides, Elizabeth was not one who accepted anything resembling rejection very lightly, and it mattered little to her when conflicting obligations arose in the lives of others. To her, she was infinitely more important than any other concern which I might encounter. Such was the spoiled nature and character of the woman to whom I was betrothed.

With my house restored to order, and with many

particulars for my journey gathered and stored neatly in a downstairs bedchamber, I paid the carpenter and the two maids for their labor and saw them to the door. No sooner than I had dressed for the dinner party, a carriage arrived to carry me to the event. The carriage had been dispatched by Elizabeth's father, as it had been for all previous dinner parties.

My Darling, Elizabeth

As a fair and prestigious Baltimore debutante, my fiancée, Elizabeth Anne Cunningham, maintained a respectable and elite, yet somewhat condescending, position among the pretentious and influential socialites of coastal Maryland. Her mother had died when she was but ten years of age, and her father had raised her during the years since. He had overindulged her terribly, giving in to her every whim and fancy. Her father, Charles Elliott Cunningham, III, had already accumulated a rather significant fortune from the shipyards which he owned in Baltimore Harbor, and his elevated position among society's dignitaries there was well established. Presidents Thomas Jefferson and James Madison had dined as guests in his home numerous times, as had several other political dignitaries. President James Monroe had composed his inauguration address while staying as a guest there. As many times as I had attended these pomp dinners before, I had not as yet achieved a feeling of comfort when I was in the presence of Mr. Cunningham, or about his household, even though I had been a regular guest at their frequent dinner parties for over six months and had been betrothed to his daughter, Elizabeth, for over four months. He was often discourteous, coarse, and boastful in conversation, causing me to take great care in my choice of words, and necessarily reluctant in speaking my mind. Judiciously, I had to guard my every word. I was always thankful and relieved when our dinner was brought forth to the table, for Charles spoke very little when there was food in front of him, and I rejoiced whenever he was not spewing forth the latest society gossip, or paying nauseating verbal tribute to his latest financial accomplishments. He was a terribly obese man, and yet, because of his wealth, he employed many courtesans as well as a mistress, which only corroborated my opinion that there were some women willing to participate zealously in disgustingly lewd behavior as long as there was adequate monetary compensation for their conduct. One of his courtesans was scarcely older than his own daughter, Elizabeth. I had always held great disdain for men who chose much younger women as the objects of their affection – the very concept seemed sinful in and of itself. His behavior was disgracefully vulgar, I thought. However, when I stopped to consider my own outlandish behavior, how could I possibly think of my own personal conduct as being higher in standard than that of his mistresses? My relationship with Elizabeth was driven primarily by a desire to lay future claim to a share of her father's wealth, therefore, my motives were easily as prostitorial and disgraceful as that of Mr. Cunningham's concubines.

Attempting to keep my own personal sexual transgressions as inconspicuous as possible, I had initially accessed Elizabeth's bedchamber by way of her balcony on our first fleshly liaison after college. When I had eventually tired of climbing trees in order to reach her balcony, she had secretly given me a key to a rear door of her house. The door was at the very foot of a stairway which led upstairs to her bedchamber. I was familiar with the house, and equally as familiar with the carnal behavior of both Elizabeth and her father. I had very little conscience about my promiscuous behavior during our engagement – as did Elizabeth. I maintained my relationship with Elizabeth in hopes of gaining future wealth as my compensation. In turn, she used me as a means of upholding her stellar image of purity within her circle of friends. Her purity was only a façade. Displaying me in public, as one would display a pedigree dog or cat, or a thoroughbred racing horse. Beyond anything, Elizabeth was proud of her social image, and I can only suppose that my station in life as her fiancé, was to maintain that stellar image. I had always been taken by many in Baltimore society to be of handsome physique and stainless character, yet I never saw myself as such. Nay, my character was far from flawless, and handsomeness lies only in the eyes of the beholder, for I never saw even a trace of handsomeness when I gazed upon myself in a mirror – persons sometimes bear stains which cannot be seen on the surface, and such was equally as true for me, as it was Elizabeth.

At the dinner table that evening, Elizabeth was quite curious about the strange satchel which I had sat on the floor beside my chair. I merely told her that it contained important manuscripts which I had intended to study if the opportunity had presented itself. She still thought it queer that I would bring such an unsightly thing to a proper dinner party. Having told her enough to satisfy her inquisitous curiosity, she soon dismissed the issue from her mind. Elizabeth was overflowing with outward beauty, to be sure, but her personality and wit was somewhat shallow. Perhaps that was a trait which was shared to some degree by all fair maidens in Baltimore's more prestigious and snobbish society circles, for in all of my courtships I had yet to happen upon a member of the feminine gender capable of entertaining me with meaningful conversation. I had suffered for years, enduring pretentious conversations with charlatans masquerading as intelligent, innocent debutantes. Perhaps my courtships had been performed in the wrong circles. I had always felt slightly ill at ease with Elizabeth, yet her hand had been very highly sought after among Baltimore's aspiring, young bachelors. Winning her hand should have been viewed as a superlative accomplishment by most observers' consideration. Oddly, I felt no such pride in winning her hand. However, she was her father's only child, and some day his wealth would most likely be hers.

Nevertheless, I felt strongly that a good marriage was best conceived when the two hearts were in harmony with one another and brought together by a mutual admiration and sincere love. In my mind's eye, a man, and a woman were equal in the eyes of God, and to me, the promise of eventual wealth should never have been as important to me as love. But, a question had loomed above me since Elizabeth and I first became betrothed; did I in fact, have any trace of love within my heart for Elizabeth? Deep within the depths of my heart I knew that I did not. Although admittedly, I also knew that I was unsure of what love really was, or even felt like at the time. But the mere fact that I had grave misgivings bore testament to the fact that I had some serious doubt regarding the survivability of our future marriage. I felt an extreme void in the pit of my stomach whenever I was with her, but thought that, in time, these uneasy feelings of emptiness would vanish, and give way to feelings of sincere love. As of yet, they had not. Things had only gotten progressively worse from my perspeective, as Elizabeth began to demonstrate the pronounced pious attitude that she now "*owned*" me... lock, stock, and barrel... as if I had been purchased by her father and given to her as a gift so that she would be in possession of a penis for her bedchamber, and a mannequin whom she could randomly take out of storage and place on display at her elegant dinner parties. I was certain that my innermost feelings were of no consequence to her. My thoughts of Elizabeth were easily diverted by my own restless nature, and her thoughts of me were easily overshadowed by her own vanity. I was but a marionette in our relationship, with Elizabeth and her father pulling the strings to make me dance at their will. I felt as though I was drowning, and would reach out for any lifeline thrown my way. My father's mission seemed to present just such a lifeline, and it seemed to have arrived just before I sank hopelessly below the surface.

After dining that evening, Elizabeth and I went to her front porch for meaningless and boring conversation and tea, as we usually did following our meal. It was an unusually warm and pleasant evening for early March, and we sat beside one another at a table with our tea. Her father always gave me an expensive imported cigar after we ate, but Elizabeth would not permit it to be smoked in her presence, so I would always put it in my pocket to be smoked at a later time. She had always dominated our conversations with vacant, irrelevant chatter, and I had always been content to let her do so – influenced greatly by keeping my '*eyes on the prize*' of her father's wealth. This evening, however, would be somewhat different. Unpleasant as it was, our short conversation would ultimately mark a turning point and an abrupt conclusion to a relationship in which I had never felt comfortable since its inception. Sitting beside her on the porch with our tea, Elizabeth said, "It's been five days now since you last visited my bedchamber, John. I will be expecting you to come to me tonight... will you?"

I did not answer her question. Instead, I acted as though I hadn't heard her, and decided to reveal the prospects of my impending, extended absence to her as gently as I could.

"Elizabeth... dear... it grieves me to tell you this, but I must leave on a mission to finish my father's business in the Northwest Territories, and close his interests there before returning to Baltimore. I shall be leaving on the eighth morrow."

"How long shall you be gone, John?"

"It's difficult to say for sure, I'm likely to be gone throughout the spring and summer, my dear... hopefully to return by October."

"October? Hopefully? Our wedding is supposed to take place in October! What shall I do if you've not returned by then? Sit here, alone, looking foolish in front of my friends?"

"I'll be back as quickly as I can, my dear. I promise you. This is something I must do for my father, Elizabeth. Please understand."

"And you would leave me here, like this, knowing that your absence at such a time will cause me great distress?"

"Would you deny me the opportunity to satisfy my father's last request, Elizabeth? Surely you would not."

"Would you deny *my* request... that you stay here with me and forget about this foolishness? Your allegiance is with a dead man, John? A father whom you never even knew as a child? One who abandoned you and your mother!"

"Elizabeth, please! Allow me to explain..."

"Your father's dead, John! I'm not! I do not want you to leave Baltimore! I forbid it! I'll not permit you to go off on some stupid folly, and leave me here to look foolish!"

"*Permit me*? You won't *permit me*? Perhaps I've misjudged you, Elizabeth. Is it really your belief that you have some sort of supreme authority over me? Do you really feel like you can contain me at your will... as though I were another of your possessions? Another one of your servants? Is your heart really that cold? Are you really so spoiled that you must always have your way, with never a consideration given to the feelings of others?"

"I refuse to discuss this matter any further, John! It's upsetting me! You may either go, or stay. The choice is yours!"

"Well! That being the case, the choice has been made all the more simple for me. This has been a most enlightening evening, Elizabeth. Incredibly short, but enlightening nonetheless! I am most thankful to you for having exposed yourself before me like this. I would have been heart sickened had you revealed your true self only after we had wed! I shall cause you no further distress, Elizabeth!"

"You would rob me of my virtue and then leave me alone like this? And dare to call yourself a gentleman?"

"Rob you of your virtue? Elizabeth, my dear… The thief who robbed you of your virtue, as you call it, had crossed the threshold of your bedchamber long before my initial crossing! And I strongly suspect there were many such crossings… by many such thieves! Don't insult me by assuming that I am as stupid as they!"

"Come back here this minute, John! You cannot leave me here like this!"

"Oh? I can't? Watch me! Goodbye, Elizabeth! And please, allow me to return the key to your rear door. You may pass it on to some poor fellow who is more tolerant of your wickedness than I… if such a fellow exists!"

"Come back here this minute, John!"

"And just one other thing before I leave tonight, my dear… a word of friendly advice, as it were; When you are indulging in the pleasures of the flesh with your next victim, some indication of physical enjoyment on your part would be greatly appreciated by him, I'm sure! As it would have been by me! And here, please return your father's cigar… perhaps he can give it to one of his young whores!"

"How dare you say things like this to me!"

Without waiting for one of her father's coachmen to take me home, I turned and walked away toward the damp cobblestone streets of Baltimore. As I walked out of the gate, she again cried out, demanding that I come back, but I never acknowledged that I had even heard her. Her yell was not a request, but more in the issue of a command, as one might talk to a dog, and her commands were falling on deaf ears. Elizabeth was a beautiful woman outwardly, but her contemptuous heart had revealed the true unyielding ugliness of her inner character to me that night, and I would not allow myself to be tethered any longer to a relationship which only provided me with discomfort. I felt vindicated from an association which had never stemmed from love, nor even deep admiration. It had been a betrothal of convenience, of status, and of vanity… for both of us. We had never spoken those magical words, '*I love you*' to each other, because neither of us knew their meaning. As far as her virtue was concerned; I was quite certain that it had been forfeited years before I had met her, and that she cleverly feigned its existence as a means of entrapping some unsuspecting young bachelor in a web of matrimony. I was never stupid enough to believe in her imaginary carnal purity from the very first moments of my very first midnight visit to her bedchamber balcony, yet said nothing to her because the matter was inconsequential to me. I was not the first to pluck a pedal from Elizabeth's rose, nor would I be the last to experience the prick of her thorns. Corporal relations between Elizabeth and me seemed to have been astonishingly boring events for her, consequently depriving me of the gratification of having brought sensuous pleasure to her as a partner – an element of unification which was important to me. I would not regret the absence of these insincere and unfulfilling relations from my life. I would sooner visit the brothels of Baker Street than to ever cross her threshold again.

    Every day thereafter, before I departed, Elizabeth would send a coachman to my door carrying a perfumed envelope. They were each addressed, *My Dearest John*, and accompanied by two roses. For three days, I refused each of them, and instructed the coachman to carry them back to Elizabeth. I will admit to being somewhat curious of the content of her letters, but had come to recognize the cunningness and deception she was capable of, and cared not to expose myself to it by actually reading her deceitful words. I supposed that she was giving me her generous "*permission*" for me to embark on my mission… or, God forbid, offering to accompany me. She was not pursuing me because of any romantic sentiment which she might have felt… she was pursuing me in order to avoid the social embarrassment she would incur as a result of an aborted betrothal. I felt as though sincere love was an emotion which Elizabeth was incapable of, and I even held great doubts of my own capacity for love. I was truly finished with her, and free to pursue my growing interest in completing my father's mission. Had Elizabeth and I wed, as we had planned, I am convinced that my life would have become disgustingly miserable and intolerable. I could have even been driven to strong drink. Most people would proclaim my cessation of our betrothal as an irresponsible forfeiture of assured future wealth. I felt that it was a necessary separation in order to preserve my sanity, and rid myself of feeling as though I had sold my soul to the devil. I was both young and ambitious, but my soul was not for sale… at any price. I wondered if I would ever be blessed by experiencing a romantic relationship which was sincerely felt from the heart. I wondered if such a thing was even possible, and if so, what it would feel like. I presumed that it would be somewhat difficult to find a prospective woman who would love me for who I was, for within the depths of my heart and soul, I held very little fondness for myself, and the person who I was. I had come to terms with the fact that I had almost married into a nightmare, solely for the sake of money, and I was sorely ashamed of myself.

    I was astonished to discover that within my father's worn leather satchel, there were envelopes tucked in a leather pouch at the very bottom, containing more than six thousand dollars... six thousand, four hundred and thirty-four dollars, to be exact. This was a fortune in and of itself, and more than enough money to fund four well-equipped expeditions into the Northwest Territory. Instead of using the money to fund an expedition, I could have used the money for my own immediate betterment and disregarded Father's mysterious mission as an old man's idiocy. I could have purchased stock in the rapidly expanding railroad industry and possibly lived in opulence with the handsome dividends I would receive. I could have used the money to start a business for myself here in Baltimore, or perhaps nearby in Washington. Washington would undoubtedly offer better prospects, for I felt certain that Mr. Cunningham would now use his considerable influence in opposition to any endeavor I may wish to pursue in Baltimore, since finding out that I had disgraced his only daughter by severing our relationship. Perhaps it was high time for me to leave Baltimore. The opportunity to see the vastness of the Northwest Territory with my own eyes was beginning to drive me insane with anticipation.

    The sincerity in Father's voice as he lay there dying in my home had somehow impassioned me with a desire to fulfill his request and follow it through to its end, even if it would cost the entire amount which was contained in the satchel. Perhaps it would prove to be a disappointing folly, just as Elizabeth had suggested, but the adventure offered me a respite from the boredom of my stagnant social eminence in Baltimore. The fact that my home had been broken into and ransacked, only added credibility to Father's claim, and fueled my desire to see this entire matter to its conclusion. I studied books and manuscripts at the Baltimore Library, gaining as much information as I possibly could, and spent many hours in planning for my journey. My research even carried me to the Congressional Library in Washington, where, by special permission, I searched through the journals of both Meriwether Lewis and William Clark, as well as transcripts from the journals of Alexander Mackenzie. I revisited my friend, Marcus Attenborough, absorbing every vestige of information I could. I left no stone unturned in my quest for knowledge in matters of travel and the geography of the Northwest Territory as well as information pertaining to the indigenous savages who resided there. I paid particular interest to references made to the many different tribes of savages residing in the region and the particular eccentricities of each. However, I found all reference material pertaining to these people to be woefully insufficient and non-descript. If I wanted to learn more about them I would have to obtain my knowledge first hand when I arrived at their villages. However, Mr. Attenborough had given me the journal of a Scotch-Canadian trapper named, *Silas Macgregor*, who had lived among the Indians for twenty-one years, and wrote candidly and meticulously about their culture, their animal-like carnality, and their mysterious pagan beliefs. Most of his accounts were so lewd and vulgar in content that they were disgusting to read. Such as five days which chronicled therein:

<u>*Twelfth day of August, 1778*</u>*: Entered the larger Arikara village today, nine miles northwest of the juncture of the Knife River and Little Fort Creek. We were greeted by their chief, White Eagle Flying, and three lesser chiefs. I gave them each four blankets and a twist of tobacco and also presented White Eagle Flying with a bracelet of copper and iron.*

<u>*Thirteenth day of August, 1778*</u>*: ...During the heat of the summer months, the native women of the Arikara avail themselves scearce of garments and wear nothing above their wastes to conceal their nakedness. This brings great discomfiture to Daniel and myself as we attempt to conduct commerce among their men people. Their breechcloths accomplish verry little additional coverment.*[sic] *Their fondness of visitors is neither subdued by shame or humility nor does it appear to be diminished any noticeable amount when they are in the presence of their husbands, who seem not*

disconcerted or jealous of their wives licentious behavior and moreover encourage it as a gesture of friendship. My determination to remain celeste in this village has been greatly tested by the handsomeness of these indigenous females. They follow us and touch us with their hands so as to solicit and encourage our proximate participation in the benefaction of their contentment.

<u>*Fourteenth day of August, 1778*</u>*: Daniel and I took abode in the lodge of White Eagle Flying of evening last. My bed was contained of two damsels and myself. Daniel's bed was thusly occupied in similar to my own. My sleep was greatly interfered upon with each Indian woman insistent upon attention before sleep was permitted me. I fear that there will be but little rest acquired by us as long as we reside in this village. White men are sought with wanton eagerness by the women here.*

<u>*Fifteenth day of August, 1778*</u>*: No entry.*

<u>*Sixteenth day of August, 1778*</u>*: I am with great misery and tiredness. I am fearful that if we habitate here longer we will be depleted of our strength and vitalness for our attendance seems forever in demand. We took our horses and our stores and departed soon after meridian hour on the third day.*

Silas Macgregor – 1771 "A Scotsman In The Shining Mountains"

    Although his journal had been recorded sixty years previous, I would digest these terrible accounts for what they were worth, and make my own assessments when I would meet these savages face to face. I gave considerable attention to the journals of Alexander Mackenzie, who had explored the Northwest Territory into Canada thirteen years prior to Captains Lewis and Clark, and the Corps of Discovery. Everything which I read, compelled me to go forward with my mission. I was a bit apprehensive in regards to some of the accounts of Indian attacks; their merciless slaughter of trappers and immigrants, yet would use this information for the benefit of my own safety alertness. I was prepared for such encounters, and perfectly well-armed for any such occurrence, or so I thought. Such confidence was merely a reflection of my own arrogance, for I truly had no idea of what might befall me during my journey into such a strange and foreboding land, nor my ability to survive in such a place.

The maps and travel directions contained inside of Father's satchel appeared to be all that I would need to guide me to the special place which he mentioned in his letter… a small, narrow canyon somewhere on the eastern slopes of the great western mountains where a lake separated the mountains from a vast plain. His maps and related documents appeared to be quite detailed, and I felt reasonably assured that I would have little difficulty following the directions. I made arrangements with my neighbors in Baltimore to oversee the wellbeing of my house, my horses, and my carriage. I purchased a Remington .50 caliber rifle, and two newly invented revolvers which matched in a .44 caliber, and a third, smaller pistol which could be carried on my person. The smaller revolver, was in the .36 caliber, and easily concealed under my coat. These weapons had all been modified to receive the new percussion caps, as the firing catalyst, instead of the less reliable and weather vulnerable, flint lock firing mechanism. I would make no further purchases of supplies until I had arrived at the end of the rail line in St. Louis. Once there, I would purchase the rest of the provisions I would need and see to the task of obtaining a large canoe, as per my father's instructions. Everything would then be loaded aboard a riverboat which would take me up the Mississippi River, then forthwith on a northwestward course, up the Great Missouri River as far as Fort Saint Joseph. At Fort Saint Joseph, I would seek to procure a man servant who would provide the additional labor required to propel a canoe against the strong currents of the Missouri River. From Fort Saint Joseph, I would have to paddle my way more than two hundred and seventy-five miles to the purported outpost of the Frenchman. From the outpost, all traveling would be accomplished by horseback, into the extreme wilderness of the Northwest Territories. In Father's notes, he had said that I could obtain horses, either at the outpost or at the nearby village of a tribe of people called, *the Arikara*, but he cautioned me of their treachery and thievery. These were the same iniquitous savages who were mentioned repeatedly in the journals of Silas Macgregor and Meriwether Lewis.

In his notes, Father had explicitly warned me of the Frenchman who owned and operated the outpost, writing;

The Frenchman who owns the outpost, Francois Brěaux, is not a man to be trusted. He is an evil man, and great caution must be practiced when negotiating with him. To be safe, trust no Frenchman.

In fact, throughout Father's documents there were warnings which were so numerous that they seemed to be coming from a man who was almost delusional, and perhaps obsessively over-cautious – as if he had been hell bent on berating the ethics and morality of the French people as a whole. Although I would pay necessary heed to his many cautions, I would make my own judgments as to the character of those who I would encounter, regardless of their lineage.

By this time, the word of my ended betrothal to Elizabeth seemed to have reached almost every ear in Baltimore. I had received numerous visits from friends expressing their most sincere regrets. During these visits, I forced myself to appear saddened by the forfeiture of Elizabeth's hand, but inside, I remained gleefully confident that I had done the right thing. In my heart, I felt as though I wanted to laugh, yet I did not. In a way, I felt sorry for Elizabeth. Her personality and her moral behavior were products of her upbringing, and now, as a young adult, she had become the shadow image of her father. As I had expected, most of my visitors were of the impression that it was Elizabeth herself who had ended our relationship... a story which I am sure Elizabeth had fabricated in a pious effort to preserve her precious dignity. I advised no one otherwise, preferring to allow her to languish in her own guilt. Her lies had brought no shame to me, and only reinforced my opinion of her shallow, deceitful, and greedy character.

    There were twenty-nine pages of instructions in Father's small leather satchel, with each page representing a different segment of the journey which lay before me. There was a page which gave reference to my traveling from Baltimore to St. Louis, another page which dealt specifically with what I should do once I had arrived in St. Louis, and so on. Some of the papers seemed irrelevant to the overall mission, yet I felt as though they might have been of some future importance, so I kept them with the others. After all, if they really had been irrelevant, why would Father have bothered to include them in his satchel? I employed a local seamstress to come into my home before leaving Baltimore and alter the lining of my jacket in order to permit ample storage pockets for the twenty-nine pages of instructions and the four maps within, accordingly making it possible that these valuable documents could be concealed on my person. Some of the currency which Father had bequeathed me to fund my expedition would also be carefully carried in an inner pocket of the coat. I packed only two portmanteaus for the expedition, carefully selecting the contents of each. I purchased some durable clothing and other accessories which were appropriate for an expedition of this type and an exquisite medical kit which was equipped with many medicines and implements. I disassembled the rifle and removed the barrel, so that it would fit into one of the leather portmanteaus, and stored two of the revolvers in a portmanteau as well. My powder, percussion caps, and bullets were also packed in a portmanteau in protective wax containers along with my clothing. The other revolver would be carried on my person at all times, concealed within a special pocket of my coat, behind the left lapel, from where it could rapidly be retrieved and used in the case of emergency. I then stuffed Father's empty satchel with newspapers and empty medicine bottles, and would continue to carry it with me to be used as a possible decoy for those whom I might encounter along the duration of my journey who may harbor ill intentions.

St. Louis

With the planning phase of my mission having been completed, and the care of my Baltimore home left in good hands, on April 8, 1836, I boarded a steam train bound for St. Louis. Elizabeth must have finally relented to my true wishes, for she did not come to the station to bid me what could have been an embarrassing farewell. As for me, I felt that the farewell which I had bade her on the evening of our dinner party was quite sufficient in ending our courtship. However, Elizabeth's coachman was at the train station, and had watched as I boarded the train. I'm quite certain that it was his duty to report my departure back to her, and I had fully expected as much. I felt a strange satisfaction in knowing that my departure would not only formalize our permanent separation, it would also formally clear the way for countless other suitors to vie for her affections; poor devils. If only they knew that she was incapable of true affections for anyone other than herself! I also felt confident that Elizabeth would be successful in rapidly ensnaring another candidate for betrothal, under the ruse of her non-existent virtue, and thusly fill the present vacancy in her bedchamber. Her hand was undoubtedly the most sought-after hand in all of Baltimore. If only my fellow competitors knew her as I did... ahhh, but soon enough they will find out for themselves.

   Elizabeth never returned the ring which I had given her for our engagement. Even though I had paid a great deal of money for the ring, I did not ask for its return. The money which I had spent for the ring was well spent when considering the education which I had received in return. My final words to her may have seemed cruel and insensitive, but I felt as though they were necessary to clear the air between us, and I had certainly been long overdue in expressing my true sentiments to her. Still, deep within my heart, I wished that I could have severed our relationship without the harshness of anger, and the exchange of cruel words. So be it.

Over the previous eight or ten years, I had learned to converse quite impressively among the socialites there in Baltimore... always being careful to choose the correct words... words which were chosen in an attempt to impress listeners with my proper command of the English language. My university education had enabled me to achieve great acceptance among the sophisticated and elite of Baltimore. In the process of achieving this great level of social recognition, I had unwittingly become another of its anonymous victims... robbing myself of the simpler pleasures of life. I was ill at ease with the man who I had become. I had reached a juncture in my life when I knew that it was time for an uncertain transformation of some type – a reckoning. Perhaps my deep involvement in my father's mission would permit me the opportunity to become the man who I wanted to be. Perhaps it would be an opportunity for me to nourish and encourage that person inside of me who was yearning to express himself. Perhaps when I returned home, I could chance to meet a young lady whom I could admire as a person, respect, cherish, and love. If I did choose to pursue such a sincere relationship with a lady when I returned, I would search for one well outside of the contemptuous evilment of Baltimore. Perhaps there would be better prospects in the countryside surrounding Baltimore or Washington. I longed for a life companion with a virtuous heart... if such a person actually existed. Would it indeed be possible for me to find a young woman whose heart was not wrought with conceit and bitterness, greed and contempt? Probably not, but I would continue to carry such hope in my heart rather than face a future of disappointment. I had only just come to realize, that I was not only a very discontented man, but a terribly lonely one as well. I had no family or close confidante with whom I could confide in. I truly was alone, and felt as though I was by myself in a barren sea of emptiness.

After the attempted theft at my home, I had taken Father's warnings much more serious, and at times, perhaps too serious. There were so many aspects of this new adventure which were completely ambiguous and unfamiliar to me. I endeavored to acquaint myself with as many particulars of a venture such as this as I possibly could. I would be traveling outside of the protective climate of Baltimore's noble society, where a watchman or a constable were most often readily available, and into a world where the possibility of personal harm was more of a practical and foreseeable eventuality. These possible harms could fall upon me in ways which were completely unfamiliar to me. I had never before been the intended victim of an evil-minded person, other than Elizabeth of course, and did not know exactly what I should expect. It had never been necessary for me to deal directly with, nor confront, villains or thieves. Further, there were no vicious wild animals roaming about the streets of Baltimore, save for the many greedy politicians and solicitors lurking thereabouts on Court Street. Therefore, if were to expect that which was unexpected, I had to formulate a means of confronting such threats as well. Father's instructions had clearly warned of thieves and bandits, savage Indians and wild animals along the journey, and I had taken his warnings very much to heart. For two weeks I felt as though I was constantly being watched, and remained suspicious of the many persons whom I met on the street. In his letter, Father had said:

"Others are aware that this fortune exists, and will not hesitate to bring harm to you in order to learn of its location. Trust no one. Confide in no one. Always be aware that your enemies may be anywhere about you."

These words were beginning to instill a sense of awareness upon me which made me suspicious of all strangers, and would be the words which I would use to guide my every action until my journey had been completed. After all, the sanctity of my very home had been invaded, and had the satchel of documents been there, I am sure that it would have been stolen. There was someone, somewhere, who truly wanted these manuscripts and maps. I was convinced of their authenticity, and curious of their unknown value. I studied everyone who was about me, and in doing so, I began to notice that there was a gentleman riding in the same train coach as I who seemed to be paying a great deal of attention to me. Every time I glanced in his direction, he would quickly turn his head to look the other way. He was obviously a novice at remaining undetected, yet had it not been for my heightened state of awareness, I too, may have easily overlooked him as a potential threat to my wellbeing. I felt as though he was following me, but I had no proof to that effect. Was it possible that I was over-reacting? I had an eerie sense that I could feel his eyes upon the back of my neck as I sat in my coach seat, yet forced myself to maintain a casual, relaxed outwardly appearance in order not to appear alerted. I did not wish to inform the man of my suspicions. To have alerted him to my suspicions would have only complicated my situation.

   I sat there in my train coach, viewing the countryside as it passed by my window, trying to conceive of a method whereby I could determine the true character and true intentions of this mysterious traveler. Were my feelings correct, or had I merely become paranoid and delusional because of Father's repeated warnings? The conductor had announced to all of the passengers that there would be a scheduled, one hour stop at *Hagerstown Station* in order to afford all of the passengers the benefit of dining while the train was resupplied with fuel and water. I was convinced that a stop such as this would supply ample opportunity for me to take some kind of action... exactly what kind of action, I was not sure. Hagerstown was the final destination for a few of the passengers on the train, and a few new passengers would be boarding there to continue westward toward St. Louis. The conductor told us that there was an inn just a short walk from the station, so most passengers exited the coach to go to the inn for dining. It was drizzling rain outside, and the conductor passed out umbrellas to the male passengers and parasols to the ladies as they disembarked the train. In a voice which was purposely loud enough to be heard by the suspicious character, I asked the conductor,

"May I leave my satchel on the train, here? There are documents inside which I would like to keep dry from the rain."

"Yes, sir. You can put it under your seat. It will be safe there until you return from dining."

In an intentionally obvious manner, I placed the satchel under my seat, stepped off of the train, and began the walk to the inn with the other passengers. The suspicious gentleman was still seated in the coach, his head turned toward his window, when I stepped off of the train. Once I had walked a safe distance away, I retired to a position at the station behind some luggage carts where I could observe the train coach without being seen. Under the porch roof of the train station, I folded my umbrella and stepped back in the shadows, out of sight. Workmen at the station loaded items aboard the train while others saw to the maintenance of the steam train's engine. Two new passengers boarded the train in different coaches as I continued to wait in the shadows and observe the activity from my hiding place there.

My suspicions of the curious gentleman had been well founded. I saw him dash off of the train and hurriedly walk away in the rain, in the opposite direction of the inn, and disappear into the streets of Hagerstown with something bulky tucked under his coat… something that I knew to be my father's satchel. I quickly caught up with him and followed along behind him at a safe distance, but lost vision of him as he entered an alleyway between two buildings. Very shortly, a carriage emerged from the alleyway and hastily disappeared from sight, heading northward. Walking on to the inn, I dined quickly at the inn, and hurried back to the train coach to see if the gentleman would attempt to re-board the coach and travel on. He did not, and the train was once again on its way to St. Louis. Of course, as I had predicted, the satchel was missing from under my seat. I imagined that the thief had fled a great distance in his carriage before he finally felt at ease and stopped to inspect the satchel's contents. In a place where he must have felt safe, he probably opened the satchel for the first time and only then noticed that he had been bamboozled. I mused over the fact that he had fled with only a worn-out satchel filled with old newspapers and empty medicine bottles. I could imagine the look that he must have had on his face when he discovered his blunder. I felt as though my ploy had been well conceived, and although apparently successful, I was resolved to maintain a continual vigil in order to deal appropriately with other such threats. Should they arise. I realized that further incidents such as this were a distinct possibility now, and I would remain observant, paying due heed to Father's warnings. To impede other such attempts would require vigilance and cunning on my part. However, I could not help but chuckle frequently each time that I imagined the villain's utter disappointment. For a short moment, I even arrogantly thought of myself as having been amazingly clever in thwarting the rascal's plan to rob me of Father's documents.

As if to add further annoyance to my travel, a family had boarded the train in Hagerstown, and had sat directly behind me. Their children were among the rudest and most disruptive children I had ever seen. Frustrating me greatly, was the fact that the parents of the ill-mannered children seemed not to care that their children's behavior was causing a nuisance among the other passengers. Eventually, I moved to a seat at the very rear of the coach, and still, the noise of the children was very disruptive to my comfiture. I have always loved children, but I do not think highly of parents who mistreat their children, nor do I think very highly of children who mistreat their parents. Proper behavior is a characteristic which should be learned from one's parents... a duty which these parents had evidently shirked. What a pity, for the children's sake, I thought. For it was quite likely that their rude behavior would most likely accompany them through later life.

The train continued onward, and made a seemingly endless number of stops at various stations along the way. I would critically scrutinize each new passenger who boarded the train, trying to determine if any appeared to pose a threat. Having been driven from my seat to the rear of the coach proved to be a blessing, for I could easily observe the entire coach from this position without having to turn my head to do so.

During my journey on the train, I could not help but have occasional thoughts of Elizabeth. I was not obsessively curious as to her present state of mind, but still, I did wonder about her from time to time. Did she weep when her coachman had told her of my final departure? Perish the thought! I had never seen Elizabeth weep over anything. Had she already chosen her next victim? Had she already presented him with the key to her rear door? Perhaps. If she had, it was of no consequence to me. I was my own man now, and I had cleansed myself of her wickedness forever. The rest of my life lay before me, now, and I was determined to make the best of it. From this moment on, I was free to become the man that I wanted to be.

During the next four days, my steam train journey was much less eventful, and at times, painfully boring. There were many miles of travel which were made very uncomfortable when the smoke expelled from the steam engine seemed to permeate the air inside the coach with a bitter, nauseating smoke. According to the conductor, this occurred when the train was accompanied by a strong tail wind. Passengers were forced to cover their mouths and nostrils with their handkerchiefs in order not to breathe the putrid smoke. The smoke seemed to be more intense toward the rear of the coach, where my new position was, but I was so satisfied with the view that I tolerated the terrible smoke. I was very pleased when the train finally arrived in St. Louis, yet remained apprehensive as to what possible dangers may have been awaiting me there. I continued to assume that anonymous assailants lay in wait around each corner. Accordingly, I wasted no time lollygagging at the station. I immediately hired a coachman, loaded my two large portmanteaus aboard his coach, and instructed the teamster to take me to the Sutton House Inn, on the west side of upper St. Louis. There were three other hotels which were closer to the station and the river, but I felt that there was a greater possibility that if I was still being sought after, they were being watched. These other hotels would be the most likely choice for most travelers. My pursuers, if there actually were any at this point, would not expect me to seek lodging that far away from the train station. My portmanteaus were placed in a room there at the Sutton House Inn, and I retired for the evening shortly after dinner without incident.

Continuing to follow my father's written instructions, I was to locate a Captain Phillip McBride at the river waterfront, and engage his assistance in obtaining the rest of the supplies which I would need. Captain McBride piloted a steam vessel, known as the "*Puritan Enterprise*," which supplied several outposts along the lower Missouri River where the water depth would permit such a large vessel, and according to Father, McBride was a man in whom I could feel confident in placing my utmost trust. I was puzzled somewhat by Father's instructions, however. In his letter to me, he had specifically said for me to "*trust no one*." Yet, further along in his instructions, he said that Captain McBride was a man who could be trusted above all others. I reconciled that Father had meant that I should not reveal the true object of my journey to anyone, yet I should completely trust Captain McBride with assisting me in the preparation of my expedition and the procurement of supplies. At his riverboat office, I was informed that the Captain was presently engaged in a voyage, and was not expected to return until the morrow. I returned early the following day and waited at the dock for more than two hours before first seeing the appearance of his boat, approaching from the north. It was a moderately large-sized steamer, with a paddle wheel on either side, and a very shallow draft and internal keel which allowed it to voyage in much shallower depths of water than some of the other boat designs. Once the vessel had docked and secured with mooring ropes, I walked up the plank and introduced myself to the Captain.

Meeting Captain McBride reinforced my trust in Father's instructions… as well as Father's judgment of men. He was a large-framed man, perhaps thirty-five or forty years of age, with a jovial, likeable personality and a warm, friendly demeanor. He was eloquent of speech, and in my assessment, a very well-educated man. With rosy cheeks and a briarwood tobacco pipe in his mouth, and at six feet, two inches, he was an imposing figure of a man. Even without his captain's hat and a seaman's over-jacket, he could have clearly been recognized as the commanding figure aboard his vessel. Even his deep tone of voice seemed to add emphasis to his authority. We sat together in the wheelhouse of the *Puritan Enterprise* and had quiet conversation there as his crew made preparations to unload his cargo of cotton, tobacco, and wheat. His cargo had been brought to St. Louis from many storage facilities along the upper Missouri river, and was being transported to recipient merchants there in St. Louis. He seemed genuinely saddened, if not surprised, to hear of Father's death, and offered comforting words to me as we spoke.

"Your father came through here six weeks ago and told me that he was on his way to Baltimore, to see you. He said that it would be his first visit there in nearly twenty-one years. He was weak, frail, and barely able to stand by himself. Yet when I saw him the previous spring he appeared fit and healthy for a man of sixty four years. I helped him settle some business issues up river at Fort Saint Joseph, and when we got back to St. Louis, I arranged for his train passage to Baltimore. I also hired a '*gentleman's assistant*' to accompany him. He said that he desperately needed to speak with you as soon as possible. That was the last I saw of him."

"When Father was here, did he tell you that he was dying?"

"No, John, but judging by his weakened appearance, I suspected as much, John."

"He arrived at my home and died shortly after his arrival. We only spoke a few words to each other before he passed. There is so much more that I wanted to know about him. Many of my questions have gone unanswered with his passing."

"Your father was a good man at heart, John, and even though he was among the kindest people who I ever met, he was also among the saddest at times. Occasionally, I could see the sadness in his eyes and hear it in his voice."

"Why do you think he was so sad at times, Captain?"

"I never knew the cause of his extreme happiness or his occasional sadness, although I always suspected that his sadness was due to the fact that he missed his family in Baltimore so much. He talked about you and your mother a lot. He had sources in Baltimore who kept him informed of your wellbeing. There were always many letters waiting for him at Fort Saint Joseph, each time he would arrive there for supplies. Yet he was always compelled to return to the mountains with the greatest of haste for some reason... as if he had found something there which had made him very happy."

"If he missed Mother and me so much, I wonder why he never bothered to come home to see us? And I wonder why he was not present at my mother's passing? *Absence* would seem to be a queer way of expressing one's love of one's family, wouldn't you say?"

"I'm afraid that I can't answer that, my son. He spent a lot of time in the Northwest Territory somewhere, and I only saw him in the spring of each year when he would come into Fort Saint Joseph for supplies. We would often meet there and spend several hours talking while I helped him purchase the items he needed. He told me and everyone else that he was trapping, but in all those years I never once witnessed him buying supplies which would be beneficial to a trapper. Nor did I ever see him return bearing any furs. *No*, I suspect that he was prospecting for gold or silver, but he never did volunteer, and I never did ask. I figured that if he wanted me to know what he was doing all those years he would have told me. Yet, I knew that something had happened that had affected his life in some very important way."

"What do you mean, Captain?"

"About twelve or thirteen years ago I observed that a tremendous change had come over him from the previous four years. He seemed different. It seemed as though he had achieved some great inner peace and contentment in his life... like he had been '*reborn*' in some strange way."

"And what was the cause of this *great change* in him?"

"I don't know, John. And I suppose I will never know."

"So, Captain... what did you and my father talk about when you were with him?"

"Oh, mostly he wanted to know what was going on in the outside world. If any new states had been added to the union, what was going on in Washington, and such things as that. I brought him many newspapers to read. He also picked up any mail which had come to Fort Saint Joseph for him, got his yearly haircut, and that sort of thing. William Horace Welch... my goodness... I'm going to miss seeing him and talking to him."

"Mother and I missed seeing him and talking to him for twenty-one years."

"I know, son, and I'm truly sorry."

"So, he came to Fort Saint Joseph once a year for the primary purpose of having conversation with you and getting his hair cut?"

"Oh, no. His main reason behind his yearly trips to Fort Saint Joseph was to buy goods and supplies... lots of them. We would meet, I would help him purchase his goods and pack the items away on his *pirogue*, and then, as I mentioned, he would always be in a great hurry to get back to wherever he lived."

"And where did he live, exactly?"

"He never volunteered to say, and I never presumed to ask. He was a kind and generous man, but a secretive man as well... very protective of something, but I do not know what it was. Now, I suppose it will remain a secret forever."

"And you, Captain... do you have a wife and children?"

"I would like to settle down someday. I would like to find the right person and get married... raise a family somewhere. But as of yet, I remain a bachelor... one who is far too dedicated to his work to raise a family at the present time. Perhaps one day, that will change."

"Would you consent to accompany me, and assist me in procuring the supplies that I need? Your advice would be greatly appreciated."

"I would be more than delighted to help you in any way that I can, John."

Captain McBride accompanied me the following day and assisted with the procurement of my supplies. Over the last six years, I had developed an insatiable fondness for tea, so I purchased a sixty-five pound bag of tea leaves which had been imported from the West Indies. I did not know if tea leaves would be available at the French outpost, so I thought it best to purchase them here. Upon the Captain's recommendation, I purchased one hundred cans of pemmican; a food which was made with buffalo, cranberries, wheat grain and fat. The Captain also helped me purchase a large canoe, and the good Captain made arrangements with the seller to have it transported to his steam boat. The canoe, which had been built there in St. Louis, was twenty-three feet in length, and had a beam of nearly six feet at mid-ship. Due to its large size, it was very heavy, and took two strong men to carry it when it was out of the water. It would be impossible for one man to portage or otherwise handle a canoe of this size.

The Captain's steamboat was being maintained at the river dock, and loaded with wood to fuel his next voyage up the Mississippi River, and then, up the Missouri River to Fort Saint Joseph. Once at Fort Saint Joseph, Captain McBride had agreed to assist me in the hiring or purchase of a man-servant, consistent with Father's instructions, who would provide the additional manpower needed to propel the large canoe from Fort Saint Joseph to the Arikara village and French outpost, and to assist with portaging when necessary. So far, the journey was coming to fruition just as Father had detailed in his instructions, but I knew full well that travel and accommodations would become much more difficult when I left Saint Joseph in a canoe. My outdoor explorations in the countryside of Baltimore had all been single-day excursions. My current adventure represented something far more serious and demanding. My mettle would be put to the test as it never had before. Would I rise to the challenge, or would I prove to be a pathetic and wretched failure?

With a series of three blasts of the steamboat's mighty whistle, we departed St. Louis on schedule, and proceeded northward for fifteen miles to the confluence of the Missouri River. There, we embarked on a westerly course and it was very late that evening when Captain McBride moored his vessel close to the eastern bank of the river for the night. River navigation after dark was entirely too dangerous because of floating logs, sand and gravel bars, and occasional rocks, so mooring overnight was a conventional practice on the upper Mississippi and lower Missouri Rivers. I would spend the better part of my days in the wheelhouse with the good Captain, and we would always take our meals together and enjoy very pleasant conversation as we ate. He was a sincere and interesting fellow to speak with, and as I mentioned previously, very well educated. Accommodations were generally comfortable, yet the nights, when the boat was moored, were an absolute unpleasantness to endure because of the incessant hordes of mosquitoes which sometimes arrived in great numbers to pester us. These ubiquitous demons were a constant torment when the sun set in the evenings. It was entirely too warm at night to close the windows of the tiny cabin, and because the windows had to remain open, it was therefore impossible to completely escape the mosquitoes. The nights when there was very little wind outside were the most difficult nights to contend with. When there was a gentle breeze outside, the mosquitoes were almost tolerable. Beds were equipped with mosquito bars, but great care needed to be exercised when lowering them, lest mosquitoes would be trapped inside with the occupant. Not sleeping well at night, I supplemented my rest by taking frequent naps during the day when there were no mosquitoes about the vessel. I also spent a great deal of time in my stateroom, studying over my maps and planning for the part of my journey which would eventually take place on dry land.

    The second evening, while walking about the deck of the boat, I discovered a young woman with two small children huddled in an aft corner of the deck near the large bins where the boat's mooring ropes were stored. She was fanning her sleeping children with a folded newspaper in order to keep the mosquitoes at bay while her children slept – indicative of a mother's love. I inquired as to why they were sleeping on the deck and she hesitantly offered a variety of untruthful excuses, until she finally admitted that she did not have enough money to pay for a stateroom. They were on their way to meet her husband in Fort Saint Joseph, where he was employed nearby at a grist mill of some sort. I quickly went to the Captain and paid for an extra stateroom. Returning to the distressed woman, I presented her with a key and ushered her and her children into their room, where they could have a greater degree of comfort for the remainder of their voyage. The children were both sleeping soundly, so I carried one and she carried the other. She was nervously reluctant to accept my generosity at first, perhaps thinking that as a consequence, I would be expectant of some fashion of sexual compensation for the deed. I showed her how to raise and lower the mosquito bars around their bed and fetched a bag of biscuits and dried beef from my room. Once she had come to recognize that her suspicions of my honor were unjustified, and that my true concern was for the welfare of her and her children, she thanked me repeatedly and wished me God's blessing with tearful eyes as I turned to retire to my own stateroom.

Four days later, on the day which our boat docked at Fort Saint Joseph, Captain McBride and I ventured into the streets in search of an establishment in which we could obtain possession of a man-servant. Fort Saint Joseph was a thriving young city. The city outside of the fort was growing quickly. Every building, every factory, and every church appeared to be newly constructed. There were several Indians about the city, but I saw none which were dressed in the more traditional attire of a true wilderness tribe. Except for their distinguishable facial features, they appeared much the same as the many frontiersmen who were walking about the streets. Everywhere Captain McBride and I walked, new buildings were being constructed. There were two banking institutions, and at least four or five hotels, and practically every other kind of establishment one could want for. Merchants, vending food and various implements for farming and trapping, were everywhere, selling their wares from tents, and the walkways and streets were alive with commerce. The city, in size, dwarfed the fort itself. One could have easily thought they were in Baltimore, had it not been for the deplorable condition of the muddy streets and avenues, and the noticeable absence of buildings constructed with brick.

Having great difficulty finding a man servant, we eventually located the owner of a large wood yard near the river who was willing to sell one of his man-servants, but, at an altogether extremely high price. I had an adequate supply of money to use as barter, but was not yet desperate enough to allow myself to be swindled. However, the gentleman had probably detected eagerness in my voice, and shrewdly stood his ground on the price, thinking that I would relent to his demands at any moment. I was in dire need of additional manpower in order to propel my canoe against the strong currents of the river and assist with other work, but I steadfastly refused to be taken advantage of. We bid the gentleman good day, and turned to leave, and he immediately began to lower his price to a more reasonable sum. After much negotiation, I took interest in an older, dark-skinned male whose hair was beginning to turn grey around his ears. He lacked several teeth, and was missing an index finger on his left hand, but otherwise, he appeared stout and strong. As an additional asset, he spoke perfectly understandable English, although in its most basic mode. I told the owner that I wished to speak with the servant in private before making my decision as to whether or not to buy him. He agreed, so the servant, Oscar, and I walked a short distance and spoke.

"Do you understand me?"

"You ain't said nothing yet, boss."

"How long have you been a slave, Oscar?"

"I always been one, boss."

"How would you like to be granted your freedom?"

"Yes, sir. I'd like that a whole lot, boss."

"Are you strong enough to paddle a boat?"

"Yes, sir, boss!"

"I'm going to buy you from the man who now owns you. If you will help me paddle my boat up the Missouri River, I will free you and give you twenty-five dollars in gold when we get to where I want to go. Do you want to go with me?"

"Why would you set me free? Why would you do this for old Oscar, boss?"

"My reasons are my own. Answer my question... Do you want to go with me and earn your freedom?"

"Yes, sir, boss! Old Oscar wants to go with you mighty bad!"

"Very well, then... do not call me, 'boss.' My name is, 'John.' Understand?"

"Yes, sir... Mister John... Yes, sir..."

I liked Oscar from the onset. His eyes and general appearance told me that he had endured a harsh existence in his life to this point, and I felt as though it would bring great joy to him if he was granted his freedom. I did not try to negotiate the price for Oscar any lower. I simply paid the price, received the signed and witnessed ownership documents from the Taskmaster at the wood yard, and Captain McBride, Oscar, and I walked back into the streets of Fort Saint Joseph. We walked back to the river at my insistence, where we found a private place where Oscar could bathe. He was quite odorous, and smelled as though he had possibly not bathed in months. Once he was clean, he redressed, and we visited a clothier, and purchased some proper clothes and boots for him. He had been dressed poorly to embark on a journey such as we were about to engage. Once he was properly attired, we returned to the boat to supervise the unloading of my merchandise from Captain McBride's vessel. By the time everything had been loaded into the large canoe which Oscar and I would depart in, it was too late in the evening to begin our journey up the Missouri. As badly as I wanted to depart, good judgment prevailed, and instead, we slept aboard the steamboat, with the intention of leaving at first light in the morning. As I walked toward the gangplank to go up to the stateroom, I was approached by a family at the dock. I recognized the woman and two children as being the ones whom I had purchased a stateroom for earlier in the week. I heard the woman tell her husband,

"That's the man, right there, Timothy!" My first thought was that the woman had perhaps told her husband that I had made improper amorous advances of some type when I had purchased the stateroom for her and the children, or that I had somehow soiled her reputation. I soon found out otherwise when the man approached me closer.

"Excuse me, sir. May I speak with you for a moment?"

"My name is John Welch. How may I help you?"

"My wife, Rebecca here, told me what you did for her and our children on the boat... I just wanted to thank you personally for what you did, and shake your hand, sir."

"If what I did helped in any way, then I am glad I could have been there... and your name?"

"I'm Timothy O'Brien, sir. I am indebted to you for your Christian kindness. If you will tell me how I may post a letter to you, perhaps I can repay you when I am paid my wages at the end of this month."

I could clearly see that Mr. O'Brien and his family were of destitute means. They even looked gaunt and hungry to me... all of them. They had probably spent the last of their money in order to afford passage so that they could be together as a family once more. Fumbling in my pocket, I held four twenty dollar gold pieces in my hand and put them in his shirt pocket.

"Mr. O'Brien, no repayment is necessary, sir. Please regard this as a gift for you and your wonderful family, and receive it with my blessings. You have a lovely family, sir, and I wish you good fortune and much happiness."

Mr. O'Brien and his wife were truly shaken by this gesture of good fortune. I received warm hugs from him and his wife and continued on my way. O'Brien had made a comment in our brief conversation which gave me pause for thought. He said that he had appreciated my *Christian kindness*. *Christian kindness*? I had been accused of many things before... but never of such a thing as, *Christian kindness*! I had never done such a thing before in my life, and was almost overcome with a sense of joyousness. Is this what it feels like to contribute to the relief of those who are less fortunate? Is this really what it feels like to help someone that is in need? If so, it was indeed, gratifying. They probably used the money to buy food for their family, and I felt like it was more than enough money to carry them until his wages were paid, and most likely two or three months additional. I was delighted by the warm feeling which I had received in knowing that I had done something which would undoubtedly contribute to their happiness. This was a new concept for me, and one which I was anxious to embrace again. I had always been a "*taker*" in life, and had never experienced the joy of giving.

With Oscar following closely behind me, we went aboard the boat and up to our stateroom. I prepared a sleeping mat on the floor next to my bed on which Oscar could sleep, and then locked us both in the small stateroom there, tucking the key in my shirt pocket. That way, I felt that it was unlikely that Oscar would flee during the night and abandon me. I kept my revolver at my side, and slept lightly that night, for I was unsure of Oscar's trustworthiness or his general character at that point. Had he been of poor character, or an evil man, he could have easily fallen upon me during the night and murdered me in my bed. Oscar did not speak much during the daylight hours, but at night, while he slept, he constantly emitted a torrent of ungodly noises as he snored. It was a horrible thing to listen to. I woke him repeatedly, and he would turn upon his side, and thusly he would cease snoring. However, moments later he would be on his back again and resume his hailstorm of vocal noises. I finally resolved myself that it was of no use to continue to wake him. We were not terribly bothered by the mosquitoes that night, and I attributed it to the possibility that Oscar's snoring had driven the little devils far away from the

Missouri River. It was an inhumanly, irritating sound, which interfered greatly with my sleep.

Oscar and I ate a hearty breakfast the morning of our departure from Fort Saint Joseph, and I judged that it may very well have been the finest breakfast which Oscar had ever eaten. Likewise, it was indeed one of the finest breakfasts that I had ever eaten, but breakfast had not been taken without some irritating degree of difficulty. The owner of the restaurant would not permit Oscar to dine inside with Captain McBride and me. I bitterly objected and began to argue vehemently with the owner until three men arose from their table and threatened to take me outside and beat me. Having won boxing championships when I was in college, I was ready to take on the three ruffians, but Captain McBride intervened, and convinced me to compromise by allowing Oscar to eat at the back door of the restaurant while he and I dined inside. I reluctantly agreed, and the three angry men soon sat back down at their table. Hateful stares from the three hooligans persisted during our entire meal. We ate our meal and walked back to the river with Oscar following closely behind. On our walk back to the river, Captain McBride and I spoke to one another.

"John, are people such as Oscar permitted to dine in restaurants back in Baltimore?"

"No, but I had rather hoped that things would be different here."

"I'm sorry, John. I'm afraid that things are no different here."

"Captain McBride, in all of our discussions, you have not yet asked me why I am undertaking a journey so far up the Missouri River."

"I feel like you would have told me if you wanted me to know. Although I believe that I already know the reason for your journey."

"Oh? And why do you think I would want to make such an arduous journey, sir?"

"Just like your father, I believe that you are searching for something. Perhaps you are searching for the same thing which your father searched for. I do not care what your reasons are. I will help you any way that I can, and pray that you find whatever it is that you are looking for. Your father would have expected as much from me."

"Father was right. You are a good man, Captain McBride. Meeting you, traveling with you, and talking with you, has been an honor, sir. I sincerely hope that I have the pleasure of seeing you once more, when I return."

Soon thereafter, Oscar and I bid farewell to Captain McBride, and thanked him repeatedly for his hospitality and valued assistance. I offered to pay him for his time and trouble, but he told me that Father had assumed that I would be traveling on this journey, and had already compensated him for his time. The fact that he would accept no further compensation from me only served to elevate his gentlemanly character and trustworthiness in my reckoning. The insight which he had offered regarding my father's past only served to further confuse me, however, for it offered nothing in the way of a reasonable explanation of my father's twenty-one year absence from Mother and me.

With Oscar in the front of the large canoe and me in the rear, we pushed off from the muddy banks of Fort Saint Joseph and were on our way. I glanced over my shoulder several times to see Captain McBride standing at the bank of the river, watching intently. He was still there when we rounded a bend in the river, and the waterfront of Saint Joseph, along with Captain McBride, vanished from sight. I was now engaged in the most physically demanding part of my journey; more than two hundred and seventy-five miles of river lay before me, to be traveled by canoe. When I had attended college, I had spent many pleasant afternoons canoeing on the Potomac River in Washington. Usually, I was in the company of a lady friend, and found it to be quite relaxing and pleasurable. Now, however, with my canoe loaded heavily with merchandise, and two hundred seventy-five miles of swift water to navigate, it was very tedious, dangerous, and demanding work.

Oscar had no difficulty in paddling our canoe, despite the absence of the finger which he was missing on his left hand. He was a strong man, obedient, and he always seemed eager to please me. He often sang as we paddled and I found his deep voice to be quite spectacular, and his singing to be quite pleasing to the ear. In fact, I would occasionally find myself inadvertently singing along with him whenever he sang songs with which I was familiar. It helped to pass time as we paddled, and made the journey seem all the more cheerful. It also provided us with a rhythm of sorts which we could use to coordinate the strokes of our paddles. My arms often ached under the burden of constant paddling, yet I did not yield to the pain. I did have second thoughts, however, when my arms began to ache and throb, and I realized that we had traveled less than eight or ten miles… into a journey in which there would be more than two hundred and seventy-five miles remaining to be traveled by canoe. It made me weary just to think about it. Instead, I tried not to think about it and cheerfully sang along with Oscar.

> ♪ *Here we all work on dee Mississippi…*
> *Here we all work while dee white man play…*
> *Here we all work on dee Mississippi…*
> *Only lay down at dee end of dee day…* ♪

There were no bothersome engine noises as we navigated the river in our canoe. There were no dreadful clouds of putrid smoke and soot to choke us. The dead silence was broken only by the soft, watery sounds of our paddles as we pulled ourselves through the muddy water. We saw fewer and fewer homesteads along the river, and then, eventually there were no signs of habitation at all. We saw the ruins of two pirogues that had been broken as they attempted to navigate small waterfalls, and another that was a casualty to a log jam. They were gruesome reminders that the river could be one's friend at one moment, and a terrible, awesome enemy the next. On that first day of travel, we passed three canoes on their way back to Saint Joseph, heavily laden with what appeared to have been animal hides... possibly buffalo. We talked to no one, however, and continued earnestly in our efforts to cover as many miles as possible each day.

I tried to plan our campsites near landmarks which were indicated on my map. In doing so, I could make reasonably accurate calculations as to how far we had traveled, as well as make crude assessments as to how far we had yet to go. Struggling against the river's current as we were, and having to portage around several waterfalls and log jams, we considered ourselves fortunate on the days when we could travel thirty to thirty-five miles. One day, we accomplished less than six miles because of a series of small waterfalls and log jams. Portaging was difficult work. All of our goods had to be unloaded from the canoe, the canoe had to be carried across land to a place where it would be reintroduced to the water, and then we had to walk back and carry all of our goods up to the canoe. The entire process was slow, tedious work, yet every mile which we had successfully put behind us was one less mile which we had yet to travel. I felt as though we had reached a major milestone when we had finally covered the first hundred miles. I poured us each a small cup of strong spirits that evening to celebrate, but Oscar politely refused it after taking the first swallow and choking vigorously on it. He choked so hard that he almost became ill. I assumed that he had most likely never tasted strong spirits before, and judging by his reaction, he probably never would again. I felt that it was incumbent of me to drink both glasses... one for myself, and one on Oscar's behalf. I tried to make merriment in the evenings when we camped. I had grown to despise the mornings, knowing full well what lay in store with all the laborious, continuous paddling and portaging. But in the evenings I always felt exhilarated by having accomplished all of the difficult miles that day. I will acknowledge that there were days when I had second thoughts and serious misgivings... those days when my arms throbbed and my back was stiffened and sore. Occasionally, we would be dissuaded in our choice of camping sites when we found them to contain many snakes which appeared to be of the venomous type. Oscar was sorely afraid of snakes, and secretly, I had no love for them either. On such occasions, we would continue to survey ahead for additional locations until we found one to be suitable for our safety and peace of mind. There were many, many nights when I wondered what it would feel like to sleep in the comfort of a bed again, away from the biting insects and the hard ground. I had blisters about the skin of my palms and fingers, and the back of my neck had been burned by the sun, yet through my pain and discomfort, we continued to push on.

The muddy waters of the Missouri were plentiful of hazards and sandbars. We portaged around numerous small waterfalls and log jams and our spirits often sank to low depths when we would portage around one difficult hazard and almost immediately encounter another which required a portage. I did not complain about the swift current when the water was free of hazards and passable without delay. The many miles of quiet water gave us lifted spirits, and sufficient time for our minds to relax in preparation for the next difficulty... of which there were always many.

The Outpost

With each laborious stroke and pull of the paddle, my canoe glided farther upriver. And each day we proceeded upriver we came closer and closer to the day when we could finally depart the river and travel overland to our destination. We followed the Missouri River northwestward, passing fewer and fewer signs of civilization as we went. We had seen a few Indians from a distance, either in canoes or on the banks of the river, but we attempted no communication with them. I discovered that I was referring to my timepiece less and less for telling the time of day. Moreover, I was using the sun to assess the time of day. It was indeed the sun, which governed and dictated the start and stop times of each day. The timepiece became little more than a meaningless reminder of the triviances of civilization. Oft times, it was an extreme annoyance when my back and arms would ache from paddling and my timepiece would indicate that it was only two o'clock in the afternoon, and there were still six more hours remaining in the day before we would camp for the evening. Eventually, I ceased referring to my timepiece because it only served to add to my agony.

Paddling had become very difficult for Oscar and me as the river narrowed and the current became noticeably more opposing – always wanting to carry us in a direction opposite to our intended course. We were fortunate when we could travel fifteen to twenty miles during the course of a day. I had been told that traveling upriver took twice the number of days as traveling down river, and I could now easily understand why. On the twenty-first day of our journey, we passed a small outpost without stopping. However, I made note of its location on the map for future reference. On the map, I simply dubbed it the '*Lower Trading Post.*' My best calculations indicated that we had come more than two hundred miles, when we began to see a greater number of Indians occasionally at the river banks, just above the outpost, who were either bathing or doing various other chores. They watched us with wide-eyed curiosity as we continued to paddle up the river. One group of six or seven young men began throwing stones at us with astonishing accuracy, one almost striking Oscar in the back once. We paddled to the opposite side where we were out of their throwing range, and they soon abandoned their mal-intentioned frolic. The river was narrower here, and the current became even stronger in places. I was beginning to tire greatly, yet it was much too early in the day to stop for rest at the first outpost when we had passed by.

In one narrow stretch of very rapid water, Oscar turned and yelled at me, "Look, boss!"

I looked to see the badly decomposing body of a white man floating quickly past us, carried away by the current of the river. The odor was horrible, yet the sight was even worse. The water was much too swift for us to make any attempt to turn the canoe around and try to recover the body for burial. It would have been extremely dangerous and near impossible for us to turn around or even pause long enough to steer our canoe to the bank without risking capsizing in the swift current. Regrettably, we continued on. The incident served to remind us, however, that there were dangers lurking ahead, and life was a very fragile element, especially in the hostile world we would be traveling in. I could not help but wonder what horrible fate had descended upon the man which had cost him his life. I would never know.

My father's map indicated that the Arikara Indian village and French trading post where we would leave the river, were just ahead. Perhaps I could rest there for a day or two before we continued to travel on by horseback. I would be exceedingly happy to shed the canoe and ride a horse for a change. I was hopeful that there were people at the trading post who could speak English. I yearned to have relief from the constant paddling and to enjoy pleasant conversation with people again. I had been told by a trapper in Saint Joseph that a few of the Arikara there could speak English, but most spoke either French, or the native tongue of Arikara, or at times, an odd combination of both. *"I shall see,"* I thought, and we paddled on. I also hoped that any Indians whom we would chance to meet would be more hospitable that the hostile group who had tried to harass us by throwing the stones.

My canoe was heavily laden with goods intended for us to trade with the Indians, but Oscar never complained. He seemed perfectly content to follow my directions and sing his canorous songs. He was much stronger than I, and seemed never to tire. I tried to impress him with my eagerness to put forth as much labor as he, but if he noticed my efforts, he never made mention. According to Father's notes, the French outpost ahead was very close to the Arikara village, and the goods which I could not secure by trading with the Indians could perhaps be sold or traded to the French. I had been raised to despise the French, but would willingly barter with them if it would suit my purpose. At the wilderness outpost, I would not have the luxury of many choices of whom I could bargain with. The only choices were the Arikara and the French. My ability to speak and understand the French language was terribly limited. I understood much of the French language, but the French had the disgusting habit of pronouncing their own words very poorly, and thus making it very difficult for me to understand what words they were actually saying. I wondered how this impediment would affect the success of my obtaining the horses which I would need, yet I resolved myself not to be overly concerned until I was confronted with the issue.

Oscar had proved to be a good companion, yet our conversations were infrequent and shallow. He was a happy fellow, willing to talk, but was not capable of understanding anything but the most basic of conversations. I longed for conversation with another educated white person... someone with whom I could debate an unimportant issue, or exchange opinions with. In Baltimore, I derived much pleasure in reading, but my greatest pleasure came when I would discuss a particular book with my colleagues and friends. To have someone of reasonable intelligence with whom I could have confided in would have been of great comfort, for even as meticulous as I had been in my planning and research I still lacked confidence in my ability to successfully maneuver through conversation with the various tribes of Indians, or the French. My education had included studies of the French language, but I did not like to speak it, and therefore never received high marks for my efforts. I always felt as though the French language, when spoken, had a peculiar, nauseating sort of sound to it, and thus avoided its use whenever possible. I hoped that I had remembered enough of the language to enable me to barter with the scoundrels I would soon be confronting. I felt terribly alone, and inadequately prepared. I knew from my research that it was possible there would be very few, if any, persons whom I could confide in or have reasonably intelligent conversation with, but I had underestimated the devastating effect it would have on my fortitude. Loneliness was my constant companion. Like a demon, it hovered above me at all times.

    The map which I had purchased in St. Louis was purported to be an accurate rendering of maps which were made just six years earlier by French and American surveyors. I had, however, already noted several discrepancies along my route thus far, and found Father's maps to be of much greater accuracy than the ones which I had purchased. This bolstered my confidence in Father's documents even more. Father's map clearly showed many tributaries entering the river which were not indicated on the 1812 Government map. The river which I was navigating was known as the Great Missouri, and by all accounts it would afford me passage to the Arikara Village and outpost where I would soon depart the Great Missouri and proceed north by way of dry land. I would need horses at that point, and was prepared to purchase them at the French outpost, or the Arikara village. I searched ahead after each bend in the river with hopes of seeing the outpost at any time. It became apparent, near dark, that it was not going to happen on this day, so Oscar and I again beached the canoe and camped near the water as we had done every evening for the last twenty-two days. I hoped that the following day would be our last to spend paddling against the swift current of the river.

It would be early the next afternoon, before we finally reached the French outpost, which was owned by the French trader of ill fame by the name of, *Francois Brěaux.* He was the very man whom Father had warned me of in his notes and letters. Having traveled more than two hundred and fifty-five miles by canoe, the outpost was a welcome sight, yet looked much different than I had anticipated. It was not the thriving center of activity which I had expected it to be. They were eight or ten Arikara Indians there with their squaws and a half-dozen or so Frenchmen, but I could see no large Arikara village as I had been led to believe. A few *coureurs des bois* (trappers) were thereabouts, replenishing supplies for their next excursion into the wilderness, and tending to their packhorses nearby. The ground around the trading compound was quite muddy from recent rains, and walking about was not done without difficulty. Three or four Arikara squaws with children mingled about, evidently tending to chores of some type.

I quickly learned that the French did indeed have horses that were for sale there, and a few mules, and their trading establishment contained a vast assortment of supplies and sundries for sale which catered to wilderness travel. Beaver pelts were stored in three tall piles which almost reached the ceiling, and were stacked and bundled there in preparation of being shipped out by pirogue to Fort Saint Joseph. Steel traps hung from log beams in the ceiling and a vast array of blankets and dry goods were stored about. Kegs of salt pork and molasses were sold there as well as beans and cornmeal. There was a large keel pirogue there at the river, and the goods that it contained were being unloaded and carried into the trading post. I was disappointed to find out that none of the Frenchmen there spoke fluent English, however, Francois Brĕaux sent for an Arikara Indian whom I was told spoke reasonably good English, and we were eventually able to communicate effectively through this very adept Arikara interpreter. Everywhere about the inside of the trading post there were white men and Indians who were scanning me with suspicious, peering eyes. I had the distinct feeling that I was being dissected, piece by piece, by their inquisitive eyes... as if they were trying to discern my reason for being there among them, yet no one confronted me with honest, straightforward questions. I felt the presence of debauchery and evil all about me, and was quite relieved when I had walked away from the trading post to follow the Arikara interpreter to his village. Once there, I would endeavor to acquire horses.

    From my Arikara interpreter, I learned that the Arikara village, or the largest part of it, was nearly a half-mile north of there at a place called, Yellow Creek Bend. I made arrangements with Oscar to watch over my goods and stay with our canoe until I returned. I armed him with a knife and a stout pole, and told him to guard my goods with his life. Leaving Oscar and my canoe full of trade goods behind, I followed the Indian interpreter on a well-used trail to the Arikara village, which was a series of earthen huts with animal hides over the roofs. We passed several Indians along the way as they walked back toward the trading post. I tried very hard not to stare at the Indians whom I saw along the way, yet I could not help my fascination with seeing them at close distance with my own eyes. I asked my interpreter, "Are those men over there Arikara? They are not dressed the same as you..."

"Two of them are Delaware. The biggest one is Paiute, I think. At the trading post, we sometimes see Shoshone, Pawnee, and Lakota... even Mandan sometimes..."

The Indians I was seeing before my eyes did not appear as I had seen their likenesses portrayed in many library drawings. They were strangely handsome, wrapped in blankets that were partially draped over their shoulders. Most had long, unkempt hair which was black or very dark brown in color, and wore headbands about their foreheads. Several of them bore ornate tattoos on their faces and had odd skin piercings on their ears and nose from which various trinkets dangled, which I felt to be a hideous deformity rather than any kind of complementary facial enhancement. As we passed by each of the Indians, they seemed to look at me as though I was somewhat of an oddity, or a freak, and I suppose that I really was the odd one in their eyes.

The Indian who guided me to the village was named, *Hidessa*, which translates to mean, "*Runs too slow*," and I immediately gathered the impression that even though we had each evolved from an entirely different culture, with entirely different principles, he was most likely a trustworthy fellow. He had a peculiar sort of personality that just seemed to reflect a simple sincerity in everything that he said. When we first arrived at the outskirts of his village, I bore witness to a most dreadful display of public indecency. Shockingly, through the open doorway of a lodge in the woods, scarcely twenty yards from the trail, I glimpsed an older Indian woman inside, bent over something resembling a bundle of furs, holding her dress up above her waist, as a younger Indian man was standing behind her, engaged in a most disgusting display of carnal attendance. Why had they not drawn a blanket over the door, or made some other attempt to conceal their lewd act from public view? It was despicable behavior, and would have brought embarrassment, even unto the deviants of ancient Rome! Hidessa seemed to pay the matter no significant attention, so I inquired, "That's disgusting, Hidessa! Is that sort of thing practiced commonly here in your village?"

"The man is a Delaware... the woman is Osage, and she is earning her keep. There is no harm, and it is none of our business."

I simply turned my head and continued walking forward, and asked myself, *"Is this the way that savages commonly behave themselves?*

In his village, Hidessa introduced me to his chief, *Black Deer*, and a sickly gentleman who was his cousin, *Long Pants*, as well as several others whose names I do not recall. Hidessa's two wives had soon prepared some cornmeal cakes and fish for us, and after eating, we walked back to take Oscar some food at the canoe. Before leaving his village, Hidessa had introduced me to many residents of his village, and announced to his people that I had goods to trade at the river. His announcement seemed to have been received with great enthusiasm. Many times, I was asked, *"tá-nēha-quā" (what do you have?)* Hidessa would answer each of their questions by telling them to come to the river and see for themselves.

Hidessa spoke English very well, had a fine, gentle disposition, and we found that we shared a mutual dislike for the French. Hidessa told me that his mother had once been sold to a Frenchman who, in the heat of a drunken argument one night, had cut off the end of her nose. Hidessa said that when he had grown into a young man, he took his bow and arrows and found the Frenchman at another village and killed him. He then cut off the nose of the dead Frenchman and presented it to his mother on a leather lanyard of some type, as a keepsake I suppose. After killing the Frenchman, Hidessa carried his mother back to live with him at his lodge, where his mother lived for a few years until she died. Hidessa said that his mother was quite ugly, without a nose, and that no man wanted her for a wife after that. The Frenchman's nose hung in their lodge as a morbid memento of the event until the woman died. Hidessa told me that his mother had taken the nose with her when she died. I assumed that what he meant by such an odd comment, was that the nose had been buried with his mother so that she could carry it into the afterlife as a prize.

I commented to Hidessa that his village seemed to be scarce of younger men, as most of the Indians whom I saw were either women, children, or older men. He told me that his people had gone to war against the Mandan Nation, after the latter had raided an outlying Arikara village and killed six of their men and two women. He said that their young Arikara braves were being led by their war chief, *Kēsō-essel*, and would soon return with many horses and scalps. He said that all would be quiet after that until the Mandan people retaliated, then the younger men would go off to war again. Such was their way of life, and had been since time immemorial.

Hidessa told me that his village used to be much larger in population. He said that when the French and English first came to his village several years ago, that many of his people had died of strange sicknesses. His village now had less than half of the people who had lived there when he was a child. He said that many of the men who lived there would not offer their daughters or wives to a Frenchman because they had become smart enough to deduce that the French had been the cause of many deadly illnesses. Some, however, sold their daughters and wives to any buyer who was willing to pay their price. The very idea of buying and selling human beings sickened me. However, in Oscar's case, I knew that it would bring me great delight in granting him his freedom from slavery, but in order to do that, I first had to own him... I could not own him until I had bought him... so as much as I despised the idea of buying another human being, I begrudgingly did so. I judged Oscar to be close to fifty years of age, and I knew that it would bring me great happiness in knowing that he could spend his few remaining years as a free man. To have lived almost fifty years of his life in slavery was incomprehensible to me.

Thanks to Hidessa's superb English diction, he provided me with much needed information about the Arikara and the bartering process which they used. The Arikara did, in fact, have horses and other animals to sell or trade, as did the French, and offered a variety of other services which they were willing to provide, such as the manpower to load and unload pirogues. Hidessa soon had a multitude of Indians gathered around us at the river who were keenly interested in seeing the goods which I had in my canoe. Nearly sixty Indians accompanied Hidessa and me back to the river to view my merchandise and earnestly begin the process of trading. Many were curious observers, but at least half of them were seriously interested in trading with me. We sat on the bank of the river, above my canoe full of goods, and with Hidessa as my interpreter, the trading began. On command, I would point a long stick at an object, Oscar would then hold the item up, one-at-a-time, and at my instruction, Hidessa would entertain offers and relay them to me in English. I was trading specifically to acquire horses, and there was no other currency discussed.

The trading ritual itself was much more complicated and time-consuming than I had expected it to be. Oscar would hold up some items, and horses would be brought forth for my inspection. I was quite anxious to trade for the items which I wanted as quickly as possible, and get on with my journey. The Arikara, on the other hand, seemed to want the bargaining to last forever... as if it was an amusing source of entertainment for them. After thoroughly inspecting my goods, the Arikara and I bargained individually, one-at-a-time, and discussed each item that they wanted, and what they were offering in the way of horseflesh as payment or trade. Several Indian women were gathered there also, some of whom were prompting their husbands into bidding when they saw something which was of interest to them. There was often a great exchange of oratory between Hidessa and the Indians who were vying for my goods, and I felt assured that Hidessa was bargaining in my best interest. The process itself was long and tedious. Bargaining would appear to stall at times, yet moved along rather quickly at other times. Several more horses were brought before me for my review as bargaining intensified. Some of the horses met with my approval, and some did not. I was not an expert in judging horses, but I was smart enough to look the horses over carefully, and not let the Arikara know that I was not an expert. Even I could clearly see that some of the horses brought before me were in poor condition and some were quite old and swayed in their backs. I rejected several animals, and the ones brought before me after that were much better specimens. I suppose the Indians simply wanted to see if I was stupid enough to buy inferior animals before presenting their better stock – which was a tactic employed by any good businessmen. As darkness approached, it became obvious that the bartering session would have to be recessed, and continued in the morning. I was told that bartering could sometimes take days, and I was eager to finish the burdensome process and be on my way. The Frenchmen who were present seemed to muse jokingly at my negotiations, and although I did not have a good understanding of their language, I had little trouble understanding their disrespectful behavior and at least a few of their words. I did understand a little of the French language, but not enough to converse with them. They discussed me between themselves, and mumbled what seemed to have been obscene parodies at every trade which I made. I asked Hidessa to tell me why the Frenchmen were musing between themselves, and he only answered that the French were a disgusting lot, and that I should not let their rudeness anger me. I assumed that the Frenchmen were somewhat displeased with me because they may have felt that my bartering directly with the Indians was in some way competing with their business. Regardless, I was not the least surprised by their behavior, nor was I intimidated by it. I heard Francois Brěaux utter the words to his two companions, *"Cet Anglais est un cochon stupide!"*

Even in my extremely limited understanding of the French language, I was still aware that what he had told his comrades, was, "*This Englishman is a stupid pig.*" I had put up with about all I could take. I arose, and walked over to Brĕaux, and standing before him, scantly two feet away from his face, I said, "***Ta mère doit avoir couché avec des chiens de concevoir, comme vous!***" I expected an immediate fight with Brĕaux, and was poised to receive him or any other Frenchmen who wanted to join the fight. He seemed shocked to know that I had some cursory knowledge of what he had been saying. Instead of taking offense at my words, he turned and walked back inside of the trading post with his two putrid comrades following closely behind. I walked back to Hidessa, and sat down beside him to resume trading. Hidessa looked at me curiously and asked, "What did you tell him that made him go inside so quickly?"

"I don't think my French is very good, Hidessa, but I think I told him that his mother must have slept with dogs in order to produce a pup as ugly as him."

"I think I understand why he went inside, John Welch. Suppose he has gone inside to get a gun and will return to shoot you? Aren't you afraid?"

"No, I am not concerned. I have a gun as well, Hidessa. However, if he does come out with a gun, just move out of the way quickly. Now, let's get on with the trading. I would like to leave this awful place as quickly as I can."

Brĕaux did not come back out with a gun. In fact, he didn't come back outside at all. I remembered Marcus Attenborough telling me that a Frenchman could be a fierce fighter at times, but only fought fiercely when their opponent's back was turned.

By noon the next day, I had successfully obtained four horses by trading with the Arikara, and two more by outright cash purchase from the French. In my assessment, all six horses were fine animals. I had traded for all of the items which I needed, but still had a great deal of merchandise remaining in my canoe. I was left there, in possession of my canoe, an assortment of dry goods, and a dozen beaver traps. I told Hidessa to announce to his people that I wished to trade the canoe and all of my remaining dry goods to the person who will bring the best offer to me. I would entertain all reasonable offers. I told him to tell his people to bring their offers to me, and I would make my choice by sundown the next day.

Throughout the following morning, I painstakingly entertained several offers from the Arikara, as well as a few from the Shoshone. Mostly, they were offers of Indian women or pelts, or a combination thereof. One man offered me both of his daughters... the oldest appearing to be eleven or twelve years old. The sale and purchase of human flesh disgusted me, but conditions here far exceeded any mere disgust which I had. These people were willingly offering their own flesh and blood for sale! Their own daughters... and children, at that! How could they live with their own consciences after committing such an abomination? How could they go back to their village and face their family after doing such a thing? Had they no decency at all? They were savages! Every last one of them!

One of the Indian traders had proudly offered me two buffalo hides, and his young daughter, if I would include three of my beaver traps with my canoe and dry goods – in other words, every I had to trade. The beaver traps were only a ruse anyway... to hopefully cause some people to have the false impression that my interest in entering the region was in trapping. But regardless of the man's offering, I wanted no part in buying or trading for a woman. Especially a woman as young as this one was. Perhaps only fifteen or sixteen years of age, and a delicate beauty to be sure, but still... a woman who was this Indian man's own daughter! I was intrigued by the fair-skinned maiden who had been brought before me and offered for trade, though. There was something about her... something I could not explain. Her skin was a pleasing color which was darker than a white person, yet fairer and lighter in complexion than her father. I asked Hidessa why this maiden appeared so much lighter in complexion than her father.

"I have known this woman since she was first born, and I have known her father since he was a child. She is Arikara. Many years ago, her father shared his lodge with a Frenchman during a terrible cold winter. He shared his two wives, too. This woman that you see before you is the seed of that Frenchman. She has two older sisters, and one of them is also of a Frenchman."

"I see. Does this child's people look down upon her because she is of a Frenchman's seed, Hidessa?"

"She is not a child. She is a woman. But no, there are many women and men in our village who are of French seed, some English, too. She is only one, and there are many others. I am of English seed."

"So her father knowingly permitted another man to lay with his wife?"

"For *ohgā sá-ho*, yes. That is the way of our people. That has always been our way. Our women are friendly with all men and it is the way of my people for men to share their wives."

"Who, or what, is *ohgā sá-ho*?"

"That is when a man and woman unite to have union, you know? The woman lays down and the man lays down on top of her and takes his pēneă and..."

"You don't need to explain any further, Hidessa! I am not stupid! And such a thing is considered proper behavior by your people? For a woman to couple with a stranger... within the walls of your own lodge? In the presence of the woman's husband?"

"Yes... It is the only friendly thing to do. I have two wives. Would you like to have *ohgā-sá-ho* with one of them?"

"Hidessa! Of course not! Thank you, but, no!"

"If you wish, you may have *ohgā-sá-ho* with both of

them if you want to."

"Hidessa! Please! No, thank you!"

"Most of the men here share their wives freely, but not many are willing to share their daughters until they grow older. Some of the older women have died from illnesses and the husband cannot raise daughters by himself, so he sells them so they will have a husband to care for them. Some of the men in my village bring white men from the river into their lodge for *ohgā-sá-ho* and receive money to let the whites lay with their young daughters."

"Ahhh... the world's oldest profession, huh?"

"I do not understand."

"Forgive me, Hidessa. I am the visitor here, and I should be more respectful of your customs. I'm sorry. I mean no offense, my friend."

"When a man lays with your wife, he leaves part of his spirit inside of her with his seed. Then, when you lay with your wife his spirit comes inside of you, and you become better, more powerful man."

"Mercy... And you really believe this to be true, Hidessa?"

"Yes, I believe it because it is true."

"Have you ever considered the possibility that when the man is leaving his seed inside of your wife, in addition to his spirit, he may also be leaving syphilis and gonorrhea inside of her as well?"

"I do not know these words."

"I hope and pray to God that you never do, Hidessa, and I sincerely mean that. At any rate, such a thing is not permitted where I come from... thank God."

I was beginning to learn things about the Arikara culture which I found to be quite repulsive. Earlier, I had seen the bent-over woman being attended by the Delaware Indian, and after what Hidessa had just told me, I simply wanted to leave this heinous village as quickly as possible. Even the atmosphere here made me feel unclean. There was no wonder that venereal diseases were rampant in villages such as this. If I could just finish my business here and be quickly on my way, I could travel in the wilderness... far away from the revolting behavior of the filthy French and these iniquitous, immoral savages.

As far as the Arikara man who was offering his daughter in trade was concerned, any woman would be a terrible burden in the country which I would be traveling in, and a constant distraction I'm sure. I did not need, or want a woman, or a squaw, and if I had wanted a wife, I would certainly have sought after one who was closer to my own age than the fair maiden whom I had been offered. If I had wanted to choose a wife, I would have chosen one who was perhaps twenty or twenty-one years of age, and I would have sought one who was white, in a civilized Christian society, such as Baltimore, where English was commonly spoken and some degree of social propriety was practiced. And I would have sought one who was well-educated and intelligent; one with whom I could enjoy pleasant conversation, and one who shared my same spiritual beliefs. Although, admittedly, during the five months in which Elizabeth and I had been engaged, I could not remember a single conversation between us that was either pleasant, entertaining, or meaningful.

Out here, in the wilds of the Northwest Territory, I had observed none of the social graces to which I had become accustomed. The very idea of a savage selling their own daughter was repugnant to me, and I would not be a party to such evil doings! I felt sorry for the young girl who was being offered up as if she was bartering material. Her heart must have been broken, knowing that she was being offered up for sale, into an unknown destiny, and by her very own father... that is, if she has a heart. Perhaps these savages are all without hearts or souls. Perhaps they are merely a species of mammal... creatures that who bear a bodily resemblance to humankind... and they are devoid of a heart or soul.

I had announced to everyone who came to barter with me that I would make my decision two hours before sundown, and that I had planned to depart on a journey at first light the next morning. Shortly, I received several other offers, but they too were of no consequence to me, as the earlier offers had been much better, with the exception of any offer which had included Indian women as part of the barter. Most of the explorers and trappers who I had talked to along the way had Indian wives; some having as many as three or four. One, a European fur trader who spoke no English, had five Indian squaws. Most Europeans took on wives primarily for their carnal favors and the luxury of having inexpensive laborers at their command. Then, the unfortunate women would often be abandoned when the trappers had left with their goods. I suppose that men of no conscience could do such a thing without remorse, but I doubted that God would ever forgive them for such treachery.

Perhaps I could buy a companion/laborer, let her help me in my work, then release her back to her people when my work was done and pay her handsomely for her efforts. As far as carnal interaction was concerned, I would never stoop so low as to do such a thing with a savage! I could release the woman after my mission was completed, unharmed and unmolested, and free to go about their life as they had before I had arrived... and pay them attractively in money or trade goods for their labor. I entertained the possibility momentarily, as if the idea merited at least some cursory consideration, but then laughed to myself at how ridiculous it sounded... buying a woman... as if I was considering the purchase of a horse, or a keg of flour. On the positive side, however, an Indian woman would be an extra pair of hands, an extra pair of eyes, and a companion of sorts, if it was not for the communication impediment. As quickly as the thought entered my mind, I dismissed it. I would continue to think about my options, and try to make a decision in an hour. In the meantime, Oscar, Hidessa, and I sat and ate a meal together, and as we ate, we talked. Hidessa looked at me as though he wanted to offer me some valuable advice, and said, "You should have taken the young woman and the two buffalo hides, John Welch. She is the most beautiful woman I have ever seen."

"You mean the young child with the two buffalo hides, don't you, Hidessa?"

"She is not a child, John Welch, she is a woman, and she is a Christian, too, and she would make you a good wife. As I told you, I know her father well."

"She's a Christian, Hidessa? Out here in the wilderness like this?"

"Why do you find that so strange? Do you have to live in a white man's city to be a Christian?"

"Well, no, of course not. I just didn't know that there were any churches or cathedrals out here in the wilderness."

"Do you have to live where there is a church or that other thing you just said, to be a Christian?"

"Well, no, you don't. But it helps to reinforce one's faith by hearing God's word spoken by a Holy Priest of the cloth, or a minister of the Gospel once in a while."

"There is an Englishman who speaks Arikara well, Arapaho, too, I think. He comes to our village often and preaches, but he is not Catholic. The French are all Catholics, but the English preacher is not. Most of my people are Catholics, but some of them are Christians, too."

"Catholics are Christians, too, Hidessa. Is that girl's father a Christian?"

"Yes, he is a Christian, too."

"Well, if he is a Christian, then he's a damned poor one. Christians are not supposed to buy or sell people... like they were livestock or something. Yet he's willing to sell his own daughter? Christians don't do that, Hidessa!"

"Maybe so, but that is the way my people have always done it. That is the way that a father finds a good husband for his daughter. He is not really selling his daughter, he is making sure she has a good home. If a man can pay a good price for a daughter, than he can probably provide for her and feed her when she is his wife, and the father knows that she will have a good home and will not be hungry. The money paid is an offering to the father to assure him that his daughter will be safe and have a good home. If the father did not love his daughter, he would not do this… he would just give her away to anybody, maybe. I know this man well, and he has sold two other daughters, and they both have good husbands and plenty of food. But he has never offered a daughter to a Frenchman. He has grown to dislike the French. But as his daughter grows older, he may change his mind, for there are not many young men in our village anymore who have goods to trade for a wife, or can even feed a wife."

"Well, if he has never offered a daughter to a Frenchman, that alone tells me that he may at least has some sort of conscience. Hidessa, I don't mean to offend you, my friend, but Christians simply don't buy and sell people."

"Are you a Christian, John Welch?"

"Of course I am… why do you ask this?"

"I was just thinking that if you were a Christian, then you are a damned poor one… that's all."

"Why would you say a thing like that to me, Hidessa?"

"Oscar told me that you bought him before you came here, and Christians are not supposed to buy or sell anyone, John Welch."

"It was different in Oscar's case, Hidessa!"

"How was it different?"

"Because, I'm going to give him his freedom as soon as we get packed tomorrow morning, that's why!"

"You still bought him, didn't you?"

"Well, yes… but…"

"If Christians don't buy or sell people, how can you be a Christian if you bought Oscar?"

I discovered that it was a waste of time to try to make an

argument with Hidessa. Not because of any great lack of skill on my part, but because Hidessa possessed a great amount of wisdom within his savage framework, and was able to clearly see the hypocrisy of the white man's culture. I felt somewhat humiliated, having been ensnared by my own hypocrisy and my own injudicious and condescending words. Hidessa was overwhelmingly the winner of our impromptu debate. I found it quite ironic, that with all of the people around me at the village and the outpost, there was only one with whom I could converse with in English, and he seemed to possess far more intelligence than I. Perhaps Hidessa was right. Perhaps the Arikara way of doing things was better than the white man's way. If an Indian was destitute, and his daughters had come to age and were starving to death, would it not be best for him to pass them on to a husband who had the means of providing for them? Maybe, under certain conditions, it was the proper humanitarian thing for a father to do. But I would remain steadfast in my conviction that marriage should be based upon love, compatibility, and mutual attraction to one another, and not treated as though hearts and bodies, feelings and emotions, were "tradeable" commodities which could be sold to the highest bidder. Admittedly however, I was a pathetically incompetent authority when it came to characterizing or defining the meaning of *love*. It was, after all, an emotion which I had never experienced for myself. My conversation with Hidessa left me feeling more respectful of his simple logic. In the future, I would exercise more caution in choosing my words before I attempted to debate another issue with him, or answer any of his entrapping questions. I would also restrain myself from announcing my own pious beliefs. Perhaps it was possible that all barbarians were not as lacking in intelligence as I had initially assumed. Perhaps not all of them were as barbaric, as well.

    Still, I felt terribly uncomfortable in this strange place and was anxious to leave as quickly as possible to resume my journey. I felt somewhat confused as to what I should do at this point. Father's notes and instructions were quite detailed, but offered no help regarding the important decision which I was about to make. I would have to trust my own instincts and barter accordingly.

As the hour in which I must make a decision drew near, I began to weigh my options in a manner which would give my highest priority and utmost attention to the mission I was on; the journey to find the narrow canyon described in my father's manuscripts. My journey from Baltimore had carried me more than three quarters of the way to my final destination, but I knew full well that the most difficult and dangerous part of the journey still lay ahead of me. To this point, I had followed Father's instructions flawlessly. I had found his map and his instructions to be very descriptive, precise, and intelligible. In his notes, Father said,

When you arrive at the Arikara village, employ a trustworthy Arikara laborer to assist you in the rest of your travels. Do not employ a Frenchman or Englishman. Be kind and honest with your Arikara laborer. He will help you with the horses and assist you once you arrive at the canyon, but do not tell him the purpose of your journey nor your destination. Nor should you permit your workman to escape the confines of your employment until your mission has been completed, lest he will announce to the world the location of your fortune.

I was mentally staged to follow Father's instructions, and proceed with the employment of a laborer, yet, as Hidessa had told me, most all of the young men had gone to fight against the Mandan. Knowing this, I was certain that the only labor resource available hereabouts would regrettably be either a woman, or an older man. I would not start a journey such as this depending on an old man. I felt as though my susceptible emotions were beginning to affect my objectivity as well as my ability to reason and make sound business pronouncements, yet my available options had dwindled away at this point. The young Indian girl whom I had been offered was weighing heavily on my conscience. Could I employ her to fill the capacity of a laborer? She seemed very small in stature. Her father was not offering her up for employment... or to be rented as a laborer. Instead, he was offering her up for sale – a permanent transaction, one which frightened me. She had looked absolutely pitiful as she stood there before me in her beautifully beaded buckskin dress and moccasins... like an exquisitely innocent Indian princess with a beaded headband for a crown. She appeared to be at the mercy of the world... and she really was at the mercy of the world. She looked as though she had been brought to the executioner's block, fully aware that she had absolutely no say in what was about to transpire. It was by no fault of her own that the seed from which she sprang had been benifacted by a French donor... a Frenchman who was shamelessly allowed, and even encouraged, to impregnate her mother. I could see the fear and uncertainty on her pathetic young face as she stood there no more than twenty yards away. It was one of the most heart-rending sights which I had ever witnessed. I could only imagine what must have been going through her frightened young mind as she contemplated what would become of her. In her innocent little heart she must have felt forsaken and tormented, deserted and despondent. The culmination of the years of her youth had led her to this place to be vended, as a piece of merchandise. Her own father was willing and eager to use her for bartering material, as if she were a rifle or a saddle... or a mule. No wonder, though, for it was her very father who had permitted a Frenchman to lay with his wife. It's hard to imagine that a father would actually trade a daughter for a canoe and thirty or forty pounds of dry goods and eight beaver traps. What kind of people would do such things as this? Yet, as Hidessa had said, it was commonplace in that Arikara village, and perhaps it was conventional behavior among other Indian nations as well. I did not know. I only knew what was happening here before me, and I didn't like it at all. These were ignorant savages that I was among here! They were naught but wild and inhumane savages! All of them!

I was only beginning to learn about Indian cultures, and in them, what was right, and what was wrong, what was acceptable and what was not. I was familiar enough with the Holy Bible to know that it was a sin to enslave a person. But it was senseless for me to give the matter any further consideration, for I could not, and would not allow these horrible circumstances to distract me from my mission. I did not want or need a woman, or a squaw, and I especially did not want to employ a woman under such horrid circumstances… even a fair maiden who was as stunningly attractive as this one. She was, in fact, small in stature, and one with truly delicate features and innocent eyes. And she surely was a beautiful sight to behold, even as she trembled in her fear and anxiety. My Lord… How my heart did sympathize with her.

I was beginning to agonize over my decision. I was being intolerably haunted by an image… an image of an innocent young Indian girl. A brown-eyed beauty, who, if I didn't purchase her, would most likely be sold indiscriminately to a Frenchman by an uncaring and unsympathetic father before the next season of crops was planted. The French would have taken great pleasure in deflowering an innocent young girl such as this, perhaps brutalizing her repeatedly and then selling her abused, battered little body to someone else as if she were a horse or a pig. They would not have thought twice about exposing her to their atrocious venereal diseases, and would have given no thought to her if she had become sick and died from their horrible syphilis or gonorrhea, diphtheria or small pox. If she lived long enough to grow old, she would probably age into ill health, broken both in body and spirit.

Could a father raise a daughter, as one would raise a calf or a chicken? Knowing that their child was being raised for the sole purpose of one day carrying them to the marketplace? The French were filthy scoundrels, of this I was sure, and they had no conscience or decency about them. They were notorious for their immoral decadence, and their cruelty and abuse of their Indian wives, and I may very well be this young girl's only chance to escape such wickedness and cruelty. However, I had to keep reminding myself that I did not want a woman! Or in this case, a young girl! Yet, the way she had looked at me so pitifully while her father was trying to sell her to me was unforgettably disconcerting. She stood there speechless before me as she nervously awaited her fate. Her eyes almost spoke out to me, saying, *"Please help me, sir... Please!"* How could I depart this place without her under these conditions? How could I leave her in this evil place to be sold to the French? If I left her, knowing she would be sold to the French, would I not be a contributor to her eventual fate? How could I do such a thing? Easily, I thought. I'll just leave and forget about her. Despite her beauty, she is just another savage, like the rest of them. Her image will soon leave my mind, and I don't want a woman anyway! I need a laborer, not a woman! I'm on a mission, and I don't want to do anything that could possibly detract from my mission or retard its progression, or jeopardize its success in any way. Nothing is more important to me than my mission! Nothing! But....... My Lord... what about those sweet brown eyes that looked up at me? Could I ever get those sweet, innocent eyes out of my mind? Could I ever forget the image of her standing there before me, shivering in her fear and anxiety? Maybe she could indeed be the laborer that Father suggested. I could help her with the work that would require a strong back. She could probably be of some other use to me on my mission as well. She could be taught to cook, if she doesn't already know how. Perhaps she could kill rabbits or squirrels and turkeys. I suppose that she could gather firewood and start a fire. Perhaps she could gather fruits, nuts, and berries along the way to supplement our food stores. Maybe she could be taught to fish, wash my clothes, tend to the horses, or some other utilitarian chores. Perhaps when my mission was completed I could find her a suitable husband, an educated fellow perhaps, one who could provide for her, and keep her safe from the French, and show her love and admiration, kindness and devotion. He could provide her with a life which would be free of fear, so that she would never again have to endure something like this. They could raise a family together, and live a happy life somewhere. Maybe I could take her back to Saint Joseph and pay for her to get an education there.

I could even bring her back to Baltimore and personally oversee her education and her wellbeing. I have five empty bedchambers on the first floor of my home… She could stay in one of them while she received a proper education in a nearby school. In Baltimore, there were schools for young ladies as well as physicians to attend to her health requirements. I could do many things for her, I suppose… But I could do nothing without first buying her. I despised the idea of buying a human being. Perhaps if my motives were honorable, such as they were when I had purchased Oscar, God would forgive me for buying her. Perhaps if I abandoned her to fall into the hands of the French, God would never forgive me. Lord, please tell me what I should do…

Presently, I summoned Hidessa and asked him to fetch the Arikara man who had offered the two buffalo hides and his daughter. I told him that I wanted to see her again. There was the faintest possibility that she was not as pitiful as I had remembered. I had only seen her for a short time, and she was twenty or more yards away when I had looked upon her. Maybe if I could look at her more closely I would feel no regret for leaving her here for whatever fate might befall her. I may be able to see her as the savage that she probably is. Perhaps I would have no trouble with my conscience if I left her here to be sold to the French. There was a possibility that I had mistaken the look which I thought I saw on her face and in her eyes. Maybe she was also a savage, just like the others, and had not yet grown to appear as one. Perhaps she wouldn't mind being sold to the French. Maybe she would even want to be the wife of a Frenchman. Maybe she lies in her bed at night, longing to be the wife of a Frenchman! I knew that I could tell once I looked at her again, and saw her eyes at a closer distance. I was not familiar with the ways of the Indian, though. If I rejected her, would she feel as though she was not worth the cost of a canoe and a few other things?

Nearly an hour passed, when I saw the young girl approaching on the trail with her father. They were each carrying a buffalo hide. Hidessa was walking with them, and talking actively with the girl's father as they walked. I would use him as an interpreter again. Once they drew close enough for me to look into the young girl's eyes, and see her pale, frightened face again, my stern resolve to disassociate myself from my feelings fell completely apart and crumbled. Inside of my heart, I conceded, and voluntarily surrendered myself to my overwhelming emotions. We all sat down, and I was the first to speak.

"Hidessa, ask this man what his name is."
"This man's name is, *Necheda*. I know him well."
"This girl that he is offering in trade appears as though she has not been deformed by facial markings or piercing of the skin as many of the other women I have seen. Why is that?"
"Those things are not permitted to a woman until after she has married, and can only be done with the permission of her husband. The marks which you see on the cheeks of our women are the number of male children a woman has borne. They are marks of pride."
"You see them as marks of pride... I see them as marks of mutilation and disfiguration."
"I do not understand those words."
"Forget it, Hidessa. Tell Necheda that I accept his offer. The canoe, the dry goods, and eight beaver traps are his.

He may take them now and leave his daughter and the two buffalo hides here with me."

Hidessa translated, and the father began talking with his daughter, and her to him. They seemed to have been rushing through their conversation as though they were in a hurry. It was obvious to me that they must have been saying their goodbyes, yet they seemed to be doing so without emotion. There were no warm hugs or kisses. Neither of them shed a tear nor showed any outward sign of sadness. I thought to myself that perhaps savages lacked the ability to weep. Sadness is an emotion generated by the heart, and perhaps these savages have no heart.

"Hidessa, what is her father saying to her now?"

"He is telling her that she needs to be obedient to you or you will probably beat her badly, and that she now belongs to you forever. That's all."

"For the love of God, he's her father! Did he not tell her that he loved her, or wish her well, or anything such as that?"

"No. He did not say those things to her, John."

"Hidessa, tell Necheda to wait for a moment. I want to look at him before he leaves."

I walked up to the man, face-to-face and looked closely into his eyes. I wanted to see the look on his face for myself. I wanted to see what a man, who would sell his daughter, looked like. His face was cold, and his eyes were even colder. He was chewing on something which he held within his mouth that I assumed to be tobacco, and on his face I could see no shame or remorse whatsoever. I could see no emotion at all. I looked for the slightest hint of regret, but there was nothing there.

"Hidessa, ask this man if he would like more time to speak with his daughter before she leaves to go with me. Ask him if he would like to take her back to his lodge for tonight. I'm not leaving here until tomorrow morning."

"He said, no. His daughter is yours, and you must feed

her now."

"Hidessa, ask this man how he feels about our trade."

"He says he feels good. He wants to leave now and take his goods back to his lodge. He is finished talking."

"Very well, tell him he may leave."

Necheda left and came back shortly with three other Indians, and together they carried the canoe and all of the dry goods back to their village. The father never looked over his shoulder for one last look at his daughter, and the Indian girl did not watch her father walk away. Instead, she stared nervously at the ground and occasionally glanced up at me. She looked defeated, as though she expected to be beaten at any moment. I was left there on the river bank, standing with the Indian girl and Hidessa, and soon her father and the other men were out of sight. Oscar was watching our horses at the rear of the trading post. I motioned for the Indian girl to sit down, so that the three of us could talk. Hidessa was the first to break the silence.

"This woman belongs to you now, John. If she runs away from you, you may kill her if you want to, or you can do whatever your people do to such women when they disobey their husband... but I think she will not run away."

"I will neither kill her, nor will I hurt her in any way, and I will not force her to go with me if she wants to remain here."

"Remain where, John?"

"If she wants to go back to her family, she can do so. I will understand, and her father can keep the goods we just traded."

"She is yours now. She no longer belongs to her father. If she goes back to her family they will not feed her. No one will feed her. She will not be allowed to enter their lodge. She will disgrace herself and her family if she leaves you. She would have no choice but to earn her keep like that Osage woman was doing when you came here."

"Such a thing will not happen to this child as long as I am alive! I may never understand your customs, Hidessa. They seem a very cruel way for one human to treat another."

"Her father told me that she is a virgin."

"At her young age I should certainly hope so! And I do not wish to discuss things such as that in front of this girl, Hidessa!"

"She cannot understand what we are saying."

"She still has feelings, and I want nothing said that may hurt her feelings or cause her any distress or worry! Dear God… She has been through enough already. Tell her not to be afraid of me. I will not beat her. I will never beat her or hurt her in any way. I will protect her from harm, and I will take care of her. Go ahead and tell her that, Hidessa."

"She says that she believes you and she will not disobey you."

"Fine. Now then… ask her if she minds doing some hard work with me, Hidessa."

"She says she will work very hard for you and will not eat too much, and she will make moccasins for you."

We sat there in silence for a short time while I tried to think of appropriate questions to ask and words to say. I knew that once we had left the village to begin our journey into the wilderness, it would be unlikely that I would have an opportunity to converse with her through an interpreter. Hidessa may have been the only interpreter in this region, for all I knew. I looked at the young lady and admired her beautiful dress, with its ornate beadwork. It was possible, I thought, that she may have even created the dress with her own hands. Her eyes looked downward, as if she waited in humble obedience for my next command. Despite the reassurance I gave her that she would not be beaten, she was still trembling. I could plainly see it. I wished that I could have spoken to her with words which would have eliminated all of her fears.

"Hidessa, ask her again to please not be frightened."

"She says that she is trying very hard."

"Hidessa, ask her what her name is… what I should call her."

"She says that her people call her, *Lō-wē-já.*"

"Lo-we-ja?"

"Yes…"

"Tell her that I think her name is beautiful, and ask her if she wants to go with me to the mountains and help me with my work."

"She says that she is your éspouse now and you are her onēssē, she must do as you say and go with you wherever you go."

"Éspouse? Oh, no! She's not my wife, Hidessa! We're not married! For God sakes, Hidessa! Go ahead and tell her that! I want to make that point very clear!"

"You traded goods to her father so he would give her to you, and he did. She is your wife, now. I cannot tell her that she is not your wife, when I know it to be a lie!"

"That is not the way we do things in a Christian society, Hidessa… there must be a ceremony before a man and woman can be called husband and wife! There must be vows exchanged! And the service must be performed by a member of the cloth… There has been no such ceremony! I am her guardian, maybe, and only her guardian! Tell her that!"

"I do not know what this word, '*guardian*' is. I have never heard that word before. What does it mean?"

"A guardian is someone who will watch over her, protect her, feed her, and take care of her… and make sure she has clothes to wear."

"You call that a guardian, maybe where you come from, but here in my village we call that a *husband*."

"Hidessa, I am not her husband, and she is not my wife!"

"You don't have to call her your wife if you don't want to. She belongs to you now, so you can call her anything you want to. But she is still your wife now. You cannot say that the sun does not brighten the day when you can see your shadow in front of you, and you cannot say that this woman is not your wife when her father has given her to you and you have traded goods for her. If you don't like her, you can sell her to someone else, but you will not receive the high price that you just paid."

In the young girl's face, I saw her anxiety rising as Hidessa and I argued louder and louder, so I lowered the tone of my voice and spoke softly.

"I'll explain all of this to her on the trail, later. I don't want to waste any more time arguing like this, and I can see that this is upsetting her. Ask her where her things are."

"What things, John?"

"Her belongings. You know, like her clothes, or anything else that she wants to pack and take along with her on this journey. She will need to bring some items along with her. Ask her where they are, Hidessa."

"You traded for her and the two buffalo hides. That is all you get. She has nothing but the clothes she is wearing."

"She has nothing? Her father sold her to a stranger, and gave her nothing to take with her? My God, Hidessa! What kind of malevolent place is this?"

"I don't understand some of the words you say sometimes, John. I have never heard some of the English words you speak. Many men have come here that speak English and I understand all of the words they say, but you speak different English words than they do, sometimes."

"We can discuss this later. We need to start packing before it gets too dark and watch over our horses. I'm departing this place at dawn on the morrow, and I want to have everything organized tonight. The sooner I can leave this Godforsaken place, the better I will feel. Will you help us pack the horses, Hidessa?"

"Yes, John. I will be glad to. Your wife will help us, too."

"Stop that, Hidessa! She is not my wife!"

"I think she is. She thinks that she is, too. And I think she will make you a fine wife! You will see."

My wife? My espousa? Perhaps I should have had Hidessa explain to her father that I was not buying her so that she could be my permanent partner in life. I probably should have made that perfectly clear before accepting his offer. I had employed her services as a helper, a companion, and an assistant... perhaps even a cook... nothing more. I could not allow myself to be distracted from my purpose of being here... my mission. But at this point, what was done, was done, I thought. Somewhere along the trail I will find a way of explaining all of this to her. I will clarify her role and her duties, and perhaps she can tell me what she would like to do with the rest of her life when we return this way. I would be happy to help her any way that I could. At least she is temporarily safe from the deviance of the French and English trappers now, and a father who treats her as if she was a bag of wheat or a bushel of corn. Perhaps I could enroll her in a boarding school in Saint Joseph, or St. Louis, and maybe she could one day marry a successful businessman there. Perhaps someday she could study to become a great artist or musician. I would be more than happy to fund her future. Her large, brown eyes looked confused and frightened, and revealed her delicate vulnerability to the harshness of the world around her. I had roughly calculated that the price which I had paid her father, and considering the cost of the canoe, the beaver traps, and the dry goods, and it came to less than eighty-six dollars. Eighty-six dollars for a human life! Deplorable! It would now take from three weeks to a month to ride to my final destination; more than adequate time for me to develop some means of communicating with her. Given the same amount of time to travel back to the trading post, I would have more than two and a half months in which I could learn to communicate with Loweja. I would do my best to help her understand that our relationship was not matrimonical in nature, but purely an association of convenience, mercy, and humanitarianism. Surely I could accomplish that in two and a half months.

That evening we went about the process of getting my provisions packed and arranged for transporting by horseback. We arranged the packs in a manner which would permit us to quickly load everything onto the horses in the morning, and we would be able to hasten our departure when it came time for us to leave. Twice, I had to stop Loweja from trying to lift a heavy pack by herself, and had to get Hidessa to explain to her that I did not want her to hurt herself. It was more than obvious that Loweja was putting forth a great deal of effort in order to impress me with her hard work.

As much as I despised seeing the Frenchman again, we went into the outpost afterwards, to buy a few last minute items of food, and a few things for this young Indian girl who had nothing of her own, excepting for the clothes which she wore. Having a woman along on my journey had not been in my plans and was not what I had wanted. Having a woman with no belongings bewildered me, for I was unsure of exactly what to buy for a woman that would be traveling in the wilderness and owned nothing but the dress which she was wearing. I should have taken all of that into consideration before accepting her in trade, but I didn't.

I bought some extra woolen blankets, some thick woolen stockings for her feet, and two large canvases to be used as a tent or emergency shelter. I had Hidessa ask Loweja if she wanted anything, but I don't think she fully understood that I was offering to buy her whatever she need in order to make herself more comfortable. I took the initiative and used the opportunity to buy a few things for her which I thought may appeal to her feminine needs. A hairbrush, comb, a small bundle of cloths for sanitary purposes, two knives, and a pretty ornate silver bracelet which I thought she would like. I also bought her a large woolen pouch for her to store all of her items in, and a woolen coat in case we encountered unexpected cold weather. In addition, I bought her two more pairs of woolen stockings for her feet in the event that the weather turned cold. The Frenchman who ran the outpost, whom I had insulted earlier, *Francois Brĕaux*, was looking at Loweja's delicate body and small stature much like a wolf would look at a piece of meat before it was devoured. Knowing now that I could understand a little of the French language, he said nothing offensive, yet his eyes betrayed his profane thoughts. I felt like wringing his filthy neck. My old friend, Marcus Attenborough, was correct in his assessment of such a character as this; the French were a disgusting, uncivilized and immoral breed. I was normally not a violent person, but it was all that I could do to restrain myself from striking this Frenchman. Before leaving the trading post, I had a last-minute thought, and got Hidessa and Loweja aside to speak with them in private.

"Hidessa, ask Loweja if she needs any undergarments or anything similar to that. I will buy her anything she wants."

"I do not understand this word, *ungra..dar...mons*."

"Ask her if she needs extra things to wear under her dress... ask her in French. I believe the words are, *sous-vêtement*."

"She says that she wears nothing under her dress. She does not know what you are talking about either, and she does not know those French words either."

"Forget it. They probably don't sell that sort of thing at a wilderness outpost, anyway. Let's get all of these things carried over to Oscar and the horses before it gets dark."

I was glad when we finally finished our business at the trading post and left. It would be dark soon and we still had much work to do. Back at our camp, Hidessa offered me some words of advice.

"Sleep close to your goods tonight, my friend."

"Why, Hidessa?"

"The French like to sell you things and then sneak into your camp at night and steal them back. Sometimes they hire boys from my village to steal your things. That way, they can sell them again to someone else when you are gone. Sleep close to your horses, too. There are some boys in my village who would steal your horses if you do not watch them. They are my people, but some of them are thieves, too."

Hidessa and Oscar moved all of my horses several hundred yards away from the outpost and prepared a small camp there, where we could be safer from the French and maintain a watchful eye over our goods and horses. I asked Hidessa to tell Loweja to gather some firewood while Oscar and I carried the packs and the other heavy goods which I had purchased from the trading post into our camp. In her eagerness to please me, Loweja collected enough firewood to last a week before I took notice and motioned to her that she had gathered more than aplenty. Before leaving to go back to his lodge, Hidessa shared some bread and salt pork with us in our camp. Once Hidessa had left to go back to his lodge, I spread the two buffalo hides out on the ground, motioned for Loweja to lie down, and covered her with two of the woolen blankets which I had bought for her at the trading post. She looked up at me with thankful eyes, but said nothing. She was still frightened, and I could plainly see it in her eyes. I noticed that she was wearing the silver bracelet which I had bought for her at the trading post, and I felt a strange sense of gratification in knowing that she liked it well enough to wear it. It made me feel warm and content inside, much as I had felt when I had purchased the stateroom for the woman and her children on the riverboat. Once I had covered her over with the blankets, I looked down upon her, removed my hat, kneeled down beside her, and spoke softly and sincerely,

"Loweja, I know that you cannot understand me, and I am truly sorry that you can't. I wish that I could tell you not to be worried or frightened, but I know how I would feel if I were in your place. I will never harm you in any way… of that you can be sure. I think you are beautiful, Loweja, and I will never allow anyone to pierce your skin or put any of those hideous tattoo markings on your face. Please believe me. I will protect you, Loweja, and I will watch over you. I swear it. Goodnight, Loweja, and may God bless you."

She looked up at me with curious eyes as though she was trying to understand what I had said, and very softly issued a reply in her native tongue.

"*Vesa-mī-ena-ĕskē. So-oná-tē.*" I comprehended nothing of what she said, and greatly regretted it. But, owing to the softness of her voice when she replied, I did sense that she had at least understood the sincerity of my words, if not the words themselves. I lied down on the other buffalo hide, ten or twelve feet away from her, and covered myself. Looking up at the clear night sky, I tried to evaluate all that had happened on that confusing day. I asked myself how I had gotten into such a complicated and poorly disciplined situation; a situation which had been a result of my own making. Almost none of my research back in Baltimore had prepared me for what life was actually like in the wilderness. I had been keenly focused on my mission since leaving Baltimore, nothing else, just my mission. Yet, here I lay, in a strange land, among strange people… with a woman laying twelve feet away who is most likely scared to death of me! This is absurd, I thought. As ridiculous as it had been, Hidessa had proclaimed that Loweja was now my wife. What an ignorant thing for someone to say! She's not my wife! We didn't get married! And I still maintained the fondest hope that she could serve as an adequate laborer. She could become my trusted helper… my assistant, perhaps. She's young, and strong. She has been impressively active in the work which we have done so far in preparation for our journey. And as far as the language barrier is concerned, I'll just have to find some way to teach her to speak English. Perhaps I can even learn to comprehend some Arikara words as well…

With those comforting thoughts on my mind, I relaxed somewhat and eventually drifted off to sleep. Had I known what awaited me in the morning, I would not have thought that the day had been so confusing after all.

In the morning, before full daylight, I opened my eyes to see the dark figures of two men looming over me. Thinking they were perhaps French thieves, I rolled to my side and quickly arose. My revolver was nearby, but I had inadvertently rolled away from it without picking it up first. My rifle and my knife were wrapped and tied in a blanket and would have been impossible for me to retrieve in time to use in my defense. Defense wasn't necessary, however, for the unknown dark figures were that of Hidessa and Oscar.

"I did not mean to scare you, John."

"Hidessa! I didn't know it was you and Oscar! I thought for a moment that you were two French thieves about to rob me!"

"I don't think we look much like thieves, and I am sure that we do not look like we are French!"

"I'm sorry. I did not mean to insult you, my friend."

I looked around in the dim light of predawn and saw that Loweja was gone. She had neatly folded her blankets and rolled up her buffalo hide before departing. I felt perplexed, and had unsettling sentiments about her sudden departure. It may have been of great benefit to my mission, I thought, if she has run away to go back to her people, yet I felt strangely wounded deep inside because I would not be able to watch over her and protect her and to keep her innocent virtue far away from the iniquitous French and English trappers. A sense of extreme sadness fell upon me. For some reason I felt vacant and disappointed... alone and abandoned. Had her beauty really affected me that severely? Was I really so affected by an Indian girl that I could feel this damaged? This despondent? I mentioned to Hidessa that she had apparently fled back to her people.

"Loweja must have run away back to her village sometime during the night, Hidessa."

"No, I don't think so, John. I think she is over in the bushes taking care of a woman's morning business."

"How do you know that, Hidessa?"

"Because I saw her over there just now. She was squatting down among the bushes and I think I know what she was probably doing."

At his words, I felt an immense sense of relief. Presently, my heart and spirits rose even higher as Loweja walked back into camp and the four of us built a fire and ate a meal before packing the horses. Loweja did not eat very much. I offered her more, but she quietly shook her head, indicating her rejection. She seldom took her eyes off of me, as if she constantly awaited my next need... my next command. I did not want to become overly charmed by Loweja, despite her prodigious beauty. Infatuation could only lead to a damaged sense of objectivity, and I wished to make no excessive allowances for her. She was a worker who was expected to carry her own weight, a helper, and her beauty would have no bearing on the assignment of tasks. To allow myself to show such partiality would only detract from my mission and possibly contaminate my judgment. I couldn't allow that to happen. Yet, I felt strangely sympathetic when I looked at her. And sometimes I would catch her looking at me with an innocent observing stare. I began to notice a curiously appealing sensation when I looked deeply into her eyes, so I avoided doing so. I had felt sorry for her when I had bartered with her father because her eyes had looked so pitiful. I saw less fear in her eyes now, as if she was beginning to recognize that she was in no danger with me. Regardless of any peculiar sensations, I shrugged it off as best I could, and asked Hidessa,

"Ask her if she knows any English words at all." Hidessa complied, and she answered,

"White man... piège... horse... mari... knife... food... éspousa. Da-eeme-ta-nechu?"

"That is good, but some of those words are French."

"She can speak a little French, but not very much. She wants to know what you would like for her to call you. Onēssē?"

"What does Onēssē mean?"

"It means, husband, John."

"Hell no! I do not want her to call me that! She's right, though, I should have introduced myself to her yesterday. I'm sorry. Tell her that I am sorry that I did not do that. I am *John*, and you are *Loweja*. Tell her that I want her to call me, *John*, please," I said, while pointing first to myself, and then to her.

"*Joan?*" This was the first time I had heard her speak directly to me, other than the strange words she had said last evening, and it came as an extreme delight. Her voice was softly feminine, yet very clear and very pleasing to the ear.

"That's good! That's real good, Loweja!"

For the next half hour or so, we busied ourselves getting everything loaded onto the pack horses. Hidessa had told me that there was only one more outpost in the direction we would be traveling. Beyond that, to the northwest, nobody knew exactly what was there. Before departing, I had one more issue of business to address; that of granting Oscar's freedom which I had promised him.

"Oscar?"

"Yes, sir, Mr. John."

"I promised you your freedom if you would help me get this far, and you have. Here is the ownership documents, and I have signed it. You are a free man now."

"Where do you want me to go, boss?"

"Where would you like to go?"

"Can I come with you, boss?"

"Oscar, I can pay for your transportation anywhere you want to go. You tell me where you want to go, and I'll make the arrangements at the outpost. Now, where would you like to go?"

"Can I come with you, boss?"

"I suppose so. If you will stop calling me, boss! My name is, John."

Now I was faced with a very real predicament. Oscar had been loyal, trustworthy, and a hard worker. He had never talked back to me and he had always followed my every command. How could I possibly leave him behind in such a confused state of mind? I called Hidessa over and we talked for a good long while. If I took Oscar with me, I would have to buy another horse or two, and a few extra provisions, but I knew that Oscar could possibly be of great assistance to me on my mission. In fact, had I known that Oscar wished to go with me, I would most likely not have traded for Loweja – although fate had done me a tremendous service when I had acquired Loweja, and time would show me just how fortunate I had been.

After three hours of additional bartering with the Arikara, and purchasing four additional horses, the four of us were on our way. Yes, *four* of us. I had purchased an Arikara wife for Oscar as a companion, and even allowed for him to select the one of his choice from three women who were brought before me. Oscar did not show much enthusiasm, and he certainly did not choose the same woman for himself that I would have selected, but both he and his new companion seemed moderately pleased with the alliance. I had figured that if Oscar had a close companion, then she could occupy some of his attention and he would ask fewer bothersome questions of me. He chose a woman who had been widowed… one closer to his own age, named, '*Octeenchaha.*' It was one of the most confusing, disorganized, and frustrating days of my life, and had been even worse than the day before when I had bartered for Loweja. But the confusion was over for now. Before departing, I spoke with Hidessa.

"Hidessa, I am very proud to have met you. You have helped me greatly here, and I hope that you will do me the honor of considering me as a friend. I've certainly come to know you as a friend."

"You *are* my friend, John Welch. I do not understand some of the words that you say sometimes, but you are still my friend. And even though you buy people sometimes, I think you are a Christian, too."

"Thank you, and God bless you, Hidessa." I handed Hidessa two twenty dollar gold pieces as a token of my appreciation. Eventually, everyone mounted their horses, and we were finally ready to leave, albeit at a later hour of the day than I would have preferred. We were an odd looking group when we departed, and I had spent more money than I had planned, but Father had provided more than ample funds for the mission. Loweja and I bid our farewell to Hidessa, and the four of us started on our northwestern journey in earnest.

Every Indian in the village knew that we would be departing that morning. Several, out of curiosity, had congregated to see us off, yet none of Loweja's family came to bid her farewell or wish her good fortune. It seemed like a very crass and cold-hearted gesture to me, but the matter was out of my control. I saw Loweja turn around in her saddle and look back once, and when she turned back around, there was a tear on her cheek, but she never uttered a word. After seeing Loweja's tear I knew that it was indeed possible for an Indian to feel mental anguish, and even cry. If Loweja had uttered some sort of words which would somehow describe what she was feeling in her heart, it wouldn't have done any good for me to hear them. I wouldn't have understood her if she had spoken. Although, within my heart, I felt as though I did understand how she must have felt inside. I wanted to ease the pain which must have been in her heart, but I could not. I felt helpless, but again, I swore an oath to myself that I would protect her and watch over her. Maybe I could find some way to introduce a little happiness into this girl's life after the heart-wrenching ordeal she had just gone through. The grief and anxiety that she must have been feeling weighed heavily upon my heart as we rode off to the northwest.

Our pack horses were loaded very light. In the event that one or two of our horses became lame, the remaining horses could be packed with heavier loads. To have embarked on a journey such as this with fewer horses would have been foolhardy.

I had made meticulous plans when I had first started putting the conceivements of my journey together in Baltimore. I could never have imagined that I would have been proceeding overland with eight horses, an Arikara Indian woman, an Arikara Indian girl, and a freed slave. It was simply not what I had envisioned when I had formulated my plans. To further complicate the issue, I could only have very basic conversation with one of them... I could not converse with the other two at all. I could not even ask the women if they needed to stop along the way at opportune times to relieve themselves. With Loweja riding by my side, I could only take advantage of the opportunity to try to teach her some simple English words. I would point to items, and speak their names clearly to her.

"Tree. John. Loweja. Nose. Horse."

I tested her often, by pointing to certain objects without citing their names, and Loweja would think about the English name and call it out to me. Sometimes I would have to correct her, but most of the time she could recall the proper name without me having to correct her. In the mornings, I would often quiz her about the words which she had learned the previous day, and she would astound me with her ability to retain English words. It was apparent that she was putting forth a great deal of sincere effort to learn the language. Perhaps this was an indication that she wanted to be able to converse with me as badly as I wanted to converse with her.

On the Trail

During that first day on the trail, our journey was pleasantly uneventful. We never passed by the other outpost that Hidessa had mentioned, and I could only assume that the trail which we were on was a different one than Hidessa had described. There had been a divergence in the trail, where another trail turned abruptly eastward. I presumed that the other outpost was east of us on that trail, at an unknown distance. Our trail turned sharply westward, and we rode for many miles through a great expanse of open grassland, as was indicated on Father's map. The grassland seemed as though it was never-ending, and waved in the gentle breezes like a giant undulant sea before us. As we rode, I continued to try to teach Loweja some very simple English words, like '*hand, foot, ear, smile,*' etc., and felt like I would only confuse her if I tried to teach her too many new words at one time. We practiced saying the words, "*yes, no, good and bad,*" and I taught her the meaning of each word. She was quick to learn these words, and I could tell that she was putting forth a great deal of effort to learn my language in sufficient understanding. Her face reflected an obvious interest, and she struggled earnestly to pronounce English words as I said them. In my heart, I felt as though she was not going to be the burden which I had originally thought she would be. I knew that she was probably heart sickened by leaving the family that had raised her, so I spent a good bit of my time smiling at her and trying to encourage her to smile back at me as we rode. My efforts however, seemed ineffective. She looked at me as though she had no understanding of the meaning of a smile. It was possible, I thought, that she had never experienced a smile. The smiles which I so earnestly displayed served only to confuse her. Perhaps she even thought that her father had sold her to a madman, or a lunatic. She looked at me with wide-eyed curiosity, but I felt that in her heart, she was probably still scared to death of me, and I understood why. If I had been her, I would have undoubtedly felt the same way. She could very well be thinking that as my wife, I would come to her bed soon, whether she wanted me to or not, and that she could be cruelly dishonored any night now. And by the frightened look on her face, she was probably wondering if tonight would be the night. If that be the case, her fears were completely unfounded. Her virtue was safe with me, and I wished that I could have given her some comfort and reassurance by telling her as much. I desperately wanted to, but couldn't. Given her small body and delicate features, she would be at the complete mercy of any ruffian wishing to abuse her, however, anyone wishing to do so now, would have to reckon with me beforehand. I was here to protect her, and I would defend her with my life, if need be.

Before noon hour, we encountered a rattlesnake in the trail, and before I could intervene, Loweja jumped from her horse, handed me her reins, and quickly dispatched the snake with a rock. My cries for her to stop fell on deaf ears, for she did not understand what I was saying. It had all happened so quickly, that I hardly had time to react. She removed the snake's head with one of the knives which I had bought for her and put the dead reptile into one of her saddle bags, I supposed to be saved there for our dinner. She took her horse's reins from my hand and remounted, looking at me with eyes which were clearly expectant of me to announce my approval. Still somewhat stunned by the suddenness of the event, I managed to muster a broad smile, and declared, "Good, Loweja! Good!" In exchange, Loweja almost smiled back at me. I did not want her to dispatch another rattlesnake, though. I feared that such things put her in danger of being bitten. Yet I was completely helpless in telling her as much. Once again, I practiced saying, "*yes and no*," with her, and reiterated the meanings. It was my hopes that if we should encounter another poisonous snake that I could stop her from getting too close to the serpent by simply yelling, "*No!*"

Near mid-afternoon, Loweja quickly sprang out of her saddle again, handed me the reins of her horse, and started running back in the direction of her village. I searched ahead of her in the trail to see if she was going to dispatch another snake, but saw no such snake. She ran past Oscar and Octeenchaha who were directly behind us, and my heart sank, as I watched her running away. I felt a sudden rush of extreme sadness fall upon me, as if I was about to lose something very precious and dear to me. Then, to my surprise, she stopped after running only a short distance past Oscar and Octeenchaha and reached down to the ground and picked something up from the trail. She turned, and began running back to me. She came beside my horse and handed me my compass which I had carelessly dropped. She took her horse's reins from my hand and very quickly remounted her horse and looked at me, with eyes that were yearning to see my repeated approval for what she had just done. I was momentarily dumbfounded. I had no words to properly express my gratitude to her for finding my compass, and I was greatly relieved that she had not run away. So as not to disappoint her, I looked over at her from atop my horse, smiled broadly, and said, "Thank you, Loweja! That was good! Thank you!"

"*Kōá sā jees*. Good, Joan?"

"Yes, Loweja! Good!"

I hadn't the faintest clue as to what she had just said to me, but I believed that I saw the faintest hint of a proud smile on her face that time. She had probably told me that I should be more careful, and that losing such an important item was both negligent and stupid on my part. She may have even been telling me that I was a clumsy oaf, for all I knew, and she would have had every right to tell me that. Secretly, I was extremely relieved that she had not been running away as I had first thought. She was such a sweet and charming kind of person that I would have been terribly heartbroken if she had left. I would have been deprived of the ability to oversee her protection and fund her future. However, if she had indeed been running away, I would not have sought to force her to stay with me. I would have simply accepted her decision to leave, given her a horse to depart on, and miserably wallowed in my own grief. The compass was invaluable to me. It could have cost us hours if it had been necessary to come back looking for it. My very mission depended on my compass to guide me. Even so, I felt an even greater sense of comfort in the fact that Loweja had not run away than I had felt with the return of the compass. I tried to tell myself that the reason I felt such a strange attachment to Loweja was because of the efficiency she was showing as a worker and able assistant. There were, however, other reasons which were rapidly gaining magnitude. Although these reasons were very real, they were reasons that I did not care to consider or even acknowledge at this time. This young woman was enticingly beautiful… and I had to remind myself that regardless of her beauty, she was still a savage, and she was also a child.

That evening, we made our first camp in a seemingly endless sea of tall grass, at the edge of a small stream. Much of the area bore evidence that there had been a great herd of buffalo passing through the region in recent days, yet there were none to be seen nearby. There were a few trees near the stream with enough dead limbs and branches on the ground to furnish us with enough firewood for the evening and following morning. We had to build our fire right at the very edge of the creek, so as not to risk setting the tall grass afire. There was grass aplenty and water for the horses, and the place would offer me a good opportunity to study my maps to be sure we were maintaining the course which I had intended. At first, when I studied the maps, I did so in private, removing them from the pocket inside of my coat, and then quickly returning them. As we rode farther into the wilderness I exercised less caution, and viewed the maps freely in front of the others. Loweja and Octeenchaha made some kind of crude bread out of cornmeal that evening, and Loweja quickly skinned the snake that she had killed and placed it on a spit above the fire to cook. I brewed a pot of tea and a large pot of beans, showing Loweja exactly how many tea leaves should be placed in the water to boil. Loweja tasted of the tea, but did not seem to like it very much at first until I added some sugar to hers. She was somewhat reluctant to taste of it a second time, but at my insistence, she raised the cup to her lips and proceeded to take a sip. When she tasted of it the second time, the sweet taste of sugar had an instant effect. The expression on her face changed immediately, and she smiled and readily took another sip. Then, she smiled an ever greater smile. It was the first definitive smile which I had ever seen cross her face, and it was a delightful sight to behold! It was the first time that I had seen her wonderful white teeth. They glowed as brilliantly as shining pearls. Her face shown like a beacon in the night when she smiled and it gave me great satisfaction to see her appear to be happy, if only for a few brief moments at a time.

  Loweja was diligent in the duties she performed in camp, and it was good to see that she did not have to be prompted in any way to attend to her work. Once she had learned the routine of travel and camp, she knew exactly what she had to do, and she simply did it without being instructed. When I needed an extra hand to fasten the ropes on the packs she was always right there at my side, eager to help. In a way, I felt like she was a more capable worker than most men would have been. She was amazingly strong for her small size, and seemingly tireless. She seemed to always be poised to attend the next task, and I only had to intervene when it appeared that she was going to attempt to lift something which I felt was too heavy for her to lift alone. The first time that she helped me secure the ropes on the pack horses, she stood directly by my side, and I judged her height to be about five feet, one inch... certainly, not much more. She was my precious little Indian princess, and I was her guardian... pro tempore, of course.

The snake proved to be a surprisingly delicious supplement to our beans and cornmeal, and I did my best to convey my delight to Loweja. I noticed that she had removed the snake's rattles, and placed them in her possibles bag to be used for some later purpose, perhaps. Whatever her reasons, I hoped that they would not be used in any manner for the preparation of our food. The snake's meat was delicious, but I could not imagine the rattles as being edible. When thoroughly cooked, the meat of the rattlesnake could easily be pulled from the bones by using one's fingers.

In camp that first evening as I studied over Loweja, I became aware of a rather peculiar happenstance. As she bent over to pick up her possibles pouch from the ground, she distinctly passed bodily wind in the process of stooping. I was grievously embarrassed for her, and yet I pretended as though I had heard nothing, but, from the corner of my eye, I saw no noticeable signs of discomfiture upon her face. In fact, she showed no type of reaction at all. Of course, I said nothing, out of respect for her feminine dignity and self-esteem, but noticed that she seemed to pay no consideration to the event whatsoever. I thought that perhaps she had not heard herself as I had, and she had not realized that it had happened. An hour or so later, she repeated the phenomena as she bent to pick up a pail of water, and still showed no signs of embarrassment or humiliation even though we had made eye contact for a short time. I thought that she must surely have heard herself that time! The embarrassment that I felt was probably sufficient for both of us, yet with her having no reaction whatsoever to the incident, she had incited my curiosity. I was perplexed, but eventually shrugged the incident off as if it had not happened at all. After all, we were in a great wilderness, and not at an afternoon tea party in Baltimore. Perhaps she had never eaten beans before, I thought, and was unaware of their digestive consequences. That could not have been the case, however, as beans were a regular staple amongst Indian tribes of the region. Perhaps there is no shame in that sort of thing among the savages who live in the wilderness. I was mildly curious, but gave the matter no further deliberation. Even if I had spoken her language I would not have quizzed her about such a thing as that. It was a very personal matter, and I had no right to ask her about personal matters. I dismissed the occurrences from my mind by assuming that savages were not necessarily compliant to the social expectancies of the white man, and continued to study Father's map.

    A half hour before dark, I looked about the camp, but did not see Loweja. Oscar and Octeenchaha were collecting some firewood for the following morning as I continued to scan the area for Loweja. I did not want to intrude upon her privacy if she was somewhere in the tall grass relieving herself, and I was fully aware of the fact that all women required personal privacy at times to recompense their own particular feminine obligations, yet I was momentarily concerned for her safety and continued to search for her for my own peace of mind. My apprehension increased until I walked toward the creek, and in the fading twilight of the early evening I observed her near the creek in the tall grass. She was kneeling, with folded hands, obviously attending prayer. *"This is strange,"* I thought. Perhaps she really was a Christian, and perhaps she was even a more worthy and upright Christian than I, for I had never kneeled on my knees to pray except at the altar of our cathedral in Baltimore. Perhaps she was not a savage to the extent which I had assumed, and maybe she was not a savage at all. I chose not to disturb her. Instead, I walked quietly back to camp and left her alone to pray, for she did not pray in silence; she spoke aloud to the Great Holy Father, softly and earnestly. I did not understand the words which she spoke, even as much as I would have liked to, but I did manage to hear the name

"*Joan*" spoken clearly at least twice. What was she saying to the Great Holy Father? Was she asking him to protect her from me? Was she asking that our passage into the wilderness be a safe one? Was it possible that she was asking for some form of blessing on my behalf? I wished that I could have understood her, and I wished that I could have known why she mentioned my name to the Great Holy Father. Nevertheless, I had been touched in some unknown way by what I had seen and heard. I firmly believed that Loweja was not just an anonymous Indian worker as I had thought, but someone very, very special.

    Just as I had done at the trading post, I spread our buffalo hides out on the ground about ten or twelve feet apart, and placed our blankets on top of them. Oscar and his new bride, Octeenchaha spread their beds thirty or forty yards away, near the horses, so they could keep watch over them, and I could be at some distance from Oscar's incessant snoring. Octeenchaha didn't seem to pay any attention to Oscar's snoring which was a merciful benefaction for Octeenchaha. I had no idea if they had been intimate with one another at that point. The matter of their intimacy was their own personal business, and none of my own. If they had become intimate, they had done so discretely, after dark, and away from Loweja's innocent eyes. That was all that mattered to me. They preferred to stay somewhat off by themselves anyway, and watching over our horses at night would be their responsibility for the rest of our journey. The horses seemed not to be greatly bothered by Oscar's snoring.

    As Loweja was at the creek, cleaning the tea pot and filling it with water for the morrow, I lay down and covered myself with two of the woolen blankets. I watched her return from the creek and sit upon one of the packs to take her long hair out of braids. She appeared to be using a grooved, flattened stick to straighten her hair, so I got up and showed her how the hair brush and comb were used. She evidently didn't know, but once she learned, she used both of them vigorously, every evening and every morning. For my efforts, she produced a smile and mumbled a word or two in her native tongue. I went back and got into my bed again and watched her for several minutes while pretending to have my eyes closed, until she had finished brushing her hair. When she walked over to her bed, she looked down at our sleeping arrangements, and with her wonderfully revealing facial expression, showed her pronounced disapproval with the manner in which I had prepared things. She walked over to the hide which I had spread out for her, and pulled it across the ground to a place where it was only about four feet from my own. She quietly uttered some indistinguishable words in Arikara, which sounded very much like she was softly blessing me out for putting her buffalo hide so far away from my own. Then, she lied down, covered herself with the other woolen blankets, and in the twilight of evening darkness, spoke softly to me, "*Say-ha-way*, Joan…*onēssē*." I didn't have a clue as to what she meant, but I clearly heard that word again that meant, husband, and involuntarily, I answered back, "*Say-ha-way*, Loweja."

Could these words be the Arikara equivalent of saying '*goodnight?*' Is that what she was saying to me? I did not know, but I delighted in the fact that she had spoken to me without being prompted to do so. I almost melted with delight each time she spoke to me. Maybe this was a sign that her anxieties and fears were subsiding. She certainly appeared more comfortable in her situation now. Maybe she was beginning to relax in my presence, knowing that she was not going to be beaten or mistreated in any way. I truly hoped so. My dear God, please bring comfort to her heart, and please provide me with a way and means of talking with her someday… There is so much that I would like to be able to tell her… There is so much that I would like for her to be able to tell me. I cannot fully provide for her and care for her unless we can someday talk to one another. I want to hear her tell me about the things she thinks of as we ride alongside one another on the trail. I would like to know when there is something she wants, so that I could provide it for her. I want to know who this beautiful person who I have happened upon really is. I enjoyed being with Loweja, yet I was terribly uncomfortable when I heard her say the word, "*onēssē*." I was not her husband, and as she continued to learn the English language, I vowed that I would find a way to explain this to her. In the meantime, I was very content with the way that our journey was progressing. As I lay there in my bed gazing up at a near full moon, I thought about a strange actuality which existed in my life; Elizabeth Cunningham had exquisite command of the English language and spoke fluently in French and Spanish as well. Yet, when she spoke, her words were vacant and meaningless. Loweja, on the other hand, had very few English words at her command, yet, when she spoke the simple words she knew, her words were wondrously filled with meaning, and fell upon my ears as sweet music. Even when she spoke in her native tongue her words were pleasant to listen to.

On the third day after our departure, we encountered two white men and a pack train of eight horses traveling eastward. They were not French, and although we tried very hard to communicate with one another, our efforts were completely in vain. The *coureurs des bois* (trappers) seemed to have been just as frustrated as I, that we could not have even basic conversation. I assumed them to be German by the sound of their language, but could not have been certain. We struggled to communicate for what must have surely been a half hour. They were pointing to the northeast and saying, "*no beaver*," which seemed to indicate they had found poor success in their trapping. They were friendly enough, but without being able to understand one another, we eventually waved a solemn farewell to each other and went on our separate ways.

I had always taken the privilege of communicating for granted. I had spent my life in the company of people whom I had no difficulty talking with and understanding. It is both humbling and frustrating when one has the desire to talk to another person, and cannot. It is quite distressing when you are face-to-face with someone, and want to convey a simple message... a simple greeting... or a friendly thought... and cannot. It is perhaps, the most helpless feeling I had ever experienced. It only adds to one's frustration when you can see that the other person also has a great desire to speak with you, and cannot. During my days of preparation in Baltimore, I knew that there would be difficulties along the way in communicating with others of a different culture, but I had failed to consider the extent of these difficulties, as well as the emotional discomfiture that it had brought to my state of mind. To further frustrate me, I could have reasonably basic conversation with the French, but had no desire to do so. Had they taught the language of Arikara at my university, I would have been among their most stalwart students!

Confident in our course of travel as I was, the four of us were usually on the trail very shortly after daybreak each day. As a surprise, on our fourth morning in camp, I added sugar and molasses to our cornmeal – more as an experiment than anything else. Everyone liked the sweetened taste. They were wonderful treats in the mornings when fried crispy in a pan over the fire, and became a regular staple for us during the rest of our journey. They were also delicious when taken with tea, both in the mornings, and evenings as well. Making and breaking camp had become an expediently simple task for us. The more we did it, the faster and more efficient we became. I could almost feel a hint of fall in the morning air, but still being late April, I knew that there was no truth to my feelings. I attributed the brisk mornings to the fact that we were gaining in altitude each day.

We had reached a plateau in the great grassland where there was a large escarpment of limestone which protruded a hundred feet perpendicular from the prairie. Here, we left the trail and proceeded due north without the benefit of a trail.

Subsequently, thirteen miles to the north, we arrived at a smaller trail and resumed a general northwesterly course, as was written in Father's instructions. The correctness of this course was substantiated by further landmarks which coincided with Father's maps. We found the skeletons of four persons lying near the narrow trail on our sixth day of travel. The skeletons had undoubtedly been there for some time, as the bones were scattered about, and it was impossible for me to tell if they were the remains of white people, or Indians. Each of the skulls had been crushed in at least one place, quite obviously where they had been struck with a tomahawk or some other type of blunt instrument. Oscar and I collected the bones and placed them in a mound at the side of the trail which we covered with rocks. Loweja and Octeenchaha did not assist Oscar and me with recovering the bones, refusing to touch them with their hands. However, they did assist us in the gathering of rocks and stones to cover the remains. Their refusal to touch the remains was surely rooted in some native superstition of some kind, and I was respectful of their beliefs. I said a brief prayer over the final resting place of the unknown victims. As I finished the prayer and spoke the word, '*Amen*,' I noticed that Loweja also said '*Amen*,' and made the sign of the cross in unison with me. Without further ado, we remounted and resumed our journey.

    I continued to take every opportunity to attempt to teach new words and definitions to Loweja. Having a partner was comforting, but having a partner with whom I could not share meaningful conversation with, was at times, very exasperating. I wanted to hear Loweja's thoughts, but could only do so by reading her facial expressions and listening to the tone of her voice. Loweja had wonderfully revealing facial expressions. The more relaxed she became, the more revealing her expressions became. I felt as though I could understand many of the things she said simply by reading her face and listening to the tone of her voice. When she smiled, she produced dimples at the edges of her smile which added emphasis to her spectacular beauty. She was slowly learning new words every day, and I felt as if she longed for pleasant conversation as much as I. She would hand me a bowl of food in the evenings, smile at me, and clearly say, "*Food Joan.*" In turn, I would smile back and say, "*Thank you, Loweja!*" She had also learned to say, "*thank you,*" and "*you are welcome.*" I was ready to teach her that my name was "*John,*" and not "*Joan,*" but felt no great sense of urgency to do so. For the time being, my ears rather enjoyed hearing her call me, *Joan*. As for Oscar and Octeenchaha, they seemed to have been a perfect match for each other. I talked very little to them, as most of the time I was very content to place my full attention toward helping Loweja learn new words. I often saw them looking at each other, and could faintly hear them struggling to communicate, just as Loweja and I were struggling. Oddly, it sounded as if Octeenchaha was teaching Oscar to speak Arikara, instead of Oscar teaching her to speak English. I surmised that Oscar had been told what to do all of his life, and was content to let Octeenchaha be the dominant figure in their relationship. One afternoon, I heard them laughing hysterically about something, and although curious, I never inquired as to the nature of their amusement. I continued to wonder whether or not they had experienced intimacy with one another. One morning while I was going through the documents in my pockets, I examined the ownership document which I kept for Oscar. There was a paragraph which cited descriptive information that was used for identification purposes. This was the first time that I had read the information contained within the paragraph. With sadness and guilt in my heart, I read, "*Male, five feet, ten inches, uncircumcised, emasculated in his youth, index finger of left hand missing.*" Emasculated in his youth! What a terrible thing to do to a person… slave or not! Why would someone have done such a thing?! If they were in fact being intimate with one another, I thought that it was probably not in the conventional sense. They slept together, in the same bed, and I never violated their privacy in any way. My sympathy for Oscar ran deep within my heart.

In my thoughts while on the trail, I had conceived the framework of a plan. When we had journeyed to within two or three days ride of the final destination, I would leave Oscar and Octeenchaha in a camp to await Loweja and me. Loweja and I would go together into the canyon alone, and make a determination as to whether or not there was actually any gold which existed there in the canyon. We would draw less attention if it was just her and I, and there was still a very distinct possibility that there was no gold present in the canyon – that the wealth described by my father existed only in his feeble imagination. If there was gold there, and I desperately needed Oscar's help in order to retrieve it, he would be within a day or two's ride from me and I could summon him at will. Everything else Father had written in his notes was accurate thus far, but the possibility of there being no gold could easily be a reality. For all I knew, if there was gold there, it could have already been discovered and mined since Father had been there last. I felt comfortable and confident with this plan, and felt as though it would provide the utmost safety for us all. If mining in the canyon would prove to be a laborsome, time-consuming task, I would leave, and return later with Oscar and Octeenchaha, and the four of us could work together. However, in Father's notes, he said for me to employ one helper, and one helper only. His notes seemed to indicate that great labor would not be required. With Loweja as my helper, I would continue to follow his directions and place my faith in assuming that his written words were correct.

Even though the odd composition of my group was far from anything which had been in my overall plans before leaving Baltimore, things were working out reasonably well thus far, and we were making exceedingly good time as we traveled. By the eighth day, we had come as far as I had estimated for ten days of travel. Everyone had a job to do, and went about it with earnest resolve and harmony. Loweja would often disappear from camp for a short time and return minutes later with edible roots and plants which supplemented our diet and sometimes added beneficially to the taste of our food. On one of her brief exploits she had come across a stagnant pool of water and returned to camp with nine large frogs and a turtle, and what appeared to be small, dark-green cabbage leaves. It was a delicious addition to our cook pot. It was not uncommon for her to return to camp with a rabbit or two, or a spruce chicken. Rabbits in this country were large, and could easily be approached close enough to kill with a stone or throwing stick, and the same was true with spruce chickens. Watching Loweja skin a rabbit was a sight to behold. She was extremely skilled in such tasks, and her skill gave testament to the fact that she had probably done such chores a thousand times or more. Both Loweja and Octeenchaha had a keen knowledge in determining which of the varieties of burgeons, or mushrooms, were safe to eat. How they made this determination I did not know, I just placed my trust in their judgment and enjoyed the delicious additions to our diet. In my opinion, not everything Loweja and Octeenchaha cooked was palatable. They soon learned what foods I did not like and would not eat, and avoided preparing them altogether. There was one particular food that they prepared which I found horribly unpleasant. It was a root-like vegetable similar in shape to that of a small carrot, only yellowish in color, and of the same consistency as a carrot. I could not partake of this without gagging at its bitter taste. Consequently, Loweja ceased gathering them. When I was displeased with the food they had prepared, I would simply open a can of pemmican and make do with that. Whenever it was necessary for me to open a can of pemmican it seemed to hurt Loweja's feelings... as though she had failed in her efforts to please me with her cooking. Knowing this, I limited my use of pemmican to those rare occasions when I simply could not eat the food which had been prepared.

Loweja and Octeenchaha both had a craving for sugar, and I quickly had to establish rations so that our supply of sugar would not be depleted before the end of our mission. Octeenchaha had put so much sugar in her tea one morning that she had rendered her tea to the consistency of a heavy syrup. Loweja had attached a rawhide strap to her woolen possibles pouch that I had bought for her and carried it across her shoulder most of the time. When she removed her headband at night she would store it overnight in her pouch, along with her other valuables. She did not remove her bracelet at night, and I believed it to be among her most prized possessions. It seemed as though the contents of her possibles bag were growing, as it appeared to be much bigger than it had been when it contained only her comb and hairbrush and a few other assorted items. I was curious of the contents, yet respectful of her privacy and although I was tempted to peek inside, I never did. One evening, however, the mystery was solved when she emptied the contents on her buffalo hide so that she could clean the dust and debris from inside the pouch. I saw her hairbrush and comb, two knives, some strips of rawhide, several large plant leaves which I assumed to be for personal hygiene use, several small stones for throwing at rabbits or spruce chickens, the bundle of cloth pieces which I had bought for her, the rattles from the snake she had killed, tiny bundles of roots that I had seen her chewing on from time to time, and several pieces of flint. She had offered me a root to chew on several occasions while we were riding, but I had politely declined until one morning after we broke camp. I accepted her offering with a smile and began chewing on the root. Surprisingly, it had a pleasing taste to it, vaguely similar to sweet mint, but was much too coarse to allow for swallowing. I noticed that she would discard the root after she had chewed on it for several minutes and rendered it to a stringy pulp, so I did the same. It left my mouth with a fresh, clean feeling which I enjoyed. It became a morning ritual of sorts, for her to hand me a root to chew on after we had broken camp and were on the trail together.

"Thank you, Loweja!"
"You are welcome, Joan."
"Loweja... my name is, *John*. *John*... not Joan."
"John?"
"Yes! That's it! John! Very good, Loweja!"

I found myself becoming more and more enamored by her presence, and was beginning to feel like my attempts to ignore her beauty were futile. I was beginning to feel remorseful for once having thought of her as nothing but a *savage*. I had contrived these thoughts out of my own condescending ignorance at the time. Despite her superstitions, despite her primitive understanding of a white man's world... she was no savage, by any means. She was a pleasure to travel with, yet her presence caused me occasional discomfort. The times of my greatest mental discomfort occurred during the times when I would be looking into her eyes and see a smile come across her face. I usually had little trouble resisting the charm of her beautiful eyes alone, but when they were accompanied by a smile, it came as an uneasy torment to my stalwart resolution to avoid any manner of amorous feelings toward her. The fact of the matter was, Loweja was beautiful, and her beauty was very difficult for me to ignore. I had been with Loweja now for eight days and eight nights, and aside from the strange sensations I was feeling in my heart, I had no regrets for bringing her with me. She was a joy to be with and was a very diligent worker as well. The fact that I was paying more and more attention to her as a woman seemed not to perturb me greatly, nor did it distract me from my mission, until one day in the early afternoon. We had stopped at the edge of a bluff to allow Loweja and Octeenchaha an opportunity to go into some bushes for personal reasons, and as Loweja got off of her horse, the tassel hem of her dress had entangled with the ropes which held the blankets and buffalo hides on the back of her horse. As she lowered herself to the ground, for a brief moment her dress was raised above her waist, revealing the startling fact that she indeed wore no undergarments under her dress. What she had told Hidessa and I at the trading post was true. She quickly pulled her hem out of the ropes allowing her dress to fall down into place and turned her head hastily toward me, to see if I had seen what had happened. I acted casually and quickly looked away from her, over to the southeast and down toward the ground, giving her the impression that I had seen nothing... but I had seen plenty. It had all happened so quickly that I was left with very little mental image of what I had just seen, yet my heart was racing strangely for some unknown reason. What is happening to me, I wondered? Why am I so attracted to this young person who is traveling with me? Why is it that I spend so much time during the day looking in her direction, or going out of my way to pay attention to her? And what are these strange sensations that have suddenly crept into my heart? Why can I not evacuate them? With stern resolution, I told myself, "Be strong, John... and stay focused on your mission."

When we had been on the trail for about two weeks, a tremendous change came over Loweja. It was as though her personality had changed overnight. She became very stand-offish and withdrawn from me – as though she wanted to avoid me altogether. She would not speak to me or even acknowledge me when I spoke to her. She would not assist Octeenchaha in preparing our meals, she would eat far away from me, and each evening she would drag her buffalo hide twelve or fifteen feet from mine and sleep off by herself. I was heart-sickened by her conduct, and felt as though it was due to some sort of an instinct for her to return to her inbred savage ways. Perhaps I had done something which had angered her. I was greatly perplexed because she would not talk to me, and felt as though all of my efforts to make her happy were in vain. I even thought that I may have committed some sort of unpardonable violation which had turned her against me. I worried about it continuously until after five or six days she seemed to return to her sweet, lovable self. I was thrilled to have her back with us as the person that she had been prior to this unexplainable behavior. Yet I desperately wanted to avoid repeating whatever I had done to upset her in the first place. I dismissed any further thoughts of the incident, yet remained completely bewildered by the occurrence.

I was immensely pleased with the performance, surefootedness, and stamina of our horses. I was not a great judge of horses, and the fact that we seemed to have such good horses in our possession was largely attributed to happenstance. They were all spy animals, and yet gentle in nature. I had taught Oscar how to properly prune and trim their hooves when necessary, and only rarely did I have to attend to the worst cases of hoof fraying or an occasional infection. Our horses had become very accustomed to us, and Loweja doted upon her mount, often petting its neck as she rode. She even spoke to her horse occasionally, and I would have loved to have been able to understand what she was saying to it.

One night in camp we were all suddenly awakened by the panicky whinnying and baying of our horses. We arose to find the sky glowing orange in the east and a tremendous grass fire coming toward us quickly. The line of fire was two or three miles from us, but was moving so rapidly under the force of the northeast wind that we hurriedly broke camp, packed the horses, and fled for our lives toward the northwest. The sky was so bright from the fire that we could see perfectly, even though my timepiece indicated that it was just two o'clock in the morning. We wasted no time in fleeing from what would have been a certain death if the fire was to catch us. At each rise in the land I would turn and assess the progress of the blazing fire. It seemed to be gaining on us, and appeared to be scarcely a mile behind us at one point. I could tell from my vantage point that the fire had engulfed the area where we had been camped, and was continuing to pursue us at a rapid pace. We whipped our horses into a near gallop for a mile or two, and then turned to the west toward a nearby mountain of shale and sandstone. A herd of perhaps two hundred fifty buffalo stampeded within a quarter mile of us as they fled the blazing prairie. The landscape behind us was reminiscent of hell's inferno itself, as we turned our horses up the mountain.

Climbing the slippery rocks on the north side of the mountain, we had to dismount, and lead our horses up the steep slope. We finally reached the summit and stopped there in wonderment as we watched the horrendous fire below us. There was nothing growing on the mountain which would provide fuel for a fire, so we huddled there on top with our horses and watched the fire as it reached the bottom of the mountain and slowly extinguished itself. We were forced to breathe through dampened bandanas, and still the smoke burned our throats and nostrils. The horrible fire continued westerly, around the mountain, and by daybreak, we could see no signs of fire. Only small patches of smoking debris lay in its wake. Mercifully, a gentle rain began to fall as we led our horses back down the steep slope. At the bottom, we remounted our horses and traveled back toward the main trail to resume our northwesterly course. In the distance, we could see lightning. The air was still thick with smoke and barely tolerable to breathe. We eventually passed through all signs of scorched earth and stopped early that evening to camp, eat, and give our horses a well-deserved rest. Many hours passed before the bitter smell of burning grass left our nostrils and we were able to sleep. We were all fairly exhausted from our ordeal, yet very thankful that our lives had been spared.

Having finally crossed the great grassland, we were now in an area with many scattered hills and valleys, and we began to see more and more stands of trees. Sycamore and cottonwood were in great abundance along the creeks, with good stands of pine covering the hillsides on both sides of us. In the distance, we could see higher mountains, and all along the way we began seeing increased numbers of wild animals.

We saw wapiti, deer, antelope, and buffalo in great numbers, and rabbits appeared to be just about everywhere. I seldom had trouble finding the landmarks which Father had indicated on his map, and then, I would simply use my compass to steer us toward the next one. The compass bearings on Father's map were incredibly accurate, yet if Loweja had not recovered my compass when I had dropped it, I most likely would not have been able to find any of the landmarks. Each day that we traveled, the high mountains in the distance grew closer and closer. It was now early May, and the distant mountains still had snow on their very tops. They were beautiful to see, and every day brought their beauty closer to us. The Indians called these magnificent mountains, *'as-sin-wati,'* which when translated into English means, '*Shining Rocky Mountains.*'

On a very warm and pleasant evening, on the eleventh day of our journey, we had camped near a high bluff which overlooked a small stream a hundred yards below. There was a gentle breeze out of the northwest and there was much nearby firewood scattered through the trees. Loweja had left to fetch a pail of water from the stream below us, as Oscar and I made camp and tended to the horses while Octeenchaha gathered some firewood. The sky was overcast, so I used one of the large canvas covers to erect a large lean-to for Loweja and I to sleep beneath should rain occur during the night and Oscar did the same for he and Octeenchaha. During Loweja's extended absence to get water, I began to worry about her and was leaving camp to find her when I saw her hobbling up the steep trail with a pail of water, evidently in pain. I rushed to her aid and took the pail of water from her hand and sat it on the ground. I picked her up into my arms, carried her into camp, and asked, "Loweja! What's the matter, did you hurt yourself?"

"*Shyo-nek tee-sa*, John."
"What? Tell me in French..."
"*Je me suis blessé le pied! Mon pied.* Foot."

"*laissez-moi regarder!*" I asked her in French, to let me look closely at her foot.

She sat down on one of the packs in camp and raised her leg to show me her foot. I could see blood on the outside of her moccasin. I kneeled down beside her and took her foot in my hand. A very thin chard of quartz rock had penetrated the bottom of her moccasin and was embedded in the side of her heel. She had walked all of the way up the steep hill with an injured foot and a pail full of water without a whimper, and never spilled a drop of it! I delicately removed her moccasin and looked closely at her injury. The small end of the sliver of stone was clearly visible above the surface of her skin. With my fingernails, I grasped the end of the sliver as gently as I possibly could, and pulled it out. Almost a half inch of the sharp stone had penetrated the side of her heel. Loweja looked at me with benevolent eyes and never grimaced in pain. I doubted that I could have done as much if I had been the one who had been injured. I was very concerned that, due to the location of the wound, infection could set in. After retrieving my small medical kit from the pack, I cleaned the wound with alcohol and tincture until the bleeding had stopped, and then dressed the wound with sulfur and a bandage. I cleaned the blood from the inside of her moccasin, and slipped her moccasin gently back onto her foot. Oscar and Octeenchaha had watched from a distance of ten feet or so, but said nothing. Once her moccasin was back on her foot, she looked up at me and very distinctly said, "Thank you, John. *Merci.*"

"You are welcome, Loweja. *Soyez le bienvenu.*"

"Foot better now. *Pied est bonne.*"

"Let me see the other one," I said. "*Une autre.* I had better give it a good look, too." I pointed to her other foot, and she enthusiastically raised it for me to inspect. I slipped her moccasin off and held her foot in my hand. I pretended to be inspecting the foot for any sign of injury, but my real motivation lied in the simple heavenly joy which I derived in merely touching her foot with my hand and fingers. She was impishly smiling and wiggling her toes with delight and I was being aroused tremendously by the feel of her foot in my hand. Oscar and Octeenchaha curiously looked on, unaware of what was really transpiring between Loweja and me. No one suspected the immense pleasure which I was experiencing, although I never doubted that Loweja knew. My heart was beating so strongly that I felt as if my face was flushed. Her face and her eyes were telling me that she was delighting at my touch as much as I delighted in touching her. I tried to appear as serious and nonchalant as I possibly could. I reluctantly replaced her moccasin on her foot, looked into her eyes, and nodding my head approvingly up and down, I softly said, "This is a good foot, Loweja."

"Thank you, John. *Nichee-dos*? Look at hand?" She asked as she held her hand out for me to inspect. I held her hand for a moment and looked at it, but I could feel the meddlesome stares of Oscar and Octeenchaha on the back of my neck. I wanted to shout at them and tell them to go somewhere far away and do something, and leave me alone to savor this wonderful pleasure... but I restrained myself momentarily.

"Good hand, too, Loweja."

"Thank you, John. This hand?" She asked as she held the other hand up for me to inspect.

"Yes, Loweja, this hand is a good hand, too. Much good! Oscar, is there something that you and Octeenchaha should be attending to now?"

"Yes, boss. We can take the saddles off of the horses."

"Then go and do it, please! Both of you!"

I was well embarrassed now by Loweja's prodigious smile. Her enjoyment of the event was not as concealed as mine had been. I wanted to thank her for allowing me the privilege of touching her feet and hands, but did not know how. I did not know the proper words to express myself in her language or mine. Perhaps if Oscar and Octeenchaha had not been there I may have even become more advancing in my behavior... I should hope not, but I just did not know. I had felt almost delirious with delight in touching her, and I was utterly ashamed of myself for having derived so much pleasure from such a simple thing as touching someone's foot and hand. Loweja had received a potentially serious and almost debilitating injury to her heel, but we had both used the opportunity as an excuse for touching. It became evident to me that she was flirting with me... enticing me... inviting me... I knew it, and I was almost overcome with the emotional satisfaction brought forth by the event.

    I changed the dressing on her injured foot during each evening forthcoming, and took great pleasure in inspecting her feet and hands. On the evenings when it would appear that I had forgotten to inspect her foot, she would not hesitate to remind me by asking, "Do foot, John?" As menial as it may have seemed to an onlooker, we both looked forward to our evening touching ritual, yet I was frightened to death at what it was leading to. I told myself each night that I should not be touching her in this manner. She is more of a child than a woman. She is in my care. I am her guardian and her protector. My conduct must not be impassioned or corrupted by her prodigious beauty. Yet, every night, when she would offer her foot to me for examination, I could not resist the temptation of touching her, and each time that I did so, I would feel the same wondrous sensations. One evening, I came exceptionally close to getting carried away with myself and stepping beyond the bounds of righteousness. After tending to Loweja's injured foot and cleansing the wound with alcohol and tincture, I was cheerfully satisfied that it was healing very well. She offered me her good foot to inspect, and with a very serious look on my face, I said, "This is not a very good foot here! This is a very smelly foot! This foot needs to be tickled! It needs to be tickled badly!"

    She obviously did not understand what I had just said,

but seemed concerned over the fact that I had a serious, apprehensive look on my face. Without warning, I began tickling the bottom of her foot and she winched around until she had withdrawn it from my grasp, giggling and smiling as she did so. I thought she was going to put her moccasin back on, but instead, with a sheepish smile, she once again offered her foot to me and asked, "Good foot, John?"

"No, this is bad foot!" And I began tickling her again. This exercise was repeated time after time until I finally gave in and declared her foot to be a "*Good foot!*" I could not completely understand how such a simple, childish thing, like tickling someone's foot, could create so much delight within me. It was completely beyond my explanation or my understanding.

I had thus far spent the years of my young adulthood with a heart as vacant as a bottomless cavern. I had never felt as though anyone was worthy enough to occupy even the remotest corner of my emptiness. I guarded my emptiness with near fanatical resolve. I would not have voluntarily given my permission for anyone to take up residency there. Yet magically, somehow, a remarkable young Indian maiden had gained access… and there was nothing that I could do about it, nor was there anything that I wanted to do about it.

A Chance Encounter

As Loweja's heel continued to mend quickly over the next four days, we traveled onward for the next week, pleasantly and without incident. Even though her heel had mended completely, our evening ritual of "*foot inspecting*" was repeated each evening. We continued onward, accompanied by weather which was usually quite delightful. However, we did have to seek shelter one afternoon during a sudden violent thunder storm. I was able to throw a sheet of canvas over a low tree limb, and Loweja and I quickly huddled beneath it until the storm had passed and the rain had practically ceased. With rain still falling from the leaves of the trees, we sat there under the canvas for a while. Oscar and Octeenchaha did likewise, at a tree some forty yards distant. While we were under the canvas, Loweja looked at me and smiled, with drops of rain about her beautiful face. She had a wonderful smile, and it not only added greatly to her beauty, it filled my heart with joy each time I saw it. My heart absolutely overflowed with satisfaction each time I watched her smile. I reached up to the side of her nose where a large drop of rain was perched, and gently transferred the drop of rain from her nose to my fingertip and showed it to her. Under the canvas, in the continuing rain, she asked, "Rain, John? *Ki-mi-woini*... rain?"

"Yes, Loweja, it is rain! That is very good! What is this?" I said while pointing to her lips.

"Smile? *Na-teecha toma*?"

"Yes, Loweja! Smile!"

"You *noma John*... not Joan, yes?"

"Yes, Loweja! That's right! My name is John, not Joan."

We were very close together under the small canvas cover... closer than I had ever been to her before. She raised her foot for me to inspect, and after looking around to make sure that Oscar and Octeenchaha could not see me, I gladly took her foot in my hand. This time, however, I used the opportunity to gently rub the bottom of her foot without first inspecting it. We looked into each other's eyes, deeper and longer than ever before, as I continued to gently rub her foot. I noticed that she was beginning to smile more and more, without being prompted to do so. In fact, she smiled almost continuously now, and I attributed this to the fact that she had probably come to know that she would indeed, not be mistreated in any way while she was under my care. Her current station in life gave her the freedom to be herself, and it delighted me greatly whenever she displayed her exuberance... yet at the same time, it caused me some degree of concern. I was beginning to have more and more uncomfortably warm and affectionate feelings for her... feelings which I had not predicted ... feelings which I would have preferred avoiding. I wanted to find ample satisfaction just in knowing that Loweja was showing signs of cheerfulness now ... and that her cheerfulness alone would provide me with great contentment. Beyond that, I wanted to avoid any extensive fixation with Loweja... I wanted no constraining, unnecessary emotional ties with her, and I especially wanted my romantic feelings to advance no farther than they already had. I stubbornly refused to acknowledge that my romantic sentiments had already advanced to an extent that there was probably no turning back. I could not undo what had already been done. I could only try harder in the future to contain my emotions and try not to succumb to sentimental triviances of the heart. I would often find myself looking at her in an involuntary stupor, until I was aware of the fact that she was looking back at me. I would snap out of my trance quickly, and go about my business with the uncomfortable certainty that she was not only well aware of my innermost feelings... that she somehow had the uncanny ability to read my thoughts while looking into my eyes. I felt that she knew there was something happening within my heart which was beginning to overpower me... that she knew I would soon break down and surrender myself to her without compunction. If I could only talk to her... Yet, even if I could talk to her, what would I possibly say?

On the twentieth day of our journey, we met a traveler and his Indian wife. I was beginning to think that perhaps every white man in the western hemisphere had an Indian squaw or two, for it seemed far more commonplace to see Indian wives than white wives. Yet, when I considered the unavailability of eligible white women in this region of the country, and the over-abundance of indigenous women, it only stood to reason that most wives were Indian. When I compared Indian women with the caliber of women which I had known in Baltimore, I felt it was indeed possible that Indian women could make better wives than some white women... although I wasn't quite sure of why I was beginning to feel that way. This traveler who we had happened upon was perhaps in his mid-thirties, and his Indian wife was probably about twenty-five or twenty-six years of age. She was of a darker complexion than my bronzed-skinned Loweja, but a very attractive woman, nonetheless, save for a deep scar about the side of her face and cheek. The scar ran from the corner of her lips almost all the way to her ear. It was not a hideous mutation by any means, nor was it a significant distraction from her beauty and her congenial personality, but certainly it was a scar which bore testament to the fact that she had received a serious injury at one time in her life. Both the man and his wife were attired in buckskin garments adorned with much Indian beadwork and trinkets. He wore a pressed beaver-hair hat, much the same as the one that I wore. Together, they were an adventurous looking man and woman who made for a quite handsome couple. When I had first seen him I had briefly mistaken him for a Frenchman, but after our initial conversation I quickly learned that he was an Englishman. He had come to America from a place not far from my ancestral home in South Wales. We were two Welshmen, who happened to come upon one another in a great wilderness area. There were four pack horses behind them that appeared heavily laden with goods of some kind. They were returning to their home in the mountains after a trip to purchase supplies, and judging by the size of their packs, they had most likely bought enough provisions to last for months... perhaps longer. I was pleasantly surprised to learn that the man's wife was also Arikara, like Loweja, and spoke fluent English as well as Ree, Mandan, and French. I explained the communication difficulties between Loweja and me, and the man suggested that we pitch a camp nearby and spend an evening letting his wife tutor Loweja while he and I talked. Even though it seemed too early to stop for the day, I thought that it was a splendid idea, and thanked him immensely for his offering. We had made good progress on the trail thus far, and I was eager for Loweja to learn any new words that Mrs. Parker could teach her. Since leaving the Missouri River, there had been so many things that I had wanted to ask Loweja, and here before me was a grand opportunity to do just that. Foremost among my questions would be the issue of Loweja's age; was she a child or an adult? Thinking that there was a good possibility that my question would soon be answered, I said a silent prayer, hoping that I would discover that Loweja was a young adult, and not a child as I had feared. Additionally, having the opportunity to speak English with another white man offered prospects that I was unable to resist.

    The gentleman, Earl Parker, and I sat far away from Loweja and Mrs. Parker, so as not to disturb their intense schooling. Mrs. Parker told me that the most important words for Loweja to learn in the beginning were, "Yes"... "No"... "I do not understand"... and, "Yes, I understand." She said that everything else would come to her quickly after that. Oscar and Octeenchaha sat far away from us and seemed content to be off by themselves with the horses. Mr. Parker was more than willing to offer advice to me on traveling the northeast route that I had charted. I showed him the map which I had purchased, but did not show him the map that Father had given me. The map that Father had given me had our route clearly marked, and I did not want to tell anyone the exact location of my ultimate destination. We looked at the map together as Mr. Parker spoke.

"Once you get up here where these two rivers fork, don't go no farther west. If you do, you'll likely run into a bunch of Sioux or Crow Indians, and they ain't exactly noted for their hospitality in these here parts. Where exactly are ya headed?"

"Here, in the foothills of these mountains." I had lied, somewhat, with my true destination being fifteen or twenty miles to the northeast from where I had indicated on the map.

"I don't hardly think you're gonna do much trapping there. I went through them parts a few years ago, and I never seen nary a beaver, nowhere. Both the Hudson's Bay Company and the American Fur Company went through there eight or ten years ago and cleaned out all the beaver. I did see a bunch of bears up there, but no beaver."

"I'm sure you're right, Mr. Parker, but I'm going to give it a try anyway. I'm just *hard headed*, I suppose." I remembered the words of my father in his manuscripts, where he wrote, '*Do not tell anyone what your true mission is.*' But there were many strange passages in Fathers manuscripts as well. Passages that left me puzzled as to their real meaning. One passage read, '*You will not know what your true mission really was until it has been completed. Only then will you recognize the true wealth of your discovery.*' These bits and pieces of mysterious passages were strewn all throughout his notes, and kept me in wonderment of their meaning... references like, '*You will find not only that your purse has been filled, your heart will be filled with something far more valuable than silver or gold.*' Was it a coded message of some type? I could only go forward with the faith that Father had provided good directions without the need to confuse me with any such coded messages.

Mr. Parker had been a member of a geological expedition fourteen years earlier which had been funded by the United States Government, and was commissioned just six years after the Corps of Discovery Expedition. When the expedition had ended, Mr. Parker had decided to remain in the west. He said that he had fallen in love with the mountains and would never be content to live anywhere else. He was passionate about his love of the mountains, and equally as passionate about his love for *Mrs. Parker*. They seemed to have been a perfectly matched couple. I rolled up my map and put it away while asking, "How did you meet your wonderful wife, Earl?"

"Well John, this is the way it happened... I came on a camp one night where she and this French trapper was. She weren't no more than thirteen or fourteen years old at the time... that's been six or seven years ago, I suppose. This French trapper feller was a loud, nasty bastard... a real sonuvabitch! He got all drunked up that night. She burned her fingers at the fire and spilled a pot of beans by mistake... that's all she did, was to spill a damned old pot of beans. Then, that bastard jumped up quicker than I could stop him and sliced her face open with a skinning knife and commenced to cursing at her. That's where that scar came from that she has across her cheek. Then he started kicking her in the stomach and spitting on her while she was down on the ground crying her heart out. I jumped up and kicked him in his balls and got the knife away from him and thought I had kilt him with it. I stuck him in the gut two or three times while he laid there holding his balls and speaking a bunch of French nonsense. Then I throwed him aside and went over to help her. She was bleeding bad... I mean really bad! She was just a little thing... sitting there crying her sweet little heart out. Next thing I knew, I was crying worse than she was! I got her to hold the skin on her face together while I got a needle and thread and stitched her up. I did a pretty damn good job of it, too... even if I do say so. I worked on her for a few minutes and finally got the bleeding to stop. It had to hurt like hell when I stitched her up, but she only looked at me with thankful eyes, and never flinched one time when I sowed her up! No, sir! Not one blessed time! Anyhow, me and her heard the French bastard start moaning about that time, and we both went over to him and sent his ugly ass to hell... me with a knife to his chest, and her with a big old rock to his ugly head. We both just stood there looking at each other for a good long while over his dead body. We was a sight, we was... We was both covered with blood... some of it was his'n, but most of it was her'n. I put a dressing on her face, we washed away most of the blood we had got on us, and the two of us left out of there the next morning. We rolled his body over the hill, and took his horses, rifle, traps, and anything else that was there. We only went a couple of miles before things started getting even worse. She commenced to bleeding again real bad, only this time she was bleeding from her crotch. I made camp again and started a fire and laid her down on a blanket. I pulled her dress up and seen that she was trying to have a baby, but the little thing was dead. It wasn't much bigger than a chipmunk. She had been carrying a baby inside of her and that dirty bastard had kicked her in the stomach! I took her dress off to wash the blood from it, and got a wet rag to wipe the blood off of her legs, and I couldn't believe my eyes! Her legs and her back-side was covered with bruises from where she'd been beat. Anyhow, we stayed there a couple of days until she rested up and quit bleeding and was able to ride. We've been together ever since then, and you won't find another man and woman on this here earth who love each other more than me and her, by God! It took several weeks for her face to heal enough so's I could finally kiss her, but when we finally could kiss, we sure as hell made up for all them days that we couldn't! Ha! Ha! Ha! As far as the scar on her face is concerned, every time I see it, it just reminds me of how much I really do love her. I ain't never harmed a hair on her body, and I've always tried my best to keep her from any harm. She's nursed me through the times that I got sick, and I've done the same for her. I would have most likely lost my scalp a couple of years ago if it hadn't have been for her talking to the Indians like she does. I still love her as much today as I did when we first met... No, by God, come to think of it, I believe I love her even more!"

"That's quite a story, Earl! I'm glad you have so much love for each other. I would have done the same thing that you did, Earl. If you had not been there that French bastard may have even killed her. I do not have any tolerance for any man who would mistreat a woman! Did you teach your wife to speak English, Earl?"

"Yep. Took me almost three months, and she still needs for me to explain a word or two every now and then, but now there's times when I think she speaks a whole lot better English than I do!"

"Do you and Mrs. Parker have any children, Earl?"

"She can't have children. That French bastard saw to that when he kicked her in the belly that night. We've tried, but whatever he did to her when he kicked her, messed her up inside, I suppose. That don't make no nevermind to us, though... we still love each other. We've talked about it a lot, and when we get to the point when we want to have children, she's gonna help me pick out a second wife... one that she likes. Ya see, when a man takes on a second or third wife, it's mighty important that the wives like each other and can get along without a bunch of fighting between themselves. That sure is a pretty little wife that you have, John!"

"Wife? Oh, you mean, *Loweja*. Thank you, Earl. She's not just pretty on the outside, inside, she's got a heart of pure gold on the inside."

Earl Parker didn't talk often, but when he did, his words flowed freely. I was not appalled by what he had just told me, and I understood why they had killed the Frenchman. I felt that their actions against the Frenchman were not only justified, they were commendable. To strike, beat, or brutally disfigure a woman may be acceptable behavior among some of the European and barbarian cultures, but it was repugnant behavior among men of conscience, and in the eyes of God. Anyone who would come to the aid of someone being mistreated like that had my sincerest admiration and respect.

For hours, I could see Loweja and Mrs. Parker working diligently on Loweja's first formal introduction to the English language. I could see them gesticulating and studying with earnest effort, and I was terribly anxious to hear the results. Finally, in the glow of an early evening campfire, Mrs. Parker and Loweja walked up to the fire after more than two and a half hours of serious tutoring and sat down to join Mr. Parker and me. Loweja had the smile of pride upon her face, and I felt as though I was going to be pleasantly surprised. Mrs. Parker was the first to speak.

"Mr. Welch, you have done well, teaching Loweja some of the English words. Now, I want you to listen to what I have taught her. Listen to what your wife has to say to you, please. Go ahead, Loweja."

"Hello, John Welch. My name Loweja. I am wife of you."

"I can't believe it! This is wonderful! What else can she say?"

"Go ahead, Loweja, tell your husband more."

"Shall we eat? I need to pee, can we stop, please? This is good food, *ce-na-chuá*. I will kill rabbit for us. Do you like me, *John Welch*? I like you."

"Mrs. Parker, this is wonderful! I am truly amazed! I can't believe that you accomplished all of that in just a few hours! Does she just say the words, or does she truly understand what they mean?"

"She understands everything she just said to you. Loweja is learning very fast. She is very eager to be able to talk to you. She thinks you are someone very special."

"I think she is someone very special, too, Mrs. Parker, I really do. Could you please ask Loweja how old she is? It is very important for me to know this."

"She won't know for sure how old she is in years, like white people do."

"Why not? I don't understand."

"The Arikara and the Pawnee do not count years the same as white people do. A person's age in years is not important. You are either young, or you are old, that is all that matters."

"It seems ridiculous to me that a person would not know how old they are. I cannot imagine a person going through life, not knowing how old they are, and only thinking that they were either young or old, and nothing else."

"Why?"

"Well, because it's common for one person to ask another person how old they are... in years."

"What good would it do a person to know how many years old they were? No one has ever asked me how old I was in years."

"Well... maybe it's not as important out here in the wilderness, but it's important in a white man's world. What would you suppose Loweja's age to be in years, if you had to guess?"

"Let me speak with her in Arikara for a little while, and I may be able to answer your question."

They spoke at some length in their native tongues, and Mrs. Parker turned to address me, saying, "Loweja is probably between seventeen and eighteen years old. But you still have not answered my question; why is this important to you? What difference does it make?"

"Believe me! It makes a big difference to me. If you really feel like she is seventeen or eighteen years old, then she's only about four or five years younger than me... that's wonderful!"

"So, what difference does that make? She's your wife, even if she was only twelve."

"My Lord! She's not that young is she!?"

"No. She is well past the age where she should be married, like I said, she has seen seventeen or eighteen winters, but I still don't know what difference all of that makes. You are young and Loweja is young. Nothing else matters. Why have you not been with her? She says you haven't been with her yet. She thinks you don't like her very much."

"Been with her? I've been with her ever since we left the Missouri River... about twenty days now. I've been with her almost every minute of every day, and I do like her... very much."

"Have you had *ohgā-sá-ho* with her? She says that you haven't."

"I still don't understand. It seems to me that I have heard that word before but I don't remember what it means."

"Make baby... you know?"

"Oh! No, I haven't done anything like that to her! I swear to the Almighty above that I haven't!"

"Why? Is there something wrong with your *pēneă*? She is your wife. Don't you like her very much?"

"Yes... I do... I like her very much! I just... Well, I'm just kind of confused right now about the way Indians go about this whole husband-wife matter. And I can assure you that there is nothing wrong with my *pēneă*, Mrs. Parker! I would rather not talk about this sort of thing any longer if you don't mind, Mrs. Parker... especially with Loweja sitting here listening to us like this. And please don't say that word again that means to make babies. I'm afraid that she may understand what we're saying and I'd rather she didn't hear anything like that."

"Loweja told me that she wants you to be husband for her, but thinks that you don't like her very much."

"That's not true! As I just told you, I like her a lot! I just need some time to think things over, that's all. I'm just not comfortable with the idea of being romantic with someone as young as she is. I promised her that I would take care of her, and keep her from any harm, and that's exactly what I'm going to do!"

In his confusion, John thought, '*Loweja wants me to be a husband for her? How could she possibly think that I don't like her? What have I done to make her feel that way? Is it because I have not demanded my marital privileges? I don't have that right! We're not really married! I don't want her to think that I don't like her. It's just not true. I've liked her since I first saw her... and she keeps growing on me every day; so much so, that I'm almost agonized by how much I really do like her. I like her so much that I just don't want to do anything that will bring disrespect to her in any way. I've never known a woman in Baltimore that I truly respected in any way at all... but I do respect Loweja, more than anyone I've ever known!*'

And so it went, all evening. Little by little, Loweja was learning some English, and learning it faster than I could have ever imagined. I knew that Loweja was a sweet and kind person, but I was only now beginning to realize that she was also a very intelligent person as well. Every new word she learned thrilled me... except for that '*ohgā sá-ho*' word. Mrs. Parker had worked wonders with her in such a short time. Mrs. Parker told me that I should talk to her a lot... the more, the better. She said that I should continue to encourage her to learn and say new words, and try to use as many of the words which she already knew as possible, and in frequent conversation, lest she forget them. She said that even "*meaningless*" conversation would help Loweja to learn English faster, and while casual conversation may have seemed unimportant to me, it was very important for Loweja. At one point, while we were preparing a meal, I was able to get Mrs. Parker aside from the others and privately ask her, "Mrs. Parker, on the trail coming up here, Loweja seemed to go through a puzzling time. She ate very little, she would not help Octeenchaha prepare our meals, she would not sleep near me, and she didn't even want to talk to me. She would not even answer me when I would ask her a question. Would you have any idea what brought all that on? It only lasted for about five or six days, and after that she was fine, and started to sleep near me again and talk to me at will."

"She was just making her blood, that is all. Our people call it, '*nī-misquoi*.' White people call it, '*men-straighten*,' or something like that. In her village, women are not permitted to touch food that will be eaten by someone else when they are making their blood, or the people who eat the food could get sick and die, or a demon could come and take her husband from her. She is also not permitted to be in the bed of her husband then. Our people used to believe that she could not even talk to her husband during that time or he would die at the hands of his enemy. If she talked to her husband while she was making her blood and he was killed in battle, she could be put to death. It could be said that she murdered him. She was trying to protect you when she stayed away from you and didn't talk to you."

"Protect me? I see. I should have known something like that was going on, but I just didn't think about it at the time. Do you believe in all of that superstitious nonsense, Mrs. Parker?"

"No, John. I believed it when I was a young girl because that is what I was told by my mother, but I have learned different. Earl has taught me that these things are not true."

"Would you please explain this to Loweja before we leave? It breaks my heart when she behaves like that. I feel like I have died inside when she doesn't want to speak to me."

"Yes, John. I will explain this to her. I will be happy to. She should know these things are not true, and I will be glad to tell her for you."

"Mrs. Parker, answer this for me if you would, every morning Loweja gives me a root to chew on. It has a pleasant taste to it, but it cannot be swallowed. Is that some kind of morning ritual or something?"

"No. It helps to keep your teeth clean and makes your mouth feel good inside. Our people call it, *'sassafras'* root. It can also be boiled in water and made into a tea. It is very good. If you have sugar to put in the tea it has a good taste. But if you drink too much of it at night you will have to get up a lot to pee."

"I have another question, and I hope I don't embarrass you by asking it."

"Ask me anything. I don't mind. If I can help Loweja learn more about you, and help you learn more about her, maybe you can stop this foolishness and start being a husband for her. She thinks she is not worthy of you and that is why you don't like her very much."

"That's not true! I like her more than I have ever liked anyone or anything in my entire life, Mrs. Parker, and she is worthy of anyone. If anything, it is I who am not worthy of her."

"What question did you want to ask me?"

"Well, I've noticed that Loweja sometimes... uhhh... she sometimes she passes wind, and seems not to be ashamed when it happens. Among your people, is this something that is permissible for a lady to do around others?"

"Why should she be ashamed to let her wind out? Why would something like a fart embarrass anyone?"

"Well, it's just that in a white man's world... I mean, in a civilized society, it's not considered to be a proper thing for a lady or a man to do, at least in the presence of others, that is."

"What do white people do, hold it inside of them?"

"Well, yes, that's exactly what they do... when they are around other people."

"White people do some very strange things sometimes, but this is one of the strangest things that I have ever heard about. I don't know what else to tell you about that."

"Let me ask you this... What does *'say-ha-way'* mean?"

"It can mean several things, but mostly, it means, '*I am yours,*' or '*I belong to you.*' Why do you ask this?"

"She says that to me every night when we turn in. I thought it may have meant, *goodnight*."

"What do you say to her in return when she says this?"

"I say the same thing, *say-ha-way*."

"She belongs to you. You don't belong to her! One night, try saying, *necu-ta-say-ha*, instead, and see what happens."

"*Necu-ta-say-ha*? It's very strange that you should say those words, Mrs. Parker... My father said those very same words to me just before he died. What do they mean?"

"They can also mean several different things, but mostly, they mean the same thing as saying, *I love you*."

My father had told me in English that he loved me before he died... but why had he spoken these words a second time in the native tongue of the Arikara? Why would he speak these words to me in the language of an Indian? My thoughts were redirected back to Loweja and Mrs. Parker. I thanked Mrs. Parker for all of her help, but I really wasn't certain that I was ready to say something as profound as '*I love you*' to Loweja. Or was I? I was enamored and infatuated no doubt... I knew that I liked her a lot... She was such a sensitive and kind person, how could I help but like her? But are these feelings and sensations that I have developed for Loweja really, *love*? I don't know... I've never felt anything even vaguely similar to this for a woman before. I had thought that she was much too young to be the object of my love... but since speaking with Mrs. Parker, I wasn't so sure anymore. I was gentlemanly predisposed enough to be in control of my behavior, and my passions. I would not permit my body to be aroused by some sort of perverted lust for a mere child. Yet, at times, I did not see a child when I looked into her eyes. I saw a wonderful, mature human being whom I felt was my equal. I wondered how old she really was. My confusion over the matter haunted and tormented me continuously. My youthful escapades with the ladies of Baltimore had been driven solely by my craving and lust of the feminine flesh. I had indulged women purely for my own physical gratification. The feelings which I had now developed for Loweja were powered by a different type of desire. I felt more of a mysterious *'spiritual'* attraction to Loweja which seemed to weigh equally with my physical desire to be with her, as if my heart and body was calling out to her in unison. Yet I could not permit my bodily desires to lure me into doing something unconscionable, something which I might regret later. I could not allow myself to succumb to these yearnings without knowing for certain in my heart that Loweja had similar feelings toward me.

"Let me ask you a question, John Welch."
"Certainly, Mrs. Parker, what is it?"
"How would you feel if I told you that I thought Loweja was twenty or twenty-one years old? Would you go to her as a husband then?"
"I would feel wonderful! I would be delighted! And yes, I would like nothing more than to go to her as her husband! But you are just saying that, aren't you, Mrs. Parker? You don't really believe that she is a day over seventeen, do you?"
"I'm trying to get you to see that you are letting a few foolish words keep you from being with your wife... only a few foolish words... words that don't mean anything important! You are acting like stupid man! You go around thinking in your mind that you will like this person because she is this many years old, and you will not like that person because she is not old enough for you to like... People have hearts, John Welch! Does Loweja not have a heart because she is only seventeen or eighteen years old? No! Loweja has a heart! She has a good heart! And you are punishing her for no reason! You need to think about that and stop hurting Loweja's heart! Whether or not you want to admit it, you are being cruel to her when you hurt her heart! Love does not

come to everyone, John Welch! Only very fortunate people ever get to feel real love in their hearts. It has come to your heart now, but you only want to drive it away with stupid excuses! Only a stupid man would do such a thing! You think about that, John Welch!"

"I will, Mrs. Parker... I promise. And thank you for the scolding you just gave me. I suppose I deserved it. I swear that I'll think about everything you just said. Perhaps you are right."

"I won't bother you about that anymore. Loweja tells me that you are best man who ever lived on this earth. I think maybe you are the most stupid man, but I will hold my tongue and say no more, but I would like to ask you one more question first."

"Go ahead, Mrs. Parker... I'll try to answer as best I can."

"How many children follow along behind you on this trail?"

"Children? I don't understand the question. There are no children following behind us on this trail that I am aware of. There is no one but the four of us."

"I don't believe you. I think you tell big lie. I think there are children that follow behind you."

"Believe what you like, Mrs. Parker! There are only the four of us... two men, and two women! There are no children following along behind us! I don't understand why you are saying these things to me!"

"Do you realize, John Welch, that you just called Loweja a woman?"

"Huh? Uhhh... I did, didn't I? To be so young, you are a very clever person, Mrs. Parker. You just tricked me into saying that!"

"Maybe so, but I think you just gave me an honest answer from your mind. In your mind you see Loweja as the woman she really is. Why can't you see her as a woman in your heart? You seem to do well when you are thinking with your mind... yet you do very poorly when it comes to loving with your heart. You have not had much love in your life before Loweja, have you John Welch? I can tell that this is true, and I am very sorry for you."

"I don't believe I have ever spoken with a person who was more capable of getting their point across, Mrs. Parker! You are truly a wise and wonderful woman. You have opened my eyes to a lot of things here today. Thank you... and I mean that from the bottom of my heart."

I had an eerie sense about me that I was in the presence of a truly amazing woman. It seemed as though she could almost read my mind and see the anguish and confusion which had resided within my heart for years. The evening offered a refreshing amount of conversation for all of us, and gave me a lot to think about. Loweja and Mrs. Parker had talked vigorously throughout the evening in their native tongue, and surprisingly, I heard Loweja using several English words in their conversation, and it gave me great pleasure to hear Loweja laugh out loud for the first time. She had a very pleasant, and almost *'musical'* giggle to her laugh which I hadn't heard before, and it sounded almost as if she was singing as she laughed. I also heard Loweja mention the name, "*John*" several times in her conversations with Mrs. Parker, and wondered what they were talking about. As far as Loweja occasionally passing wind was concerned... the more I thought about it, the more convinced I was that Mrs. Parker was right. Why should she be ashamed? And why should I be embarrassed to hear it? White people really are strange, and do strange things, I thought. The more I learned about the unassuming, natural ways of the Arikara, the more uncomfortable I felt about the arrogant, supercilious, and condescending ways of the white man. I wondered what was happening to me. I had been in the wilderness now for more than twenty days, yet I no longer yearned for the creature comforts which I had left behind in Baltimore. The prestige and opulence of my Baltimore social life seemed as if it were fading into my distant past as an unpleasant memory, and I felt much more at ease and at home here, in the wilderness with Loweja than I had ever felt in Baltimore. *'My God, can this really be happening to me?'*

Oscar and Octeenchaha had turned in an hour earlier. The embers of our campfire had diminished into a soft glow. When the evening had ended, and the Parkers had turned in on their laid out blankets, I once again spread our buffalo hides out on the ground... this time, only about a foot apart. Loweja pulled hers closer, as she usually did, until it was actually touching mine. After covering herself, she smiled at me and said to me as she usually did, "*Say-ha-way*, John Welch."

"I.... I... *Say-ha-way*, Loweja. Goodnight."

"Goodnight, John Welch."

"Loweja?"

"Yes, John?"

"I am very proud of you, Loweja?"

"I do not understand words."

"I know... and I'm very sorry that you don't. Goodnight, Loweja."

"Goodnight, John Welch."

I was beginning to think that I really did want to say more to her... right then and there, and just couldn't bring myself to do it, especially in the presence of the Parkers, who were laying only three or four feet from us on their blankets. Loweja's charm and beauty was breaking down all of the barriers which had encased my heart since childhood. The wall which I had so steadfastly constructed around my emotions and my superfluous rectitude was crumbling, brick by brick. I had never known feelings such as I was experiencing now. This was all new to me. I would have given everything that I owned to know her true sentiments, and her true age! Everything! One moment I would look upon her as a mere child, an adolescent... The next, I would see the beautiful woman that she really was. Maybe I was better off by not knowing her true age. If I had known her true age in years I may have felt even more shame over my desire to go to her. Perhaps Mrs. Parker was right. Perhaps the difference in our ages really didn't matter at all. Loweja and I were both young, just like Mrs. Parker had said. That is all that should matter. In my mind's eye, I made involuntary comparisons between Loweja and Elizabeth Cunningham, both as a person and as a woman. Elizabeth's merits paled in comparison to those of Loweja! In her innocence, Loweja was the most beautiful and complete person I had ever known. I could see compassion and tenderness in her eyes, traits which were completely foreign to Elizabeth. Yet, Loweja's presence seemed to complicate my situation. *'Exactly what was my situation now, really,'* I asked myself. Exactly who was this fellow, John Welch, who lay here upon a buffalo hide in the wilderness? Loweja was not really my wife now, was she? Did I really "*own*" her, as one could own a piece of property? In the eyes of God, how could one person own another? Loweja is a living and breathing person with a wonderful mind and a soul of her own. I was agonizing with these types of thoughts and questions, but was slowly coming to the startling realization that... **No!** I did not own Loweja! I did not own her at all! In truth, it was the other way around. **In truth, it was really she who now owned me.** I knew this in the depths of my heart, and I was at peace with it. I felt comfort in finally admitting that she owned both me and my heart. I firmly decided that I would find the right time and place to tell her how I felt inside. I would speak the words which Mrs. Parker had taught me, "*Necu-ta-say-ha.*" But I would force myself to patiently wait for the time that I could do so without the need for an interpreter, or the presence of a nearby audience. I wanted to say the words to her myself, in private, but only when the time was right. I wanted to bear my soul to her and present my heart to her, and be man enough to accept her rejection, if such a thing would be forthcoming.

In the light of a full moon, I turned my head to the side and saw that Loweja was laying there, apparently awake and studying my face. I could see the moon glistening in her beautiful brown eyes. I smiled at her and she immediately returned my smile. Her face showed brightly in the full moon, and I'm sure that mine did, too. She was only two feet from me, and I wanted badly to reach out and touch her face, but did not. I knew that if I touched her in any way while I felt enamored like this, that I would fall apart, then and there. I could see in her eyes that she really did want me to come to her... but this was neither the time nor the place to let something like that happen. As we lay there looking at each other, we heard soft moaning and scuffling from where the Parkers were lying, scarcely three feet from us. Both Loweja and I rose up slightly and looked toward the Parkers, to see Mr. Parker was atop his wife, under the privacy of their blanket. They were quite obviously bound together in marital union, while kissing wildly. Loweja and I looked at each other and then looked back at the Parkers. Briefly, I wished that the moon had been darker, so that the Parkers could have performed their act without Loweja or me seeing them. Immensely embarrassed, I lied back down and turned my head out of consideration for the Parker's privacy, but Loweja seemed enchanted by what she was seeing – as if she was receiving some sort of continued education from Mrs. Parker, and perhaps she was. Loweja continued to watch with obvious attentiveness and innocent curiosity until the Parkers had completed their brief unification. Then she lied back down and turned her head to look at me again. My heart was beating wildly and I wanted Loweja terribly, but I was much too embarrassed by the presence of the Parkers, and had the presence of mind to keep my feelings contained. Momentarily, I entertained the possibility of dragging our buffalo hides far away from the Parkers and allowing my passion to flow freely... but I did not. We continued to look into each other's eyes, but said nothing before finally drifting off to sleep. Sometime during the dead of night I awoke briefly and looked at Loweja's beautiful face as she slept in the moonlight. I quietly reached over and gently took a braid of her hair in my hand and held it. She was not asleep as I had thought, and gently moved her hand to lay on top of mine and we both faded off to sleep again. Later in the night, I felt Loweja's foot slide under my blanket and touch my leg. I slept very little after that. I realized that she had done so in her sleep, and rather than fall back asleep myself, I preferred to lie there, having pleasant thoughts about my wonderful little Indian princess.

  We sat down for tea and breakfast the next morning, and Mr. Parker gruffly asked, "Did ya'll hear all that ruckus last night?" At first, I was terribly taken aback, because I thought he was referring to the noises which he and Mrs. Parker had made during the heat of their passion of the night, and I was briefly at a loss for words to say. I finally said, "No, Earl, I didn't hear a blessed thing. What kind of ruckus was it?"

"Hell, I don't know... It sounded like someone was killing a hog or something! Or maybe even a whole bunch of people killing a whole bunch of hogs!"

"Oh... That. That was just Oscar, snoring. That's why he and Octeenchaha usually sleep far away from Loweja and me."

"By God, I ain't never heard nothing quite like it! That will sure as hell keep the bears out of your camp at night!"

During the hustle of breaking camp and getting our horses ready to travel again, I was once more able to get Mrs. Parker aside and whisper a question to her.

"Were you able to tell Loweja the truth about all those superstitions regarding her cycle of bleeding? Did you tell her they were all a bunch of nonsense?"

"Yes, John, I did. She now understands the foolishness in those beliefs, and is very sorry you had to see her acting like that. She did not mean to hurt your feelings, she was only trying to protect you from getting sick or hurt."

"I understand now... Thank you! Mrs. Parker... would you please tell me again what those Arikara words are that mean, *I love you*? I want to make sure that I don't forget them."

"Why? Are you finally going to say those words to Loweja?"

"Yes, Mrs. Parker... I am... but only when the time is right. I really do love her, Mrs. Parker... I swear to the Almighty that I do. I love her more than anything in this world, and I'm going to tell her as much!"

"*Necu-ta-say-ha* is the words. You are going to make her very happy when you tell her this, John! And it makes me happy to know that you will say this to her."

"What do those words actually mean in Arikara?"

"They mean the same thing as saying, *I love you,* but the words actually say, *my feelings for you are good, and come from deep within my heart.*"

"Thank you, Mrs. Parker... for everything you have done for Loweja and me!"

"I'm sorry for the way I talked to you so cruel last night, John Welch... Please forgive me for my hurtful words."

"I'm not sorry at all for the way you talked to me last night, Mrs. Parker. I'm very thankful for the way you talked to me. It's kind of strange, but..."

"But what?"

"You may be the wisest person I have ever known, Mrs. Parker, and I mean that sincerely. Meeting you and talking with you like this has been an honor for me, and I shall never forget you."

After breakfast, I thanked both of the Parkers for the time they had spent with us and the questions which Mrs. Parker had so painstakingly answered for me. We said our farewells to them and rode on. Before leaving earshot of the

Parkers, Loweja delighted me greatly by turning back in her saddle and clearly shouting, "Goodbye," to the Parkers.

"*Chin-contè-sa*, Loweja," I said.

"*Chin-contè-sa*, John Welch!"

"Good morning, Loweja!"

"Good morning, John Welch!"

"You are very pretty this morning, Loweja!"

"You are very pretty this morning, too, John Welch!"

"Do you need to pee, Loweja?"

"No, John. Not now! *Ben-eck-tulinch-tá*."

"Will you tell me when you do, so we can stop?"

"Yes, John. You are good man, John Welch! Good *onēssē*, too!"

"...and Loweja is good woman... perhaps the most complete and charming woman I've ever known..."

"Not understand too many words you say, John Welch."

"I know, Loweja... I know..."

I said a prayer to thank God for the privilege of finally being able to have some basic conversation with Loweja. My associates in Baltimore would have laughed at hearing our simple, elementary conversations. They would have characterized them as being the ignorant and simple babbling between fools. But to me, they were the most satisfying conversations which I had ever experienced. We had scarcely been gone from the Parkers for an hour, and I must have thought of a hundred more questions that I would have liked to have asked Mrs. Parker, but I eventually focused my attention back on our journey.

I was still quite confident in our course of travel as we gained altitude each day and pushed onward. Oscar was becoming somewhat of a thorn in my side at times. He must have asked me twenty times a day how much farther we would have to travel before we got to wherever we were going. I always answered with words that seemed to pacify him briefly, but an hour later he would ask the same question again. I exercised patience with him though, for a journey such as this must have been a frightening experience for him. In contrast to Oscar, Loweja seemed delighted with our journey. A smile was almost ever-present on her lovely face. She enjoyed looking at this new country, and I enjoyed looking at her. She rode up beside me, and with a broad smile she handed me my morning root to chew.

"Thank you, Loweja!"

"You are welcome, John! Do you like *sassafras*?"

"Yes, Loweja… very much… and I like you, too!"

"Loweja like John Welch, too! Very much. *Tī-sū-ata! Eitonyo-sī-hinnáh! Geá-tõn sá-sā nōōchá tā!*"

"Please speak English words, Loweja."

"Not know English words…"

"Then let's work on our English words some more, alright?"

For the next eight days, our journey led us toward higher elevation, and through beautiful, unspoiled country. The forest was filled with hemlock and fir, and occasional lodge-pole pine. I saw much evidence of grizzly bear activity, as well as wapiti, deer, antelope, and a variety of small animals. I had seen glimpses of several grizzlies moving through the forest well ahead of us, but none came close enough to pose a threat. The grasses were thick and lush in this country, and water was abundant here. This was the most beautiful land which I had ever seen in my life. There were stands of enormous fir trees scattered throughout the hills, and a beautiful new tree with white, paper-like bark which I had never seen before. The air was fresh and clean, the breezes light and pleasant, and a variety of colorful birds were all about. It was the kind of country that made a man feel alive inside. Small fields of wildflowers were scattered between the woodlands and hillsides, and the sky loomed above with its seemingly endless azure-blue deepness. We stopped once to rest the horses and I watched Loweja stroll into a small field of wildflowers. She picked a few, held them to her nose, and inhaled their wondrous fragrance. There were brightly-colored butterflies fluttering about her, and it will remain in my mind as being one of the most beautiful sights I have ever beheld. I wished that I could have commissioned an artist to capture the scene on canvas, but realized that even the best rendering, by the best artist in the world, could never have portrayed the real beauty as it appeared before me here in this place. Every night that we camped, our buffalo hides would be laid out side by side and I would reach to her and take a braid of her hair in my hand and she would clasp her hand onto mine before saying goodnight. Most nights, she would hand me a braid of her hair and then hold my hand as we fell asleep. On the nights when she took her hair out of braids, I would simply reach over and grasp a handful. It became the most pleasurable event in my day, and seemed to have a like effect on her as well.

A Most Unusual Cure

It was during the early morning hours of our twenty-third day of travel, two days after leaving the Parkers, when I first became aware that an illness of some sort had come upon me. I was both nauseous and quite ill in my bowels, and weakened to such a degree that I felt as though I could not travel. In the darkness before dawn I had rushed into the bushes from my bed several times to relieve the distress which had invaded my bowels. Loweja was aware of my illness immediately, and without me saying anything to her, she had risen and started a fire to boil some water for tea. In the light of the fire, I could see the immense concern for my welfare which was on her face. In the cool pre-dawn air the water for the tea finally boiled and Loweja frantically steeped the tea leaves until she had rendered enough for a cup of strong tea. Out of concern for me, she was shaking so badly that she spilled some of the tea as she handed it to me, and I took the cup from her trembling hands and drank some.

"Thank you, Loweja. Thank you very much."
"You are welcome, John. Please drink."
"I will… I will…"

Within a very few minutes, severe cramps ensued, and I was doubled over with pain as Loweja continued to work at the fire. It was apparent to me that she was busily preparing some sort of mysterious primordial concoction for me to take as a remedy for my agony. If that be the case, she was making poor use of her time, for I would not partake of any such crude, archaic remedy without knowing its composition. Twice more I had to rush into the bushes to relieve the incessant torment of my bowels. Loweja was now at the point of shedding tears, and singing a chant of some sort as she continued frantically to prepare something in the small cooking pot. I had neither the strength nor the inclination to ask her what she was preparing. She ground a substance of some sort, using a makeshift stone pestle and mortar, to a fine dust and poured it into the pot, where she stirred it until it had boiled. Once it had boiled, she strained some of the liquid through a cloth and she poured some of the strained contents into a cup, let it cool for a moment or two, and then handed it to me.

"Drink, John!"

"No, Loweja, I do not care to drink that... whatever it might be."

"Please drink, John! Do this, please!"

"No, Loweja! Thank you, but I will not drink that! I feel very sick! Please, just leave me alone."

"This make John feel good! Please drink, John!"

"God only knows what you must have put in there, Loweja, and I will not drink it!"

Her persistence was admirable, if not grievously annoying. She cried terribly and persisted to beg me to drink the contents of the cup, and as the severity of my stomach cramps became even more intense I took the cup into my hands and drank the bitter contents, purely for the benefit of dismissing her anxiety, and to encourage her to leave me alone. The elixirs which I had brought along on our journey may have done me some good, but they were buried deeply within one of the packs and I did not have the strength to stand long enough to search for them in the darkness. I looked at Loweja and tried to muster a smile in order to calm her fears. She stayed by my side and wiped my forehead with a damp cloth. In the soft glow of our campfire I could plainly see the streaks upon her cheeks that had been left by her tears. Our yelling at one another had awakened Oscar and Octeenchaha, and they had come to the fire to render any needed assistance. They built the fire up as Loweja continued to wipe my forehead. In a compassionate voice, Loweja spoke softly to me.

"John is good man. John is good man. John will be better soon. *Tena-soo-wionē-teth.*"

Loweja knelt beside me and prayed aloud to the Great Holy Father in her native tongue, undoubtedly asking him to extricate this sudden illness which had come over me. Even in my suffering I was touched by Loweja's concern and her prayer. When she had finished her prayer, she wiped my forehead again and held my hand as Oscar and Octeenchaha continued to tend the fire. In a very few moments I began to notice a curious, yet unexplainable sensation. The pain from my stomach cramps were subsiding, and my nausea and bowel distress was mercifully beginning to abate. I continued to be greatly weakened, but with the worst of the pain having diminished, I closed my eyes and slept, with my head in Loweja's lap.

When I awoke, according to my timepiece, it was approaching nine o'clock in the morning. Oscar and Octeenchaha were eating near the fire, and Loweja was still sitting next to my buffalo hide bed looking down upon me and holding my hand. Her face immediately brightened when she saw that I was now awake.

"John good now?"

"Oh my God… yes, Loweja. I feel much better, and much stronger, too. Thank you for helping me get over my illness. You were very good to me last night, and I will never forget what you did to help me. Thank you."

"You are welcome, John Welch! You help me much when I hurt foot, so now I help you when you hurt. *Je peux vous aider.*"

"Oscar, after you finish eating, you and Octeenchaha start putting the packs on the horses and get ready to break camp. We have lost several hours here this morning and I want to get back on the trail as quickly as possible."

"Yes, boss."

I drank a cup of hot tea and washed up at a nearby spring. My stomach was still too sensitive for food, so I ate nothing, despite Loweja's pleas for me to eat. By ten o'clock we were back on the trail and proceeding as if nothing had ever happened. My pain and suffering was but a memory now, and I felt fully invigorated, thanks to Loweja and that mysterious miracle concoction which she had forced me to drink. I was very appreciative of the kindness and attention which Loweja had rendered to me during my hour of need and I was extremely curious of the ingredients she had used in preparing my '*cure.*' On the trail, riding alongside one another, my curiosity finally got the better of me, and I asked her, "Loweja, what was in that drink that you made for me last night?"

"*Tena-soo-wionē, ejionne-ěsteech*, John. Med-sin."

It took several minutes of laborsome hand signals and explanations before she was finally able to communicate to me that she had ground the rattles of a rattlesnake to a fine powder, added some sassafras root and another root which I could not understand the name, boiled it all together, then strained the debris from the mixture and given it to me to drink. It was only then that I remembered reading in the journal of Meriwether Lewis that the same remedy was administered to *Sacagawea*, the Indian woman who had guided his party into the Northwest Territory in 1803. *Sacagawea* had also suffered from severe stomach cramps and bowel distress and had almost died. The strange concoction had given her relief as well, and saved her life. Whatever the contents, I could not have been more delighted with the almost immediate healing effect it had on me.

"Loweja, I want to thank you again for helping me back there."

"You are welcome, John Welch. You are good to Loweja, and Loweja want to be good wife to you. *Tena-soo-wionē-teth*. John much sick... bad sick..."

I found myself occasionally searching the trail ahead for rattlesnakes. Loweja's miracle remedy had worked so well that I thought it would be prudent for us to have a few of the rattles on hand in the event that someone else were to fall victim to a similar disorder.

Loweja's understanding and elementary use of the English language improved notably each day, and I rejoiced in the fact that we were finally able to have simple conversations, as long as I kept my words as basic as possible. When I spoke a word which she did not understand, she would tell me so, and I would try to explain the definition to her. Much of our communications were enhanced by the way we looked and smiled at one another as we talked. For example;

"*John hungry?*" Would be asked with a questioning expression on her face.

"*Yes, I am!*" Would be answered with an affirming nod of my head and a subtle smile on my face.

"Is Loweja hungry, too?"

"Yes, I am, John, much hungry!"

"What will we eat tonight, Loweja?"

"Rabbit? Is that good?"

"Yes, Loweja! Rabbit sounds good to me! Mmmm!"

I often found myself marveling over how much I had underestimated the contribution to my mission which Loweja would be capable of making. She had proven herself to be a competent laborer whenever there was work to be done, an excellent cook, successful hunter of small game, and even a fairly good physician. However, if she had been incapable of doing any of those things, I still loved her more each day, simply for the person she was.

On the twenty-eighth day of our journey we spotted three approaching riders from the north. We had not seen a solitary soul since we had left the Parkers. I removed my rifle from its scabbard and laid it across my lap and reached over to my side where I could feel of my revolver. Loweja and the others were close behind me. I felt as though I should have taken the precaution days earlier of arming Oscar and teaching him the fundamentals of shooting. Two armed men would have presented a much more formidable appearance than one. On the other hand, if Oscar became nervous and shot prematurely, the accident could result in an unnecessary fight. I had no idea of his dependability in the face of conflict. As the riders grew closer, I could see that they were Indians, and they were clearly not Arikara in my opinion. They looked much different. They were fearsome, yet extraordinarily handsome in appearance. I became nervous as we came closer and closer together, but I saw no outward indication of aggression on their part. We approached each other with great caution. I raised my right arm as I had been instructed by Hidessa, as a universal symbol of peace and goodwill, with no ill intent. We paused, scarcely ten feet apart, and their leader evidently recognized me as the man in charge and spoke to me directly.

"*Da-conta-say-moyka!*"

"I'm sorry. I do not understand. Do you speak English? How about, *Chin-contè-sa*? How about French? *Parlè vous Francē*?"

Clearly, he did not understand what I had just said. I felt terribly nervous, and devoid of what words to say next, when Loweja came to my rescue by moving her horse forward and saying,

"*Da-conta-say-moyka. Gy-teoka-say-na-voo.* Pawnee *ĕshē-tá... tūálá...*"

The group of Indians were looking curiously at our possessions which were visible to them. They also paid great attention to Oscar, for they had probably never seen a man of his dark skin before. They mumbled between themselves and looked admiringly upon him. I remained tense with anxiety, at these magnificent looking Indians, handsomely dressed in their ornate native attire. They carried bows and arrows in decorative quivers at their sides, and the brightly colored feathers of many birds adorned their heads and headbands. Their leader carried an older long rifle across his lap as well. Loweja took the initiative to speak again.

"*Dūo-sõn-tee-chūna.*"

"Do you understand them, Loweja?"

"Yes, John… little, maybe."

"What do they want?"

"They want to know if you come here to kill all their… deer."

"Tell them, '*no*.' Tell them that we are just passing through. And we will only kill rabbits to eat."

"I do not understand all you say, John."

"I'm sorry. Tell them, '*no*.' We just ride this way."

Loweja continued to speak with them, and relayed to me that the Indians had a desire to trade with us if we happened to have items which would interest them. I let Loweja handle most of the negotiations, and after a few minutes, with my approval, she traded a pound of lead bullets and a small sack of sugar for three rattlesnake rattles and a pair of moccasins. I could not help but admire the way that Loweja had successfully bargained for the things that she wanted, and she did so without my interference, and seemed to have done a much better job than I possibly could have. When the trading was completed, their leader addressed Loweja by saying,

"*Teesha-too-rohă. Eĕn-neka-ta.*"

"*Chin-contè-sa.*"

"*Chin-contè-sa.*"

With that, the group of Indians slowly went on their way, and we slowly went on ours as well. When we had ridden a good distance from the Indians I turned to look back at them once more, but they were gone from sight. It was almost as if they had simply vanished. I was relieved, and very thankful that Loweja had saved the day. I even felt as though she may have saved our scalps as well.

"Thank you, Loweja."

"You are welcome, John Welch."

"What people were they? They looked very different from the Arikara people I have seen."

"They are *Pawnee* people, John."

I had been warned that the Pawnee were a fearsome people, showing little tolerance for trespassers, yet these three fellows were friendly enough, and seemed to have been very pleased with the results of our brief trading session. They seemed curious, and had every right to be, but they did not seem threatening to us in any way. I only felt comfort during their presence. I was very thankful that Loweja had been able to communicate with them and bargain so effectively. Oscar and Octeenchaha looked as though they were frightened out of their wits during the encounter, but Loweja had remained perfectly calm and whatever she had said, seemed to satisfy them. I was proud of her, and told her so.

"You are good woman, Loweja!"

"John good man... and have good heart."

"Loweja, I can't tell you how happy I am just to be here at your side with you this morning. You just wouldn't understand me if I tried. But I'm going to tell you something right now, darling... You have the most beautiful eyes that I have ever seen! I have not seen your legs yet, except for that one very brief time when your dress got caught on the blanket ropes. My Lord! I saw plenty then... a lot more than just legs, and I think you are absolutely the most beautiful person that I have ever seen! I will never forget the way that you cared for me when I was sick that night. I love the way you hold my hand at night, too! I feel like you are my very own special little Indian princess, my dear. It's remarkable how I've come to admire you so much! In fact, '*admire*' is not nearly a strong enough word... I know the words I want to tell you, Loweja. Mrs. Parker taught them to me, and I'm going to say them to you, very soon! I swear before the Almighty that I will!"

"What words you say, John? I do not understand words you say. You say too much words. You say words too fast for Loweja."

"I am sorry. I know my words confused you, but it was something I had to say or I would have burst. You are good, Loweja! You are good for John!"

"John good, too! Do you like me, John?"

"Oh, yes, Loweja, I like you much! Very much!"

"Can I pee, John?"

"Yes, Loweja... I will be honored to hold your horse while you go pee."

On the twenty-ninth day of our journey, we arrived at the edge of a creek which was marked very clearly on one of the maps which Father had given me. We were in higher country now, and it was truly breath-taking country to see. We were no longer viewing the mountains from a great distance, we were in their very midst. From Father's maps, I estimated that we were less than a day and a half away from our final destination, and as I had planned, I did not want to go all of the way into the narrow canyon with four people and twelve horses. It was too dangerous. It would simply attract too much attention if we should happen upon someone, and possibly jeopardize my mission and endanger the lives of Loweja and my friends. We camped there at the creek that night, and very early the next morning, right at dawn, I instructed Oscar and Octeenchaha to maintain a camp there while Loweja and I pushed onward. I told them that Loweja and I would return within three weeks and we would then journey back to the Missouri River together. Oscar was frightened over the prospects of staying there alone, but already Octeenchaha was becoming the dominant figure in their relationship and she assured Loweja and me that they would be just fine there until we returned. There were plenty of fish in the creek and lots of rabbits and spruce chickens about, and in addition, Loweja and I had left ample provisions with them... perhaps more than we had taken for ourselves.

We also left one of my revolvers with them, primed and loaded, before we pushed on.

I was not completely at ease with the idea of leaving Oscar and Octeenchaha by themselves for three weeks, yet I did feel strongly that doing so would enable Loweja and me to approach Father's canyon with the least amount of obviousness if there happened to be cowans or thieves about the area. Additionally, I was desperately in need of spending some private time with Loweja. She was the most compelling force in my life now, and I wanted us to acquaint ourselves with each other apart from the constant interruptions which had accompanied us on the trail. Separated from all other humanity, we could be at peace to become more honest and open with each other. I wanted to talk to her freely, without any distractions. In my mind, I kept repeating the words which Mrs. Parker had taught me. I longed for the time that I could say them aloud... to Loweja, without compunction.

It was early, on the thirtieth day of our journey when Loweja and I entered a small valley in the foothills very near our destination. The narrow canyon which Father had described in his manuscripts was at the far end of this valley. We had just left Oscar and Octeenchaha alone at a lower camp and pushed on together. Loweja and I had gotten to a point where we could have simple conversation and actually understand one another. I was extremely proud of how quickly she had learned the many English words which she now had in her vocabulary... and all within a mere four-week period of time. I was beginning to lose passion somewhat for my mission, however, as I was realizing more and more that the feelings I had in my heart for Loweja, was undeniably and overwhelmingly, nothing less than '*sincere love.*' I could no longer keep my feeling hidden, yet I was unsure of exactly how to announce my feelings to her because of communication difficulties in choosing words which would accurately describe my emotions. If Loweja had a better understanding of the

English language, it would have been a simple matter of my choosing the correct words and telling her outright how I felt. Arikara culture was far more complicated than that. The Arikara vocabulary, according to Mrs. Parker, did not have words that translated to mean the same thing as passion, emotion, and deep admiration, yet they did have the words to describe *love*. Was Loweja capable of feeling *love* the same way that I was? Certainly! She had to be capable of feeling love. I saw love in her eyes every time I looked deeply into them... but was the love which I saw in her eyes really for me? Yes! I'm sure that it was. I could sense it when we held hands at night. I knew in my heart that sometime between now and the time we would rejoin Oscar and Octeenchaha, that I would reveal my true feelings to her. We were alone now... just her and me. There were no excuses now and no defenses left in the armory of my heart... they had been extricated by love, and I wanted her for my wife. I felt as though I could no longer live without telling her so.

Loweja and I had arrived at a creek, well hidden from the trail. We located a beautiful, secluded depression which would offer the perfect camping site for a day or two. I knew when we were setting up our camp, that this would be the place where I would somehow find both the words and the courage to express my love to Loweja. Her eyes clearly told me that she was also aware of what would happen here between us, and she wanted it to happen just as badly as I. My final destination was less than two miles due north from where we were now camped. I decided that we would stay in this beautiful valley for a couple of days, and I would do some scouting ahead on foot to assess what work Loweja and I would have to do in order to find and collect the gold which Father said was there, if, in fact, there really was any gold there. More importantly, I would also assess whether or not Loweja and I would be safe there in Father's narrow canyon while we went about our work to process and collect the gold. I would not jeopardize

Loweja's safety at any price. I would gladly abort my mission altogether and forfeit any claim to my father's wealth before risking her safety. Had someone already discovered the location? Had they already taken all of the gold which Father said was there? Is someone there right now? Are they waiting there to kill anyone who approaches? I would not expose Loweja to any such potential danger. I did not want to leave her behind in camp, but felt that she would be much safer right there at the creek for the time being, as long as she didn't wander around. I felt that it would be safe for me to leave her for four or even as much as five hours... any longer than that would cause me great anxiety.

After setting up our camp in the secluded depression next to the creek where there was a small waterfall, not visible from the trail above, I asked Loweja to stay there in camp while I did some scouting, and told her that I would be back early that afternoon. I left one of my other revolvers with her and asked that she remain well hidden near the creek while I was gone.

"Loweja, are you sure that you will be alright here by yourself until I get back?"

"Yes, John. I will fish here and find food for us. We eat good fish when you come back. Do you like me much, John?"

"Yes, Loweja. Yes, I do. And when I get back, I am going to try to tell you how much I really do like you. I want to say things to you from my heart when I get back. Do you understand me?"

"Yes, John. I understand you good. I will tell you much things from my heart, too. I have much to tell you. *Eèss-tu-callá, onēssē."*

Now, I had just fully committed myself. I had just told Loweja that I would be telling her something from my heart when I returned. She knew what I was going to be telling her. I could see it in her eyes, and I was sure that by this time, my own eyes were capable of concealing very little of my true emotion. In her native tongue, she had spoken the word, *onēssē* again, meaning *husband*, and although I did not understand the context in which she had said it, it fell upon my ear as a very pleasing sound. I hesitated leaving, and almost bore my heart to her then and there, but decided that there would not be a more opportune time for me to scout the canyon above than right now. I told her not to venture back toward the trail. Together, we hid our horses in tall bushes near the creek and before leaving, I cautioned her again to be careful while I was gone. I felt as though I was being terribly torn between two forces. My mission was pulling me toward Father's canyon, and my heart was begging me to stay with Loweja.

    Reluctantly, I left on foot to travel northward for a mile or two, then westward where Father's map indicated the confluence of two small creeks. Just as it had been with all the other landmarks on Father's map, I found the confluence with little difficulty and followed the smaller of the two creeks into a narrow canyon. Father's map was incredibly accurate. There was only a tiny passageway that led into the canyon and no other passageway leading in or out. The steep walls which loomed above me could not be climbed, nor could they be ascended by intruders. I felt as though this may have been the most private place in the world. At the very north end of the canyon there were a series of small, natural caverns. One of the caverns was large enough to camp in, and would offer us perfect protection from the elements of nature. In the northwest corner of the small canyon, I found a crevice below two large rocks where there was a good spring, and plentiful grass for the horses nearby. The area was filled with black sand and small rocks in the narrow creek bed. I would take my shovel and pan a sample here to see if my father's claim had been true. But when I started to dig in the black sand, my heart almost jumped out of my chest when I looked down to see gold nuggets lying about in the black sand... there were literally hundreds of them! Lying there within plain sight! Some were just small slivers, while others were the size of small peas... and a few were the size of apricots! This was it! This was the place that Father had told me about! This is the place where I would gather a fortune, and fund a future for Loweja and me! There was enough gold just lying on the surface of the small stream bed to make several men rich for life! I paused and looked around, fearful of what may happen if others were aware of this place. The canyon walls were impenetrably steep and the narrow opening to the canyon was constricted by large rocks and hard to find. There were great thickets of serviceberry bushes which obscured the entrance to the canyon. This place could have easily been overlooked by anyone passing by. From forty yards away it appeared as though there was no entrance there at all. Without a map it would have been very difficult, or even impossible for anyone to find the entrance. Even with the aid of a map, the entrance could have easily been overlooked by someone who was not sure of what they were looking for. Somehow, Father had stumbled upon this place and found the fortune which was contained therein.

I formulated a plan in my mind as I looked at the glittering yellow nuggets in the sand below my feet. I would walk back to our camp and bring Loweja and all of our possessions back into this place where we were not likely to be seen or disturbed. Here, we could go about our work, uninterrupted, in relative safety, and complete privacy. We could collect an enormous fortune for ourselves... right here, and live the rest of our lives in relative comfort!

With a few tree limbs laid across the entrance to the canyon our horses could be contained safely within, without a need to tether or hobble them. There was dry firewood aplenty along the banks of the creek and mustard plants were growing in various patches. All that I needed to do in order to get started was to go back to camp and bring Loweja and our horses into this unique little canyon. Leaving my shovel and a few tools behind, I rushed back to get Loweja.

I was in a hurry to get back to the camp where I had left

Loweja. I had been gone for more than three and a half hours and had felt ill at ease the entire time I was gone. I had taken an oath to protect her, and I could not do that if I was not with her. Now that I knew that we could go about our work in the canyon safely, I was regretful that I had left Loweja alone at the creek. I wished that I had brought her here with me on my initial visit. I had to get back to her quickly. Much of the way back, I ran, pausing only long enough to catch my breath on a few occasions. I had almost run directly into a large female grizzly with two cubs along the way, but was able to stop myself in time for her to scamper up the bank and flee with her young ones. I was careful not to stumble and fall as I ran, for a broken foot or a broken leg in this wilderness could easily cost a man his life.

As I ran back along the tiny pathway toward our camp and drew closer to where I had left Loweja, I came around a bend in the creek where I had an unobstructed view of our camp just thirty yards away. Loweja was standing in the middle of the wide creek, fishing... unaware of my presence because of the noise made by the rippling waterfall above her. She had not heard me running along the pathway. I was awestruck by the sight before me, but my first sensation was that of thankfulness that she was safe. She was completely unclothed, save for the silver bracelet which I had bought for her. To my knowledge, she had not removed the bracelet since I had first given it to her, thirty-one days ago, and it glimmered brightly in the afternoon sunshine. She had a long spear in her hand, which she had obviously whittled from a sapling, and was slowly and intently driving fish toward the shallower water, then spearing them with remarkable stealth and accuracy. It was the first time that I had seen my lovely Loweja completely naked. Her beautiful dark hair was out of braids and hanging wet against her body. Her hair hung all the way down to her waist in back. She had evidently used the opportunity to bathe as well as fish, for her whole body was wet with beads of water. In the mid-afternoon sunshine her light bronze skin showed beautifully before me. The tiny droplets of water about her shoulders and back sparkled like the reflection of little stars in the sunshine. This was no child who stood here before me! How could I have ever thought of this beautiful woman as being no more than a child? This was my wonderful Loweja standing there... the woman who I loved! Why had I not noticed Loweja's exquisite breasts before? Could it have been because of her native buckskin dress which she always wore? Did the dress somehow hide them from me? Did the dress somehow compress them against her body? Or could it have been because my attention was always being drawn to her enchanting eyes and her beautiful smile... her impish dimples and her gorgeous white teeth? I desperately wanted to run out into the creek and take her into my arms at that very moment, but felt that my sudden appearance in the presence of her nakedness would have alarmed her. Instead, I sat quietly upon a rock, and watched through the bushes with extreme delight as she continued to fish. I sat there spellbound, for what must have been nearly a half an hour, watching and studying over her beauty as she remained unaware of my presence. I was mesmerized as I watched. I knew full well what I wanted to say to her now and was ready to say it, whether she fully understood my every word or not. I would take my chances! Maybe she could read my eyes, and somehow interpret what my heart really wanted to say to her. She had already told Mrs. Parker that she "*wanted*" me more than two weeks ago. And now, I was finally ready to give myself to her – wholly and completely. And I did not wish for her to submit to my passions because she felt like she was '*owned*' by me. I refused to look upon her as a possession which I owned. As badly as I wanted her, I did not want her to give herself to me because she felt that it was her duty as a '*purchased*' wife to do so. I wanted her as an equal and willing partner... not an obedient servant. She was a beautiful human being, with a heart, and with a soul, and with a wonderful mind of her own. I felt a burning deep inside which was more intense than any feeling I had ever experienced in my life. I was deeply in love with her, and I knew it! I was no longer afraid to admit it now, to myself or to her... or the entire world. I wanted her badly, and was now ready to try to tell her in a manner that she could hopefully understand. I wanted to use words which would help her to understand that my love was not driven by selfish, carnal lust.

      I watched Loweja spear several large fish, and lay them on the bank, one by one. As I sat there in absolute splendor watching and studying over her, my eyes detected dark movement of some sort within the bushes at the far bank. I saw the tops of several bushes moving. With a sudden attack of horror, I saw a tremendously large black bear silently stepped from the bushes and into the shallow waters of the creek scarcely twenty-five yards behind Loweja, who had her attention fully on the fish which she stalked. She was completely unaware that she, herself was being stalked! The huge bear started taking slow, deliberate steps toward Loweja, who still did not hear the bear approaching her because of the noise made by the small waterfall. Quickly, I raised my rifle and carefully took aim at the behemoth just as Loweja turned and saw the huge beast behind her. She dropped her spear and stood there, frozen in shock as the current of the water carried her spear downstream. "**Click!**" The gun did not fire! I re-cocked and squeezed the trigger a second time! "**Click!**" The loud metallic click had drawn the bear's attention to my direction. In a panicky state of mind, I threw the rifle aside, grabbed my knife from its sheath and ran into the creek, yelling as loudly as I could to keep the bear's attention focused on me instead of Loweja! Loweja remained frozen in fear as I continued yelling and closing the distance between me and the bear... running as fast as I could in the knee-deep water... stumbling over hidden boulders and falling down twice. My aggressive presence, along with my yelling, must have confused and startled the bear. He stood erect on his hind legs and loomed above me as I ran closer and closer. It was only now that I realized just how huge the bear really was! My dear God! He was a good three feet taller than Loweja! He was as big, if not bigger, than any grizzly I had ever seen! He was clearly two feet taller than me when standing on his hind legs! Suddenly, the beast dropped down on all four feet and quickly ran away when I had come to within five feet of him, and disappeared back into the bushes from whence he had come. My heart was beating so strongly that I thought my chest would explode at any moment. I stood there momentarily with my knife held firmly in my hand to make sure that the bear was not going to return... and then I replaced the knife in its sheath and turned to face Loweja. I thanked God that the bear had not been a grizzly, for it was unlikely that a grizzly would have backed down from a confrontation such as that. Had it been a grizzly, however, I would have done the same thing. Perhaps when he was busy killing me, Loweja might have had time to make good an escape. But that sacrifice had proven not to be necessary, for the huge, black beast had fled in terror. I had never seen such a large black bear, either before or since!

Loweja was so frightened by the event that she just stood there trembling in water which came almost to her knees. I rushed to her but fell in the water again before reaching her. I felt like a clumsy oaf as I picked myself up and came to her. I held her in my arms as she began to shake and weep with pitiful sobs. I pulled her close against my chest, and with my face in her wonderful wet hair, spoke softly to her.

"That's alright, Loweja! Everything is going to be fine now. I'm here now. I'm sorry that I left you alone like this, but John is here now. You're safe now, Loweja! I'll take care of you! John will always take care of you!" I felt her arms around me, squeezing tightly, and as much as I wanted to provide reassurance for her, I was overwhelmed by the comfort and reassurance that she was providing to me, with her arms locked so tightly around me. This was my wonderful Loweja who I was finally holding in my arms. I had never touched her before like this. I love her! And I will always protect her! I was still terribly shaken by what had just happened, but wanted to remain strong for her, so that she would not see the fear which had overtaken my composure. Finally able to speak, she sobbed, "John! *Kaes-tay! Kaes-tay! Masqua!*"

"I know, Loweja, I know. It's alright, now, It's alright. *Masqua* is gone away now. *Masqua* is gone. And I will not allow *Masqua* to harm you."

I picked her naked and trembling body up in my arms, and with her arms still locked tightly around my neck, I carried her back to the bank where she could dress herself. While she dressed, I walked back up the pathway to retrieve my rifle and came back to help her collect the fish which were laying on the bank. A horrified look was still upon her pitiful face and she still trembled as I tried to raise her spirits.

"Loweja, you've got some nice fish here!" But she was still too shaken to answer. Her bottom lip quivered as she looked at me. Again, I commented on her fishing prowess.

"Loweja is good fisher! Real good fisher! Loweja is pretty fisher, too! Very much pretty!"

I noticed that she hardly took her eyes off of me as we walked slowly back to camp, as if she was held in awe by some sort of heroic action on my part. My actions were not heroic. They were merely an instantaneous reaction to a desperate situation. I was simply willing to do anything that I had to do in order to prevent any harm from coming to her. I had taken an oath to that effect. A short while later, after tending to some chores about camp and still in my wet clothes, I checked my rifle and replaced the old powder and percussion cap to reassure myself that the next time it was needed it would be functional. I turned to look at Loweja and saw her sitting on the edge of a rock near our packs, facing me. She was brushing her wet hair so that it would dry in the warm afternoon breeze. I removed all of my wet clothes and wringed water from them, without prudishly and senselessly going back into the bushes to do so.

I was not afraid for Loweja to see me for what I really was, just as I had already seen her. I was merely a man... a desperate and fragile man... a man who was alone in the wilderness with the woman whom he loved. She stopped brushing her hair and simply sat there staring at me in obvious wonderment and loving admiration. Her eyes inquisitively followed me as I hung my wet clothes on a limb to dry in the evening sun and stood there for several moments, hanging my boots on tree boughs and squeezing water from my stockings. I turned to her, and said, "Britches are wet, Loweja. All of my clothes are wet."

I made no squeamish attempt to conceal myself from her curious eyes. I was her husband. She was my wife. Instead, I remained unclad and went to the creek to clean the fish that Loweja had caught. She watched me intently during this entire time, with wide eyes and the hint of an adoring smile. I had seen her nakedness, and now she had seen mine. I did not want to hide anything from her any longer. My love was far too intense to permit immature boyish modesty. I walked back up from the creek and arranged my wet clothes on the tree limbs differently, shaking them again so that they would possibly dry in less time, hopefully before dark. I tried to wring more water from my britches, shook them off, and hung them back on the tree branches to finish drying. When I looked back at Loweja, I saw that she was still brushing her hair, but her dress was draped over a nearby tree limb, and she too, was unclad. She softly spoke to me,

"*Tagná* is wet, too. *Nig-snī-tequoīs*. John is good to Loweja. John is *quoi-natch-inini*, beautiful man... beautiful *onēssē*."

"Loweja is good to John, and you are a very beautiful woman."

I walked over and saw how she was twisting her hair into braids and gently reached down to take over the task, but instead, I untwisted the braids and picked up her hairbrush and began brushing her hair again. Her long, beautiful brown-black hair felt good in my hands, just as it had felt during the ‚any nights we had spent on the trail when I had held a braid of it in my hand. I looked around at her eyes as I brushed her hair to find that they were closed, in obvious delight. Her dark hair glimmered and sparkled in the last moments of the evening sun. Then, I asked her,

"Will you leave your hair out of braids tonight... for me?"

"Yes, John. *Pin-ack-wani*? Stay like this, yes?"

"Yes, please, Loweja."

I continued brushing her hair, and it slowly dried. I handed her brush back to her and she rose to face me.

"Thank you, John Welch."

"You are welcome, Loweja. Did you like that?"

"Yes, John. Much like. Loweja much like you, too."

I spread our buffalo hides out, side-by-side, and as usual, I placed my revolver near the top of my buffalo hide, along with my rifle where they could be easily reached during the night if needed. Loweja walked over and pulled her buffalo hide onto the top of mine and spread two blankets on top. Then she folded one corner of the blankets over and stared seriously into my eyes. This gesture did not puzzle me, even for a brief moment. I clearly understood the message as well as the invitation which she was sending. She was telling me in her own wonderful way that she wanted to receive me as her husband... for us to sleep together upon the same buffalo hide... as husband and wife. As Mrs. Parker had said; we had both endured enough of this foolish, unnecessary nonsense of abstinence and self-denial... all because of my stubborn reluctance to express my love openly and freely, and to accept her for who she really was... my wife... my good wife... Now was the time for it to happen, and this was the place.

"*Say-ha-way*, John. *Stěssă-tā-ummo ot-tāko onēssē.*"

In Baltimore, I had courted some of the most

sophisticated and prestigious ladies which Baltimore society had to offer, with never a nervous moment's hesitation in their bedchamber. But as I stood here before Loweja, and was about to speak from the greatest depths of my heart, for the first time in my life, I found myself feeling quite nervous. I was about to bare my soul and tell this woman that I loved her. It briefly, but vividly, occurred to me again that Elizabeth and I had never spoken such words as, *'I love you'* to each other... and for good reason... we did not love each other! I, in fact, had never spoken those words to anyone in my life except to my father as he lay upon his death bed. Those words were meaningless, unless they were offered from the heart. But here, before me now, was the one wonderful person in this world who was truly the object of my love, and I was about to tell her as much. Nervously, I answered, remembering the words which Mrs. Parker had taught me... words which I had repeated in my mind, over and over again.

"Loweja?"

"Yes, John?"

"I have something that I want to say to you... from my heart. Will you please hold my hands while I tell you the words?"

"Yes, John. I will tell you words from my heart, too."

"Loweja, *necu-ta-say-ha*. That means that I love you with all of my heart." Immediately I saw tears of emotion beginning to form in the corners of her eyes, and she softly answered back with words which magically transcended the language barrier and touched my very soul, "I pray to Great Holy Father for many days that I hear you say that to me. *Nek-tonoma sao,* John. My heart hurt even, to hear you say that."

"I should have said those words to you much sooner, Loweja. I'm sorry that I did not. I have loved you since I first saw you at your village. I stand here before you now as a man who loves you from the bottom of his heart. *Necu-ta-say-ha*, Loweja, I love you!"

"I never know man good like you. You are beautiful man. You are man with heart that is very much good and you have make my heart feel good, too, with these words."

I really did love her, and I would no longer try to ignore my feelings for the sake of my mission, or anything else for that matter. My mission was not as important to me anymore as Loweja was, even after seeing the gold with my own eyes and knowing that it was there just waiting to be picked up. My eyes enjoyed looking into Loweja's eyes much more than seeing all of the gold in the world. In the final glimmers of the evening light, we stood before one another. In near frenzy, she leaped upon me and we firmly embraced. With her arms locked tightly around my neck, she raised her legs and wrapped them fervently around my waist. I could feel her heart beating strongly as I kissed her neck. She sighed loudly, almost wailing with delight, then said, "*Necu-ta-say-ha*, John Welch! You are my husband! You are man with good heart!"

"Yes, Loweja… I *am* your husband… your… *onēssē*, and I'm proud to say it, too!"

Loweja and I got under the woolen blankets together, for the first time as husband and wife, and learned to kiss, in a manner which was quite possibly unique to only Loweja and me. Our kisses defined the very nature and intensity of our love for each other. I had kissed many young ladies in Baltimore… many. Some of the kisses I had thought to have been quite passionate at the time. But none of the kisses which I had ever experienced before in my life had even come close to preparing me for the wildly intense kisses of Loweja. Her kisses brought new definition to words of passion and delight. Her kisses were so passionate, and so physically extreme, that they were almost violent, almost animalistic in nature, yet immensely rewarding, extremely enjoyable, and fulfilling beyond description! She bit my neck time after time… so hard that they were almost painful bites, yet sublimely pleasurable. I had never experienced anything like it before! It was as though I had been cast into a sea of delightful extremes which had been previously unknown to me! I had never known that pleasures such as these even existed! Together, we crossed the boundaries of conventional fulfillment, and went far beyond. I was mesmerized by the touch of her fingers as she explored me, and my body involuntarily contorted in loving reaction to her every touch.

I had known long before this night that Loweja loved me, and I had also know that I loved her as well. This remarkable night of love declarations would mark an end to my previous hesitations, and it would also mark a beginning of a new life – a life in which I was now privileged to live with my wife, Loweja Welch.

In the growing darkness of the wonderful night, we gave ourselves to each other in a frenzy of wild and uninhibited pleasures. Loweja was very vocal in her delight, and her unrestrained noises of passion only served to elevate my own pleasures to unimaginable heights. Under the woolen blankets that night, and the pleasant, comforting music of a nearby waterfall, our hearts were melded into one, and my love for Loweja was finally released to run unsuppressed, unbridled, and unashamed.

Daylight the next morning found us both very reluctant to emerge from beneath our warm woolen blankets. The air was crisp and cool. We could see our breath in the air. We had remained tightly embraced during the entire night, sharing passions with one another in the darkness, where the darkness had denied us the pleasure of looking into one another's eyes. Now, as daylight crept through the trees, we made love again, and this time we were able to see into each other's eyes. Her eyes looked adoringly happy, yet invitingly impish at times. This had been Loweja's maiden voyage into intimacy, and she was more than simply awestruck by the profoundness of such a new and delightful way of expressing her love. For me, even though I had experienced pleasures of the flesh before, I found that when these passions are performed with someone a person loves, the delight is magnified tenfold.

The frigid mountain air prevented us from fully exposing ourselves from beneath the woolen blankets that early, and we were content to remain there for a while longer... touching, feeling, looking into each other's eyes, kissing, again and again. Loweja was so beautiful. Without knowing all of the proper words to express ourselves to one another, we exchanged pleasant and delightful moans to communicate our pleasures to each other. They became our voices of love; our verbal notification to each other, which signified our approval of the other's advances. They were our *"language of love,"* and they were not rendered vague because of a language barrier... they sent the same, distinct message, in her language or mine.

"John?"

"Yes, Loweja?"

"Why you wait long time to be husband for me? I love you much for many days and want you for husband so much... and you make my heart hurt you wait so long. You hold my hand and you hold my hair and you tickle my foot, but I wait much long time for you to be real husband to me. Why you wait? Did you not like Loweja before?"

"Oh, no, Loweja, I have loved you since I first saw you. I'm sorry that I hurt your heart, but I wanted to be sure that you loved me, and that you wanted to be my wife, because I do love you so much."

"I never be wife with man before now, ever, and I want to be wife much with you, but I did not know words to tell you, so I wait for you to come to me as husband. Eètnă-ĕsh tell me not to come to you as wife. She say wait for you to come to me as husband, then I can be wife, so I wait. It take you long time, but now you come to me and I am happy. I am much happy! Now that you are my husband and we do this, can we do this much now? *Eeno-su-ma Stĕssă-tā-ummo ot-tāko onēssē?"*

"We can do this as much as we like, any time that we

like, Loweja. You are my wife now, and I am your husband. Neither of us will ever have to wait again, and I will spend the rest of my life trying to see that nothing hurts your heart again."

"Do I make you happy, John?"

"Oh, Yes, Loweja! You make me happy much! I don't think I could ever describe how much pleasure you have brought into my life, darling! I feel like I have been reborn. Did you understand any of that?"

"Yes. Some of what you say I understand good. Can I touch you much now with hands?"

"You are my wife, Loweja... my *espousa*... You can touch me as much as you like, anytime you like. Can I ask you a question, Loweja?"

"Yes, John."

"Last night, and many times this morning, you said that you loved me, right?"

"Yes, John. That is truth! Great Holy Father know I speak truth! I love you!"

"Who taught you how to say the words, *I love you*?"

"Eètnă-ĕsh... Mrs. Parker... teach me words, but she tell me never to say words to you until you say it first. It means same thing as *necu-ta-say-ha*, and it is good when I say it to you. *Necu-ta-say-ha*, John Welch! I love you, John. Do you want morning food now? I will make good morning food for you! We did not eat before we be wife and husband."

"You are right, Loweja. We forgot to eat last night, didn't we?"

"No, I did not forgot last night... but I wanted to be with husband. We can eat now, if John is hungry."

Eventually the air warmed and Loweja and I arose to go about the new day, confident in the sovereignty of the love we now shared for each other and thankful that we had finally expressed our feelings openly and unconditionally. We were bound together now. She was my wife... for now and forever more. I was her husband... for now and forever more. I saw large purplish marks about her neck and breasts that I had made during the night by kissing her so hard. I was burdened with enormous guilt that my passion had not permitted me to be more gentle and considerate, even though we had both been guilty of extremely aggressive behavior during the night. Our zealous onslaught had been a product of the sudden release of emotion that had been suppressed far too long, and then allowed to run rampant and uncontrolled all at once. I should have known better, and constrained my emotions somewhat, but I was so deeply in love with her that I had lost control of any ability to restrain myself.

"Loweja, I'm sorry if I hurt you, darling."

"Hurt, no! Feel only good! *Necu-ta-say-ha*, John! **John! Look what Loweja do!**" She said, as she gently touched my neck in several places.

"What, Loweja? What's the matter?"

"I bite you too much here. I am sorry, John! I bite you bad!" She was of course referring to marks upon my neck which she had created during her own ecstasy... marks which were probably similar to the many marks which I had made on her neck and breasts. I smiled, and eased her guilt by telling her that I had done the same thing to her neck.

"Do not cry, Loweja, do not make tears, please. You can bite my neck anytime you want to... alright? John likes for Loweja to bite his neck!"

I had been wanting to tell Loweja that I loved her for more than twenty-three days now. Now that I was free to do so, I couldn't seem to say it enough. Our love for each other was defined by absolute trust and adoration, and a wild passion which had brought an uncorrupted, pure love into our lives. I knew that I would be a changed person after this. I knew that my life would never be the same as it had been before I met Loweja, and I could never live without her again. Besides, I did not want to be the same man that I was before Loweja came into my life. I did not like the man who I had been. I felt as though I had been completely reborn into a new world where I could experience unquestionable love for the first time in my life; love which was pure and uncontaminated by the filth of evil thoughts and the wicked prejudices of society. And my wonderful Loweja was the most important thing to me in this new world.

Loweja's dress had dried completely during the night, but my buckskin clothes remained damp. Nevertheless, we dressed and proceeded to confront the new day. We went about our camp duties together, and I prepared to move our camp into the narrow canyon where we could remain unseen by any conceivable travelers, and where we could embark on the labor which we needed to perform in order to harvest our fortune. Loweja cooked the fish she had caught the day before and we ate them for breakfast, along with some porridge and tea, before moving our camp, and in the process, we seldom took our eyes off of one another. We readied all of our items to be loaded on the pack horses as we cleaned up the area where we had camped.

Any trivial sense of modesty which had ever existed between us before had been completely exiled by our love for each other… in one very eventful and memorable night. We had nothing to hide from one another. We were truly, man and wife now. Our hearts were as one now. Loweja was deeply in love with me, and I with her. We were equally enchanted with the bodily pleasures which we had brought to one another, and neither of us hesitated to take advantage of any opportunity to express our love physically when we recognized a desire within one another to do so. After that first night, our love making was often spontaneous, unpredictable, and always satisfyingly enjoyable. Touching one another added greatly to our communicating. We seldom came within arm's reach that we didn't both reach out and touch.

While we were breaking camp that morning, Loweja's mood seemed to change for a moment, as if she was giving something a great deal of melancholy thought. She approached me and looked deeply and seriously into my eyes... almost to the point of being tearful. She reached to me and took me by the hands. Something very onerous was on her mind... I could see it clearly in her eyes.

"Loweja... What's the matter, darling?"
"John... you die for me, yes?"
"What do you mean? I don't understand."
"You fight big bear with only knife for me. You die for me, yes?"
"Oh, that... Yes, Loweja! If I had to, I would die for you... gladly!"
"I love you, John! I die for you too!"

I would be taking Loweja and all of our belongings with me on this trip, as I began to feel extremely uneasy about ever leaving her alone for even short periods of time after the incident with the bear. It was only a black bear, but many men in this country had been killed by black bears, and the one in the creek could have just as easily been a grizzly. I had never seen such a tremendous beast before. I shuddered each time I contemplated the fact that if I had been as much as a half-hour later in returning to our camp that morning, Loweja would have been killed, and probably eaten. If the bear had not eaten her completely, the wolves would have soon found her body and eaten all that remained. I thanked God for the mercy which he had extended us. There was a possibility of many dangers out here in the wilderness. In addition to the black bears, there were horrible grizzly bears and ravenous packs of wolves. There was also the threat of harm at the hands of savages or thieves, although we had encountered very few people on the trail below. Loweja would be such an easy prey if someone wanted to bring harm to her, and this was always foremost in my mind. I gave her one of my revolvers to carry with her at all times. After she learned the fundamentals of shooting, I loaded her weapon. We never actually shot the gun, for I did not want the noise of an unnecessary gunshot to signal our location to any listening humans, Indian or white. In those mountains a gunshot could have been heard for miles, although, I would not have hesitated for a moment to shoot a weapon in order to prevent any kind of harm to Loweja.

We had finished our morning meal and cleaned our camp. Ashes from our fires were thrown into the river and the area was made to look as though no one had ever been there. I even picked up the manure from the horses and disposed of it in the bushes. We got everything packed on the horses and traveled up the narrow pathway toward the canyon. With the horses, we had to detour slightly from the path which I had taken the previous day due to thick tangles of serviceberry bushes. We entered the canyon after less than two hours of riding and began setting up a camp there, as inconspicuously as possible. I could see a concerned look on Loweja's face as she tried to make some sort of sense out of what I was doing and why we were camping there in that particular place. Once our camp was established, and the horses were grazing peacefully, I took Loweja by the hand and tried to explain why we were there. I took her to the small creek with the black sand and began picking up nuggets and putting them in one of the small cotton sacks which I had brought. She soon realized what I was doing as well as what I was looking for, and began helping me. Loweja's keen eyesight enabled her to see the tiniest specks of gold... of course, she expected praise and a kiss from me every time she found one, and I would gladly provide her with kisses, whether she found gold or not. Her eyes would beam with joy over each nugget she found. We picked up nuggets for less than two hours, until we had one of the sacks almost filled. It was amazing to see how quickly the first bag was being filled. Some of the nuggets were mere specks of gold. Others were the size of peas, and a few were a big as blackberries. I would push over a large rock and Loweja would pick up the nuggets which had been trapped below. There was a fortune here, and we had not even finished scratching the surface. We had collected almost two sacks full, almost ten pounds worth, without using the shovel once! And we had done this on our very first day in the canyon. There was a vast fortune there, beneath our feet, and it was free for the taking! My father had been right all along! In fact, everything that he had written in his notes had been accurate. Yet I was greatly bewildered by all of this. With such great wealth here, why did Father not return to Baltimore and live the remainder of his life as a rich man? Why had he not returned to live with Mother and me in a world of luxurious opulence and prosperity? It didn't make any sense to me.

Loweja wanted to take a pail from the pack and walk back to where we had seen all of the serviceberry bushes to see if she could find any which had ripened, but I would not permit it. I knew that she would not find any of the berries to be ripened because it was much too early in the year. Also, serviceberries were among some of the favorite foods of the grizzly bear, and I had seen hundreds of tracks along the trail which gave witness to the fact that there were great numbers of bears in the area. The notion quickly left her head as soon as I mentioned the word, "*Masqua*." I supposed that it made a great deal more sense to Loweja to collect something which we could actually eat, rather than picking up the yellow particles that were inedible. I promised her that we would check to see if the berries had ripened when we left to go home. I could tell that she had some difficulty understanding why someone would put forth so much effort to collect the gold, and I could not find the words that she would comprehend to offer her an understandable explanation. Still, she delighted in pleasing me by continuing to gather the strange yellowish substance and collect her kisses.

Father had been right when he had advised me to hire only one helper, for the mining and collection of this gold was not a terribly laborious process. I tended to all of the work which required a strong back, and Loweja attended to the rest.

We always stopped our work in the early evenings, so that we would have ample time to prepare our meals and spend affectionate time together. When mornings arrived, we were fully rested and ready to commence working again. Loweja seemed to be tireless, and never voiced a complaint with the work that we did. We worked continuously each day until early evening, collecting and washing the gold. Our gold bags were filling very quickly by the fourth day with very few disturbances to interrupt our work. Three wolves entered the canyon one morning and I thought for a moment that I would be forced to shoot one of them. I held my rifle poised to shoot at any moment, when the pack turned and walked back out of the small, narrow canyon. The presence of the wolves had startled our horses terribly, but they gathered in a corner and watched as the wolves left. Even though they had left, I remained vigilant, especially at night. I kept my rifle and my revolver close at hand at all times. We camped in a small cavern under a ledge of rock. I slept at the entrance, and Loweja slept directly behind me. Any danger which might have approached would be met by me, and could not harm Loweja without first dealing with me.

    Loweja and I talked frequently throughout the days, and I continued to introduce her to as much of the English language as possible. It was remarkable, how well versed she was becoming. Our conversations became more and more in-depth, and we understood each other's feelings much better. Each night found us tightly embraced upon our wonderful buffalo hides in the cavern, where we shared many pleasant hours of conversation. With each conversation, we learned more about each other. Her evening prayers were still spoken in her native tongue, and mine were offered silently. Loweja was a very superstitious person, yet little-by-little I tried to dispel some of her superstitions without belittling her for her primitive beliefs. She told me that when a relative or someone who was very much loved had died, that those who mourned would sometimes cut off a finger, or impose some other fashion of self-mutilation to express their sorrow. I was quite vivid in showing my disdain for such futile and senseless behavior. Loweja understood my argument, and soon came to realize the act was indeed, both pointless, and stupid.

Every day revealed that Loweja and I had an ever growing stockpile of gold... and an ever growing love for each other. As a precaution, we only made a fire in a sheltered area, and only in the dead of night, so that the smoke could not be seen from a distance. We made no fires on nights of a bright moon, and we made no fires during the day for fear that the smoke could be seen in the sky overhead. Our stockpile of gold was hidden in a crevice on the opposite side of the small canyon from our cavern, and the number of filled bags continued to grow. I shoveled material from the creek bed which contained high quantities of gold. I taught Loweja how to pan this material in order to find the smallest particles of gold, and she became quite proficient at it in a short time. She was much faster and efficient at panning than me, yet she still seemed somewhat puzzled as to why we would put forth all of the effort just to collect the yellow substance. What was it good for, anyway? She had heard the word 'gold' before, but had no concept of its value, or the dreadful extremes that mankind would go to in order to obtain it.

"Why we get this gold, John?"
"This gold can be traded for many good things, Loweja."
"What good things can this gold get?"
"Food, clothes, medicine... just about anything we want."
"Can you get sugar with this gold?"
"Yes, Loweja. We can get a lot of sugar with this gold!"

During the beginning of our third week in the canyon, our provisions were getting low, we had filled all of the sacks which I had brought, and I was beginning to realize that we had harvested a huge fortune from the earth... more than I had ever imagined in my most undisciplined dreams. I had estimated that we would stay in the canyon harvesting gold for three weeks, but I had no idea that we could have possibly accrued that much gold in just two weeks. I did not know exactly how much we had accumulated, as I had failed to pack in a device to weigh our gold. Further, I did not know what price I may expect to receive when I cashed it in. However, I did know, with reasonable certainty, that we had amassed nearly two hundred pounds, in total weight. To stay longer, would be to risk starvation, and would be an acknowledgement of pure greed. We had more than enough to remain comfortable for the rest of our lives. Loweja and I had eaten no meat for the previous two weeks, when our supply of salt pork had been exhausted, save for three rabbits which Loweja had killed with stones. We had some dried beans and some corn meal left, but weevils had gotten into the corn meal and mice had nearly ruined the beans. Loweja was able to pick some of the weevils out of the cornmeal and salvage a little of the meal, but if we did not start back now, our situation could become critical. With Loweja, I did not want to take any chances with her wellbeing. Had it not been for her, I could have easily succumbed to foolish greediness and quite possibly stayed until I had starved.

Our preparations to leave the narrow canyon had taken more than an entire day. The gold had been equally divided between the two pack horses, with dry goods and other belongings packed on top, so that the gold would be unnoticed and well hidden. There was about eighty pounds of gold on each side of each of the pack horses. We dressed the area up, to make it look as pristine as it had looked when we had first entered the little canyon, and once we were all packed up, we began our journey back. Loweja still could not comprehend the reasons we had worked so hard for almost three weeks, but she had enough faith in me that she believed that what we had done, we had done for a good reason. With everything finally loaded, we mounted our horses and started to travel south, out of the canyon. Loweja looked at me and asked, "We leave here now, John?"

"Yes, Loweja.... We leave here now."

"Where we go now, John?"

"Baltimore, maybe."

"Where is this Baw-de-more place, John?"

"A long, long way from here, darling. Many, many days of long travel."

We left the canyon cautiously, and covered each mile with apprehension. I kept both my revolver and my rifle close at hand. It was as though I had expected to see a bandit lurking behind every tree or every bush. Ever since my home in Baltimore had been ransacked, and I had encountered the thief on the train, I had felt a continuing strange sensation that there was an evil presence in pursuit of this wealth. Now that I had obtained the gold, I felt this sensation even stronger. Loweja still wanted to take the time to search for ripe serviceberries but I objected. I wanted to leave the area as quickly and as quietly as possible. It was still too early in the year for the serviceberries to have ripened anyway. The wealth contained within our packs would have been a tremendous incentive for someone wishing to do us harm. Yet each mile we traveled without incident gave me more confidence that our journey would be uneventful and pleasant. Still, we made no fires at night, unless we happened upon a place which offered us adequate seclusion from the surrounding mountains. If a fire was seen at night by savages or thieves it would only serve to lead them directly to us.

I could not help but consider what would happen if the location of Father's golden canyon became common knowledge to the outside world. There would be a deluge of miners and prospectors arriving almost overnight. The beautiful landscape would be destroyed, the wild game would eventually be killed, and this country would be infected with elements of evil which were unimaginable. Trees would be cut for houses and firewood. Thieves and villains would flock to the area in great numbers to predate upon those who would collect the gold by honest means. Boomtowns would spring up from nowhere, and the quietness and serenity of these peaceful mountains would be lost for all time.   Loweja and I had not taken all of the gold from Father's canyon. A vast fortune still remained there. Loweja and I had taken most of the easiest gold to collect, yes, but there remained a lot more which was hidden below the surface. It's possible that we took less than a quarter of what was there, farther beneath the surface. We had taken enough for ourselves and any children which we may have in the future, and behind us, we had left a canyon which looked as though it had not been touched by the hands of mankind. If we ever had to return for more gold, we could easily do so. Now, all we had to do is rejoin Oscar and Octeenchaha, and the four of us could make our way back to the Missouri River.

"Where we go now, John?"

"Back to get Oscar and Octeenchaha."

"Where we go then?"

"Back to your village and the river, Loweja."

"Where we go then?"

"We will buy a canoe and start down the river."

"Where we go then?"

"Down the river to Fort Saint Joseph."

"Where we go then?"

"Loweja, you're not going to turn into one of those aggravating wives who ends up driving their poor husbands insane by asking questions all the time, are you?"

"I do not understand what you say, John..."

The Passage Home

On the second day after leaving that special canyon, we neared the creek where we had left Oscar and Octeenchaha. But when we searched for them, they were nowhere to be found. We searched for clues, but found none, save for the remains of an old campfire where we had originally left them. I judged that there had not been a fire in that place for more than two weeks. Had they left of their own accord? Had they been attacked and killed? We searched every inch of the area of the camp, looking for some indication of the reason for their departure; some clue as to why they had had not remained here as I had instructed. We found nothing. Slowly, we proceeded downstream, looking along the banks as we went. Again, we found nothing. Puzzled and frightened, after three hours of searching, we reluctantly went on our way with hopes that we would find them back at the trading post when we arrived there. Perhaps they had squandered their provisions and departed early. The trail back to the Missouri River was easy to follow, so perhaps Oscar's wife had tired of him and demanded that he take her home. Perhaps thieves that had searched for me had found them by mistake. That seemed unlikely, as there was no evidence to support that possibility. There were numerous possibilities; too numerous to arrive at any one logical assumption. We went on, with the hope that we would find them along the trail somewhere or at the trading post when we arrived there. On the trail southeast, we continued to look for any signs of our missing comrades, but continued to find nothing.

    Loweja and I talked more and more freely while we were on the trail, and every day we got to know more about each other. She was the love of my life now, and I wanted to know as much about her as I possibly could. I could not have imagined living life without her. I felt as though my life before her had lacked definition and purpose. She had brought so many wonderful things into my life that I felt as though my very existence was now dependent on her happiness. It was strange that I should feel that way. I had never before cared for anyone enough to place their welfare and happiness above my own. My love for Loweja had changed all of that. I had never felt as though I was a complete person before... always aware that something was missing from my life, yet never having a clue as to what it was. More than two thousand miles from Baltimore, in a remote wilderness area, filled with savages and wild beasts, I had found that which was missing from my life... and her name was, Loweja.

"Loweja, I want you to promise me something."

"What thing you want, John? I promise you anything."

"Promise me that you will never put any ugly marks on your beautiful face. I saw women at your village who had ugly marks on their faces, and I never want you to do such a thing."

"I promise I will not do that. I think it is ugly thing for woman to do, too, John."

"Loweja, did your father ever beat you?"

"Yes. He beat me much times. He beat me bad sometimes. When I was little girl the big brothers of my father's other wife try to do *ohgā-sá-ho* to me. One hold me and the other get on me and try, but I bite his nose bad and it almost come off and make much *estoo-cas* and I make them go away and they tell lie to my father and he beat me real bad. I could not walk for many days."

"Your own brothers tried to do that to you? God Almighty... You have had a hard life, Loweja, and I'm very sorry. I will never beat you. I will protect you, and I will love you for as long as I live. I will kill anyone who tries to harm you. I make that promise to you."

"You will tickle me, maybe? Sometimes?"

"Yes, I will tickle you often, and I will make good love

to you, but I will never beat you."

"I will always be good wife for you! You will see that I speak truth to you!"

"I love you more each moment we are together, Loweja."

On the fifth day, after leaving the valley where we had discovered the gold, I was beginning to give a lot of thought to Loweja and me... our relationship... and our future. Loweja and I had been together for forty-eight days now. We had been living together as man and wife for the preceding four weeks, and we loved each other dearly. I felt tormented each time that she was out of my sight. I wanted to marry her, in a Christian ceremony, as a symbol of the undying respect and love that I had for her as a person, and I wanted to take her home, somewhere. I wanted to take her to a home where we could live our lives together in peace and harmony, and raise a family together. But where was my home? Loweja would be fascinated with Baltimore and my home there, I thought, and the conveniences of living in the city would be a delight to her... for a while, maybe. But she would soon tire of it and become restless, I felt. I had seen the look in her eyes when she stood in a field of wild flowers in the morning sun. I had seen the look in her eyes when she tasted of a mountain stream. I had watched her silently stalking fish with a sapling spear in her hand, and the gleam of pride in her eyes when returning to camp with a rabbit or two. Could she be happy in Baltimore? Could I be happy in Baltimore, now that I have seen the western slopes? Now that I have tasted of the clear mountain brooks? I felt as though I could be happy anywhere, as long as I was with Loweja, and she was happy. Her happiness was all that was important to me now. I swore an oath to myself that her happiness would be the driving force in my life from here on.

On the sixth day of our journey back to the Great Missouri, while on our horses, side-by-side, I tried to speak with Loweja about our future together. I wanted to know where she would feel the happiest.

"Loweja, where would you like to live, if you could live anywhere in the world that you wanted to?"

"With you, John. No one else. Just with you."

"I mean where would you like for you and me to live?"

"Together... Always together. John and Loweja."

"OK, let me try to put it another way... Where would you like for me and you to live together?"

"If we are together, John, it does not matter where we live. *heen-dos-beecha-at-tay*."

"I really don't understand those last Arikara words you said, but I suppose you're right, if we're together, it really doesn't matter where we live. I would really like to have some fish to eat tonight. If we stop early, do you think you can get some fish for us?" (*Silence*)

"Loweja, did you hear me?"

But she didn't answer... she looked past me with wide eyes and a frightened, concerned look upon her face. I turned to see what she was looking at, and saw three figures approaching on horseback in the distance. I could see that they were Indians. This was the second time in which we had encountered Indians in this country. I drew my rifle from its scabbard and laid it across my lap in anticipation of what may happen next. I reached down and placed my right hand on my revolver as the trio of Indians drew closer. In the back of my mind I thought of the miss-fire of my rifle when I had tried to shoot the bear that had threatened Loweja. Would my rifle miss-fire again if I needed to use it? Would I even need to use it? When they were close enough, I was greatly surprised and relieved to see that it was the same three Indians who we had passed on our journey northwest. Here they were again as we journeyed back southeastward. Our first encounter had ended peacefully, and perhaps this one would end peacefully as well. As they drew closer and we paused to talk, Loweja conversed with them vigorously. Judging by the expressions on their faces there was no bitterness or animosity being exchanged, only curious, friendly conversation. The encounter was more of a friendly bit of dialogue, with the Pawnee simply wanting to know more about us. Their spokesman, *Lectūschemă*, (Three Wolves) seemed to be an inquisitive fellow who was somewhat annoyed with having to converse through an interpretor, especially one who also happened to be an Arikara woman. Nevertheless, with Loweja's basic understanding of the Pawnee language, and a very basic understanding of the English language, we were able to communicate once more, albeit with some degree of difficulty. As it turned out, the Indians were far away from their usual homeland village. For us to have encountered each other twice already, in such a vast area, seemed a strange coincidence to the Indians, and me as well. Their curiosity stirred them into further conversation.

"They want to know what you are called by your people," said Loweja, and I spoke up immediately, answering,

"My name is John Welch," I said, as I pointed to myself. The Indians looked at each other strangely, talked between themselves for a short while, and their leader, Lectūschemă, pointed to the west, speaking, "William Welch, *Nu-conta-een-jaw-nee.*"

Why had he so distictly spoken the name of my father? Could I have misheard him? Why were they pointing to the west? Had they known my father? Lectūschemă had very clearly spoken his name. But why?

"Loweja, ask them why they spoke the name of *William Welch*."

"They say old white man *William Welch* live in mountains over there with Indian wives and children, and he is good man."

"Ask them if they will tell me how to find this old man, William Welch. Tell them that I want to talk to him." After much discussion between the Indians, they answered Loweja, and she relayed their message to me.

"They say that they will take us to him, John. *Nous vous wii.*"

With no further disscussion, Loweja and I followed two of the Indians who rode ahead, while the third Indian rode behind us. I returned my rifle to it's scabbard, as I felt unusually comfortable with these fellows for some reason... as if I knew them to be trustworthy people. They were rather fierce and formidable looking people, yet I felt safe and secure in following them. Oddly, I felt as though Loweja and I were under their protection while we were with them, and I was not concerned about the safekeeping of our gold or the wellbeing of Loweja and me. I was reluctant to leave the eastern trail only because I felt an urgency to get the gold into a safe place as soon as possible, yet I could not resist the urge to meet this strange man who was using the same name as my father. I would probably never travel this way again, and this could be my only opportunity to learn why this man was using the same name as my father. If I did not learn the answers to my questions this puzzle may haunt me for years to come.

We traveled over two small mountains, crossed a series of large creeks, through a great forest, and into a wonderously lush and green valley – a fertil land, a land of amazing beauty. We rode for several miles, until we arrived at a large meadow. In this place, there was a series of log structures and a small log home with smoke rising from it's chimney. There was one very small log structure which was apparently a chicken house, with thirty or forty chickens close by pecking at the ground, and four larger log lean-to structures, one with a coral fence around it. There were several other earthen huts with shaked roofs, apparently used for cool storage. Three medium-sized brown and black-spotted dogs ran from the porch of the house to greet us, and barked briefly as we rode slowly toward the house. It was a beautiful place with a large creek flowing nearby and thirty or forty young fruit trees growing on a hillside in an orchard. There was a large garden at the edge of the creek with corn and many other vegetables contained within. There were two young Indian girls standing near the house with two older Indian boys, and as we rode up to the house, a very attractive young Indian woman, perhaps twenty-two or twenty-three years of age, emerged to greet us. She was holding a rifle, as though she was poised to stage a defense if we had posed a threat. As we came closer, she handed the rifle to the largest of the two boys who quickly took it back inside of the house. She was small in stature, perhaps only an inch or two taller than Loweja. I looked around for the enigmatic man who called himself *William Welch*, but saw only the children and the young Indian woman who stood on the porch. The woman evidently knew Lectūschemă quite well, for they greeted each other cordially, and with smiles upon their faces they spoke fluently in the tongue of the Pawnee. They spoke to each other enthusiastically for several moments before the young woman turned to face me. I beckoned for Loweja to come forward and she bid the young woman good morning.

"*Chin-contè-sa. Bonjour.*"

"*Chin-contè-sa. Bonjour,*" the woman replied.

"Loweja, would you please tell this woman that I would like to see William Welch."

I wanted to meet this strange and suspicious man who used the same name as my father. I wanted to question him. We were in a great wilderness area here, and yet there was a man here who called himself, *William Welch*. I sat there in my saddle planning the questions which I would ask him and wondered what he would look like, and why he was using the same name as my father. Could it be a strange coincidence that two men had the same name? I did not think so. I think this fellow here might be up to no good… perhaps posing as my father for malicious purposes. And why would this man be living here so close to where my father had discovered the riches in the small canyon just a few days to the north? I felt very suspicious; like something odd and clandestine was going on here, and I felt compelled to get to the bottom of the mystery. Loweja conversed pleasantly with the woman, then turned to me and said, "She says that William Welch is not here."

"Oh? Then please ask her when William Welch will return, Loweja."

"She says that she wants to know why you want to see him."

"Tell her that I need to speak to him about some important business concerns."

"I do not understand those words, John." Loweja replied.

"I'm sorry. Just tell her that I need to speak with him… *parler*."

"She said that he is not here, and will not come back. She says that he has gone far away to his white son's house to die in a place called, *Baw-de-more*."

It was as though I had received a damaging blow to my stomach. With that one dramatic statement by the Indian woman, the answer to the mystery of my father's other life had been suddenly revealed to me. The home which was here before me had been the home of my father. This is where he had lived for the many years of my youth… here, with these people, in this place. I sat on my horse for some time, and bowed my head, trying to absorb the shocking impact of the news which I had just received. And still, I was overwhelmed to know that through an odd twist of fate, I had unwittingly discovered the place where my father had spent the last twenty years of his life… the very years in which I had yearned to see him walk through my doorway in Baltimore. Why would Father choose to live here, instead of being with Mother and me in Baltimore? Why? And who was this young woman who was telling us this? She knew that Father had returned to Baltimore to die, so she must be telling me the truth. Could she have been my father's Indian daughter? Could she have possibly been a young wife of my father? Probably not, at her young age, but there appeared to be no men around other than the two young Indian boys who were staring suspiciously at me. Still, this woman was much too young to be my father's wife. She was very close to my own age, I thought. I needed to know more about what I had just heard. She had answered one important question for me, but in doing so, she had created many more questions in the process.

"Loweja, please ask her who she is."

"She says that she is the wife of William Welch, and wants to know who you are... *qui êtes-vous*."

The wife of William Welch? *Espousa*? Could this beautiful young woman really have been the wife of my father!? How could that be? She was much too young to be the wife of the grey-haired old man who had returned to my house to die. She was not much older than I, if any. I was shaken to my core by what I was being told here, and tried desperately to absorb everything which I had heard. Nothing which I was hearing seemed to make sense to me. How could this be? An involuntary tear crossed my cheek...

"John? Did you hear me? She wants to know who you are. *Qui êtes-vous*."

"Tell her that my name is, *John Welch*, from Baltimore, and I am the white child of her husband... *Fils de William Welch*."

But Loweja's translation of my words wasn't necessary, for the young Indian woman who stood before me turned pale with lack of color upon hearing my words, and spoke back to me in perfectly clear and understandable English.

"You are welcome here in this house, John Welch, son of my husband." I was surprised at how distinctly she had spoken to me in English, but I shouldn't have been surprised at all. If my father really had spent so many years of his life here, it only made sense that his Indian family could speak some English, and I could only suppose that her reluctance to speak in English from the beginning, was due to caution on her part. I was a stranger to her, and could have represented a threat to her and the children. She seemed to be very shaken when she learned my identity, and even held on to the porch post for support, as if she was about to faint.

Still in stunned disbelief, I looked about me at the young Indian girls and boys gathered there. These were not just young Indians here, they were my half-brothers and sisters. Four of them! They were beautiful children...they were my kin... my relatives. The young Indian woman was darker in complexion that the children, and darker in complexion than Loweja. Father's influence was undoubtedly the reason for the lighter complexion of the children. I sat there and looked around me at my relatives. I had somehow gone from having no living family in this world, to having a family before me whom I had never known.

Loweja and I thanked our Pawnee guides for having brought us there. I searched through one of the packs and gave them each a hatchet, a knife, a box of clay trade pipes, and a long length of rope. They seemed puzzled by my emotional reaction to the situation, but after receiving my gifts, they bid us a cordial farewell and rode off, leaving Loweja and me alone with my new family. Loweja, on the other hand, was not puzzled or perplexed by anything which had happened. She knew exactly what had taken place there and looked at me with sympathetic eyes... eyes which were understanding of my bewildered emotions. I looked back at the young woman who stood there before me on the cabin porch and tearfully asked,

"What name may we call you?"
"I am *Steechánay*, but my people call me, *Mrs. Welch*."
"What name would you prefer for us to call you?"
"Steechánay, please. That is my name."
"Steechánay, this is my wonderful wife, *Loweja*. May we dismount and speak to you for a while?"
"You are my husband's oldest son?"

"Yes... I suppose I am... Up till now, I always considered myself the only son of William Welch..."

"This was my husband's house, so it is your house, too. You are welcome here, John Welch and Loweja. Please come inside and we will talk."

Loweja's face showed extreme pride when I had introduced her as *'my wonderful wife'*... my first such opportunity to do so. Loweja and I dismounted as Steechánay shouted to her boys,

"*Kwīnahā, kooch-ta sĕ-rees-a*! I told them to take care of your horses. They will put them in the corral. Will you come inside with me so we can talk, please?"

"Yes, Steechánay. We would like that very much, thank you."

"I have no tea or sugar left, John Welch. It has all been gone for many days now."

"I have a good supply of tea and sugar in our packs. I will bring it inside."

Once inside of the small home, I looked around and sensed the coziness and warmth which must have been shared within these walls. There was a stone fireplace with a large cooking pot hanging nearby. Animal hides adorned the inside walls as well as the floor, and there was a large bed near the fireplace. Wapiti and deer antlers hung from the upper rafters, as did strips of rawhide and rope. This had been my father's bed, I thought to myself. It was a large bed covered with bear hides and woolen blankets. A cluster of steel animal traps hung from a support post and there was an axe and a worn shovel leaning against the wall in the corner. There was a large loft area which overlooked the fireplace... undoubtably where the children slept, and a narrow ladder which afforded access to the loft. The rails of the ladder were worn smoothe by hands which had grasped them many times as the ladder was climbed. We sat at a small table covered with deerskins to speak after Steechánay put a kettle of water on the fire to boil.

"Did my husband, William Welch, die in that *Bought-a-more* place, John?"

"Yes, Steechánay. He died in my house, as I held his hand. I'm sorry to be the one to tell you this."

"Was he in great pain when he died?"

"No, Steechánay. He was in no pain... none at all. He died quietly and peacefully."

"Did he get to speak with you before he died?"

"Yes. We spoke very briefly before he died. I had many questions which I had wanted to ask him, but he died before we could speak that long. I am very hopeful that you may be able to answer some of my questions."

"I will try to answer your questions. I'm glad he talked to you. He always loved you very much, and wanted to speak to you before he died. That is why he left here. I am happy he talked to you and happy that I did not see him die. Did he say my name to you before he died?"

"Yes, Steechánay. He told me to tell you that he loved you." I lied terribly, saying words which I thought would bring comfort to the young woman. My words did seem to bring some peace to her eyes and a subtle smile to her lips.

"Did he live a good life here, Steechánay?"

"Yes. We both lived a good life here, in this house together, and I think we had love here in this house, too." She said, as her expression turned very sullen.

"Did he teach you to speak English so well, Steechánay?"

"Yes. He taught me many things, and I taught him many things also. I have not spoken English words since your father went away to die. There are no people here who speak English. It feels good for me to speak the words again so I do not forget how."

"Did my father learn to speak your language?"

"He learned to speak Pawnee very well, Arikara, not so good."

"What Indian Nation are you from?"

"My mother was Arikara, and my father was Shoshone, but I have lived with the Pawnee most of my life."

"How did your mother and father meet, being from two different nations like that?"

"My mother was captured by a Pawnee war party and taken back to live with them. My father was Shoshone, but he had been with the warriors who had captured my mother. The Pawnee gave her to him because of his courage in battle. But then my father was killed soon and… that is all that I know…"

"I see. Do the Pawnee and Arikara speak a different language?"

"Yes. But they can talk to each other, and understand each other sometimes. Maybe even most of the time."

"Are the four children outside your children, Steechánay?"

"Three are from me, and from your father. The oldest, *Kwīnahā*, is from your father and his other wife."

"Other wife? What do you mean?"

"I cannot speak her name, because she was not a Christian. It is bad to speak the name of a dead person unless they were a Christian. But she is dead now. She die too, last season of snow. I have raised Kwīnahā as if he was my own."

"Steechánay, are you saying that my father had two wives, at the same time?"

"I think he had three wives at same time. Me and his dead wife, and another one who was a white woman, your mother, who lived far away in a place called, *Bought-a-More*."

"My Lord! Do the children speak English?"

"Little, sometimes. Not as much as me. We have not spoken English since William Welch went away to die."

"How long have you and my father lived here as husband and wife, Steechánay?"

"We did not count the seasons, John Welch. We just lived here, that's all… but I think it was maybe six winters…"

"How did you meet my father?"

"He gave my father many things so that he could have

me for wife. I was very young then, and he was already very old, and his dead wife was also very old, many seasons ago."

"You are still a very young woman, Steechánay."

"Maybe so, but sometimes I do not feel young anymore. I am not happy here without husband now. I love my children, but my heart still hurts sometimes."

"Was my father well liked by the Pawnee?"

"He was well liked by everyone who knew him. We never saw many other white men here except for the French. Your father would not permit the French to come close to the house because they brought bad sickness to Indians sometimes. But each season he would journey somewhere and come back with many gifts for everyone, and much great medicine and food, too."

"Did my father ever beat you, or hurt you in any way?"

"No! He was gentle man. Always kind to me."

"You mentioned the word, *love*, earlier. Do you know what the English word, '*love*' means, Steechánay?"

"Yes... William Welch taught me what it means. Why do you ask that?"

"Did you and my father love each other?"

"No, not at first. I did not want to go away from my village with old man. I want to go with young man only, but my father sold me to William Welch because he had been good to our people, and gave my father many great gifts. I went with him because he bought me and I had to go with him. But after our first season together, I think we had some love for each other. As I told you, he did not beat me. He was always kind to me... yes, I think we had some love. I was much younger than Loweja when he bought me, much younger, but he was gentle to me and I grew to love him. His other wife did not like me, and she tried to beat me many times, but he would not let her hurt me. He tell her that if she beat me, he would beat her, so she stop trying after he tell her that. I loved him, *yes*, because he did not hurt me."

"And because he did not beat you, you think that is the

same thing as *love*?"

"Maybe so, I think... but I don't know..."

"Who watches over you and the children now that William Welch is gone?"

"There is no one to watch over us. I have brother who comes here sometimes from Pawnee village. That is all."

She seemed to become more depressed as we talked about her situation in Father's absence, so I tried to change the subject. I could clearly tell that she was deeply bothered by the uncertainty of her future there in the wilderness as a widow with four children. Loweja sat there quietly listening to Steechánay and me talk. She was surely absorbing everything which was said between us, for I noticed the glimmer of a tear in her eye as we talked. Strangely, I felt no overwhelming urge to condemn Father for choosing to live his life here among these people rather than in Baltimore with Mother and me. My mother could be a strange and demanding person at times, and often indignant and offending. Even though she was my mother, in my heart I knew that she would have been a difficult person for a man to live with, much less, love. Deep down, I felt as though I understood the reasons that Father had made his choice, and I held no bitterness in my heart, other than the resentment I had for Father marrying Steechánay at such a young age. I was beginning to see a sort of brutal truth in the lives of Indians which does not exist among the whites. This home, which had been my father's home, seemed to speak to me... echoing the happiness which had once been here. The walls seemed to be talking to me, and the message which I was receiving was not necessarily that of love, as much as it was contentment and peace.

"Steechánay, how young were you when my father bought you?"

"I was not yet woman. I was just young girl. I had only just made my first blood, and did not know what to think of it. I cry even, and his other wife laugh at me when I cry."

"And my father impregnated you when you were just a young girl like that? Please tell me that is not so, Steechánay!"

"I do not know this word you say, John. I am sorry."

"My father had *ohgā-sá-ho* with you when you were just a young girl?"

"Yes, but he was gentle with me, and kind to me, and he put Joseph inside of me then, and I soon loved him because he did that. Then he put Kwesha inside of me and then, Pokeem... my youngest child, and I think I loved him even more then."

"Did his other wife know that he was having *ohgā-sá-ho* with you when you were just a child like that?"

"Yes. She was there each time. She show me what I must do to be wife, and I just did it while she watch your father and me. When I had Joseph, my first child, my body was too young to make good milk, so your father made his other wife give Joseph her milk so that he would live. I want to give him my own milk, but my body would not make it."

"My dear God! I'm sorry to hear that my father would do such a thing to a child! It is hard for me to believe. It makes me very sad to hear this. From my heart, Steechánay, I am truly very, very sorry."

"You make tears, John... please do not. Do not be sorry, John. I have Joseph and the other children now. I would not have them if your father had not put them in me, and I loved your father because he give me children. Do you have such good love for Loweja?"

"Yes, Steechánay, I love Loweja very much. Very much. She is a good wife to me."

"Does Loweja have such love for you?" But before I could answer, Loweja answered for me,

"Yes! Very, very much love, Steechánay. I love John Welch. I die for him, even! He is best husband in all of earth!"

"That is good, Loweja. That is very good. I am happy for both of you." Steechánay stood up and announced,

"I will make a meal for us, the water is now ready for tea." and Loweja quickly spoke up, saying,

"I will help you, Steechánay." I sensed some sort of mysterious bond which had already taken place between Steechánay and Loweja during our brief conversation... some sort of sistorship of their spirits, perhaps. I think that it was because of the sincerity which was in their eyes as they spoke to one another. Loweja seemed to have great compassion for Steechánay, and regreted the lonliness which she was experiencing in my father's absence. I struggled to come to terms with the fact that my own father had introduced premature copulative relations with a girl who was just a minor at the time... probably just twelve or thirteen years old! In my mind, I wanted to forgive him, yet I could not. If Steechánay was a small woman now, at twenty or twenty-one years, she must have surely been much smaller in stature when she was at twelve or thirteen years of age. My heart would not forgive him for what he had done. Then, it occurred to me that it was not me who needed to forgive him, but God. At Steechánay's table, I lowered my head and silently asked God to forgive him for what he had done. Steechánay and Loweja knew that I was in prayer, and said nothing while I prayed. When I had finished, I raised my head and asked,

"Steechánay, may I go outside and see the children, please?"

"They are your family, John Welch. They will be happy to see you. They are good children. When you come to know them, you will love them just as I do."

As Loweja and Steechánay started to prepare a meal, I stepped outside to see my four new brothers and sisters. I wanted to meet them and see them closely. They were huddled in a group, quietly talking to each other. As I approached, they ceased talking and focused their attention on me. They looked frightened at first. I smiled and sat down beneath a tree where I could be at eye-level with them, and motioned for them to join me. Reluctantly, they each slowly walked toward me and sat down just a few feet away. For a while, I said nothing. I just sat there and looked at each of them. I judged that the two boys were probably ten and thirteen years of age, and the two girls were most likely eight and nine. The boy who looked to be ten years old was Steechánay's first child, Joseph. I felt another momentary rush of disgust in my father's decadent behavior, knowing that Steechánay must have been barely in her teenaged years when Father had impregnated her. But I let my evil thoughts pass, and focused my exclusive attention on the children before me. They were such beautiful children. I smiled an even broader smile, pointed to myself, and said, "I am John."

The children clearly recognized that I was making an attempt to introduce myself, and one-by-one they said,

"I am Kwīnahā"
"I am Kwesha"
"I am Joseph"
"I am Pokeem"

"Those are mighty beautiful names! Can you teach me this game that you play?"

It wasn't long before I felt completely at ease with the children, and they with me. They showed me how to play a game which involved balancing a stick on the sharp point of a rock, and then seeing who could be the first to knock it off by throwing small stones. I tried as hard as I could to impress the children with my throwing accuracy, but they won the game every time, and I soon found their laughter to be quite contagious. Their presence and their cheerfulness gave me tremendous delight. It suddenly occurred to me that there was no father figure in their life now, only their mother, Steechánay. This was worrisome to me. These children needed the presence of a father in their lives. Every child needs a father in their life. Having been deprived of one myself, no one could appreciate that more than I. Perhaps Steechánay would re-marry soon, and the children would once again have a father. Soon, Loweja called for me and told me that our meal was ready. It was customary for the children to eat after the adults had eaten, so I excused myself from the games and walked back into the house. When I had entered, Steechánay asked me, "Will you and Loweja be staying here?"

"We would like to stay for the night, if you would allow us to, that is. We need to leave early tomorrow, for we have a great distance to travel."

"Do you want me to leave, John?"

"Do I want you to leave? Leave to go where? What do you mean, Steechánay?"

"You are your father's oldest son. This is your house now. You can make me go, if you want to."

"Steechánay, I would never do such a cruel thing as that! This is your house, now. Not mine. It is my wish that you stay here as long as you want. Understand?"

"You are a kind man, John Welch, just like your father. The children and I will sleep under the lean-to tonight so that you and Loweja may sleep here, in your father's bed. It is where your father and I slept."

"Loweja and I will sleep under the lean-to tonight! Your place is here, with your children, in your own home."

When the children came up to the house to eat, Loweja and I sat nearby drinking our tea and watching them as they ate. They were all so well-mannered and polite. It was obvious that Steechánay had been teaching them well. I took great delight in watching them eat, but wondered in the depths of my mind what the future held in store for them, with no father. And what did the future hold in store for Steechánay, with no husband? I found the prospects quite bothersome.

That evening, Loweja and I spread our buffalo hides out under the larger lean-to and made a cozy bed there. The night air was turning chilly. I knew that the cooler weather of fall would be upon us at any time. As much as I wanted to stay here longer, I was reluctant to do so for fear of being stranded by early winter snows if they were to come. As we lay together under the lean-to, I asked Loweja, "Do you like it here, in this place, Loweja?"

"I like any place where you are, John... but yes, I do like this place. I much like this place, and I like Steechánay and children, too! She is nice woman, but she have unhappy eyes."

"I noticed that, too, Loweja."

"What does '*noticed*' mean?"

"It means that I saw the unhappiness in her eyes too, Loweja."

"My heart hurts for Steechánay."

"Loweja, let me ask you a question."

"Yes, John?"

"Men around here can buy wives when they want one, right?"

"Man can marry daughter if he can give mother of woman good gifts like horses or furs, like gifts you gave to my father to have me for wife. Why do you ask this?"

"Do women ever buy a husband when they need one?"

"No, John. That is not done. Ever. Man must pay father and mother for woman. Woman cannot pay father and mother for son. That is not done."

"It was just a thought that I had. I thought maybe I could buy a husband for Steechánay before we left here... but I suppose not."

Loweja and I were on our horses and ready to leave very early the next morning. Kwīnahā had helped me prepare our horses. But before leaving, I asked Steechánay a question which had been weighing heavily on my mind ever since Loweja and I had discovered that Oscar and Octeenchaha were not in the camp where we had left them on the creek.

"Steechánay, Loweja and I were supposed to meet a couple of people four days north of here just a few days ago, but they were not there. Have you heard anything about a dark-colored man with an Arikara wife passing near here?"

"Many days ago, yes."

"What do you know?"

"I heard that the Pawnee had killed a man with very dark skin and took his woman. They take dead man and his woman to their village to show people man with dark skin. That is all I hear."

"The Pawnee did that?"

"That is what I heard. The Pawnee have been very good to your father, and to me. They only kill when there is a reason to kill. Did you know the man with dark skin that they killed?"

"Yes, I did, and I'm sorry to hear that he's dead. Thank you for telling me about this, Steechánay."

"Will you and Loweja be coming back here?"

"I don't know. I would like to come back some day, but right now, I just don't know for sure. We've got business which we need to tend to far away from here. If we do come back, is there anything you would like for us to bring to you?"

"Sugar, please, and maybe some tea leaves, too."

"If we do come back, we will be glad to bring you those things. Goodbye, Steechánay, and thank you for receiving us so warmly. You are a good woman, and we wish you a happy life here."

"You are a good man, John Welch… and Loweja is a good wife. I hope you do come back. I hope you do… and I will ask Great Holy Father to protect you on your journey."

After our farewells to Steechánay and the children, Loweja and I re-traced our route back to the main eastern trail, and then continued southeastward towards the Arikara village and the trading post. I grieved terribly over Oscar's death, and only found comfort in knowing that I had tried my best to bring some happiness into his life by giving him his freedom from slavery. I prayed that God would have mercy on his soul and forgive me for unknowingly leading him into the place of his death. I also prayed that God would have mercy on Octeenchaha, and that her captors would not treat her with brutality. I did not know Octeenchaha very well, we did not speak to each other very much, but she seemed to always have a very pleasant smile upon her face. I wondered why the Pawnee would kill such an easy-natured fellow as Oscar, and yet permit Loweja and me to pass through their country without difficulty. I would remain puzzled over the occurrence.

It took fourteen more days of continuous travel for Loweja and I to reach the Arikara village. The vast grassland which had been so badly scorched by the great fire had healed, and the burned, dry grass had been replaced with lush, green grass. The beautiful mountain valley where Father had spent the last twenty years of his life remained vivid in my mind. It was a wonderful place, and I understood perfectly why Father had fallen in love with both the valley, and Steechánay. I felt sorrow in my heart for Steechánay. She was a beautiful, young, vibrant woman, who had not yet reached the prime of her life, and she had no husband to rely on and without a husband, a very questionable future ahead of her. Loneliness was written all about her face and in her eyes. I hoped that she would not be over-eager for the companionship of a man and perhaps bring a filthy European trapper into her home with my wonderful half-brothers and sisters. I could not live with myself if I knew something like that would happen. I wanted the best for Steechánay, but was helpless in the matter. I could only hope and pray.

As the Arikara village came into view, I studied Loweja's facial expression to see if I could detect sadness in her eyes, or any sign that she was homesick. I thought that perhaps she was missing her family, and as we came closer to the village, I asked her, "Loweja, would you like to visit your family while we're here in your village?"

"No! You are my only family, John. *Say-ha-way*. You are the only one I want to be with. You are the only one who would die for me. You are my husband. I love you. My father and my mother beat me much, but John only loves Loweja."

"And I will always love you, Loweja. I just thought you might want to see your mother and father again before we leave. Maybe you could tell them you are happy now, so they would not worry."

"I said goodbye before. I was never happy here. I am happy now… want to be with you only. If I see them now, I will only think of times they beat me much."

"Did your mother and father beat your brothers as badly as they beat you?"

"Young boys in our village cannot be beat by father or mother. It is a sin for a father or mother to beat a son… it is not done. Only girls and women get beat. When I was little girl I was sorry to be girl. I wanted to be boy so I would not get beat. Now that you are my husband I am happy I am not a boy."

"I'm happy that you're not a boy, too, Loweja! I am much, much, much happy!"

I often wished that Loweja could speak perfect English, instead of fragmented bits and pieces, although I felt as though I was able to hear and understand things in her simple words which perhaps did not need a glossary of explicit language to properly convey. She was a deep, caring person, and I wanted to please her more than anything in this world… She was my life's blood now. She was right; I would die for her.

At the trading post, I had Loweja wait outside with our horses while I bartered inside for a canoe. I still had a goodly amount of paper currency and gold coin on my person as well as the horses to bargain with. Still, I negotiated shrewdly with the Frenchman so that he would not recognize me as being overly wealthy, and an easy person to steal from. Negotiations took over an hour before we finally came to an agreement. It was all that I could do to control my temper when the scoundrel saw Loweja with our horses in the distance and offered to buy her. Despite the overwhelming urge to shoot him dead, I forced myself to laugh at his offer. After the bartering process was completed, I looked up to see the familiar, smiling face of Hidessa approaching. He graciously offered to help load our goods onto the canoe and I quickly accepted his offer.

"I see that Loweja is still with you, John Welch."

"She is my wife, Hidessa. Of course she's still with me."

"You seem to like her a lot more now than you did before."

"I love her, Hidessa. Like I said, she is my wife, and I will always love her."

"Where is Oscar, and the Arikara woman who traveled with him?"

"Oscar is dead, and the woman who traveled with him has been taken captive by the Pawnee."

"I am sorry to learn this. Things have also happened here in my village while you were gone. I must tell you, there have been three white men with guns here at the trading post and my village who have asked many questions about you, John Welch."

"Oh? What kind of questions, Hidessa?"

"They wanted to know if anyone knew where you had gone when you left here. They said that they needed to speak with you badly. They offered much money for someone to tell them. They even paid me much money to tell them where you went, so I told them. But they were evil men and I could see the evil in their eyes when I told them how they could find you."

"What did you tell them? I have seen no such men."

"I told them that you were going to go twenty-three days west and eight days northwest, to where the great mountains part and the snow never goes away."

"Thank you, Hidessa. I don't know what they would find if they followed those directions, but it surely wasn't me. What will you do when they find out you sent them to the wrong place, if they come back to seek revenge on you?"

"They will not come back, if they went where I told them to go."

"Why?"

"Have you ever heard of the Blackfeet people?"

"Yes, I have."

"Well, that is where I sent them. No white man or Indian will return from there. Even the Shoshone and the Flatheads fear them."

I wondered if the thieves had followed Hidessa's directions, but I was indeed grateful that he had conceived a diversion for my pursuers. I wondered if the shady character whom I had encountered on the train was among the three men who Hidessa had talked to. Regardless, I was very thankful that Hidessa had misdirected my assailants. With little fanfare, Hidessa, Loweja, and I soon had our goods loaded aboard the canoe and turned two of our horses over to the French scoundrel, Francois Brĕaux as payment for the canoe. I gave Hidessa a twenty-dollar gold piece for his efforts in foiling my enemies, and also gave him the other two horses. He felt as though he was the richest man in the world, or certainly the richest man in his village.

"What will you do with all of that money, Hidessa?"

"I think I will buy another wife, maybe."

"I thought you already had two wives."

"I do indeed, but they are getting older, like me, and they don't like to talk to me much, anymore. I think I would like to have a young wife, maybe."

"Do you think a young wife will talk to you more than your old wives?"

"I am going to look for a young wife who likes to talk, John."

With our farewells completed, Loweja and I pushed our heavily laden canoe off into the current of the Missouri River and began our trip to Saint Joseph. Loweja quickly learned how to paddle. It was the first time that she had been in a boat of any kind, and although she was frightened at first, she soon showed remarkable skill in steering from the front. The canoe teetered several times, and almost capsized twice, but Loweja soon mastered the art of maintaining one's balance when in a canoe. We were traveling with the current this time, which took much less effort. The canoe moved swiftly down the river. Several times, we ran onto sand bars and had to drag the canoe to deeper water. Although she did not know where we were going, or what she would find when we got there, Loweja worked diligently with her paddle. She seemed to always work very hard to please me, and in every respect, she never failed. She always pleased me!

"Where do we go now, John?"

"Baltimore... maybe... I'm not so sure anymore..."

"What is this place, *Baw-de-more*? Can you tell me, John?"

"It's where my home is. Do you want to go there with me?"

"Yes! I want to go with you! Is Baw-de-more beautiful place? Like where Steechánay live in valley?"

"Well, I used to think it was a beautiful place... but I'm starting to have second thoughts now, Loweja."

"Does it have fish, and rabbits, and mountains?"

"Well... not exactly."

Loweja seemed to be enjoying our adventure. Seeing country which she had never seen before, seeing the mighty mud-burdened Missouri River growing wider and wider as we continued downstream... it was all new to her. Perhaps she would be thrilled to see the lively city of Baltimore... its bustling streets, its harbor with all of the magnificent sailing ships. Maybe she would enjoy going to the opera, or dining in a fine restaurant there. If I could get all of the gold to a bank, I would be a very wealthy man now. She could have a maid to cater to her every need. She could have the finest clothes that money could buy and live in absolute comfort for the rest of her life. I would not hesitate to give her anything that she wanted. Anything. I even entertained the thought of funding a formal education for Loweja... if that would be to her liking. My life's mission now was in the pursuit of happiness for Loweja and me. Nothing else was important to me anymore.

When Loweja had asked me if Baltimore had fish and rabbits and mountains, I could not bring myself to tell her what Baltimore was really like. In asking her question, however, she had inadvertently revealed to me what she had pictured in her mind as the perfect place for us to live; her image of the Garden of Eden, so to speak. In the back of my cluttered mind, I could almost envision the wonderful place she described. It was a place of peace and solitude. It was a place of wondrous beauty and love. It was a place which seemed to be very much like my father's valley. I had never seen another place like my father's valley. It was a place that made me feel like I belonged there. But it was so far away from anything that I was familiar with. I would remember that special valley. Hopefully, someday Loweja and I could go back to visit Steechánay. And if we did, I hoped that we would find her happy. If she remarried, I hoped that she would find someone who would be gentle to her and love her sincerely. She was such a kind and loving person that she deserved any and all happiness which would come her way. If she did remarry, I hoped that it would be with someone who would love and watch over the children as well. They were such wonderful children. Lord, please watch over them and bring happiness into their lives.

We were quickly on our way now to Fort Saint Joseph. If Loweja liked the bustling city of Fort Saint Joseph, perhaps she could learn to like Baltimore as well. We would soon see. We dodged sand bars, log jams, and other obstructions, making great haste on the "*Big Muddy*." With the assistance of recent rains, the river was running fast and deep. We traveled three times faster descending the river than Oscar and I had traveled going upstream, and we were doing so with much less effort. Many of the small waterfalls which Oscar and I had to portage around were now covered by the deeper water and Loweja and I simply glided over them with no problem at all.

Fort Saint Joseph

Fall had started to take complete control of the weather. Colorful fallen leaves were all about the surface of the muddy river. Loweja and I had kept our two buffalo hides and all of our blankets with us on our trip. Our buffalo hides were among our most prized possessions now. In the evenings, we would beach the canoe and camp, just as I had done during my journey upriver. The weather was cool enough that we seldom had to worry about pesky mosquitoes or other biting insects. The food that we had purchased at the trading post and brought along with us would surely last us until we reached Ft. Saint Joseph. There, we could dine in fine restaurants and live in elegant hotels until we decided where to go from there. Perhaps Loweja would want to cross the Atlantic and tour Europe. Money would be no object now. We could do anything that she wanted to. I wanted to do anything that would make Loweja happy.

I loved Loweja greatly, and wanted to marry her in a Christian ceremony… either in Fort Saint Joseph or Baltimore. I felt as though a Christian marriage ceremony would be necessary in order for me to feel like I had done the proper thing, and to show her that I respected her in addition to loving her. I felt like I owed her as much, if that was what she wanted. In camp one evening, over the glow of our evening campfire, I asked Loweja how she felt about a marriage ceremony, or at least I tried to.

"Loweja, we will be getting to Ft. Saint Joseph in about two days… will you marry me there?"

"We are already married, John. You did not know this?"

"In the white man's world where we are going, there is a

ceremony which must be performed before a man and a woman are truly married. Will you do that ceremony with me when we get to Fort Saint Joseph?"

"What does this ceremony mean, John?"

"It means that we love each other, Loweja."

"We already love each other. I love you... Do you love me?"

"Well, yes. Of course I do. I love you more than anything on this earth, you know that. I just...."

"See? We already love each other. We do not need this ceremony that you speak of, John."

"You are a Christian, aren't you?"

"Yes, John. I believe in Jesus and the Great Holy Father above. White preacher even get me baptim-ized when I was little girl."

"Well, how about you and I standing before the Great Holy Father and telling him how much we love each other? Would you do that for me?"

"The Great Holy Father already knows how much we love each other... he knows everything. He is everywhere and He sees everything and He hears everything, too."

"Yes, but... well, I never came out and formally asked you if you would marry me."

"Marry? Ask? I do not understand. In village you buy me for wife. At creek you ask me to be wife and I say yes. You do *ohgā-sá-ho* as husband with me many times now. You tell Steechánay that I am your wife. You tell me *I love you*. I tell you *I love you*. You tell Hidessa you love me. Why you ask me to marry you now? I do not understand."

"You sure do have a way of using my own idiotic words against me, don't you? Has Hidessa or Mrs. Parker been giving you lessons on how to trap me with my own tongue?"

"I do not understand. Did I say wrong thing?"

"No, Loweja. Come to think of it, what you said makes a lot more sense than what I said. We better go ahead and eat something. We have a hard day ahead of us tomorrow." Loweja looked as though she was thinking long and hard about something. She took me by the hands, looked deeply into my eyes, and asked, "John?"

"Yes, Loweja?"

"If we do not have this ceremony thing, will you not love me as much?"

"Loweja, forget about the stupid ceremony. You are right, and I was wrong. We became husband and wife in the eyes of the Great Holy Father when we made our vows that evening in the mountains. There is no ceremony on earth that could ever measure up to that. Do you understand everything that I just said?"

"Yes. I love you with my heart, John Welch!"

I was a changed person from the man that I had been before I met Loweja. I had found so many truths within the Indian culture that disputed the vanity, hypocrisy, and insensitivity of the white man that I knew I would have great difficulty returning to Baltimore and living among all of the evilness there again. Being around the Indians and sampling their simple, truthful way of life had changed my life completely. I thought about how close I had come to marrying Elizabeth Cunningham and I shuddered at the very thought. Had I stayed in Baltimore, and married Elizabeth, I would have never ventured west... and I would never have met my wonderful Loweja. She was the love of my life now. I had bought her from her father for a few dollars' worth of meaningless material, and she was the most valuable thing in my life.

Before we turned in that night, I saw Loweja, a short distance from camp, down on her knees praying to the Great Holy Father. Instead of turning and walking away as I usually did, I walked over and knelt beside her and thanked the Great Holy Father myself... aloud, with her. Again, I heard her use my name as she prayed in Arikara. As we walked back to camp, I asked her, "Loweja, what did you say to Great Holy Father when you spoke to him just now?"

"I ask him to keep your heart happy and not let hurt come to you ever. I did not tell him that I love you because he already know that."

For the next two days we continued downstream, drawing closer and closer to Fort Saint Joseph. We began to see houses and tents along the upper banks of the river, and Loweja paid particular attention to each of them. There were great piles of logs which had been cut in nearby forests and stockpiled at the river's edge in preparation of being transported to Fort Saint Joseph or beyond. We passed a variety of small pirogues and canoes either headed to, or coming from, the markets in Fort Saint Joseph. Loweja was frightened out of her wits by the time we approached the river wharf at Fort Saint Joseph. She had never seen anything like it in her life… buildings, buggies, streets, and the hordes of busy people milling about. Workmen seemed to be busy everywhere, constructing new buildings. I tried desperately to console her, but the city and the sights were overwhelming to her. After we tied the canoe off at the dock, I finally got her calmed down to the point that she was able to disembark and step off on the platform. I quickly employed a coachman and we transferred all of our goods to the coach as Loweja continued to look around in every direction, in stunned disbelief at what she was seeing. She never had any idea that a place such as this even existed. She was afraid to get inside of the coach at first. I had to enter first, to show her that it was safe to do so, and then she entered and sat beside me… squeezing my hand tightly from the fear she had inside. I had the coachman take us to the Bank of Fort Saint Joseph, where I solicited a local constable to help us unload twenty-two bags of gold. The constable told me that he had never seen that much gold in his life. Once inside the bank, Loweja and I, along with our gold, were quickly ushered into an open office where two clerks and the bank's manager closed the door and weighed our gold in front of us. Every eye in the bank was on Loweja and me as we walked toward the office. I supposed they had never seen an Indian in her native attire before, and certainly not one in a beautifully ornate buckskin dress. After much calculating, and each clerk had double-checked his figures, the bank manager left and returned shortly with the president of the bank. They all reviewed their final calculations and the president of the bank cleared his throat and announced, "Mr. Welch, you have brought four thousand and twelve ounces of gold here, sir. At nineteen dollars and fifty cents per ounce, that comes to seventy eight thousand two hundred and thirty four dollars. What would you like to do with all of this gold, sir? We are the biggest bank in Fort Saint Joseph, but we do not have the cash on hand to buy this much gold, sir."

"I wish to deposit all of it into your bank, except for twelve thousand dollars-worth, which I would like in paper currency or gold coin, sir."

"Mr. Welch, I'm sorry, sir, but we simply don't have that much paper currency or gold coin here in the bank. It would take me a week to get that much paper currency, sir. Our depository is in St. Louis, and I would have to send for it. Armed guards would have to accompany the money the entire way. I could arrange for this, sir, but it will take from five to seven days for it to get here."

"How much paper currency do you have available here in Fort Saint Joseph?"

"Perhaps six or eight thousand, sir, at the very most. We have never had a transaction this large before, sir. Not in the history of the bank!"

"Very well. Give me just four thousand in paper currency and two thousand in gold coin now, and I'll be back in a week for the rest. Can you accommodate that?"

"Yes, sir! Thank you, Mr. Welch! I'll get your currency and your coins now, and a certificate of deposit! Thank you, sir! Thank you!"

During this proceeding, Loweja sat quietly in the corner, stunned and confused by everything which was going on around her, and most likely understanding none of it. I wished that there had been some way that I could have introduced her to civilization in a slower manner, without scaring her half to death, but if there was a better way, I surely didn't know what it was. As we walked out of the bank, all of the patrons stared at Loweja in her beautiful buckskins and beadwork, a gesture which I'm sure only added to her general discomfort. Many of them had probably never seen such a beautiful Indian woman before... much less a maiden of Loweja's beauty. We climbed aboard our coach and I instructed the coachman to take us to the finest hotel in Fort Saint Joseph. As fortune would have it, the hotel was next door to a large clothier. We bought Loweja a couple of fine dresses and I purchased a new suit of clothes. Then we retired to our hotel for a hot bath. Two of the hotel maids had agreed to help Loweja bathe and dress her in one of her new outfits while I dashed across the street for a haircut and a shave. Soon, after all of the confusion had died down, Loweja and I were alone in our suite, facing each other in our new attire and ready to go out for a grand dinner. Loweja's hair was out of braids and fixed as a bun on the top of her head. The ribbons in her hair matched in color to the dress which she was wearing. She looked at me, and saw me standing before her, clean-shaven for the first time, and seemed to be almost disappointed with my appearance. Perhaps it was because I looked somewhat unfamiliar to her. Oddly, I was equally displeased with my appearance. The mirror reflected an image of a person who did not look like me... Or more accurately, the image did not look like the man I *wanted* to be.

Strangely, Loweja's eyes looked very sad, instead of happy. She forced herself to smile several times, but her smiles were superficial and meaningless... even fraudulent. She looked so different to me standing there in her brilliant red dress and her hair up in ribbons. When she had a smile on her face, it only magnified her beauty. But when she was sad, she looked pitifully different and despondent. As she stood before me, I could tell that she was not only frightened, she was heartbroken about something as well. She was totally unfamiliar with her surroundings and everything which had happened to her. I stood at the mirror for a moment, and in its reflection I saw Loweja walk over to where her buckskin dress lay on the bed. She picked it up and smelled of it… then sadly laid it back down and walked over to me.

"Loweja, what's the matter, darling? Are you sad?"

"If you like this place, John, I will stay here with you until I die."

I looked at Loweja and felt tremendously ashamed of myself. Staying in a place such as this would have been an eventual death sentence for her, yet she was willing to sacrifice her life if it would make me happy. Yes, I was deeply ashamed of myself. Not only was she frightened, she was desperately confused. She was dressed in beautiful attire, standing in the most elegant hotel in Fort Saint Joseph, and looked saddened by her unfamiliar surroundings. She had looked into a mirror for the first time in her life and for some unknown reason, did not approve of what she had seen there. She seemed to be afraid of her image. She probably felt as though she was looking into the eyes of a stranger in the mirror. And that was the same feeling that I had when I had looked at myself. Dresses in our stunningly perfect attire, we were nothing more than performers in a charade. This is not who we were.

I had not seen her naturally warm and wonderful smile since before we had arrived in Saint Joseph, and I missed it. The newness of all these surroundings had been thrust upon her so quickly that she was woefully frightened and confused. I stood there and looked at her, thinking, what have I done? What have I done to my wonderful, sweet, Loweja? The woman whom I had sworn to protect, not destroy. She was dressed flawlessly in her elegant dress and slippers. She was dressed appropriately to dine with royalty. Yet, somehow, I preferred seeing her in her Indian attire… her beautiful dress with the beadwork… the moccasins which she had made with her own hands and worn on her small feet… her hair in braids, tied with simple leather laces, and most of all, I preferred seeing her with a warm smile – the type of smile that only she could produce. The reality of what I had done to her sank in, and I was greatly ashamed of myself for thinking she could possibly be happy or even mildly content in a place such as this. She was willing to forfeit her happiness and suffer a life of misery in this place if it would bring happiness to me. My Lord… What have I done to my wonderful little princess?

"Loweja?"

"Yes, John."

"You don't like this place very much, do you?"

"I love you, John Welch. If you like this place I will stay here with you until I die. I tell you that already."

"I know you would, sweetheart. I know you would."

"You make tear, John. Why?"

"I think it's because I love you so much, Loweja, and I do not like this place we are in any more than you do, sweetheart. There are no creeks to fish in, there are no rabbits to kill for our dinner, and there are no mountains to look upon. Only ugly people. I do not like this place. I want to see you fish naked again. I want to drink tea with you in the mornings and watch the sunrise in the east. I want to make love with you in a field of flowers again. I do not like this place here."

"You say truth to me? You don't like this place, John?"

"No, darling, I do not like this place at all!"

"What will we do? Is *Baw-de-more* a better place?"

"Baltimore is a much worse place than this, Loweja. Much worse."

"What will we do, John?"

"Loweja, can you bear to stay here six more days with me while I take care of the business that I need to tend to?"

"I will stay with you forever. You are my husband. Where will we go in six days, John?"

"Where would you like for us to go?"

"Home. Away from this bad place. If John say we can."

"Back to your people's village? Is that where you want to go?"

"No, John. That is not the home of my husband."

"Where, then?"

"We can make home, in mountains, maybe… you and me, and have children in mountains."

"Near Steechánay and her children? Would you like that?"

"Yes, John! Can we go there in six days? Please, John, can we?"

"Yes, Loweja. We can go there in six days. And we can live the rest of our lives there, together. I would love to live our lives where we can be close enough to help Steechánay raise her children, and we could have children of our own! I love you, Loweja!"

"I love you, John! You know I say truth! I want to be with Steechánay and children, too! We will be happy there, me and you."

Loweja and I did not take a coach to an elegant French restaurant that evening. I had the hotel keeper deliver our meal to our room, and we ate right there in sequestered quietness and comfort, while sitting partially naked on a rug on the floor. Once again, there was a smile upon Loweja's wonderful face, and seeing her smile had become one of my greatest pleasures in life. It was my mission now, to cause her to smile as much as I possibly could. We sat there eating our food and smiling at each other. Loweja wore nothing to cover her breasts, and the only garment she wore was a pair of lady's underwear, with ruffled edges and puffy legs which came down to her knees. She stood up and walked across the floor to stand in front of the mirror. I almost laughed at how ridiculous she looked in the flashy undergarment, but managed to stifle my laughter. With a puzzled expression upon her face, she asked, "John, what do you call this thing?"

"Those are called, bloomers, I think. I'm not exactly an expert on women's attire, especially when it comes to undergarments."

"Do all white women wear this bloomers thing?"

"Well, I should certainly hope so."

"Why do they wear this thing?"

"Well… I suppose they wear them to hide their body."

"Dress already hide body good enough. Why do white women wear these and then cover them with dress? And how do they pee when they have this thing on? I do not understand this. I think it is very *mysho-tee-ma esta eel-ek.* I do not like that other thing, too!"

"What other thing?"

"This thing, John… here."

"I am of the belief that it is called a corset, Loweja."

"Why do white women wear this thing?"

"I suppose it helps some women to keep their bellies tucked in and their seins from flopping all over the place, I don't really know for sure, Loweja."

"I do not like the way it feel on *mon seins.*"

"I tend to agree with you, darling. I like to see your wonderful seins just like they are right now. You can throw those away any of those things which you don't like, if that's what you want to do."

"Forever more?"

"Yes, Loweja… forever more."

She seemed fascinated over the simplest of items which were about us there in our stateroom… items which I had never paid much attention to before. Like the softness of the bed, the elegance of the furnishings, and the brilliant glow of light which emitted from the oil lamps. I would suppose that in her heart, she was much like a person who attended a circus for the first time; it was fascinating and interesting for a while, yes, but who would want to live there? The paintings which hung from the walls were of particular interest to her, and she seemed to appreciate the things that were around her much more with the knowledge that she would soon be returning to a simpler life, far away from all of the confusion and indifference of the city. Far enough away that a person could relax in body and spirit. I wanted to be in that faraway place as well, with my wonderful Loweja and my Indian family. It was my new dream. To make this dream come true, I had much preparation and hard work ahead of me, and we only had six days left in which to do it.

Late that night, I became aware that Loweja was still awake, staring up at the ceiling as we lay there in bed together.

"Loweja, what's the matter? You're not sleeping."

"I want to sleep on *tonka-peaux*."

"I don't understand."

She took my hand and rubbed it over the sheets of our bed, and again said, "*Tonka-peaux*."

"You mean that you miss our buffalo hides?"

"Yes, John, *buffalo hides*."

"You know what, I think that I miss them too. I'll get one of our buffalo hides in the morning out of our canoe and bring it here for us. In the meantime, put your head over here on my chest and try to get some sleep."

On the first morning, while Loweja waited patiently in our room, I went to the riverfront and bargained with a pirogue broker for a large pirogue. The one which I eventually bought would require the manpower of six polemen and a pilot to navigate against the current of the river, but there were a seemingly endless number of young men available for hire. I made several other stops that morning, dashing in and out of the hotel frequently to check on Loweja's welfare. I delivered one of our buffalo hides to our room, where Loweja spread it over the bed for us to sleep on. She was right. I missed our buffalo hides also. When I came into the hotel the first time that morning to check on Loweja, the hotel manager took me aside and told me that someone had been seen throwing lady's undergarments out of our stateroom window and onto the boardwalk below. Rather than try to explain, I simply apologized, and assured him that it would not happen again. Then, I hastened to our room and asked Loweja not to throw anything else out of the window. We were both in a truly foreign world here in the city, and we were both equally as enthusiastic about leaving as soon as possible.

Loweja accompanied me on a buying trip long enough to visit several merchants where we made a number of purchases. We were buying items which we would require when we settled in the mountains. After each purchase, I would arrange to have the merchandise delivered and stored aboard our large vessel moored at the waterfront. I purchased several of the newest firearms, and ammunition a plenty. We bought some bolts of material to be carried back to Steechánay, and we bought several large sacks of sugar for her as well. We purchased tea leaves, medicines, bandages, tonics and elixirs, shovels, axes, several large boxes of striking matches in waxed containers, and hammers and nails. Loweja and I visited a jeweler and purchased gold wedding rings. She delighted greatly in looking at the rings we wore.

Every day that we waited for our currency to arrive at the bank we were buying, planning, or packing for our departure. I knew now beyond a certainty that I could never go back to Baltimore. After seeing the little valley where Steechánay and Father had lived I don't think that I could have been truly happy anywhere else on earth. Loweja was right… that was the place for us. I had no family ties in Baltimore. My only family tie at the present was Loweja, and my father's family in the mountains; my little half-brothers and sisters. Each day as we awoke, Loweja would always say, 'I love you, John.' The very next thing she would say is, "We have five days now, and then we leave this place, yes, John?" Then it was four days, then it was three days……….

One evening while Loweja and I were packing some items aboard our pirogue, Captain McBride pulled into port aboard his steamboat, *Puritan Enterprise*. When he had stepped ashore, Loweja and I walked over to greet him.

"Captain McBride!"

"Well! Hello, John! This is a pleasant surprise!"

"Captain McBride, I would like for you to meet my lovely wife, Loweja Welch."

"Well, I think 'lovely' is an extreme understatement! Your wife is absolutely beautiful, John! I'm very pleased to meet you, Mrs. Welch!" The Captain said, as he surprised Loweja by kissing her on the hand.

"I am very pleased to meet you, too!"

"Would you and Mrs. Welch do me the honor of dining with me?"

"We would be delighted!"

It was an opportunity for Captain McBride and me to bring each other up to date on what had been going on in our lives. He immediately summoned a coachman who carried us to a fine restaurant, not far from the hotel where Loweja and I were staying. It was a pleasant evening, and although quite nervous, Loweja was the perfect lady during dinner. Her eyes continuously looked at everything around her. I had taught her to eat with a fork and not her fingers when we were on the trail. She rebelled somewhat on the trail, preferring to use her fingers whenever possible, but sensed that it was now necessary to practice formal etiquette in order to comply with these new and unfamiliar social expectancies. She paid close attention to how the people around her were using their forks, and ate with equally proper etiquette. I looked across the table and into her eyes and, reading her thoughts as best I could, I plainly saw that she would rather have been fishing while naked, in a mountain creek. I admired her ability to act prim and proper, despite the discomfort which I knew it was causing her. I mused over the fact that I was the only person in the restaurant, other than Loweja, aware of the fact that she wore no corset or bloomers beneath her stunning dress. I was bursting with pride at the very privilage of being in her presence. Every eye in the restaurant was on her. Her beauty was spectacular! In the middle of taking a sip of wine from my glass I momentarily thought back to the times when Loweja had innocently passed wind in camp… and I thought about what the reaction might have been among the patrons of this fine restraunt if she were to do so, loudly, here and now. My laughter was spontaneous and uncontrollable, and I spilled a good portion of my wine on the front of my shirt as I laughed. Having lost control of myself, I laughed until I had tears in my eyes! I even had a hysterical vision of Loweja raising a leg and turning one lose! The more I thought about it, the harder I laughed! I imagined the looks that the patrons would have had on their faces! Captain McBride and Loweja looked at me with wide eyes, surprised and puzzled by my sudden exultant outburst. They looked at me as though they suspected that I had temporarily lost my mind!

"What is it, John? Are you alright, son?"

"Yes, Captain… I'm fine. I apologize for my rudeness."

"Would you care to share the object of your laughter?"

"No, sir. I'm very sorry… Please accept my apology."

Shortly thereafter, Captain McBride excused himself for a moment when one of his crewman approached to ask him a question, and I talked quietly with Loweja while he was gone.

"What do you think of the food here, Loweja?"

"If you like this food, then I like this, too. Why all these people look at me, John? It make me feel bad in my heart. Can we go back to that other place?"

"What other place, Loweja?"

"Where we sleep and where our clothes are."

"Ah, the hotel! Yes, we can go back there. Don't let these people bother you, Loweja... they are all wild savages, and they just can't help themselves. They don't know how to act around civilized people like you and me... or Hidessa and Lectūschemă... or Steechánay. And besides, these people here have never before seen anyone as beautiful as you are, my dear."

Captain McBride told us that he would be at the dock the next day to see us off. I summoned a coachman, and Loweja and I returned to our hotel room. Once inside, and our uncomfortable clothes had been removed, Loweja looked at me and asked, "Is my name Loweja Welch, now, or is my name, Mrs. Welch?"

"What name do you prefer?"

"I like both of them!"

"Then feel free to use either one of them any time you want."

"You are good to me, John. Will we see Steechánay and children soon, and are we really going home tomorrow?"

"Yes, Loweja... We're really going home, and we will soon see Steechánay and the children again. I hope and pray that we will find them safe and happy."

"Are you happy that we are going home, John?"

"Yes, very happy! Are you?"

"Yes! Very much happy! Can we leave these bad clothes here when we go back to mountains?"

"Yes, we can leave them here, but we cannot throw them out of the window, alright?"

As he had promised, the bank president had the remainder of my currency ready and waiting for me as soon as I had arrived at the bank. I had purchased a leather pouch which was attached to a belt to fit around my waist to carry most of the money in, which was stuffed completely full. The remaining money was placed in pockets inside of my coat. I went to the United States Postal Service Office and posted some letters to acquaintances in Baltimore and settled my bill at the hotel. When a carriage brought Loweja and me to the dock, Captain McBride was there waiting for us along with two newspaper reporters, the six polemen and a pilot whom I had hired, as well as several dozen curious spectators. I was dressed in my buckskin expedition attire, and Loweja was dressed in her beautiful, familiar buckskin dress. Despite their persistence, I did not care to converse with the reporters. There was absolutely nothing which I wished to say to them. I simply wanted to whisk Loweja away from all of the confusion as quickly as possible and be on our way. I managed to maintain my composure quite well, I thought, until one of the reporters rudely asked, "What are your feelings about having a wild Indian for a wife now, Mr. Welch?"

    A well-placed thrust of my clinched fist sent the obtuse reporter backwards, and onto the street, sprawled out like a rag doll. I waited for the ill-mannered fiend to stand again, but Captain McBride and Loweja both pulled me away and hastened me onto our vessel, where my foolish temper dissipated somewhat. It was not like me, to display my temper in public like I had done, and I regretted my outburst as soon as Loweja and I had boarded our vessel. As the polemen loaded their personal belongings aboard our pirogue, Loweja and I said our most sincere farewells to Captain McBride. Captain McBride gave Loweja a kiss on her hand again and gave me a friendly handshake and hug. The dock ropes were untied, and soon our vessel was going northward, upstream, with the noise and confusion of Fort Saint Joseph fading in the distance behind us. Loweja and I were finally on our way home. We sat there on the deck for some time while Loweja studied me with her inquisitive eyes. Finally, she broke her silence, gave me a puzzled look, and said, "You hit man pretty hard, John."

"Yes, I suppose I did... I'm sorry you had to see that, Loweja. I should have been able to control myself better than that."

"John have blood."

"What?"

"On your hand, John have blood. *Estoo-cas. Sang.*"

"Oh... It's nothing... I just cut my knuckles when I hit that man back there, that's all."

"What did man do, John?"

"I felt like his question was disrespectful... that's all."

"I do not understand this word... disrespectful."

"Let's just forget about it. I'm sorry it happened, and I just want to go back to where things are more peaceful."

"Can you just tell me why Captain kiss my hand?"

"A gentleman will often kiss the hand of a lady. It's a way for a man to show his respect to a lady."

"Am I lady, John?"

"You are the most wonderfully exquisite and beautiful lady I have ever known, Loweja."

"I have many, many names now. I am lady, I am Mrs. Welch, I am Loweja, and I am Loweja Welch!"

In the tiny cabin on our vessel I had prepared a cushioned mat atop some boxes of goods where Loweja and I could sleep, and spread one of our buffalo hides out there. There were curtains across the forward and aft doorways, and a pail which Loweja could use to relieve herself when necessary. I would leave by the aft doorway whenever it was necessary for me to empty her pail. Our quarters there were very small, but we had easy access to the aft deck when we wanted to sit outside, and I had brought along two chairs which I had hoped to transport by packhorse to our new home... wherever that might be. The polemen and pilot would sleep on shore at night when the vessel was moored. When it was necessary for Loweja to do something more than pee, she would do so at night, when we would take a short walk on shore together, far away from the crew. If an emergency arose during the day, I would order the pilot to take us straightaway to the shore.

Progress on the river was slow, due to the heavy weight of the vessel, the current of the river, and the north November wind which seemed to blow relentlessly. It was risky to travel on the river at this time of year, because of the threat of early snow conditions or the possibility of the river freezing over as we went farther upstream. Despite the cold wind, Loweja managed to stay warm with the other buffalo hide which she had retrieved from one of the storage boxes. I think it was the very same buffalo hides which Loweja had laid upon when we first met, and I believed that the hides were among her most prized possessions. Truth be known, one of them was the very hide which Loweja had laid upon when we had shared our passions for the first time, and it was among my most prized possessions as well. The crew had brought ample clothing and blankets to keep them warm, and seldom complained about the cold wind or the driving force of the current. They were young and strong, and had done this many times before. The vessel was affixed with a sail, but with a strong north wind, the sail could not have been deployed. Only a southerly or easterly wind would have benefitted us under sail. In extremely shallow water, the crew and I would disembark, and the vessel would be pulled along from shore with long ropes called, *cordons*. When this was necessary, it was slow, laborsome work. Several times during the voyage, channels had to be dug by hand through sandbars, affording us the draft which we required in order for the vessel to make passage.

On the twelfth day of our journey home, a blowing snowstorm had fallen upon us and the pilot could hardly see well enough to steer the pirogue. There were waves on the river caused by the blowing wind, and conditions were miserable. Our vessel was tossed around for more than two hours while the polemen struggled to make way against the wind and keep the pirogue under control. I often had to use a bucket to bail water from the bilge of the vessel. When the lower trading post came into view it offered a temporary respite from the blowing snow. I had passed this trading post before, but had never stopped there. On an evening such as this, it offered an irresistible promise of comfort, and an opportunity for a hot meal and beverage. I ordered the pilot to make way to the outpost, and once the pirogue had been secured to trees on shore, I went into the cabin to check on Loweja. She was wrapped up tightly within the buffalo hides, but was not asleep.

"Loweja, honey, we've pulled up to the shore, darling. The lower trading post is here and I thought maybe we could get something hot to eat and drink. It will do us all well to get off of the water for a few hours. Why don't you put my coat over you and lets you and me walk up there? Alright?"

"I will stay here, John. You go eat and drink, please."

"Loweja? Is something wrong, honey? Are you alright?"

"I am just a little sick, John. That is all."

Once we were tied to the dock and the trees, I hollered for the crew to go on into the trading post. I told them that I would be along directly, and I immediately went back into the cabin to see about Loweja. She looked weak and pale, and I couldn't help but be concerned for her well-being.

"Loweja? Is there anything I can get for you?"

"I will be alright soon. I'm just sick from the pirogue moving up and down so much... and maybe just a little bit from the baby."

"How about if I brought you a hot... **wait a minute**... **Baby!?** What do you mean, **baby**?"

"You and me, John, *an-jioko*. You give me baby when we make love. We are going to have baby, *an-jioko*."

"Loweja! Why didn't you tell me this? I would never have started a trip like this if I had known that you were going to have a baby!"

"I know, John. That is why I said nothing. The baby

will not come until winter is over, maybe even spring. I'm just a little sick right now from the pirogue moving up and down, John."

"Oh, Loweja. I love you so much, darling. If you say the word, I'll have the crew turn the pirogue around right now. We could get back to one of those small towns we passed and be there in less than four or five days. Maybe there's a physician there! If not, I can have you back in Fort Saint Joseph in less than eight days!"

"No! No, John! Please don't do that! I already feel a little better since the pirogue stop moving around so much. I will be better in just a little while I think."

"I can't believe you're going to have a baby!"

"That is what happen, John… when man and woman have *ohgā-sá-ho* together. Man puts baby in woman. You did not know that?"

"Well, of course I knew that! I just didn't expect… I mean, I didn't think that it was all going to happen this soon, that's all. A baby! Me and you! I love you, Loweja… You are what I have been waiting for all of my life, darling!"

Loweja was right. She did recover in just a little while. We walked up to the trading post together and had some hot tea and stew, and she began to feel much better. I believed that the constant rocking of the pirogue had caused her to be ill; '*sea-sickness*,' as they had called it in Baltimore. Walking on the firm ground seemed to help her immensely. This trading post was also owned by a Frenchman, *Pierre Després*, but he seemed to be a much more trustworthy and pleasant fellow than any of the French scoundrels whom I had met previously. Perhaps all Frenchmen were not as evil as I had thought. Després even appeared to show compassion when I explained to him that Loweja was pregnant with child. Even though he spoke broken English, and I spoke very broken French, we were able to communicate with very little difficulty. The trading post had a place for the crew to sleep overnight in a covered storage area, and the Frenchman rented a small cabin to Loweja and me while we waited for the storm to subside. She waited in the warmth of the trading post while I went into the cabin and built a fire in the woodstove there. I would never have left her in the presence of Francois Brĕaux, at the upper trading post for as much as a minute. But this fellow here seemed to have excellent character and good Christian morals. Soon, the cabin was warm and cozy and I brought Loweja inside for the night. She slept comfortably for most of that night, while I sat in a chair nearby and watched over her. I kept wood in the stove as a bitter cold wind continued to blow outside. The wind howled like a pack of hungry wolves outside, but we remained quite comfortable inside. Sometime in the middle of the night, Loweja called out to me, apparently from the appearance of a sudden nightmare, and then the sheer terror of waking up to find that I was not asleep at her side.

"John! *Na-teek-esh-lacnoo! Masqua! Masqua!*"

"That's alright, Loweja… There is no *masqua* here… Just John! I'm right here!"

"John, please come here to bed with me. I cannot sleep well without you next to me. *Necu-ta-say-ha*, John."

"I'm right here in bed with you now… go back to sleep, Loweja."

"I dream big bear kill me."

"I know you did, darling. There is no bear here. Only John. John will watch over you. John will protect you. Go to sleep now."

I did lay down with her, and we both slept well for the remainder of the night. By dawn, the bitter cold wind had ceased and the little snow which had fallen did not affect river travel. There was a thin crust of ice at the very edges of the riverbank, but the main channel was completely open for travel. At Loweja's insistence, after a hearty breakfast at the trading post, we were all back on board the pirogue and pushing up the river toward the Arikara village and the French trading post.

Loweja was showing no further signs of being sick, which brought a great deal of relief to me. The fact that she was going to have a baby was just beginning to sink in. I wanted to be a father... I really did. As a boy, I had never had a father... someone to guide and direct me, watch over me, and love me. I wanted to be the kind of father who could provide all of those things for his children. I would have chosen another time and another place for Loweja's sake, but we would have to make the best of things as they were. I had a fortune in money. I could have afforded the best physicians in the world to watch over Loweja. But there were no physicians where we would be going. I could not help but worry.

We were blessed with a delightful change in the weather for the remainder of the trip, and even experienced a southerly wind that allowed us to deploy our sail. This came as a great relief to our polemen, who did not have to work nearly as hard against the current. The days were pleasantly warm, and we discovered that when Loweja sat in a chair on the aft deck in the fresh air, she seldom felt any sickness at all. It was only when she lay down in the confinement of the cabin when the pirogue was moving that she became ill. I was confident that her discomfort was due to the motion of the pirogue, and not a physical infirmity or serious ailment. I was pleased with the performance and dedication of our crew and pilot. Captain McBride had done well in helping me select able-bodied and trustworthy men with good dispositions. As strong and fit as they were, I'm sure that they shared in mine and Loweja's joy when we finally rounded a bend in the river and the French outpost of Francois Brěaux came into view. The warm days had melted most of the snow from the ground, but it was only the first of December, and winter had not yet arrived in full force. We had scarcely been at the dock for a minute or two when I saw the familiar face of Hidessa approaching.

"Chin-contè-sa, John Welch! Welcome!"

"Hello, Hidessa! Chin-contè-sa! It's good to see you

again, my friend!"

"Welcome, Loweja!"

"Chin-contè-sa, Hidessa!"

It was good to see Hidessa's friendly face again, and it was especially good to have the long pirogue journey behind us. When we walked into the outpost, we found that my crew and pilot had already gathered inside and purchased a small keg of rum. The ugly Frenchman, Francois Brĕaux, still owned the outpost, and appeared to have retained his rude mannerisms as well, although he was careful in choosing his words when speaking to me. He seemed to sense that all that I needed was the slightest of excuses to tear him to shreds. Rather than to barter with the Frenchman for the horses we would need, I preferred to barter with the Arikara first, and only buy from the Frenchman what we could not obtain from the Arikara. The Arikara had become quite accustomed to dealing with currency by this time, because they had learned that the currency could be used to purchase anything they needed or wanted at the trading post. Hidessa was sent to arrange for a bartering session with the Arikara while I bought food and more wine for my crew and pilot... and food for Loweja and me as well. With the Frenchman, I arranged for the rental of a small storage cabin behind the outpost so that Loweja could rest comfortably while I made all of the arrangements for our journey by horseback to the valley of my father's wife, Steechánay, and my many brothers and sisters there. After I made Loweja comfortable in the small cabin, I spoke with her before going to barter with the Arikara.

"Loweja, I'm going up to your people's village to do some trading. You have your revolver with you, and I want you to lock this door as soon as I leave. I'll be back as soon as I can. Loweja, is that a tear I see on your cheek? Do you make a tear?"

"Yes, I cannot help it."

"Why do you make a tear? I'll be back soon. I'm

only going to be gone for an hour or two."

"You will buy another wife to take with us, won't you, John?"

"Another wife? Are you serious, Loweja? Is that what you think I'm going to trade for?"

"If you want to have two wives, I will understand, and I will still love you forever more."

"Look at me Loweja, darling, and stop this nonsense right now. I want one wife, and one wife only! The only wife I ever want is you! No one else! I love you, Loweja, and no one else. I'm going to your village to trade for some horses – not wives! Do you understand, darling?"

"Yes, John. I love you, too. I have very much love!"

"Well, I'm glad we got that all straightened out."

"Make love with me now, John? *Ohgā-sá-ho?*"

"When I get back we will, if you feel like it. I need to go now, and get us some horses. Horses! Not wives! OK? Hidessa is waiting for me outside. Don't forget to lock the door after I leave, darling. *Necu-ta-say-ha,* Loweja."

Another wife? I was sometimes amazed at how Loweja's innocent mind worked. I have no idea what put a silly notion such as that in her lovely little head, but I was glad to have dismissed any such idea from her mind before I had left to go to the village. This was a dreadful time of year to travel. The weather was a constant aggravation, the days were much shorter, and in the cold weather every task seemed to be made all the more difficult. The general gloominess and harshness of the weather was most likely the cause for Loweja's depressed spirit and her erroneous thoughts that I was going to bargain for another wife.

By early afternoon I had successfully obtained eight horses, three additional buffalo hides, and four deer hides. The Arikara had no mules available to sell, so I purchased four more horses from the Frenchman, giving me a total of twelve horses to take with us. My crew and pilot were kept busy unloading merchandise from the pirogue and preparing them to be carried by pack horse. The two wooden chairs from the pirogue would be secured atop two of the pack horses. I took great care in safeguarding the chairs, knowing that they would seem like a luxury when we finally arrived in the mountains. I hired two young Arikara men to ride with Loweja and me, and to assist with managing the horses and any other work which had to be addressed. I would personally attend to all remaining chores just prior to our departure in the morning. Hidessa walked back to the cabin with me and we went inside with Loweja to talk for a while. He was somewhat familiar with the general location of my father's valley, and offered some valuable advice.

"This time of the year the wapiti will be out of the high mountains and down in the lower valleys. You will have little trouble shooting some for your winter meat. In the spring and early summer there are many mussels in the creek and they can be gathered by the children and women. There will be plenty of fish and rabbits all year long. The grizzlies can be of much trouble to you all year long, except for the dead of winter when they are all asleep. It is best to teach the children to always watch for bears and wolves and eagles."

"Do the Blackfeet or Crow ever come into that area?"

"I have not heard that the Blackfeet or Crow ever come there... no, I don't think so. The Pawnee come there sometimes only, but I don't think the Blackfeet or Crow come beyond the mountain with the hole in it, or the creek that runs yellow."

"Did you buy another wife with the money I gave you?"

"Yes. I have three wives now."

"Is your new wife young, Hidessa?"

"She is much younger than my other wives, that is all that matters. Her husband was killed by a bear, so I did not have to pay much for her. She is happy to live in my lodge and she makes better food than my other wives."

"Are you happy now?"

"Yes, I am very happy, John!"

We continued to talk until darkness began to approach, and Hidessa left to walk back to his lodge. Loweja had said very little as she sat there staring at the oil lamp.

"Loweja, do you need anything?"

"No thank you, John."

"What's the matter, Loweja? You look sad. It does not make me happy when I see my wonderful Loweja looking sad."

"Would you like to buy another wife to take with us tomorrow?"

"Another wife? Not that again! I thought we talked about this yesterday."

"She could make you feel good when I am sick with child. Hidessa have three wives now. John only have me. I want you to buy one if you want to, John. I will still love you."

"Loweja... Listen to me again, darling, because I am only going to say this one more time. You are all I want. You are all that I will ever need. *Necu-ta-say-ha*, Loweja! And no one else! Just you! Remember that, please?"

"*Necu-ta-say-ha*, John! I love you, too!"

"Now, show me that pretty smile of yours... that's it... that's the way I want you to look forever! And I never want to hear another word about this *'other wife'* business again!"

Loweja had been worried that she was not pleasing me, and nothing could have been farther from the truth. She always pleased me, but she pleased me even more when she had a smile on her face. I wanted her to be happy... always, because she had brought so much happiness to me. Perhaps I had slighted her somewhat during the time when I had been so busy making all of the arrangements for our journey. I hoped that I hadn't, but vowed to myself that I would always take the time to tell her how much I loved her, regardless of how busy I was. She had a tender heart, and I would do anything within my power to see that it was not broken.

We are back!

Winter had given us a rare and welcome respite from her normally cruel and cold winds of November and early December. At dawn, everyone made the final preparations for our journey back to the happy little valley of my family. Horses were loaded with their packs, bindings were secured, and last-minute items were purchased from the outpost. Hidessa had brought his newest wife along to help in our preparations. She appeared to be even younger than Loweja, and perhaps twenty years younger than Hidessa. As soon as I saw the young woman, I realized that Hidessa was the weasel in the henhouse when it came to women, but made no comment on the matter out of respect for our friendship. Besides, the young girl appeared to be as happy as a meadowlark and seemed to smile continuously. She even hummed as she adjusted one of the bindings on a packsaddle. Once the horses were packed, cinches were tightened, and our water kegs were filled, I released my crew and pilot from their obligations and paid them their wages, plus a bonus. Their orders were to take the pirogue back to Fort Saint Joseph and leave it in the care of Captain McBride, whom I had made previous arrangements with to winter the vessel in dry dock, and hire another crew and pilot when I came back to Saint Joseph the following summer for my annual supplies, just as my father had done so many times before. With our farewells having been completed, Loweja and I, along with our two young Arikara helpers, rode away to the northwest, to the valley where Loweja and I hoped to call home. I prayed that Steechánay would be safe and sound, and that she would be agreeable to let Loweja and I make a home in the same valley, somewhere nearby, so that I could play some sort of role in raising her boys and helping her as a need occurred.

By now, Loweja and I had made the trip north enough times that we had become familiar with the landscape and never found a need to refer to my maps or use my compass. Loweja was in good spirits to be on horseback again, and smiled often when she looked at me. Her belly remained taut and flat... showing no indication as of yet of the life which she carried inside of her. Riding on a horse seemed not to bother her, or cause her any great discomfort as did the ride in the pirogue. I was concerned that our horses would occasionally slip or stumble in the mud and snow, and fearful that Loweja may have fallen, but my concerns were unfounded as we traveled on northward on our sure-footed mounts without incident. Loweja seemed at home when she was on a horse. She maintained excellent control over the most stubborn of animals, and watching her mount and dismount was a sight to behold. She seemed to be able to spring from the ground and into the saddle with one fluid motion. When she dismounted, she jumped from the horse and landed beautifully on her feet. However, I had cautioned her not to jump from the horse while she was with child, for obvious reasons. These were by far the best horses that I had ever bought, and throughout the journey north I studied over them so that I would keep the best of the lot when our journey was completed. Our camps seemed bitter cold at night, but I had purchased additional buffalo hides in anticipation of the colder weather, and our Indian companions seemed to never complain about anything. There was little conversation exchanged during the trip, except for that which took place between Loweja and me, in English and sometimes in an odd mixture of Arikara, English, and French. Of course, the Arikara boys talked freely in their native tongue to each other, but I never understood very much of what they were saying. Loweja's command of the English language had progressed to the point that I felt we could talk about anything and everything without me having to select only the simplest of words. I was impressed with the eagerness displayed by the two young Arikara men as they went about their daily tasks and said as much to Loweja. She laughed when I told her that the men were eager to perform their tasks.

"What are you laughing at, Loweja?"

"I am laughing at what you said about the men being eager to work."

"So? What is so funny about that?"

"They are eager, alright. But they are not eager to do work. They are going to use the money you pay them to get wives when they get back to their village. They are eager for *ohgā-sá-ho*... maybe, but that is all!"

"Oh. Well... In that case, I'm glad to know that they are going to use the money for a good purpose! How do you know they will spend the money for wives? And how do you know they are so eager for *ohgā-sá-ho*?"

"Because, I hear them talking yesterday when they think I not hear."

"Loweja, can I ask you something?"

"Yes, John... anything."

"When we first met, you said that you were my wife because I owned you. Do you remember saying that to me?"

"Yes, John. *Say-ha-way*."

"Do you really feel like I own you?"

"Yes, you do own me. But I feel that it is not because of the goods you paid my father to buy me. You own me because our spirits are one in the same now. I am part of you and you are part of me. Because I am part of you now, you own me."

"And do you feel like you own me, because our spirits are one in the same and I am part of you?"

"Yes, John. That is the way that I feel. Am I wrong to feel that way?"

"No, Loweja, you're not wrong to feel that way. You are not wrong at all! I don't think I could have said it that well if I had tried. You know, you are not only very beautiful...

You are also very smart, too!"

Twice during our journey home we had to make detours to get around creeks which had swollen from the mountain rains at the higher elevations, but nevertheless, we eventually crossed a small ridge and were on the trail once more which led into Steechánay's obscure valley. Darkness and deeper snow prevented us from going any farther that evening, and we were forced to camp one last time before entering the valley. It was with great anticipation, very early the next morning that the cabin of *Mrs. Steechánay Welch* came into view. As they did at our last visit, the three dogs rushed to greet us at the edge of the woods. The personality of the valley looked much different in the dead of winter. The leaves were gone from the trees and there was a light coating of wet snow on the ground. Smoke was rising from the cabin chimney, a herd of thirty or forty wapiti was grazing on the winter grass which was not covered by the snow across the meadow, and my two young half-brothers were carrying armloads of firewood onto the porch. Upon seeing us, they dropped the wood they had been carrying and ran inside, most likely to alert their mother. Soon, Steechánay was on the porch to greet her visitors. When we had ridden within a hundred yards of her cabin she suddenly recognized Loweja and me, and a broad smile crossed her face that I could see clearly from a hundred yards distant. Loweja was beside herself with joy to see Steechánay again, and I was elated beyond words to be returning to this beautiful place! Loweja surprised me by whipping her horse into a gallop ahead of me. I soon had my horse at a gallop as well, following closely behind her, and we both rode joyfully up to the house. Magically, I felt a strange sensation of comfort fall upon me. It was almost as though I had been on a tiresome journey all of my life and I was only now coming home. Everything that gave me comfort and happiness seemed to be here in this precious little valley, the valley of my father.

Steechánay and the children greeted us warmly.

Loweja was the first to jump from her horse and embrace Steechánay. Together, they walked hand-in-hand inside the small house while the Arikara helpers and I tended to our animals and began the task of unloading the vast amount of merchandise which I had brought. We placed most of it under a lean-to near the one where Loweja and I had slept when we had been there two months earlier. Knowing that the two Arikara helpers would not be leaving until the morrow, we prepared a sleeping place for them next to my goods. When the outside tasks were completed, I removed a large sack of sugar and a ten-pound bag of tea leaves from my goods and walked up to the cabin where I was well received with warm hugs from everyone. Steechánay and the children were delighted to see that I had remembered to bring some sugar. They had not tasted sugar since Loweja and I had last been there. I had also brought gifts for the children, but with Christmas day only three days away, I decided to wait to give them their gifts. Instead, I gave each of the children a piece of candy and an orange. After everyone had settled down somewhat, Loweja, Steechánay, and I engaged in pleasant conversation over our tea. With the mellow heart of friendship, I said, "Steechánay, it is good to see you and the children again! Loweja and I are glad to be here! As I look around, it would seem to me as though you have not remarried yet."

"No, John. I have not."

"Well it sure does my heart good to see you all again! Everyone looks so healthy and happy!"

"It is good to see you and Loweja again, too, John! Every time I see you and Loweja it makes me happy inside of my heart. I asked Loweja how long you would be staying this time and she said that I should ask you. So, how long will you stay here with us, John?"

"How long would you permit us to stay, Steechánay? Loweja and I have decided that we want to live here, somewhere near this valley, so that we can watch over you and the children, and help you when you need help. I can build a home for Loweja and me somewhere, but we would need some place to stay in the meantime. Can we stay here with you and the children for a while?"

"This is your house. It is I, who should be asking how long you will permit me to stay."

"Steechánay, as I told you the last time I was here, this is your house now, and it always will be. So, with that in mind, how long would you permit us to stay here?"

"The children and I... would like for you and Loweja to stay here in this house with us forever and for always, that is, if you want to and you will, please."

I could not speak. I was almost breathless. Maybe it was the pleading tone of her voice, or maybe it was because of the sincerity in which she said it. Perhaps it was the words which she used when she said, *'forever and for always.'* Either way, I was deeply affected by Steechánay's invitation to stay there forever. Loweja came to me and put a sympathetic hand on my shoulder, and yet I still could not speak. I looked about me and saw the shining faces of the four children in the loft looking down at me, puzzled as to why a tear was appearing in a grown man's eye. I had always been a great planner and organizer, yet I had neither planned nor anticipated that I would lose control of my emotions as I had. I struggled to regain control of myself as I saw a tear streak down the face of Steechánay. Both her, and Loweja knew what I was feeling inside of me and they thoughtfully gave me time to compose myself. Finally, I cleared my throat and answered with a broken voice.

"Steechánay, Loweja and I would like to stay here with you and the children... forever and for always. We both love every one of you and we would like to live here and watch over all of you. I will protect you and care for you, if you will allow us to stay here."

The three of us stood and hugged one another while the

children in the loft still tried to make some sense of what was going on. I knew that tears only served to worry children, so I looked up at them and gave them my broadest smile ever, which immediately put a smile on their faces. They were adorable as their bright little faces looked down upon us from the loft.

"Would it be possible for us to somehow live in the house here, with you and the children, Steechánay? Is there room for Loweja and me here with you until I can build a bigger place for us, or perhaps add a room?"

"I will prepare a bed for myself in the loft with the children and you and Loweja can take this bed here for your own. You can make much happiness in this bed, and that will make me very happy. That is the way that I want it to be. There is plenty of room in the house here, and there is plenty of room in our hearts, too."

We politely argued somewhat over those particular sleeping arrangements because Loweja and I felt ill at ease about taking over Steechánay's comfortable bed, but Steechánay was insistent, and would have it no other way. She said that it brought her great happiness, knowing that there would be much love shared in that bed. I know that my father must have seen great love within Steechánay's heart, for I had no trouble seeing it for myself. I only wish that Father had waited for Steechánay to come of age before sleeping with her as his wife. As I had assessed before when I was there, judging by the ages of the children, Steechánay must have been barely twelve or thirteen years old when she and Father met, and he must have been well over forty-five years old at the time. Yet, I no longer harbored ill feelings toward my father. Most men would have been overwhelmingly attracted to Steechánay's beauty, just as I had succumbed to Loweja's beauty. In my heart I hoped that she would find a husband soon. She was in the prime of her young womanhood, and it pained me to see the unhappiness in her eyes or hear it in her voice.

Steechánay looked at me and said, "John. Your father asked me to give you something before he left here to die. He told me that if you ever came to this valley looking for him that I was to give you a paper that he made marks on. I forgot about it when you were here before."

"What does the paper say?"

"I cannot read words from a paper and I cannot make words on a paper either."

"Where is the paper?"

"I will get it for you."

Steechánay climbed into the loft and rummaged through a small chest. Soon, she climbed back down the ladder and handed the paper to me. I walked closer to the doorway where the light from outside would allow me to read, and opened the folded paper.

My Dear Son John,

If my wife has given you this letter it means that I am dead and you have found my home and my beautiful valley.

I found a great fortune in gold, and have given you instructions so that you may find your fortune as well. In the letters I left for you, I said that there are treasures to be had which are far greater than that of gold. You must now choose the thing which brings you the most happiness. Is it the gold, or is it something else?

The valley that you are in right now, and my family here were my greatest treasure in life. I could not force myself to leave them or my valley to return to Baltimore. I tried, but I could not.

If you have found my valley, then you are now among the richest men on earth.

Always remember that I loved you.   William Welch

Father was right. I was indeed, among the richest men on earth now. I was at home now. I was in the very place where I wanted to spend the rest of my life. What greater treasure could there ever be for me on this earth than to have the privilege of living my life here with the people I loved, and in this beautiful place? This was indeed the ultimate treasure which Father had so mysteriously eluded to in his manuscripts and letters.

"What does my husband's words say, John?"

"It's a letter to me, from my father, William Welch, telling me that he loved you and the children more than anything on this earth."

"Thank you, John. May I keep it?"

"Yes, Steechánay, you may keep it."

The Indian boys left early the next morning to go back to their village. I gave them each a horse and a twenty-dollar gold piece, which would make them seem rich in the eyes of their people. More importantly, they would each have plenty of bargaining power to acquisition a wife. That could possibly mean that there would soon be two less Indian maidens to fall victim to the devilish Europeans. I could only imagine the speed at which the two young men must have traveled back to their village! I hoped that their marriages would be as happy as mine. We spent the next few days changing things around somewhat inside of the house to make room for Loweja and me. Loweja and I wanted to make things as comfortable as possible up in the loft for Steechánay, as we both felt remorseful that she had to sleep in the loft with the children. It seemed demeaning to me, but the house was small, and Steechánay would have it no other way. We moved some items out of the loft and built a proper, comfortable bed for her up there and placed one of the two chairs that we had brought, upstairs for Steechánay to sit in as she dressed each day. I designed and built a new ladder for the loft which was much easier for her to climb and descend.

We took four of our buffalo hides and spread them on the floor of the loft and made very comfortable sleeping places for the children as well. Steechánay and Loweja made a privacy curtain for the loft from the deer hides which I had purchased at the trading post, and I made a larger table and some bench seats so that we could all eat together as a family with the children. I was not comfortable eating while the children had to wait patiently for their turn at the small table, and I enjoyed their presence during our mealtimes immensely. I found great delight in watching them eat their meals.

On Christmas day, I gave Pokeem and Kwesha each a stuffed rag doll and a flute, and Joseph and Kwīnahā each a slingshot and a folding knife. They were beside themselves with delight. The boys learned rather quickly how to stalk and kill rabbits with their new slingshots, and Loweja saved each of the rabbit pelts for making boot-liners and mittens. I felt as though Kwīnahā was nearly old enough for me to give him a rifle, but decided to wait until I was sure. Loweja and I gave Steechánay some hair ribbons and a brush and comb, along with a tiny music box. The tiny music box became the family's favorite item. At first, it was played continuously, until I almost dreaded to hear it play. Shortly though, Steechánay kept it in a special place in the loft and it was only brought out to be played on rare evenings, just before the children went to bed. Pokeem and Kwesha were only allowed to play their flutes outside, as the noise was terribly irritating when they were constantly played inside. Of all the gifts that I gave the children, the slingshots proved to be the most beneficial for the family. One of the more serious problems which we were confronted with in the valley was not the bears or the wolves. Of all things, our most serious enemy was proving to be the mice. They consistently invaded our food stores in the storage shed, and sometimes did great damage. Kwīnahā and Joseph became deadly adversaries to the mice. Sitting atop our storage crates with their slingshots, they became masters at controlling the population of mice, often killing thirty or forty of the little devils in a single day. Of course, they expected due praise for such fine accomplishments and the family was always glad to oblige.

When we had been in our new home for about two weeks, I shot two wapiti, and the whole family pitched in to get the meat back to a shed where it was hung to cure. One evening, after we had been there for about three weeks, in front of the fireplace, after the children had climbed into the loft, Loweja, Steechánay, and I talked about the baby that Loweja was carrying.

"Steechánay, I'm worried about what to do when the time comes for Loweja to have our baby."

"There is only one thing that you must do, John."

"What is that?"

"You must go out and stay out of our way. Loweja and I will do the rest. I know what has to be done. I have done this three times for myself, and I have helped my mother when she helped many other women. Most women need no help at all. Don't worry."

"Loweja, are you frightened?"

"Frightened? I do not know this word, John."

"Scared."

"No, John. I am not scared. Steechánay has had three babies… She will show me what to do, but I think I already know."

"Your father and I were on the trail to come here to this valley to live when I had Joseph… my first. I was much younger than Loweja. I was still a young girl. Your father was very nervous, just like you are, but he spread out a blanket on the ground and walked away with Kwīnahā and his other wife. Kwīnahā was just a small boy then and I did not want him to see me have a baby, so your father and his other wife took him for a walk and I just sat down by the side of the trail and had Joseph. He was my first. I wrapped him in a blanket and came up here to this place your father had built for us. As I told you before, my body was too young to make milk, so your father made his other wife give her milk to Joseph. She did not want to do that. That made me very sad, but your father made her do that so that Joseph would live. She did not want to share her milk. When I have Kwesha, I have plenty of milk for her in my body. Loweja will have good milk, I can tell, and your baby will be happy."

"Have you ever thought about getting married again, Steechánay?"

"Yes, John. I have thought very much about it. I have maybe even dreamed about it some. Most of the time I think about it when I am alone in bed. That is the worse time. I reach around me to feel man and only feel my bed and my heart hurts to be with man. With you and Loweja being here, it is almost like I have husband again and that makes me happy during the day. At night there is still no one there for me to touch."

"But you are still so young, Steechánay, you have many good years left ahead of you. You should have a husband. What about the young men at the Pawnee village? Is there not a young man there who would make a good husband for you?"

"I think there may be many *oskīnîgui* there who would make good husband, maybe, but no man would want a wife who already has four children with her, and I would die before I left my children just to be with man. Kwīnahā is not of me, but I love him like he was of me."

"You would make a good wife for a man, Steechánay… I know this in my heart, and my heart is sad for you," Loweja said.

"Sometimes I…"

"Sometimes what, Steechánay?"

"Sometimes I dream to have a man in my bed, and to receive him as my husband, but there is no man in my bed… just me. I think I will grow old without man now." A trace of a tear arrived upon her cheek.

"You are a very good woman, Steechánay," Loweja said.

"Yes, she is, Loweja. My heart hurts for you, too, Steechánay."

"I pray to Great Holy Father that he sends husband for you and makes your heart happy and takes tears away," Loweja said.

"I will pray to Great Holy Father, also, Steechánay. You are a fine young woman, and I think that someday the Great Holy Father will provide a good husband for you. I just feel that in my heart."

Steechánay's tears flowed freely that evening. It seemed as if she was releasing many months of mental anguish before Loweja and me, and I hastened to change the subject of our conversation, for I could clearly see that she was tormented greatly by her loneliness. Discussing the matter seemed to draw her torment out into the open, yet only served to make things worse for her. Loweja was right, Steechánay would make a fine wife for any man. But in the vastness of a great wilderness like this, there were few men. There were fewer yet, who wanted to take on the responsibility of having four children to feed who were not even of his own blood. In the raw wilderness, it was frequently difficult to feed oneself, let alone a wife and four children. In the winter, conditions became even more austere. Now that I was here in the valley, I would watch over and comfort them. I would provide for them, and I would love them all. They were my family now… for now and forever more. I looked at Steechánay and Loweja as they sat at our table, and said, "Tomorrow I will have much work to do. I have some goods to unpack and make sure everything under the lean-to is safe from the weather. Kwīnahā and Joseph can help me."

"Is there any food among the items in your packs, John?"

"Yes, Steechánay. There is much food! Most of what

is stored in the shed is food. There is much corn meal, flour, sugar, salt, tea leaves, and dried beans, vegetable and melon seeds, rice, and some other things, too. I have molasses, wheat grain, salt pork, and many things such as that. Why do you ask?"

"Those things cannot be left under the lean-to when the spring comes. That's when the great bears will come."

"Great bears?"

"William Welch called them, *grizzly bears*. They awaken in the early spring and they come in great numbers sometimes. The children must remain close to the house and food cannot be left outside. There are many people from my village who were killed by these big bears. The dogs will let us know when bears or wolves come close, but they cannot keep them away... the bears are too big, and the wolves will circle around a dog, and kill it quickly. Maybe you can move your goods into one of the log huts, where it can be safe from bears. The log storage shed would be a good place. That is what William used to do."

"Then that is what I will do as well."

"You must also take great care to protect your things from the mice. They can ruin as much food as the bears."

Following Steechánay's advice on how to properly protect our food stores from the bears, I would re-enforce the doors and windows of the storage hut and move our supplies inside. Six weeks after our arrival, I had worked on the repairs to the storage hut during most of the daylight hours. I had to patch several holes in the roof, build a new door, and reinforce the windows. I saw a lot of old evidence where bears had tried to enter the hut in the past; clawing and chewing on the door and window frames. Inside, the room was dry, and our goods and food would be safe there. There was also enough room inside to hang our winter supply of wapiti and antelope meat until I could prepare one of the other huts to be used exclusively for meat storage. With Kwīnahā's help, in just ten days of hard work, we had completed the repairs and moved all of our items inside. By the end of the fourth week we had practically finished our work. When we had finished most of our repair work and had moved almost all of our goods inside, Loweja came into the hut to help Kwīnahā and me cover our supplies with layers of heavy canvas material, and I could tell by the serious look on her face that there was something very grave which she wanted to talk to me about. Sensing as much, I sent Kwīnahā to the wood shed to cut some wood. I said nothing to Loweja at first, preferring to let her tell me what was on her mind when she felt the time was right, but my curiosity was agonizing. I had learned that sometimes, when Loweja had something very important to say, she would take a lot of time in planning her words so that I could better understand her. She could also be very cunning and conniving at times, knowing by this time that I easily succumbed to her requests when she charmed me with her eyes, showed me a teardrop, or was flirtatious with me. When I would fall under her spell, I was like clay in her hands, and she could almost always get anything she wanted from me. I was keenly aware of this, and never rushed her as she chose her words. Finally, she seemed to muster up some courage and softly spoke to me.

"John?"

"Yes, Loweja. What is it?"

"May I talk to you about something? Please?"

"You can always talk to me, darling, anytime you want to. What is it that you would like to talk to me about?"

"Will you hold my hands as we talk, and look into my eyes like we do sometimes?" When she asked this, I knew that there was either something very serious on her mind, or she was going to put forth all of her charms in order to get me to do something for her, so I braced myself for the worst and asked, "Yes, Loweja, What is it? You look worried about something. Is everything alright?"

"Do you like our bed here, in this house, John, the one we sleep in at night?"

"Of course, I like our bed, darling, especially when we are in it together. That's an odd question. Why do you ask me something such as this? What's going on?"

"I think our bed is very big for us. Do you think our bed is very big for us, too, John?"

"Well, yes. I think it's very big, too, I suppose. I haven't thought much about it. What are you trying to say? I think you are trying to charm me into something... and you're just crafty and conniving enough to know that you have plenty of charm to do it, and get anything you want from me."

"I do not understand all of the words you say, but... please listen to me... do you love me, John?"

"Do I love you? Come on Loweja, you know that I love you more than anything in the world, dear. You're leading up to something aren't you? It's something big this time, isn't it? You are not just asking for more tea and sugar this time, are you? I can see it in your eyes. What is it? Go ahead and tell me, and get it over with. I have much work to do here."

"You have very big heart, *othai-messhá*, John. Very big, and I love you so much! I would do anything for you! I even die for you!"

"Loweja... What's the matter? I know you want to tell me something, or ask me something. Like I said, I have much work to do here. So just tell me what it is so I can get back to my work. Please don't be afraid to tell me."

"My heart hurts for Steechánay, John. I love her. She have very big heart, too. She is good woman, *ki-jai-ich-quois*, and my heart hurts for her to be happy. I cannot be happy I think until Steechánay is happy again, too, maybe."

"I know she is a good woman, Loweja. I love her too. But I do not think that you came down here to tell me that Steechánay is a good woman. There is something else on your mind. What is it?"

"Do you think Steechánay is beautiful woman?"

"Oh, Loweja....... Yes, I think she is very beautiful. I

think you are very beautiful, too. I think the children are very beautiful, too. I think our valley is very beautiful. Why do you ask all of these questions? I'm sorry, but I'm beginning to get a little angry, so please tell me what it is so I can get on with my work here."

"You make Loweja very happy if you let me do something. Will you, John? Please! I love you! I much love you!"

"Well, of course, sweetheart. If it will make you very happy then it will make me very happy, too. You may do anything you want. Now, what is it that you want to do?"

"I want to bring Steechánay into our bed."

"What? I don't understand what you're saying, Loweja. What do you mean, bring her into our bed?"

"I want Steechánay to sleep with us, forever more and not sleep in loft with children."

"**Loweja!?** Are you asking for the three of us to share the same bed at night? Loweja, you know that you and I sleep naked under our blankets. How could we have Steechánay in our bed with us while we are naked? How could we make love with her laying there with us? What would me and you do when we wanted to make love, go outside in the cold? We need our privacy! This doesn't make any sense to me, Loweja."

"John, Please listen to me. I love you, John. And I love Steechánay, too, in a different kind of way, like sister maybe, only much, much more. She is very lonely at night and must sleep in loft with children. Steechánay is not a children! She is woman! She need to sleep with *onēssē*. You are good *onēssē*, John. You are only man here that can be *onēssē*!"

"What about you? You are my wife! Not Steechánay! I mean, how could that possibly work, Loweja? I don't think Steechánay would ever want to join us in our bed at night and be there with us when we make love! Steechánay's heart hurts to be with a man... I know that! And it would only make her heart hurt more if she had to lay there next to us each night while we made love. I don't think you should ask her to do that! I think she would be very angry if you asked her to do something like that!"

"You would have two wives. That's all. You would make Steechánay and Loweja very happy!"

"Two wives? Me? **Absolutely not!** It's out of the question!"

"Please, John! Please say you will do this! Please say that you will do this for Steechánay and for me!"

"You mean to tell me that you would actually *want* for me to have Steechánay as my wife... in our bed... with us? You really want me to have two wives?"

"Yes, John. I want this much, and Steechánay want this much, too. Please do this thing for me and for Steechánay."

"And how would it make you feel if I had two wives? At the trading post you were worried that I may have bought another wife there. You even made tears about it then because it made you unhappy. Don't you remember that, Loweja?"

"If your wives were Steechánay and me I would be very happy. Steechánay and Loweja... no other wife! Do you want Steechánay and me to be very happy, John?"

"You know that I want you both to be happy, Loweja. We're already a family here, but something like this may make Steechánay very unhappy. She may even ask us to leave this valley if she knew we were talking this way. I don't think that she would want to do anything like that, and I could never ask her if she wanted to do such a thing as that. I just couldn't bring myself to do that!"

"Steechánay and me already talk about this for long time. Many weeks now... many weeks. And she wants to come into our bed and be with us. She wants bad to do this and to touch you and be wife again. She want to be wife for you just like I am wife for you."

"What? You and Steechánay have already talked about us doing this? About her coming into our bed? About her becoming my wife and me being her *onēssē*? The two of you have already talked about this?"

"Yes, we even pray about it to Great Holy Father together... her and me. Many times now."

"And she wants to sleep with us? Would she expect me to make love with her, too, to have *ohgā-sá-ho* with her?"

"Yes, John, please! Her heart hurts and my heart hurts!"

"Oh, my God. I can't believe this is happening. And how would it make you feel, laying there beside us while I was making love with Steechánay? Have you thought about that? Have you thought about what that would feel like in your heart?"

"It make me feel very happy in my heart because I love you, and I love Steechánay, too. Please, John. Do this thing for me. My heart break and Steechánay heart break if you do not do this thing for us."

"And Steechánay really wants me to have *ohgā-sá-ho* with her... make love to her? Did she say that? Did she really come right out and say that with her own words?"

"Yes, John. She tell me her heart hurts very bad to do this thing with you, and now my heart hurts too for you to do it."

"And you and her have already talked about all of this? You've talked to her about me making love with her while you lay there watching and listening?"

"Yes, John. For many days now we talk about this. She hear us when we make love in our bed and she makes tears in her bed while she hear us. She hear us being happy and doing *ohgā-sá-ho* and tickling, and she hurts to be with us. Her heart hurts to be with us very bad and makes many tears."

"Loweja, don't cry. Please don't cry. You know how I hate to see you cry like this."

"Please, John! You tell me before that you have me in your heart."

"Loweja............. I do have you in my heart. I will

always have you in my heart."

"Can Steechánay come into your heart with me? Please, John. I love you! Will you do this for me and will you do this for Steechánay?"

"She was the wife of my father, Loweja. I don't know how I would feel about making love to her. I already love her greatly, yes, but I'm not sure I would even be able to do something like that with her. I just don't know... This whole idea is a shattering revelation to me!"

"I do not understand those words, John."

"I'm in shock, Loweja... I just don't know what to think about all of this. I just didn't see this coming at all!"

"I am young, John. Steechánay is still young, too. She has no man to be with. Her heart will die soon and she will just be old woman! You can make Steechánay very happy, and make me very happy, too... if you do this. You are only man in whole earth that can make us happy."

"Loweja. Darling. I've never known anyone with such a warm, caring heart, as big as the one you have, that you would be willing to do something like this for Steechánay. You must love her even more than I knew. I just don't know if I could be a good *onēssē* for both of you...."

"Please, John! Steechánay is already in my heart with you. Can she come into your heart with me?"

"Loweja, I love you more than anything in this world. I love Steechánay, too, she is already in my heart, but I could never love anyone as much as I love you. You have so much love in your heart that you would bring Steechánay into our marriage... to share me with her, for the sake of easing her pain? Is that what you are saying?"

"Yes, John, because I love her and I love you. That is the way that I feel. But my heart also tell me that if you do this thing you will be happy too. I know this in my heart. I want bad for you to do this thing. Steechánay and me pray together that you will want to do this, too."

"Loweja... If you've already talked with Steechánay

about this, and you are sure that it's what you both want… If it will make you happy, and if it will make Steechánay happy, I suppose that the least that I could do is to talk her about it. Tell Steechánay that I want to talk to her about doing this thing. I don't know what I'm going to say to her just yet, but I suppose I'll come up with something. I will talk to you and her about this together."

"I love you, John! I love you! I love you!"

"Wait… I don't want us to rush into anything like this! This thing is far too serious to rush into! I'm not saying that I will do it yet… I'm just saying that I will to talk to her about it. I want to talk to you and Steechánay together, before we make any hasty decisions. I'm still not sure of how something like this would work out. I've never even thought about doing anything like this before in my wildest dreams. We are a family here, and something like this could destroy us if we rush into it. I need to talk to Steechánay. I want her to tell me how she feels in her heart. I want to hear what she has to say with her own words and I want you to be there when I talk to her. I do not want for anyone to be hurt by this! From now on, I want nothing said about this to each other unless we are all three present to hear it. Nothing! Understand?"

"Yes, John! I understand, and I will go get her now! You make me very happy, John, and you make Steechánay very happy, too! You will see that I tell you truth!"

"Don't bring her down here to the storage hut, please. Where is she now?"

"She has gone to earth hut to gather potatoes."

"Bring her up to the house and wait for me there. I will talk to both of you there as soon as I finish what I'm doing here. Send the children to clean the henhouse, or tell them to do their chores or something. I do not want them to hear us talking! I'll be up to the house in a little while. I need a little more time to think about this."

Loweja ran excitedly out of the door, but just as quickly she returned and announced, "Snow come, John." I glanced outside to see a gentle snow falling, but could not focus my mind on anything but the proposition which Loweja had so unceremoniously placed before me. This astonishing turn of events had practically rendered me dumbstruck and shattered my concepts of conventional marriage. My knees were weak and my head was spinning. The proposal had been presented to me so unexpectedly, and so suddenly, that I was completely unprepared, and uncertain of how I should act in response. I should have been incensed. I should have felt as though I had been spousally betrayed by Loweja. I should have been outraged at the very thought of what she had proposed. I should have felt repulsed by the very suggestion of having carnal relations with a woman who had once been the young wife of my father. I should have felt all of these things in my heart and soul. But I didn't. Strangely enough, I felt entirely and completely at peace with the idea, as though it may have been the appropriate biological and spiritually correct thing to do… and perhaps it should have been done weeks earlier. Had I known earlier that Steechánay had amorous cravings of the heart for me perhaps I would have been the one to initiate the stunning suggestion of a *tri-union* marriage. I did love Steechánay… and I did love Loweja… and I did love the children as though they were my very own!

An unavoidable closeness had developed between Steechánay, Loweja, and I since we had all lived under the same roof for more than six weeks. Steechánay should not have had to suffer the indignity and the loneliness of staying within the confines of the small loft with the children… as though she was being punished for some transgression. It was demeaning. She should not have had to stay in the loft, behind the privacy curtains in the mornings, while I was given ample time to dress before she came down. Loweja was right… I was the only man here. And I was probably the only man on earth who would be willing to serve as father for Steechánay's children. Out here in the wilderness, far away from the hypocrisy of the white man and the peering eyes and vicious tongues of the self-righteous, I felt at peace with the concept as long as it would not cause emotional stress, or create a division of any type between Loweja and me. I would never permit that to happen. I would move away from the valley of my dreams before permitting such dissention to enter our hearts. Steechánay was a beautiful woman. Except for brief moments, I had never imagined myself having any type of intimate physical relations with her. I had lived in close quarters with both Steechánay and Loweja for over a month and a half now. I could not have avoided noticing Steechánay's beauty. I could not help but see her legs as she climbed the ladder to the loft to check on the children, and feel some inkling of a physical disturbance. How could I have helped but notice her eyes when she looked at me? Steechánay had been the wife of my father, even though she was probably the same age as I. I did love Steechánay, just as I had told Loweja, but I had never considered her physical body as being something which I was even remotely entitled to, much less did I consider the potential of practicing acts of intimacy with her. Therefore, any fleeting attraction which I had felt for her physically was dismissed, and not permitted to become manifest, or blossom into unhealthy thoughts of carnality. Yet, if she and Loweja were in soulful agreement with this new accord, I knew in my heart that I could find some way to be accepting of it as well.

    I had noticed Steechánay staring oddly at me at times, but I did not know until now that it was much more than just an idle stare… it was genuine desire… a craving to be touched by someone who loved her with their heart, and a craving to return those loving touches. She knew that Loweja and I loved her – we had told her so many times. She could probably see it in my eyes as well. I could remember the times when we had brushed by one another as we walked by the table… and the strange way that she seemed to smile with delight when we did. It all made perfect sense to me now. She must be agonizing in her desire to touch me, and to be touched in return. How could I have not been more sympathetic to her distress and spoken about this with Loweja sooner? Yet, I would never have taken the initiative to suggest her becoming my wife for fear of hurting Loweja. With Loweja having been the one who suggested the proposal to me, I felt no guilt or shame. If this is really and truly what they both want, then I should endeavor to comply accordingly. But wait... Would I be capable of engaging in a marital relationship with one woman while the other looked on? Would I be too ashamed or embarrassed when the time came? Should I ask them to take turns sleeping in the loft with the children? No... that could only lead to resentment and distrust. We could only maintain unity as a family as long as the three of us did everything together... absolutely everything, with no secrets between us. The very idea shattered all of my concepts of a conventional marital union. I was almost delirious as I tried to organize my thoughts and conceive the words which I would present to Steechánay and Loweja.

Then, a very compelling and disturbing thought entered my mind. If I were to reject this proposal, and demand that the idea be abandoned... Suppose at some point in the near future, out of loneliness and desperation, Steechánay should marry an anonymous stranger... someone who was without a compassionate heart, and without love for the children? If they moved away from the valley, I would perhaps never see Steechánay and the children again. Could I stand by and allow something such as that to happen? No! I had grown to love them all, and had already come to accept our relationship as that of my true family. I would be miserably distraught if I could never see them again. I would continuously worry about the welfare of Steechánay and the children. Yes, more than anything I wanted them all to be safe and happy... but deep within my heart, I wanted to be the one person who provided them with their happiness and wellbeing. Even before speaking with Steechánay, I knew deeply within my heart that I wanted to be a permanent father for the children, and a permanent husband for Steechánay. Yet I continued to struggle with accepting the idea of having two wives.

    I would make my final decision only after speaking to Steechánay and hearing her words for myself. Perhaps Loweja had not accurately conveyed Steechánay's true feelings to me. Perhaps Steechánay was only asserting a desire to move her bed out of the loft. Temporarily, I lay down my tools and closed the door to the storage hut and walked slowly through the lightly falling snow toward the house, and the inevitable reckoning which awaited me there. Shortly, Loweja and Steechánay walked up from the earthen hut, each carrying baskets of potatoes, and while the children were outside tending to their daily chores, the three of us walked inside the house, closed the door, and sat at the table to talk. I stalled for time somewhat, and added wood to the fire, knowing that the time for straight talk had arrived.

    Steechánay seemed to be frightened nearly out of her wits and her emotions were in obvious shambles, as she looked across the table at me as though she expected me to reject her, and break her heart further. I knew in an instant that everything Loweja had told me was true. As quickly as Steechánay would wipe a tear from her cheek, one or two more would appear to take its place. She had been crying profusely for some amount of time, I could tell. I could not help but notice her nervousness, and sympathized with her, for I knew her to be such a kind and sensitive person with a warm, loving heart. I knew that she had been driven to me by the emptiness that she felt in her heart, and I felt ashamed that the sounds of Loweja and I making love in our bed had only added to her misery. I knew that Loweja could be very vocal at times when we made love, and I could only imagine how tormented Steechánay must have felt in her loneliness as she lay there in the loft with the children. She must have been grief-stricken as she listened to the joyous sounds of intimacy created by Loweja and me… as she lay there alone, with no one to touch or be touched by. In her agony, I could only imagine how helpless she must have felt.

I wanted to do nothing from this point on which would add in any way to Steechánay's torment. My only interest now, was in restoring her damaged heart while preserving my love for Loweja at the same time. In my ignorance, I felt extremely guilty of having denied her the sensuous attention that she had been craving… Intimacy which Loweja and I had taken for granted because we each had a partner to interact with. Steechánay had no such partner. She had no one, and even more distressing, she had no hopes of finding such a partner in the near future. It even occurred in my mind that Loweja and I had unwittingly flaunted our happy marriage in front of Steechánay, and I could not help but feel shame in having done so. We were a family, and I wanted us all to be happy. I poured myself a glass of whiskey and drank it rather quickly, hoping that it would give me support as we talked. Feeling that one glass may not supply the courage which I desperately needed at this time, I poured a second, and then a third, and sat down at the table. Once I had finished the third glass, I very awkwardly cleared my throat, and led us into conversation.

"Well… I've almost finished storing our goods away in the storage hut, and I think things will be pretty safe there. I don't think we will have a lot of trouble with the mice, either, the way I've got things fixed now."

Neither of them answered me or acknowledged that they had even heard me, but they sat there looking upon me with eyes that were expectant of me to discuss a different subject. I realized how stupid and inappropriate my comment about the storage hut must have sounded. It was simply an ineffective, nervous effort to relieve the tension that was in the air. I took a deep breath, cleared my throat again, and proceeded, as the whiskey began to loosen my tongue and embolden me to confront the real subject at hand.

"Steechánay?"

"Yes, John."

"Steechánay, will you sit closer and hold hands with Loweja and me as we talk, please?"

"Yes, John. I will do anything for you... anything."

"Steechánay, you look very frightened. Please don't be frightened, and please don't make tears. We love you, and we want to talk to you from our hearts. I'm not exactly sure of how to go about this, but Loweja and I do not want you to be afraid to talk with us about anything. Ever!"

"I will try to not be scared. But I am. I cannot help it, and I cannot stop my tears, John. Only you and Loweja can stop my tears."

"Steechánay, to tell you the truth, I'm a little scared, too, and I'll just try to say this in the best way I can. Steechánay, you know that Loweja and I love you very much. It would be hard for me to find the right words to tell you how much we really do love you. You do know that, don't you?"

"Yes, John. I know that in my heart. And I hope that you and Loweja know that I love each of you as well. My love for you has grown each day since you have first come here. I have never known anyone with hearts as good as you and Loweja. I will always love you and Loweja."

"Steechánay, Loweja is the first woman that I ever loved. I never even knew that I could love anyone as much as I love her. But since we have been living here with you and the children, I'm learning that I have more love in my heart than I ever knew existed there. Do you understand all of that so far, Steechánay?"

"Yes, John. I understand all of that very good."

"Good. Steechánay... Would you like... I mean, would you really want for me to become a husband for you, just like I am with Loweja?"

"Yes, John. If you would let me be your wife and if Loweja would let me be your wife, I would like to come into your heart as your wife. I hurt bad to be with you as wife, and I ask this thing because of bad hurt that is in my heart, and I beg you to say yes and do this for me."

"Steechánay, you said that you loved my father, didn't you?"

"Yes, John... I said that to you and Loweja when you first come here to the valley."

"Steechánay, I am not my father. I am me, *John Welch*. I am a different person than my father. I am a much different person. Is it because of my father's memory that you wish to be my wife?"

"No, John. I loved William Welch because he was William Welch. But he is gone now. I love you because you are John Welch and nobody else. I love Loweja because she is Loweja Welch and nobody else. I do not see your father when I look at you... I see you, John Welch. You are much different man than your father. You are better man than your father, even. My heart hurts because I cannot touch you and feel you at night and I cannot make this love in my heart go away. I see you each day, I am near you and I love you so much, but I cannot reach for you and touch you because I am not your wife. I am nobody. I hurt so bad to touch you. I hurt so bad for you to touch me. I tell Loweja this and she makes tears with me. I do not hurt just to have man come to me... I hurt to have man come to me that I love with my heart, and I love you with my heart, John. William Welch never kiss me. No one ever kiss me before. I see you and Loweja kiss and I see you and Loweja tickle and laugh and my heart hurts to do these things with you and Loweja... Please help me John... Please!"

Steechánay bowed her head and hid her face in her hands, sobbing terribly. I put my hand on her shoulder.

"Please do not make any more tears over this Steechánay. It hurts our hearts when we see you make tears like this because we love you so much. The reason we are talking here like this now, is because Loweja and I want to make your tears go away... forever. May I ask you a question? Please, Steechánay?"

"Yes, John."

"If you were my wife, would you want for me to... you know... have... uhhh... *ohgā-sá-ho* with you? Make love to you, as your husband?"

"Yes, John... but only when you want me, and only if Loweja say that we can. I would like that very much, but if you did not want to do it with me, could I still lay close to you and feel of you at night?"

"Steechánay... My God, woman... Laying close together at night is what husbands and wives are supposed to do, Steechánay. But when I come to bed at night, how am I to know which one of you to give my affections to? I mean which one of you to do those husband and wife things with? There may be nights that I could do those kinds of things with both of you... but there may be some nights that I could not, and I would never want to deny Loweja. How could I choose one of you without hurting the other's heart?"

"Our hearts will tell Loweja and me, and we will tell you. Loweja and me love each other so much that I know this is so. Loweja and me talk about this much. I love Loweja so much that I would not want for you to ever deny her. If you do not want to do those things with me much I will still love you. I will love you forever. I want to feel you next to me when I sleep. If you just want to do those *èlācūmás* things with me sometimes only, I think it will still make hurt go away from my heart and my belly. I will promise to be good wife. I think I will die in my heart if I cannot touch you soon."

I walked around to Steechánay's side of the table and took her up into my arms, allowing her the opportunity to touch me as she wished. Then, I beckoned for Loweja to join us, and the three of us embraced for a short time before sitting back down to resume our conversation. I looked at Loweja and asked, "Loweja, do you understand everything that has been said here this afternoon?"

"Yes, John. I understand everything good."

"Would you like to say anything at this time, Loweja?"

"I want Steechánay to be wife for you just like I am wife for you. I love Steechánay, and I think you will be much happy and there will be much love here in this house. I know this in my heart to be true."

"Loweja, do you promise that you will love Steechánay and me as if we were the same person? From now until the day that you die?"

"Yes, John. I die for both of you and I will love both of you forever more!"

"Steechánay, do you promise me that you will love Loweja and me as if we were the same person? From now until the day that you die?"

"Yes, John. I will love you both forever, and I too, would die for each one of you!"

"Steechánay, I am very sorry that you have made tears in your bed all these nights. I am ashamed of myself for the nights that you slept in the loft with children. I did not know that you made tears while you were up there until Loweja told me so today. I wish I had known this sooner. I wish that we had talked about this sooner. I love you and Loweja, Steechánay, and if this is what *you* want, and it is what *Loweja* wants…"

"Yes, John?"

"I just want to make sure that you both really understand what we're about to do here, because once we make a promise to each other there's no turning back. Is this really and truly what you both want?"

"Yes, John." …both of them answering in perfect unison.

"Then it is what I want as well. I want you to be my wife forever, Steechánay, and I want you to feel like you are welcome in our bed because it is now your bed also. I want you to lay with Loweja and me in our bed always and forever. I want you to touch me as much as you want to. If I can be the husband that you are longing for, it will bring great happiness to

Loweja and me. I love you, and I love Loweja, and I love our children. If we do this thing, we must always be three hearts as one, and we must always love each other as we love ourselves. *Say-ha-way*, Steechánay."

"*Say-ha-way,* John. *Necu-ta-say-ha.*"

"*Necu-ta-say-ha,* Steechánay. *Necu-ta-say-ha,* Loweja. I did not know until now that my heart could ever be so filled with love that I could do this. But now I know that there truly is room in my heart for both of you. I know that the people I love most in this world are here with me right now in this valley. You are my wife from now on and forever, Steechánay, and I am now your husband. I will promise to love you forever and care for you just as I will love and care for Loweja forever, until the day that I die. *Necu-ta-say-ha.* Will you show Loweja and me a big smile? It has been weeks since we have seen a good smile cross your face. Wipe away your tears now, and smile. There. That's better. We want to always see a smile on your face. No more tears. You and Loweja are the two most beautiful women in this world... but only when you are happy and smiling."

"Does this mean that you are my husband now, John?"

"Yes, Steechánay... I am your husband now."

"If you are my husband now, may I touch you with my hands now, and will you touch me with yours... and may I kiss you and Loweja?"

"Yes, Steechánay. And if there is ever any tears in your heart, we want to know about them, as soon as they come. That is the only way that we can make them go away."

The three of us stood and embraced warmly again, with tears upon our cheeks and genuine love for each other in our hearts. Steechánay actively felt of me with her hands and kissed me wildly, then turned and gently kissed Loweja. It seemed strange for a moment, to see two women, standing before me, who were kissing as they were, but I recognized it for what it really was... a sincere expression of unrepressed, innocent love. Love which came from the depths of their hearts, and could never have been understood or accepted in the narrow-minded white man's world. I had frowned on so many of the Indian customs before coming to this wilderness. I had stupidly looked down my arrogant nose at their culture and their beliefs, considering them to be the beliefs of uneducated, immoral savages. And now I was indulging in some of the very things which I had scorned, and felt no shame in what I was about to do. I only felt deep satisfaction and pride in knowing that I could ease the pain which Steechánay had carried in her heart. I had learned that there is no room for shame in a man's heart when it is filled with so much love... and I did feel unpretentious love in my heart for Steechánay as well as my darling Loweja.

"For someone who has never kissed a man before, you have very amazing kisses, Steechánay... just like Loweja!"

"That is because Loweja teach me how to do it when we go to get potatoes, John, and I like it very much."

"Oh, I see... Well, she did a very good job in teaching you! Very good, indeed! Now, if my wonderful wives will be so kind as to prepare a meal for us, I will finish my work at the storage hut. Tonight, I will promise you that there will be no tears in our house. And there will only be children in the loft from this day forward. Steechánay, please remove your things from the children's loft while I'm at the storage shed and bring them down here to store near our bed with Loweja's things... the tears that you cried may stay up there in the loft... everything else needs to be brought down here to our bed, where there is only happiness. *Necu-ta-say-ha*... both of you."

As I left to go back to work on the storage hut I still had considerable apprehension in my mind as to what this new marriage arrangement would be like in practical application. Everything which had just taken place had all happened within two hours of the time Loweja had first spoken to me about this astonishing new proposal. I was sure that it was the right thing to do, yet it was an awkward and unfamiliar concept for me because it was so radically different than anything that I had ever deemed appropriate in a civilized society. What would the next few hours bring, when we would actually put our newly established '*tri-union*' into practice, as I entered my bed for the first time with two wives awaiting me? What would the next few days, and the next few weeks yield? It continued to be foremost in my thoughts while I went back and worked at the storage hut. About an inch of freshly fallen snow covered the ground as additional snow continued to fall from the sky. The children were playing games in the snow, and I shouted for them to go to the house and dry themselves in the warmth of the fire. I watched as they went into the house, then I continued walking to the storage hut.

I fumbled around inside of the storage hut for more than an hour, but was accomplishing nothing for my efforts. I could not keep my mind focused on even the simplest of tasks. I would start to do something, and then simply forget what I was intending to do. My life had changed tremendously from what it had been just two hours earlier. I was now a man with two wives' I had become the very type of man whom I had scorned in the past, and I had not yet come to terms with this new reckoning of myself. When our evening meal had been prepared, and I was called to the house, it was with great anxiety and uncertainty that I put down my tools, inhaled a deep breath, and took those first few awkward steps toward the house to join my recently redefined family. The snow was beginning to fall much faster now. Two inches covered the ground now, and through it, I could barely see the house as I returned.

On that initial night that I would co-occupy a bed with my two wives, the minutes seemed to pass like hours as we ate our evening meal together. Afterwards, the children made their preparations for bed and scampered up the ladder to the loft. I had expected the children to notice that Steechánay's bed was missing from the loft, and start asking questions. They did not ask any questions, however, so I assumed that

Steechánay or Loweja had somehow already provided them with a sufficient explanation. After the children were in bed and settled in, Steechánay climbed the ladder to the loft and pulled the privacy curtain closed. I unconsciously studied her legs as I had never studied them before – but she was my wife now, and I felt no shame in the liberties my eyes had taken. I sat with my wives drinking tea and having quiet conversation, impatiently waiting until I was sure that the children were asleep.

We talked about things which were trivial and unimportant in nature, and I doubt if either of us heard anything that the other said. The three of us sat at the table and looked nervously, yet lovingly at each other. Loweja seemed less nervous than Steechánay or I, displaying a broad smile upon her lovely face and showing me her remarkably beautiful dimples in the shadows of the candlelight. I noticed that Loweja and Steechánay were holding hands as they sat, and I knew from the looks on their faces that by mutual agreement, Steechánay would be receiving me as her new husband on this special night. I knew that Steechánay could wait no longer, and that Loweja was equally as anxious for it to happen… perhaps as anxious as Steechánay herself, or even me. I could see it in their loving eyes as they looked at each other. Steechánay had an intense, yearning look upon her face, and Loweja had the gracious look of a loving benefactor, one who was eager to share her husband for the sake of eliminating Steechánay's horrible loneliness. Whispering, I asked, "Steechánay, did you tell the children that you would no longer be sleeping with them in the loft?"

"Yes, John, I did… Loweja and I told them before they ate their meal."

"What did they say when you told them, Steechánay?"
"They wanted to know why this was."
"What did you tell them?"
"I told them that I was your wife now… just like Loweja, and that we must sleep together for now and forever."

"Did they say anything?"

"They said they were very happy that I have husband now. They all love you and Loweja, so they are all happy, too... but I am more happy than anyone, I think, John. I feel that in my heart, and my heart beats only for you and Loweja, and our family now."

Eventually, I climbed the ladder and peeked through the privacy curtain to find that the children were all fast asleep, then I slowly descended the ladder and blew out all of the candles but one, and sat there finishing my tea in silence as Loweja and Steechánay undressed themselves in the dark shadows near our bed. They each took their long hair out of braids and brushed one another's hair. I delighted in what I was seeing, even in the dim light, as I finished the last of my tea. They stood naked before me and hugged each other warmly – a sight which fascinated me. Had it not been for Steechánay's darker skin, she and Loweja could have almost been twin sisters embracing in the shadows.

They were both beautiful before me as I watched them lie down upon our buffalo hide bed together, hug each other again, and turn to look at me. Their eyes were beckoning me to come hither... and not waste much time in doing so. I moved the candle closer to our bed and undressed. Completely enthralled, I stood there over them momentarily, and looked down upon their loving faces. Loweja was smiling happily, even showing her beautiful teeth. Steechánay looked as though she was still quite nervous and unsure of herself, yet compelled by strong, irresistible forces within her feminine emptiness to receive me. I also saw love and admiration in her eyes, and the glorious anticipation that her excruciating hunger for male companionship was about to be attenuated. I looked down upon them for a moment or two and felt my nervousness melting away – displaced by yearning.

"My wonderful, wonderful wives... Mere words cannot express how much I truly love you both. You are my family.

You are my wives. You are my very lifeblood."

As their hands reached upward to me, in the dim light of a single candle, I entered the bed between them and was immediately accepted by their warm bodies and hands from both sides. Loweja kissed me tenderly and whispered quietly into my ear, "Thank you, John... I love you. I much love you and I will forever, and I will love Steechánay, too!"

Under Loweja's generous, loving eyes, Steechánay and I familiarized ourselves as man and wife. Any nervousness that I had felt before had truly evaporated and given way to passion. Steechánay was no longer denied the pleasure of touching... or being touched, and she relished in this new wave of delight which had engulfed her, and to my surprise, just like Loweja, she didn't hesitate to vocalize her delight. After sharing a few moments of vigorous caressing and warm kisses between the three of us, I extinguished the candle, and abolished the terrible void which had lingered in Steechánay's heart. Our marriage was thusly consummated, and we were now solidified forever as *'three hearts as one.'*

In the coming months, I maintained a watchful eye on the sisterly relationship between Loweja and Steechánay after each night together. I went to great lengths each night that we lay together to divide my affections as equally as possible between the two, yet I never felt as though either of them were even slightly covetous of the attention the other was receiving. Steechánay and Loweja had always talked freely with each other, yet I had noticed that since Steechánay had come into our marriage, she and Loweja seemed to talk even more... confide in each other even more... and even laugh with each other more. I also noticed that they seemed to laugh more frequently, though I was never quite certain as to exactly what they were laughing about. It gave me a warm feeling deep inside to see the closeness which had developed between them, and to watch as it continued to grow.

I was always mindful that someday there could have been an indication of dissention which could possibly arise within our relationship. I continuously looked for any hint of jealousy or resentfulness which may have existed between Loweja and Steechánay, but it was never present. In fact, their relationship only seemed to intensify and escalate each day, with my love for each of them growing stronger as well, and strengthening the spiritual bonding of our three hearts. I seldom made love with one unless the other was present. Even during the day, when a spontaneous romantic event would take place between two of us, the other was summoned and given an equal opportunity to participate... which they enthusiastically did. I wanted no secrets between us. I did not want one of them to accidently stumble upon me making love to the other. That could have easily been mistakenly perceived as an act of betrayal, and I would never have permitted such an unbearable thing to happen. There was never a night in which the three of us were not delightfully entangled in sublime closeness. Our marital relations were never a mere act of two participants, but always a sensuous event involving all three of us. During Loweja's later months of carrying our baby, Steechánay and I partnered in union on most nights, yet we did so with the wonderful accompaniment of Loweja's magical hands and kisses. After the first two months of our new marriage, there were some nights when I was too tired from cutting wood or repairing the huts to be very amorous with either of them. On those nights, our love for each other was expressed by warm embraces and the compassionate holding of hands and tender kisses. They understood when I was tired, and remained considerate of my feelings on such occasions. Still, our deep love and sympathetic understanding of each other, and our respect for each other's feelings, remained intact and ever-growing.

With spring rapidly approaching, and last of the snows of winter melting, the time of Loweja's delivery was drawing close at hand. The children were growing like amazing little weeds before our very eyes. I felt that Kwīnahā would be a man in another year or two. Hints of spring were in the air as colorful birds began to return from their winter homes and flocks of geese flew overhead as they headed toward their summer feeding grounds. Fields of early wildflowers began to bloom and the herds of wapiti began returning to their summer homes in the higher country. With the arrival of spring, I unpacked some more items from the storage hut; rifles, powder, percussion caps, and lead. Steechánay had told me that the grizzlies would come in the spring, and I wanted to be ready to do whatever I had to do in order to protect my family and my goods. I had brought shovels and some vegetable seeds to plant as soon as I could turn the soil in the garden. There was very little hay left for our horses, and I knew that during the coming summer I would have to put up additional hay to feed them the following year because we now had more horses.

Kwīnahā and Joseph were both old enough to help with the tending of a garden and the gathering of hay as well as frequently saddling and riding the horses. They both demonstrated excellent horsemanship, and the horses responded well to their young masters. Kwīnahā was growing by leaps and bounds into a fine, handsome young man. Both of the boys seemed to follow me continuously, and were always nearby when I needed an extra hand. They spoke more and more English words each day, and I savored the conversations which we had. I had asked Steechánay and Loweja to encourage the children to speak English words as much as possible so that I could communicate better with them. I had picked up more and more Arikara and Pawnee words, but felt ill at ease in using them in general conversation. Sometimes I would find myself engaged in conversation using an odd mixture of English and Arikara. I loved the children dearly, and as we began to speak to each other more and more, our love for each other flourished.

A week or so after the day that Loweja and I had first

brought Steechánay into our marriage, I was busy one day replacing rotted shingles on the roof of the large lean-to, when Kwīnahā called up to me from the ground below, "Father?"

Kwīnahā had called me '*Father*!' It sounded so pleasing to my ear that I wanted to shout out with joy! I wanted to announce to the world that this wonderful and beautiful young man had actually called me, *Father*! Instead, I answered back very softly, "Yes, Kwīnahā?"

"Mother and Loweja say food is ready. They say you come and eat, now. Please."

"Thank you, son!"

"You are welcome, Father."

"Will you hold the ladder still while I climb down, son?" I could have easily descended the ladder without it being held, but simply wanted to hear Kwīnahā say the wonderful word, '*father*,' again.

"Yes, Father."

I was touched deeply, and very much impressed with how distinctly he had spoken to me in English. I climbed down from the roof and hugged Kwīnahā, and when I did, I could feel that he was growing into a fine young man. He would soon be as tall as I. We walked up to the house together, and after we had eaten, I talked to Steechánay and Loweja in private.

"Shut the door, please Loweja. I don't want the children to hear this."

"What is it, John? Is something wrong?" Steechánay asked.

"Steechánay, did you tell the children to call me, *Father*?"

"Yes, John. You are my husband now and they are your children. I thought you would like for them to call you '*Father*.' Does that not please you?"

"It *does* please me! It pleases me greatly! I can't even begin to tell you how much it pleases me. I just wasn't expecting it. Each of you have done so much to make me so happy here in this valley that I just wanted to say, *thank you*, and I love you both, that's all."

Steechánay smiled at me and said, "Does that mean that you will not tickle me today, I hope."

"There is no reason for me to tickle you today that I can think of. But I think maybe I will tickle you anyway! If Loweja will help me? What do you say, Loweja, will you help me tickle Steechánay?"

"Yes, John! I will help! We will tickle Steechánay together!"

Loweja and Steechánay would often take turns holding each other by a foot, while I would tickle them until tears of laughter would appear in their eyes. Steechánay quickly rose from her chair and tried to escape the confines of our small cabin, but Loweja blocked the door and I lifted Steechánay into my arms and carried her to the bed. And so… there we were… three adults, wrestling, and making joyful laughter on our bed like children. There was no shame in our adolescent behavior – there was only the purest of joy when we frolicked together, as we so often did. Frequently tickling my wives had become one of my favorite pastimes in life. I restrained myself somewhat when tickling Loweja though, because her belly was becoming very fat with child, and I was afraid of somehow accidently injuring her or the baby in our exuberance. Her belly had become so big that she was unable to wear her beautiful buckskin dress because she could not bend to reach anything on the ground or floor when she was wearing it. Together, Steechánay and Loweja had made a special dress out of a blanket which fit her more loosely and allowed her to sit and stoop with much greater comfort.

In April, when the ground became dry enough to turn the soil in our garden, Kwīnahā and I worked diligently to prepare the ground for the seeds which I had purchased in Fort Saint Joseph. Kwīnahā was a strong lad now, and I had guessed his age to be fourteen or fifteen years. I stopped digging in the garden momentarily and mused somewhat at my present situation here. Here was I, *John Welch*, rich in wealth beyond most men's wildest dreams, laboring intently in the soil to plant seeds so that my family would have something to eat... and actually performing such hard labor by choice. Loweja and Steechánay were working diligently behind me, planting seeds and laughing between themselves as they spoke in Arikara or Ree... I wasn't really sure which language they spoke.

Had I chosen to indulge myself in the spending of my fortune, perhaps back in Baltimore... or maybe St. Louis, I could have lived completely in the lap of luxury, pampered by a dozen servants tending to my every whim for the rest of my life. Perhaps I could have even married Elizabeth, and acquired even more wealth once her father had died. Perhaps I could have been the envy of all of Baltimore's elite aristocracy. I could only imagine the sorrow and unhappiness that I would have acquired in the process. There was no other place on earth where I could have possibly obtained the happiness and contentment which now surrounded me here, in my valley. There was no place on earth where such a family bond could have been replicated and nourished as it was here in my valley.

"Father, are you going to help?"

"Sorry, son! My mind just drifted away for a while."

"I do not understand, Father."

"I was just thinking about how much I love you and the rest of my family, son."

"We love you too, Father! **Father!** ***Kén-masqua*! Big Bear! Look, Father, look!**"

I turned my head to see a huge grizzly moving toward us less than a hundred yards distant. He was the biggest grizzly that I had ever seen! He was truly a frightening sight to behold, with his broad shoulders and silver-tipped guard hairs atop his back. Silently, I led Kwīnahā back to our storage hut and motioned for Loweja and Steechánay to quickly go to the house with the children. I retrieved one of the larger caliber rifles which I had purchased in Fort Saint Joseph, pulled it from the gun-box in the storage hut, loaded it quickly, and returned to the doorway of the hut where I steadied the rifle against the doorpost. The great bear came closer and closer, and when he was a scant thirty yards distant, I pulled the trigger and fired. When the smoke had cleared, I watched the huge bruin run about twenty yards and collapse. After a few short spasms and one tremendous bone-chilling growl, the beast lay there in a lifeless mound. Having heard the shot, Loweja and Steechánay left our three children in the safety of the house and came to see what was happening. I quickly recharged the rifle and once I had walked over to the huge beast and made sure that he was dead, Loweja went back to the house and gathered all of the children together.

The entire family joined in for the skinning and butchering of the great animal. Kwīnahā and Joseph fleshed out the big hide, salted it, and stretched it on the outside wall of the storage hut to cure in the sun. It was an enormous, beautiful hide with all of the hair in pristine condition. It would make a fine rug for our home or a covering for our bed when it cured. The rest of us prepared pieces of the meat to be hung to cool in the meat hut. The nights were still cool enough that the meat would keep for three or four weeks. Loweja painstakingly removed each of the bear's claws as Steechánay removed the heart and liver and took them to the house where they could be cooked for our dinner. Loweja and I tended to carving up the remaining meat while Steechánay stripped sinew from the bones and flesh to be dried in the sun and saved to use as stitching for our moccasins. We worked together, so that all of the meat could be used. Nothing but the bones and tiny bits of meat and tendon would remain. We were almost finished, when I saw Loweja rise to her feet as she tried to lift the remaining carcass, and cry out to me…

"**John!**"

"What is it, Loweja? What's the matter?"

"Baby come soon, I think!"

Quickly, I scooped her up into my arms and dashed toward the house, frantically calling out as I went, "**Steechánay! Steechánay! Steechánay!**" And all the while I ran, Loweja kept telling me in a calm voice, "I can walk to house, John. I am just going to have our baby. That is all! Let me walk, please!"

I ignored her request to walk on her own, and carried my precious little Loweja inside of the house and gently laid her on our bed. The children were curious and stood nearby, but Steechánay had soon ushered them outside of the house.

"You must go too, John. I will help Loweja."

"Steechánay, I am staying right here with you and Loweja! I will not leave her or you at a time like this! I will not!"

"Very well… I understand. If you must stay, will you help me get her dress off then?"

"Loweja, darling, are you alright?"

"Yes, John. I have baby now, that is all. I love you, John!"

With Loweja naked now, Steechánay placed a folded wool blanket under her head as a pillow and leaned over to kiss her on her forehead, then looked at me and asked, "John, get deerskin for me from hut, please."

I rushed to the storage hut and took a deer hide from the wall inside and rushed back to the house as quickly as my legs would carry me. Steechánay placed the deer skin under Loweja's pelvic area with the hair side of the hide facing downward and the skin side facing up. She again kissed Loweja on the forehead and softly spoke, "I love you, Loweja. You will do well, and I will help you."

"I love you, too, Steechánay."

Throughout the next hour and a half, Loweja sweated, obviously in pain, but never crying out with her suffering any louder than a moan. At each groan, I looked down with the expectancy of seeing our baby arrive at her opening at any moment, but it seemed as though it was never going to come. I agonized greatly with anticipation. Loweja held on to my hand tightly, and squeezed even tighter each time her body convulsed with what must have been agonizing cramps. Steechánay kept Loweja's forehead dampened with cool water and often reached down with both of her hands to stretch Loweja's opening... I assumed to make it bigger so that the baby could pass easier. It was painful for me to watch, so I simply turned my head to look away when Steechánay would do this. Steechánay applied a generous amount of grease which had been rendered from bear fat to Loweja's opening to make it slippery, and a fluid of some sort began to drip out and onto the deerskin. With each series of contractions I anguished. Over and over again, Steechánay and I told Loweja that we loved her, until I finally looked down to see a wet tuft of tiny dark hair emerging from Loweja's opening... then a head. Before my very eyes, a baby was soon brought forth... slow at first, then sliding out very quickly. Its little hands and feet were moving. Steechánay smiled broadly as she held onto the baby's tiny umbilical cord and said, "Tie this piece of string tightly... right here. That's good, John, now hand me that thing you bought for us in Fort Saint Joseph, please."

"What thing are you talking about?"
"That thing we cut cloth with."
"You mean, *scissors*?"
"Yes, *sizzas*... hand me that thing, please."

With the umbilical cut above the string, Steechánay cleaned the baby with warm water and handed the tiny child to Loweja, who wrapped it in a small sheet of cotton and held it to her body with a loving smile which could have only been produced by a caring and very proud mother. I stood there completely in awe of the wonderment which I had just witnessed. Steechánay continued to clean Loweja's opening with warm water and removed the remaining matter which had come out with the baby. When she had finished, she placed a clean, dry cloth over Loweja's opening and handed me the small water pail in which she had placed the matter in and said, "Here, John, please throw this away in the woods, far away from house."

When I returned, Loweja looked into my eyes and said, "We have baby now, John! Beautiful baby!"

Steechánay squeezed small droplets of milk from Loweja's breast onto her fingertip and gently pressed it against the baby's tiny lips. Moments later, the baby started nursing, and it came as a great delight to all of us when we saw our beautiful baby boy finally start to nurse on his own. The baby's delicate little jaws worked vigorously as it nursed! It was a wonderful sight to behold! Steechánay looked at me with loving eyes and a warm smile, and said, "Loweja makes good milk, just like I told you she would. This baby will grow to be strong man someday... like his father..."

Steechánay prepared a bed for Loweja on the floor next to our big bed where Loweja lay with the baby. Just before dark, I went outside and dragged the remaining carcass of the bear far into the woods where it would not draw wolves close to the house. I secured the doors on the storage hut and the meat hut, closed the door to the chicken house, and walked back to the house in the brisk early spring air. Once inside the house, I secured the door and windows, and in the light of several candles, I drew the children close to see their newly arrived brother. Their faces glowed with joy in the candle light as they each looked upon the baby and Loweja. They each said '*I love you*' and kissed Loweja, then scampered up the ladder to their beds in the loft. Steechánay drew the privacy curtain closed, and we each gave Loweja a tender kiss before we retired upon the bed on the floor, next to her. It had been a long day, and a very eventful day as well.

Steechánay and I wrapped ourselves in one of our warm embraces, an embrace which felt reassuring, yet somehow partially vacant without Loweja's participation. I had grown accustomed to having both of them in my arms at night. I had just about fallen asleep, when a little voice from behind the privacy curtain upstairs broke the silence. Almost in a whisper, little Kwesha called down to ask, "Father?"

"Yes, Kwesha?"

"What is the name of our little brother?"

"Name? Uhhh... That is a very good question. Let's all think about it tonight and see if we can come up with a good name in the morning. Alright, dear?"

"Yes, Father."

Kwesha's question was compelling. What would we name our son? Would '*Robert*' be a good name? *Alexander*? *David*? *Matthew*? Sometime during the night I thought of a name which I would like. I would talk to Loweja and Steechánay in the morning to see what they thought. Very late that night, Steechánay kissed me on the cheek and whispered into my ear, "John? Are you awake?"

"Yes, Steechánay, I'm still awake."

"I miss Loweja, do you miss her, too?"

"Yes, Steechánay... I miss her, too. Give me a good kiss and let's get some sleep. I have a crib to build tomorrow."

Morning found Loweja wide-eyed and happy, and busily tending to our baby. She walked to the table, nursing our little treasure, and sat there to join us for breakfast. The pleasing aroma of boiling tea filled the house along with the smell of salted pork belly frying on the skillet in the fireplace. Once I had walked around outside to make sure the area was free of any animals, the children were allowed to go outside and tend to their chores. I hung my gun up over the fireplace and sat down at the table, and as Steechánay poured our tea, I asked Loweja, "How do you feel this morning, Loweja?"

"I feel so much good, John!"

"Loweja, what are the Arikara words which mean, little bear?"

"*Wan-Masqua.*"

"And Steechánay, what are the Pawnee words which mean, little bear?"

"*Myo-Masqua*, John… why do you ask?"

"Loweja, what would you think if we named our son, *Myo-Masqua*? He came into our lives on the very day that I killed the big bear, so I think maybe he's our little bear. What do you think?" Loweja looked delighted, but offered an alternative name with the same meaning.

"Could we use the English words and call him, *Little Bear*, maybe?"

"What do you think, Steechánay?"

"You and Loweja need to be the ones who name him. I like the name, *Little Bear* too, but he is of you and Loweja… and not of me."

"Steechánay, do you remember what I told you on the day we were married, when I said that *we were now three hearts as one*?"

"Yes, John, I do."

"Loweja and I want you to be a part of everything that is in our lives now! Everything! Don't we, Loweja?"

"Yes, John, everything. We love you Steechánay."

"Steechánay, why do you make tears? Have I said something which has made you unhappy about something?"

"No, John… I only weep because you and Loweja make me so happy all of the time! I cannot help it. I think I die if you or Loweja leave me to be alone again. I love you, and this is only a very little happy tear."

If I had never taken Steechánay as a wife, Loweja and I could have still lived under tremendously happy circumstances there in the valley as man and wife. However, bringing Steechánay into our marriage had added a new dimension to the marital bond of Loweja and me, a dimension which had actually strengthened our relationship. This would have been an impossible situation if it were not for the unselfish, caring attitudes of both Steechánay and Loweja. They loved each other dearly. I could see it in their eyes when they looked at one another. We had taken a wedding oath to be *three hearts as one*. And now we truly were.

Lectūschemă

  With my marriage to two wives now, my responsibilities as both a husband, and a worthy provider had increased commensurately. I never experienced a moment of regret with my newly defined obligation. Nay... I relished in joy and contentment, even as I worked. My family members never shirked their responsibilities either. We all joined in together to work for our primary common cause; *survival in a wilderness.* It was indeed a wilderness, one which was wrought with breathtaking beauty. But it was also a wilderness in which prepared people could easily starve to death during the cold brutalities of winter. Tranquil beauty does much to fill the soul, but oft times it does precious little to fill the belly. Winters were merely a four-month test; a test to see how well or how poorly we had worked in preparation during the preceding summer and fall. My family enjoyed much time together playing games in our leisure, but when there was work to be done, our daily tasks were our highest priority.

  In the weeks leading up to my marriage of Steechánay, it was not unusual to see a small smile cross her lovely face from time to time. Yet I only discovered after we were wed, that the smiles I had seen before had been subdued and impersonally superficial. It was not until after we had married that I began to see smiles that rivaled even those of Loweja. It was as though her smiles of happiness had been placated in the past, and were only now being released in their full and unrestrained glory. In our conversations, I often tried to encourage both Loweja and Steechánay to tell me tales of their past. I felt that I knew very little about their culture and their childhood – those things which tend to mold us into the individuals we are today, and I wanted to know as much about them as I possibly could. Their past had shaped them into who they were today, and I loved both of them much too dearly to be content to remain ignorant of what they had experienced in childhood. It was also an opportunity for us to discuss rituals, beliefs, and superstitions of their culture which I deemed as being inappropriate or blasphemous. They were both keenly aware of my stance on the permanent marking or disfiguring of the human body, and they also held such things in disdain. Cleanliness is another area where we saw eye-to-eye, and regular bathing was a family event during the warmer months. Steechánay was a Christian, just like Loweja and me, but I saw her faith improve even greater as her and Loweja prayed to the Great Holy Father together. Undoubtedly, their strong faith induced me to become closer to God as well.

    Late one afternoon, my wives and I sat on the porch of the house, shelling beans and having our usual casual conversation. Through my questions that afternoon, I would make a profound discovery regarding Steechánay's family. From the time of my first visit to the valley, when Loweja and I were on our way to Fort Saint Joseph, I was impressed by the fact that my Pawnee friend, *Lectŭschemă* seemed to be very cordial whenever he greeted or spoke to Steechánay. I remembered thinking what a fine husband he would have made for Steechánay, had we not married. She had told me a lot of things about Lectŭschemă, such as the fact that he was held in very high esteem among his people. He was a mighty warrior, and would almost certainly become one of the leaders of his people one day. Lectŭschemă had always treated me with much respect, and I felt as if he was a man of whom his people could be proud, and I regarded him as a friend. While talking to Steechánay, I commented, "Lectŭschemă has not been here to visit for more than three weeks now. Every time he comes here, he invites me to his village for a visit. I like him very much. I think he is a fine man, and I think that the next time he invites me I will go to his village for a visit. I would like to know more about him and his people."

"Lectūschemă is a great man. He has always been a great man, even when we were children."

"You knew him when you were a child?"

"He was a young boy when I was born. He always look after me when I was young girl, and take care of me."

"Did you love him when you were a young girl?"

"Yes, John. We have always had much love for each other... he is my brother."

"Brother!?"

"Yes, John."

"Why did you not tell me this before?"

"I thought you knew this. He always call me '*Shy-táne,*' when he comes here and that means, *Little Sister.*"

"I have heard him call you by that name many times, but I did not know what it meant. Does he know that we are married now?"

"He has not been here since you have taken me as wife. I have not told him because I have not seen him, John."

"When he comes here, he needs to know that you are my wife now. I should be the one to tell him, but I cannot speak the language very good. We must tell him together, so you can speak my words to him."

"So be it. We will tell him together."

"I hope and pray that he does not become angry with me."

"He will not be angry with you, John... this I know..."

Another two weeks passed before Lectūschemă came for a visit. He had four braves with him. We sat on the small porch in the front of our cabin and had tea and biscuits together. I asked Steechánay to tell him that I wanted to speak with him in private, with her to speak my words. He agreed, and after mumbling some instruction to his fellow warriors, they had soon walked to the corral. The three of us went inside while

Loweja and the children entertained our other guests at the corral. Inside, at the table, I cleared my throat, and asked Steechánay to repeat my words.

"Lectūschemă... my friend. Loweja and I have been living here now with Steechánay and the children for more than nine weeks. I have fallen in love with Steechánay and the children, and have taken her as my wife. I did not know until two weeks ago that Steechánay was your sister. If I had known this, I would have spoken to you before we married, and I would have asked your permission. I am sorry that I did not know this. I would never willingly do anything which would damage our friendship in any way. Can Steechánay and I have your permission now to be husband and wife?" Steechánay relayed his reply in English words, saying, "My Brother said that my first husband went away to die, so you do not need his permission to take me for a wife. I could have told you this myself, if you had asked me..."

"Still... Lectūschemă is my friend, and I would be greatly honored, if he would give his blessing to our marriage."

"He says that you are his friend as well, and he is happy that I have a husband now, and he is even more happy that my husband is you. He says that he knew you would be a good husband for me. He says, that is why he brought you here to this place when you first come here."

My actions in requesting Lectūschemă's blessing were merely a means of paying tribute to him. My sincere respect for him was made evident that day, and I think that it was a gesture which also helped Lectūschemă to have respect for me. He knew that I loved his sister, and he also knew that I would provide for her and the children and defend them vigorously with my life. Even though our words that day had required a translator, every word exchanged was rendered with the utmost respect.

Lectūschemă often came to see us at times when he was least expected, emerging from the woods as a ghostly shadow. His visits were usually short, as he returned from a hunting party or was leaving to go after buffalo. I gave him frequent gifts from the storage shed, and he would present me with a buffalo hide or two in exchange. I began to learn more of the Pawnee language as time went by, and although I was not adept at speaking this difficult tongue, I could interject a word or two now and then so that I could feel like I was having some meaningful input into our conversations... even though Steechánay did most of the talking.

The name, "*Lectūschemă*," when translated into English, meant, "Three Wolves." It was a name which he had acquired as a boy. He and his mother were attacked by five wolves while they attempted to pick berries near their childhood village. Although mauled badly, Lectūschemă had protected his mother by killing three of the wolves with his knife, and driving the other two far back into the forest. Thereafter, he has been recognized by his people as being '*Three Wolves,*' a brave and mighty warrior. His bravery during battle with his foes has received the highest of accolades from his people. Steechánay had told me before that the banner pole at the door of his lodge was decorated with many scalps of his enemies. I acknowledged him as being a great warrior, but also recognized him in earnest as being one of my best friends.

Steechánay had told me that Lectūschemă had urged her to return to his village, along with her children, when he had first learned that her husband, *William Welch* had traveled away to a far land to die. He said that, as her brother, he could watch over and provide for them at the village, but he could not do so with her living so far away. He had been persistent in his attempts to persuade her to return to the Pawnee village, yet she refused each of his generous offers. Time after time, he had visited her and the children with extra horses to carry them all back to his village, yet she remained steadfast in her resolve to remain there in the valley. When I asked her why she had chosen to remain there by herself for such a long time instead of returning to her village, she answered with words that astounded me.

"I prayed to Great Holy Father to send me man to love me, and He told me that He would. So I wait here. Then Great Holy Father send you to me. Great Holy Father never tell lie. He send me even more than I ask for… He send me you and Loweja to love, and I am happy now."

Life in the Valley of Love

We were a family of seven before, and now, with Little Bear's arrival, we were a family of eight. I spent the biggest part of the two days following the birth of Little Bear, building a suitable crib. It was an exquisite masterpiece, if I do say so myself. It was somewhat difficult to find a place where it would fit into the small house, but I managed to make a place near our bed. Recognizing that it was high time that I do something to enlarge our cabin, three weeks later, I was cutting logs for an addition that I wanted to put on the house. It was well past time to increase the size of our living space within the house. The addition would provide an ample bedroom space for Loweja, Steechánay and I, and would also provide some improvements for some of the items which were presently in the way and underfoot. The project took weeks of hard work, and was frequently interrupted when I had to give attention to planting vegetables and tending to the garden or chasing away bears or wolves. All of my family indulged more and more in English conversation. I was now hearing much less Arikara or Pawnee spoken there, with the exception of occasional soft conversations between Loweja and Steechánay. I had learned increasingly more of the Arikara language, but was still unable to have fluid conversations in that tongue. I was curious as to what Loweja and Steechánay talked about sometimes when they spoke quietly between themselves in Arikara, so I broached the subject one day.

"Steechánay, I want to ask you and Loweja both a question, and I expect an honest answer."

"Yes, John?"

"When you both speak softly in Arikara, what do you talk about?"

"We talk about many things, but most of the time, we

talk about you."

"Why do you not speak between yourselves in English, so that I can hear you, and understand what you are saying?"

Giggling, Loweja answered, "It is because if you understand what we say, we think maybe you will tickle us!"

Steechánay tried to make a rapid dash for the door, but I blocked her escape and latched the door from within. Steechánay had been desperate to escape my tickling fingers because I had learned the exact locations of her most ticklish spots... her feet and under her arms. Loweja and Steechánay tried to keep the table between us so that I could not reach them, but I leaped over the top and caught them both in my arms. With the children working in the garden, I again wrestled them both into our bed and tickled them with relentless fervor. Steechánay tried to hide her feet from me, but it did not work. As would so often be the case, our joyful antics and laughter would transform into mild passion, evolving rather soon thereafter into serious kisses and touching. Soon, the three of us would magically melt together in the grandness of our love for one another.

As the days grew warmer, I had killed two more bears and three wolves before the arrival of May. We salvaged very little of the bear meat, because of the warm weather, and in my opinion, the wolves were not edible at all. Steechánay and Loweja didn't seem to mind the taste and toughness of wolf meat as I did. I simply could not eat it unless it was prepared in a stew with vegetables. All of the animals, however, yielded fine skins which Loweja and Steechánay could use for making clothes and moccasins. Loweja and Steechánay worked together to make me a fine necklace from the large claws of the first bear which I had killed the day Little Bear was born. I wore that necklace with the greatest of pride. My hair and my beard grew longer and longer. Loweja would keep my beard trimmed with a pair of scissors which we had bought in Fort Saint Joseph, and Steechánay made a colorful beaded headband which I wore to keep the hair out of my eyes.

    Lectūschemă and several of the Pawnee braves came once a month or more for a short visit, and we would always sit and drink tea which had been sweetened with sugar. With the help of Steechánay, I had continued to learn more and more of the Pawnee language, which helped me to have unassisted conversations with visitors when they came. The Pawnee were a friendly people, despite the dreadful things I had heard about them at the trading post. I had concluded that the Pawnee were very competent in determining whether or not a person's motives were virtuous. They were mighty warriors, but only when they had to be. Sometimes there would be only three of or four of them when they visited, other times as many as ten. They were always welcomed at my home. I gave them many gifts when they came… gifts which I had purchased in Fort Saint Joseph specifically for that purpose… hatchets, knives, marbles, colorful handkerchiefs and things such as that. They were always delighted with the gifts. As they came to trust me, they shared an abundance of helpful information with me. They told me where the wapiti could be found in the summer, where there were buffalo just four days to our southwest and where there were vast growths of berries which could be collected in the fall. They told me where their summer village was located and frequently invited me to come there to visit them.

    I had used very little of the tonics, medicines, and elixirs which I had bought in Fort Saint Joseph, and had only used them to treat minor ailments of the children. However, having them close at hand provided me with comfort in knowing that if they were needed, we had them. I had brought along four bottles of whiskey for my own personal use but after months, there was still more than three full bottles left. Pawnee culture strongly forbade the consumption of strong spirits. If a Pawnee became intoxicated he could be severely punished, and under extraordinary circumstances, even put to death. If a

Pawnee man was discovered bringing spiritous drink into his village and inducing another to partake, he would surely be put to death. When a person was put to death by the Pawnee, it was almost never quick or painless. Knowing this, I never offered spirits to any of my Pawnee visitors, nor did I drink wine or liquor when the Pawnee were near my home.

With the completion of the addition on the back of the house, Loweja, Steechánay, and I now had much improved sleeping conditions, with much more privacy. We had buffalo hides about the floor and bed, and our bed was raised to a height of about thirty inches, which allowed for the storage of some small items underneath, such as extra clothes and a rifle or two. For warmth in the winter months, I built a second stone fireplace near our bed. In the other part of the house, where our bed had been before, I built a two tiered bed for the children. The boys slept on the top tier, and the girls slept on the bottom, and it was no longer necessary for anyone to sleep up in the loft, although the loft would provide a fine temporary sleeping place if we were to have a visitor or two. Some items which were about the house had been moved up into the loft, providing us with even more living space for our family below. The crib which I had made for Little Bear sat in the corner of our bedroom, near our bed, where Loweja, Steechánay, and I could keep an ear open for any kind of disturbance which might occur during the night. The children now had space aplenty where they slept and Loweja, Steechánay, and I had an even larger bed, with all of the privacy our hearts desired. I knew that there would soon come a time in which Kwīnahā would develop into a man. When that happened, he could have the loft for his own bed instead of sharing the upper tier of the children's bed with Joseph. He would soon reach an age where it would be embarrassing for him to be thought of as a child.

As time drew on, and full summer was upon us, the stock of supplies which was in the storage hut became more and more depleted. We scarcely had more than a month and a half's worth of sugar, flour, cornmeal, tea, and dried beans remaining. I knew that a trip to Fort Saint Joseph would soon be necessary, yet I dreaded the thoughts of leaving my family for a month and a half to make such a trip. In the dim light of candles, I sat at our table and began to make a list of the supplies I would need to purchase in Fort Saint Joseph. Neither Loweja nor Steechánay had ever seen me writing on a paper, and they soon gathered around me to look at the strange markings which I was making. They watched intensely, until Loweja broke the silence by asking, "What little marks do you put on paper, John? What do the marks mean?"

"I'm making a list of some things I will need to buy when I go to Fort Saint Joseph."

"You go to Fort Saint Joseph? That bad place where we went in the boat?"

"Yes... I will not leave tomorrow or the next day, but I must be leaving soon, Loweja."

"You will leave us here to be without you? Alone?"

"Loweja, I have no other choice. I need to buy supplies for us; food, and some other things which we will soon be needing, and I cannot leave our house here empty for that long. A strange family might move in here if they think that no one lives here. Besides, Little Bear is too small to travel on such a journey. Everyone must stay here and I must go by myself."

"What will we do here without you? Who will kiss us? Who will talk to us? Who will love us like you do?"

"I will be more than happy to do all of those things when I get back from Fort Saint Joseph. Just calm down and realize that it's something that I must do. If I don't go soon, we will run out of supplies. You would have no tea or sugar. We would have no seeds to plant our next crops, and our matches and candles will soon be gone."

"How many days will you be gone? Show me with your fingers, please."

"I can't do that. I do not have that many fingers, Loweja... I'm sorry."

"Show me with your fingers and your toes."

"I do not have that many fingers and toes to count the days. I am very sorry. You should remember how long the trip takes, from the time when you went there with me before."

Now, I really did have a dilemma before me. Steechánay and Loweja were both quietly beginning to weep, and attempted to console each other as if I was going away somewhere to die, just like my father had done. Loweja and I had been together every day for the past year, and had never before been separated. I felt torn between two forces. I did not want to go. I wanted to stay here with my wonderful family forever. My heart was breaking to know that my leaving would bring such inconsolable sadness to them, as well as the misery it would surely bring to me. The journey to Fort Saint Joseph would be a terribly difficult one, and I dreaded it. But what could I do? I knew that I would miss my family and worry about them the entire time that I was gone, but I could not idly stand by and watch them starve either. I struggled greatly to arrive at a solution which would provide both comfort and security to my precious family. For almost two weeks I tried to come up with a plan, yet, with the day of my departure drawing nearer, I had conceived no such plan.

On a beautiful summer morning, five of my Pawnee friends arrived at my home, including my good friend, *Lectūschemă*. Upon their arrival, a plan had suddenly come into my mind. At the corral, after I tended to our horses, I had friendly conversation with my Pawnee friends. I could not speak much of the Pawnee language, so I had Steechánay stay with me to act as an interpreter once more. Her Pawnee linguistics were flawless, and I was confident that my words were being spoken to Lectūschemă in Pawnee accurately, and exactly as I had spoken them in English. I understood a good deal of the language, but lacked the ability to say them as quickly or as precisely as Steechánay.

"Steechánay, tell them that I have to go on a great journey to bring back food and supplies, and gifts for them. Tell Lectūschemă that I need for them to do something very important for me."

"Lectūschemă say that he want to know what you want them to do for you."

"Tell Lectūschemă that I would like for one or two of his braves to watch over my family here while I am gone, and see that they are not harmed in any way. If they will do that, I will bring them whatever they ask for when I return."

"Lectūschemă ask how long you will be gone, John."

"Tell him forty-five days, please Steechánay."

"I do not know how to say that many days. Can you make marks on ground for how many days you will be gone?"

"Yes... This many days, right here." I had made forty-five distinct marks in the soil at the edge of the corral fence.

"Lectūschemă want to know what you will give them in return."

"Steechánay, please do not make tears while we talk. It will only confuse your brother. Ask them what they want me to give them." After much discussion between themselves, they answered Steechánay.

"They want two horses and two long rifles."

"Tell Lectūschemă that I will give them four horses and four long rifles if they will do this thing for me."

"Lectūschemă say he will send two of their warriors with their wives to stay here until you come back."

"Tell him that their people can camp under the big lean-to over there, and I will leave them two rifles to have with them while I am gone."

"Lectūschemă say, when will you leave?"

"Tell him that I will leave two days from now."

"Lectūschemă say he will watch over us until you return."

"Tell him that I thank him from my heart."

Shortly, Lectūschemă and his companions rode off to make the necessary preparations in their village, and Steechánay ran up to the house, undoubtedly to confide in Loweja and explain the details of my impending departure. My mind was greatly relieved in knowing that my family would be under the watchful protection of the Pawnee. I still had to convince Steechánay and Loweja that the trip was absolutely necessary, and console them as best I could, but I still felt as though they were making a mountain out of a mole hill, and it served no useful purpose for them to become so emotional over something which was necessary for our survival.

As I worked about the storage shed to gather some items for my journey, I saw Steechánay lead Loweja by the hand and take her to the corral. I peeked around the corner, curious as to why they had gone to the corral. There, Steechánay pointed to the ground where I had made the forty-five marks representing the number of days I would be gone. Loweja looked at all of the marks and then ran to the house in tears, with Steechánay right behind her. It was heartbreaking, yet there was nothing I could do to console them. By the time I had finished a few chores and walked up to the house, Steechánay and Loweja were both teary-eyed and despondent when I walked through the doorway.

"You leave us in two days?"

"Yes, Loweja. I must go. We will need food soon. Please understand."

"I will eat bark from trees or dirt from the ground if you will stay here with us. I will eat leaves from trees……. I will eat *merde* from our horses if you will stay with Steechánay and me."

"Loweja, please don't do this. You are both breaking my heart. You and Steechánay come here for a moment, both of you. Look at me… I don't want to leave you. This is my home now, and you are all my family. I want to stay right here with you and our children. I love you all more than anything on this earth. But I am responsible for you. I am the one who is supposed to watch over you and make sure that you will have food to eat. I will be back here soon. In forty five days I will come here with the food and supplies that we need for the next year, and we will be together again… all of us. alright?"

Steechánay spoke to Loweja in Arikara for several minutes, and although I could not fully understand everything she was saying, I could understand enough to know that she was providing reassurance to Loweja. She told Loweja that her husband, William Welch had made many such journeys to get supplies, and that he always came back, just as he had promised, with plenty of food and supplies for another year. Loweja and Steechánay both dreaded my departure, but none dreaded it more than I. I remembered Captain McBride telling me that when Father came to Fort Saint Joseph for supplies he was always in a great hurry to return to his home, as if he had urgent business of some sort to attend to. I felt the same sense of urgency as my father had felt, and for the same reasons. The merriment in our household was subdued somewhat for the next two days. Twice, I discovered Loweja and Steechánay embraced and weeping when I entered the house. Upon seeing me, they would dry their tears and go about their work. It seemed that there was little I could do to console them. I could not even arouse their laughter by tickling them. They were quite adamant about the fact that they did not want to be tickled. Our joyful, happy home seemed to have taken on the same festive atmosphere as a mortuary, but there was little that I could do to change things. In Baltimore, I could have taken one of my coaches to purchase food and supplies and returned home within two hours. Here, things were different… much different.

As I had been promised by Lectūschemă, two Pawnee Indians and their wives, along with three small children, arrived at my home on the morning of my departure. The children were about the same ages as Kwesha and Pokeem, and would provide good playmates for each other during my absence. The Pawnee began setting up their camp and making themselves at home under the large lean-to. I provided them with two rifles and ammunition and started to provide them with some basic instructions of how to use the rifles, but they were already well-schooled on the use of firearms and knew exactly how to handle them. I could only suppose that they had learned their firearm skills from the two rifles which I had given Lectūschemă earlier. Loweja and Steechánay helped me pack a few provisions on a pack horse, and although occasional tears flowed from all three of us, we all knew that we were merely doing what must be done. Shortly before meridian hour I was ready to depart. The three of us embraced, and I climbed into my saddle. I sat there momentarily, looking down on my adoring family and asked, "Is there anything that you want me to bring you when I return?"

Steechánay was the first to speak, when she answered, "Yes! Bring sugar, please... I love you, John!"

"Loweja, do you want me to bring you anything?"

"Yes, please! Bring me John Welch! For he is the only man I will ever love! I die without him!"

"My Lord have mercy... I love you both... always know that in your hearts."

I rode away rather quickly, leading the pack horse behind me, until the house and my precious valley and family were all out of sight. The image of Steechánay and Loweja and all of our children crying as I left would be embedded in my memory for as long as my journey would take. Their farewell had seemed more like a mournful funeral service than the temporary *'goodbye'* that it really was. It was as if they had expected never to see me again. It was an awful, heartbreaking event for all of us, and I was left with images with I would carry in my heart for the duration of my journey.

I wasted no time while I was on the trail. I never

stopped to camp until it became almost too dark to see and I was always back on the trail at first morning light. I cooked only when I had to provide myself with ample sustenance to stay strong enough to complete my journey. I met with no travelers along the trail, and most likely would not have taken the time to converse with any if I had. I counted the days... one-by-one, as I drew closer to the Missouri River trading post. I could not seem to erase the image of my family's tearful goodbye as I had left. I would make it a point when I saw Captain McBride again, to see if anything could be done in the future in order to prevent my having to leave my wonderful family again.

Twice, I encountered heavy rains along the way, but I did not stop to seek shelter. My horse slipped in the mud on a steep slope and we fell together beside the trail with her ending up on top of me. Thankfully, neither the horse nor I were hurt, and I relentlessly pushed on toward the trading post. I remembered the long days of travel which it had taken for me to make my first and second journey to my valley, and I dreaded the difficult work which lay ahead of me on this journey. I had never missed anything in my life as much as I now missed my family. I thought many times about Loweja and Steechánay lying in our bed with my customary position between them now being vacant and void. I wondered if they were coming to terms with my absence, and if their tears had subsided. I often talked aloud to myself, first asking myself a question, and then rendering an answer. I even practiced speaking Pawnee, as a means of diverting my attention toward worthwhile things, instead of dwelling on unpleasant thoughts.

It was an enormous relief when I finally arrived at the trading post. I went immediately to the Arikara village to find my old friend, Hidessa, once again seeking his advice and assistance. He was at his lodge, sitting with his three wives as they prepared a meal. His youngest wife was pleasingly pudgy, and still appeared to be only thirteen or fourteen years old, and yet I did not look down upon Hidessa as an evil and perverted person. I had learned that condescending thoughts had no place in my heart when I thought of my friends. As he had told me before, his older wives did not speak much, but his younger wife would make up for it with her constant jibber-jabber. The young wife had an irritatingly loud and shrill voice, and I remembered Hidessa telling me that he wanted a wife who would talk to him more than his other two wives. Hidessa's greeting was warm and friendly.

"I did not recognize you at first, my friend, you have changed the way you look! You look more like Arikara now... except for the hair that is on your face."

"*Chin-contè-sa,* Hidessa! It's good to see you, my friend!"

"It is good to see you, too, John! *Chin-contè-sa!*"

"Are you enjoying life with your new wife?"

"My two old wives don't talk to me enough, and the young wife never stops talking. I believe I like the old wives better. Do you want to take my young wife with you? If you do, you may have her."

"No thank you, Hidessa! I have no need for another wife, my friend!"

"How long will you be staying here this time, John?"

"I must leave immediately for Fort Saint Joseph."

"Where is Loweja?"

"She is at my home in the mountains, with my other wife, *Steechánay.*"

"You have two wives now?"

"Yes, Hidessa, and five children... and I love them all very much. We have a good life there in the mountains."

"That is good, my friend! I am happy for you! I told you that Loweja would make a good wife for you!"

"I remember when you told me that, Hidessa. You were right, my friend, she has made me a wonderful wife, and Steechánay is an equally wonderful wife."

"Is there anything I can help you do?"

"Yes, Hidessa. I will be back from Fort Saint Joseph in about twenty or twenty-one days. When I come back, I will have many goods with me, and I will need much help getting my many packs back to my home. Do you think that you could arrange to hire eight or ten men to help me when I get back?"

"The two young men that helped you and Loweja last fall came back to the village here and bought wives with the money you paid them. I think that maybe every young man in village wants to help you now!"

"Then pick six of the strongest and most trustworthy, and have them prepared to meet me when I return. Here, I want you to take this money and buy twelve good horses for me while I am gone. When I get back, I will have my goods loaded on the horses and go back to my home as soon as possible. Can you do that for me?"

"Yes, John. I will be happy to do that."

Hidessa also agreed to watch my two horses and keep my saddle with him while I was gone. Traveling very light, I purchased a small canoe at the trading post and was soon on my way down river... and on that very same day. All the way to Fort Saint Joseph I tried to conceive a plan for the future which would enable me to obtain the merchandise which I would need in future years, without the burden of leaving my precious family behind. Each mile that I traveled, and each minute that I was away from them, anguished me greatly. However, I knew that with each mile that I traveled reduced the total miles which I would have to travel, yet it also meant that with each mile I was farther and farther away from my precious family. There was scarcely a minute that they were not on my mind. I would frequently pray to God for their safety and well-being.

I was fired upon one morning from the northern shore, but I never saw my assailant. His shot tore a hole in the stern of the canoe and passed through. The hole was well above water line, however, and did not cause the canoe to leak. I paddled quickly to get away from the location where the incident had happened, and soon felt as though the threat had passed. I kept a watchful eye toward the banks of the river, but saw no one, and there were no further incidents of hostility on my trip. Still, I could not help but wonder why someone would have taken a shot at me. The incident puzzled me for a while, but I soon released it from my mind and concentrated on closing the distance between me and Fort Saint Joseph.

I was relentless in my traveling, desiring to lessen the duration of the trip by paddling and traveling during all of the daylight hours, stopping only for brief rests during the darkness of night when I could no longer see to travel safely. With the few belongings which I had carried along with me, and with me as the only passenger, my small canoe skimmed quickly across the surface of the water. I had never seen a canoe move as swiftly. I was certain now that I could expect to cut three and maybe as much as four days off of the total duration of my trip. I came to the confluence of the Missouri River and the Agatha River late one night under a three quarter moon and did not stop to camp that night. The next night, when I did camp, I collapsed in an exhausted heap and slept till mid-morning the following day. Mile after mile, and day after day I pushed on, finally seeing the familiar sights that told me I had almost reached Fort Saint Joseph. As I drew nearer, I slowed my pace somewhat and continued at a more relaxed speed. I had made remarkably good time, and I imagined that there had never been as many miles traveled as quickly by a river traveler before – although I had nothing to base this conclusion on but my pride.

There were many pirogues, keelboats, and canoes on the river as I neared Fort Saint Joseph, and the industrious activity at the dock contributed greatly to the chaos and confusion. I did, however, find a relatively quiet corner of the dock where I was able to unload my few belongings and drag my canoe to a safe and secure location.

I was in Fort Saint Joseph, going about my business on

the first morning after my arrival, when I encountered Captain McBride, aboard his boat, *Puritan Enterprise*, returning to his waterfront docking pier. He had dry-docked my river vessel for me and had seen to its maintenance regularly while I had been in the mountains. He did not recognize me when we first met because of the length of my hair and beard, but once he did recognize me it was a joyous reunification. Before leaving the riverfront, Captain McBride and I enlisted workmen to return my pirogue to the water from dry-dock. As usual, the good Captain was of great assistance in helping me obtain and pack the goods and supplies which I wanted to obtain and take back with me. I bought such a variety of items, and so many of them, that I knew my pirogue would be heavily laden for the trip upriver. I purchased an extensive list of supplies. Among the items which I purchased, was a cast iron stove for cooking. Captain McBride and I disassembled the stove so that it could be transported by pack horse once I was back at the trading post. I bought rifles, window glass, powder and percussion caps, two oil lamps and five gallons of oil for the lamps. I bought a wedding ring for Steechánay which closely matched the ones which Loweja and I wore, and felt confident that Steechánay would appreciate such a gesture.

In addition to the other supplies, I bought our usual food items, including twenty pounds of tea and two hundred pounds of sugar. Among my purchases, were scrubbing brushes, a box of Havana smoking cigars, colorful ribbons and buttons. I bought ornate necklaces for Loweja and Steechánay and purchased 6 bolts of brightly-colored material with lots of needles, buttons, and colorful threads. I also bought hand mirrors, perfume, scissors, brushes for their teeth, and several cans of tooth powder. I bought supplies continuously, until Captain McBride told me that it would be dangerous to add the weight of more goods to the pirogue.

I still had more than six thousand dollars in paper currency, and another three thousand in gold coin, so it was not necessary for me to make a withdrawal from the bank on this trip. Captain McBride advised me that I would need six polemen and a pilot for this trip due to the extra weight we had aboard, and he once again helped me hire a capable crew. The pilot and two of the polemen were among the same ones who had worked for me the previous fall. They were all well-seasoned and able bodied men. Captain McBride and I dined together on the eve of my departure, and with all the chaos and confusion during the loading of the pirogue, dinner was the first opportunity in which we were able to speak to each other in a relaxed setting.

"John, may I tell you something?"

"Certainly, Captain, what is it?"

"You seem to have acquired great happiness and contentment, my son. I can see it when I look into your eyes. Before, you had the look of an ambitious and restless man, perhaps even showing signs of boredom at times. Now, I can see the look of a man who has achieved great satisfaction... great success in life... and great peace of mind."

"You are very perceptive, Captain. I, sir, have acquired happiness on a scale which I had never imagined humanly possible."

"Is Loweja happy, now that she has returned to the mountains?"

"Yes, Loweja is very happy now. So is *Steechánay*, and so are our five children."

"Five children!? How did you manage to do that so quickly, John? And who is *Steechánay*, if I might ask?"

"*Steechánay* is my other wife, Captain. She already had four children when we were married. Loweja and I had our first child about three months ago. A beautiful, healthy baby boy!"

"I extend my heartfelt congratulations to you, my son, both for the birth of your child and also for your marriage to Steechánay! I would truly like to meet your family someday."

"You do not look down upon me as a deviant or a

pervert because I have two wives now?"

"The number of wives that you have is of no consequence to me, John. As long as you are happy I wouldn't care if you had twenty wives. I envy you for the happiness which you have acquired. I am well acquainted with your fine character, John, and I know that whatever you have acquired, you have done so in a noble and honorable manner. It does my heart good to know that you are so happy. You have almost the same look upon your face that I used to see in upon your father's face."

"Almost?"

"Your father had found happiness somewhere, yet he was tormented by his separation from you and your mother. In your eyes, I see no such torment. I only see a great desire to get back to your wonderful family as quickly as possible. Am I right? And I would wager money that they truly are a wonderful family!"

"You are right, sir. You are right on both counts."

"Tell me, John, is there anything in the world that I can do for you? Anything at all?"

"I only wish that you could help me devise a plan whereby I could have my yearly goods and supplies delivered to me without it ever being necessary for me to leave the valley where I live. Forty-five or fifty days away from my family is more than maddening to me. I ache for them every single minute that I'm away. As my wonderful wives would say… *my heart makes tears to be with them*."

"Allow me to think for a moment, please."

"Thank you, sir." (*Long pause followed*)

After much thought, Captain McBride looked at me and asked, "Tell me something, John… Do you have a map which adequately describes how to get to this valley of yours?"

"Yes, I do, why?"

"Splendid! Suppose I were to send a rider to your valley, say… each spring… perhaps in March or April. And suppose you presented that rider with a manifest of the materials and supplies that you needed for the next eight or ten months... And suppose a crew of men with pack animals showed up in your valley each May or June, bearing all the items which you had requested. It would never again be necessary for you to leave your valley, or your family... How would something such as that work for you?"

"Captain McBride, sir, that would be a true blessing! Could you arrange for such a thing?"

"I could, John. It would take money, of course, perhaps as much as four or five hundred dollars for each delivery, depending on the expense of the goods you would order."

"If I leave you with three thousand dollars, could you make arrangements such as that for the next five years?"

"That would probably be enough to pay for the next six or seven years, I would think."

"Good! Then I will leave you with four thousand dollars for the next six years, and you keep any money that's not spent."

"I think you would be over-paying me for my time."

"That's the way that I would like it to be, Captain."

"Then you leave everything to me. Rest your mind. And go safely and quickly back to your family. God be with you, John!"

Home Again

I was but a day's journey away from the valley of my happiness. I had a team of twelve pack horses heavily loaded with supplies and gifts, with six Arikara Indian helpers. I was once again returning to my valley, and was about to burst from the excitement of knowing that I would soon be seeing my family again. I prayed repeatedly that I would find my family safe and sound. Little Bear would soon be five months old and I yearned to hold him in my arms again. I longed for the kisses of Loweja and Steechánay, and I longed to see the bright faces of the children as they looked upon the gifts which I had brought back to the valley for them. I was going home, and would soon be there. My journey had brought great exhaustion to my body. In my haste to return to my family I had pushed my body beyond its limits, and I felt as though it might be several days before I fully recovered. I had experienced frequent headaches and occasional dizziness, but was determined to push myself onward to see my family as soon as possible.

In Fort Saint Joseph, I had rushed to complete my purchases... so much that I scarcely took time to rest. Instead of the forty-five days which I had estimated the trip to take, I would be arriving home three days sooner than I had anticipated. Perhaps my early arrival would come as a delightful surprise to everyone, and I hoped that it would. As he had promised, Hidessa had made all of the arrangements which I had requested, saving me much time and confusion in the Arikara Village and trading outpost. Travel on the river had been much faster with the six polemen, and with a pleasant southerly wind, we were able to deploy the sail, which helped the polemen tremendously. There were but few interruptions or aggravations during the trip. Seven times we had to deploy the crew on land to cordon the pirogue in order to keep us from running aground on sandbars, and twice more in order to negotiate small waterfalls, yet even with those time-consuming inconveniences, we had made remarkably good time on our voyage. I was extremely pleased with how quickly I would be returning home, and even more pleased that Captain McBride had devised a plan which would enable me to procure future supplies without having to leave my precious family for extended periods of time. On the trail, I instructed the men in the pack train to follow my tracks as I turned to head northwest. I wanted to arrive at my home well ahead of the crew so that I could have some time to spend with my family in private celebration before their arrival. If I hastened, I could arrive at my home at least ten or fifteen minutes ahead of the pack train, allowing me to receive generous hugs and warm kisses from my family in private.

  I was riding my horse through a magnificent stand of large fir trees when my valley and my house first came into view. On the hillside, I dismounted and stood there for a short while looking down into the valley. This was the valley of my dreams. This was the home of the people I loved. Smoke rose from the chimney of the house. I saw two children of the Pawnee guardians at the lean-to with their mothers nearby. I saw Kwīnahā and Joseph carrying firewood toward the house and Kwesha walking from the hen house, carrying a basket. Kwīnahā must have been the first to see me, as he dropped an armload of wood on the ground and rushed inside the house. Soon, my entire family and all three of the dogs were running across the meadow to greet me. I dismounted, and led my horse by the reins as I walked slowly toward them, savoring the sight of seeing them running to greet me. Then I, too, ran quickly to meet them. Loweja was carrying Little Bear in her arms and sobbing terribly. Steechánay ran alongside of Loweja, as if she did not want to greet me ahead of Loweja, but at the same time. They were always very thoughtful to each other's feelings that way. We all met in a flurry of sobbing and emotion and walked slowly back to the house, sharing kisses and smiles along the way. Kwīnahā took my horse to the corral and I carried Little Bear in my arms as Loweja and Steechánay clung tightly to me. Our kisses were wild and furious. It was a wonderfully joyous time for all of us! My family did not want to take their hands or their eyes off of me, and I was absolutely absorbed by such adoring attention! Kwesha had jumped onto my back, and little Pokeem wrapped herself around my leg. Even our dogs were glad to see me! We were all so happy to see each other again! Sitting down at the table in the house, I looked around me, basking in the loving eyes and smiles of my family as I held Little Bear in my arms and admired how much he seemed to have grown in during the forty two days I had been gone... I spoke softly, and forced myself to look seriously melancholy... even despondent. It was high time for me to have a little fun with my wonderfully mischievous and impish wives. Sadly and mournfully, I spoke to them.

"I was not able to get any supplies or food for us. I am very sorry."

"You are home, and you are safe! That is all that is important to us!" Loweja said, while taking Little Bear from my arms and laying him on the children's bed.

"Yes, John! You are here with us now. We love you! That is all that matters to us! We will find food here in mountains and we can eat fish and otters from the creek. *Slõuyzinal-te-onya*," Steechánay added... then said, "Kwesha, get some water and some bread for your father."

"But what will we do here without sugar? Without tea? How can my wonderful wives live without these things?" I asked, as I buried my face in my hands... peeking out through my fingers while I pretended to weep.

"We will be alright here, as long as we have each other and you are here with us. Please do not make tears about this, John. Loweja and me are too happy to see you, and this does not make us happy."

"Maybe I should leave again, and try to find sugar and tea somewhere else. Maybe I can find sugar and tea in Baltimore?"

"**No! Loweja and I do not want you to go again!** We don't want any tea and sugar! We don't love tea and sugar! We just love you! *Des-inga-stooy-cam-ēkă*!"

"Steechánay say right thing, John! We want you here with us! Our hearts are tired and hurt inside! We don't want tea and sugar... we just want you! Tea and sugar are bad! *Des-inga-stooy-cam-ēkă*! I will find rabbits for us to eat!"

"Why are my wonderful wives yelling at me like this and speaking in tongues that I do not understand?"

"It is because we do not want you to go again! We love you! You are our husband and we want you to stay here with us! We do not have husband when you go away!" Then, Kwīnahā excitedly shouted, "Father! Someone's coming! There are many horses coming! With many men! Do you want your rifle?"

"Do not be concerned, Kwīnahā, it's just my men bringing the tea and sugar, and some other things. I'll go out and tell them that Loweja and Steechánay say that they only want a husband. They don't want any tea or sugar anymore. They can take it back with them! Tea and sugar are bad!"

Suddenly, I was attacked by both Steechánay and Loweja. They knocked me from my feet and onto the floor, wrestling and punching me, tickling me wildly, laughing loudly all the while! They seemed to appreciate the humor in my little joke... as if it had brought much happiness into their lives after forty two days of worry and doldrums in my absence. Even the children joined in to wrestle with me on the floor, laughing loudly. I was surprised by Kwīnahā's amazing strength as he held my hands down while Loweja and Steechánay tickled me! I was showered by kisses and overwhelmed by joy! There has never been such a homecoming! There has never been such a reunion! And... there has never been such love in any house! Anywhere! The two Pawnee men who had been guarding my family came up to the house to welcome me home and tell me that there were riders approaching. They stood in the doorway, puzzled by my family's raucous antics on the floor. I looked up, and with Steechánay translating, I told them not to be alarmed, that the approaching men were my crew, and we would soon be unpacking my goods and I would honor my promise of gifts to reward them for the protection they had provided for my family.

It took most of the remainder of the day to unpack the horses and properly store our supplies and provisions. The heavy pieces of the cook stove were unloaded from the back of a packhorse at the front of the house, where it could be reassembled. Loweja and Steechánay stored the bolts of material in the loft after admiring their beauty, and together, they prepared about ten pounds of tea leaves to be stored in our kitchen storage baskets. The box containing the five rifles was unpacked, and I gave four of the weapons to our Pawnee friends and took the other one into the house. I also gave the Pawnee two kegs of powder and several pounds of lead for bullets. Most all of the other items were stored in the storage hut and the oil lamps were carried up to the house by Loweja to be placed on our kitchen table. She was excited when she first saw them because she had remembered the wonderfully bright light which they could bring into a room, recalling the ones which had been in our hotel room in Fort Saint Joseph. When the horses were finally all unloaded, I picked out four of them and gave them to the Pawnee to be carried back to their village. I gave three horses to my Arikara helpers which they could ride, two on each horse, back to their village. As promised, I gave each of them a twenty dollar gold piece and they left quickly... anxious to return to their village with their new-found wealth. I had five horses remaining which were turned into the corral with our other horses. The Pawnee guardians of my family preferred to wait until the following morning to return to their village, and remained camped in our valley one last night under the lean-to. Loweja and Steechánay prepared a meal at the end of the day while Kwīnahā and I struggled to reassemble the new cook stove.

After my long absence, we ate dinner as a family once again, this time under the light of our new oil lamps, as we drank our tea and sugar. It was a cheery occasion. The family was enthralled over the brightness of the light which emitted from our lanterns. They had never seen the inside of our home illuminated to such a degree at night. Every time I would mention the little joke I had played on them, either Steechánay or Loweja would give me a firm punch on the shoulder and then a warm kiss on the cheek. Loweja walked outside to get a fresh pail of water, and I took the opportunity to follow her to speak in private. I reached into my pocket and produced the wedding ring which I had bought for Steechánay.

"Loweja, look at what I bought for Steechánay while I was at Fort St. Joseph."

"John! It is just like the ones that you and me wear!"

"Do you think Steechánay will like it?"

"She will like it very much! You are good husband for us! You make love to us tonight, John?"

"Yes! You bet I will! We will make great love tonight!"

"When will you give ring to Steechánay? *Ni-teela-sumit-et Steechánay?*"

"Tonight, before we make love, if that is alright with you."

"Yes! Steechánay be very happy! You will see!"

That evening, after the children had climbed into their beds, Loweja, Steechánay, and I carried one of the oil lamps into our room and closed the door behind us. Loweja sat at the edge of the bed and nursed Little Bear until he had swallowed his fill. She placed him in his little crib and went to Steechánay and they kissed. They unbraided each other's hair and undressed. I walked to them and helped brush their hair. Brushing their long, dark hair brought me such great delight because I knew that it pleasured them so much. In the light of the new oil lamp, I spoke softly to Steechánay.

"Steechánay, my wife, there's something that Loweja and I would like to talk to you about."

"What is it, John?"

"Before I left to go to Fort Saint Joseph, I saw you and Loweja holding hands one night."

"We hold each other's hand many nights. Many times while you are gone to Fort Saint Joseph we hold hands."

"When you hold hands with Loweja, do you ever look at the ring that she wears?"

"Yes, John. Why do you ask this?"

"This is from both of us, Loweja and me." I held the ring in the palm of my hand for her to see. She just stood there and looked at it for a moment or two and a broad smile crossed her face.

"Do you like it? It's a symbol of the love that we all have for each other... you and me, and Loweja."

"You make me very happy, John. No one has ever made me this happy with love like you and Loweja, not even William Welch. Loweja and me lay in our bed at night while you were gone and our hearts hurt to be with you. We say John will be home soon. We could not live without you, John! We worry much in our bed until you come back. Now you are back. Our hearts are only happy now."

"Do you like the ring, Steechánay?"

"Yes, John."

"Let me put it on you. I hope it fits... Yes! It does fit. When you look at it, just know that Loweja and I love you with all of our heart."

"I will never take it off! I will wear it until I die! I think I loved William Welch very much. We had love, maybe, but we did not have happiness in this house like the happiness that is here now. Your father and me never kiss each other. We did not laugh. We did not tickle each other. We just lived here. I think I did love your father. But no woman on earth has ever felt a better love than I feel now with you and Loweja."

Loweja came over and the three of us embraced and exchanged wonderfully undisciplined kisses with each other. Instead of blowing out the lantern, I left it softly aglow so that we could see the wonderful pleasures that we shared... pleasures which we had been denied for forty-two days and nights. In the aftermath of our bliss, I extinguished the lamp and the three of us fell fast asleep in our traditional warm and loving embrace.

Near noon hour the next day, Kwīnahā and I were still struggling to assemble the cook stove. In Fort Saint Joseph, it had not taken Captain McBride and me very long to disassemble the stove, but reassembling the stove proved to be much more difficult than I had anticipated. The tools which I had bought in Fort Saint Joseph were adequate enough, but the parts seemed to puzzle us as to where they should be attached. Little by little we continued with the project until we were left with one strange-looking part that didn't seem to fit anywhere. With the part in my hand, I moved it all around the stove, looking to see where it might attach, or what purpose it might serve, but could not seem to solve the puzzle. Steechánay walked past us to empty a pail of water and paused long enough to offer some casual advice.

"*Saw-èlta-esk-õso-deem*"
"What? Please don't speak in Arikara. I don't understand you."
"I'm sorry. That was not Arikara, John, it was Pawnee. I don't know how to say this in English."
"Say what in English?" Slightly frustrated, she sat her pail of water down and took the part out of my hand. She

turned it upside down and held it precisely where it was supposed to go. I should have been able to figure it out without Steechánay's help, but didn't. This was embarrassing for me, as I had seen hundreds of stoves in my lifetime, and this was perhaps the first and only stove which Steechánay had ever seen.

"I had it upside down, didn't I, Steechánay?"

"That is what I tried to tell you in Pawnee, John. I didn't know how to say it in English."

"Thank you, Steechánay! Thank you very much!"

"You are welcome, John."

"You are not laughing at me, are you, Steechánay?"

"No, John... well... maybe just a little, but not much."

"You won't mention this to Loweja, will you?"

"Mmmm... Maybe if you be good husband I will not say anything to her. We will see if you can be good husband."

Clearly humiliated, I was glad that the stove was finally assembled. Kwīnahā and I painstakingly moved the heavy stove inside where I installed pipes for the smoke to escape and connected them to the existing chimney. Finally, our project was completed. The stove was a welcome luxury by all of us. Having an oven, it would allow for the baking of bread and cornmeal instead of frying. Frying our bread toughened it, and sometimes rendered it hard to chew. Baking bread, rendered the bread soft and chewable. This new way of fixing bread and cornmeal was a delight to everyone. In the oven of the stove, our bread remained thicker when it was done as well. I unpacked the few pots and pans that I had bought. I arose quickly from the floor once, and suddenly felt strangely ill and weakened, and had to sit back down for a while, but I said nothing to anyone. I knew that I was very exhausted from my journey to get supplies, and hoped that I would feel better as I rested each night.

Loweja and Steechánay were thrilled with our new stove, and prepared our evening meal on it. In fact, the family was thrilled with all of the purchases which I had made on my journey. Each day, I unpacked more and more of the items which I had bought. It was like having Christmas morning each day that I unpacked our goods. I gave Loweja and Steechánay gifts of ornate silver necklaces and they were so delighted that they did not want to take them off, even at night. I had to issue a mandate of sorts on the second night, that they not wear them to bed.

"Yes, John, we will not wear them in bed again. We only wear them in bed because we think you want us to. We will not do that again. We are glad to take them off!"

After dark the second night I was home, I went to the corral to put some hay down for the new horses, and when I returned, I found Steechánay and Loweja seated at our kitchen table. Each of them were holding a hand mirror which I had bought for them and they were studying themselves in the light of our new lantern. I poured a cup of tea and sat down at the table while they continued to study over themselves. I took a sip of tea as Steechánay asked the first question, "John?"

"Yes, Steechánay?"

"Do you really think Loweja and me are pretty?"

"Of course I do! Why would you ask such a silly question?"

"I think that Loweja is pretty, and she thinks that I am pretty, but when we look into the glass at our faces, I don't think I am very pretty and Loweja thinks she is not very pretty. Do the mirrors lie?"

"Ha! Ha! Ha! Yes! Mirrors can lie terribly! Mirrors have been lying to people for a thousand years!"

Then, Loweja spoke up to ask, "If the mirrors tell lie to us, how will Steechánay and me know if we are pretty?"

"That's very easy. I will tell you, and I don't lie. Alright? Now put the mirrors away. I want to tell you both something very important. Next year in the spring I will not be going to Fort Saint Joseph."

"That is good, John. We are glad."

"A man will come in the spring and I will tell him everything we need. He will then go to Fort Saint Joseph for me and he will buy all the things we need. Men will bring them back to us on horses in the late spring, just like I did. I will not have to leave you alone. I will not have to go away like I did, ever again. Alright?"

"You have made us very happy, John! Now Steechánay and I will make you very happy, *yes*? We have something for you, John!"

"Something for me? What is it?"

"We make you shirt and britches for you, see?"

I was in a state of amazement as I looked at the beautiful shirt and britches that they had created during my absence. They were made of soft buckskin, with beautifully crafted beadwork around the pockets. They were very similar in appearance to the buckskin dresses which Loweja and Steechánay regularly wore. I was delighted, and my wives were very pleased to see that I liked their handiwork and gifts. They must surely have worked diligently on them while I was away. I told them that I would set them aside and not wear them until I had an opportunity to properly bathe in the creek. That night, after the children went to bed, Steechánay boiled a pot of tea and the three of us sat at the table to talk. Evenings like this afforded me the wonderful opportunity to speak to my wives earnestly and privately. I still felt dizzy and terribly weak, but said nothing to them about the way I was feeling. Instead, we had casual, relaxing conversation while they worked together sewing some garments for the children.

"Loweja?"

"Yes, John?"

"Do you remember that day right after we first left the trading post coming up here for the first time? You couldn't speak a word of English, and I couldn't speak Arikara. Do you remember those days well?"

"Yes, John. Those were days before you hold my hand even."

"Do you remember your dress getting caught on the saddle ropes one day when you got off of your horse and your dress came way up high?"

"I remember, but you did not see me when this happen! Did you see me?!"

"Oh, yes I did! I saw plenty that day!"

"Why you not tell me you see me? I did not want for you to see me then! *Shy-etná-umē!*"

"Do you remember that day on the trail when we were north of here and you were fishing in the creek?"

"I fish in many creeks, John. Which creek do you talk about?"

"I'm speaking of the special creek that we were at on that day when I first told you that I loved you. Do you remember that creek?"

"Yes, John. I remember that creek good. That was day that you save me from big bear and you only had knife to fight with. Big *masqua!*"

"That's right. That was also the first day that I ever saw you naked. I'll never forget that... Do you remember that?"

"Yes, John, I remember good. I was fishing in creek naked and you were in bushes sitting on rock watching me for long, long time."

"**What?** You knew that I was sitting there watching you? You knew that I was there in the bushes looking at you the whole time?"

"Yes, John. I wait for you to come long time that day so you can see me. You sit there long time watching me that day. *Masqua* watch me too, and come out of bushes to eat me, but you scare him off."

"Why did you keep on fishing if you knew that I was sitting there watching you naked all that time?"

"I want you to see me naked so maybe you will start to

love me. You not like me much until you see me naked. Then you say you love me after that. I wait for you to come to me in water but big *masqua* came first. When I saw you raise rifle I turn around and see big *masqua*."

"**Why you sly fox you!** You trapped me! You trapped me with your beautiful naked body!"

"Maybe so. But we were together for many days and you would not be husband with me or kiss me or even touch me, you only hold my hand and my hair and I was your wife then. I thought you did not like me much and I already love you much, so I did that thing to make you like me and be husband with me... and you did. I wait for you in creek that day in cold water for very long time and then I see you walk down path and sit on rock to look at me. I make you think I not see you."

"Steechánay... what do you think about all of this? What do you think about this sly fox here that I married?"

"I think maybe Loweja is much smarter than John Welch! Maybe I should have gone fishing naked, too, and let you watch me for long time! That way my heart would not have hurt for so many days in the loft with the children. I think maybe Loweja is even much smarter than me *and* you!"

Steechánay and Loweja started laughing wildly and I laughed along with them as I wrestled both of them to the bed and smothered them with kisses... tickling them repeatedly, which added greatly to our laughter. Loweja had surprised me tremendously when I learned of the cunningness which she had employed to seduce me that day at the creek, without me even knowing that I had been cleverly seduced. I had thought that I had been the initiator of our passion that day when it was really she who had lured me to her. I had walked blindly, right into her trap! I had no idea that she knew I was watching her from the bushes all of that time. She was right, however, I had been stubbornly slow in recognizing and coming to terms with my love for her. At the time, I was fearful of getting deeply involved with any such romance during our first days on the trail, thinking that she was merely a child, and I was now very thankful that she had ensnared me with her beauty the way that she had. I needed coaxing, I suppose, and Loweja knew precisely how to go about doing it. Her tactics proved to be the very catalyst which broke my foolish resolve. I would have eventually succumbed to her charm anyway, for I don't think there are many men anywhere who could have resisted her charm for as long as I did. But if I had the opportunity to live those days over again, I would have gladly succumbed to her on the very first day. Considering how happy I was now, and how much I had learned about each of them, I think that perhaps Loweja and Steechánay were both smarter than me. Much smarter!

That night, in the darkness of our bed, I turned to Loweja and asked her, "Loweja?"

"Yes, John?"

"Do you ever feel angry that your father sold you to me the way he did?"

"He do that thing to find me good husband. He find me best husband on the earth. I am not angry, I am happy, and I am glad that he did that thing."

"Steechánay, what does your name mean in Pawnee?"

"It means, *girl who swims in deep water.*"

"Loweja?"

"Yes, John?"

"I've never asked you before, but what does the name, Loweja, mean in Arikara?"

"It means, *bird with a broken wing.*"

Upon hearing Loweja's explanation of her name, Steechánay immediately protested, saying, "That is not truth, John! Loweja tell big lie! I know what name of Loweja really means, John!"

Curious, I asked, "What do you think it means, Steechánay?"

"It means, *smart woman who fishes naked and tricks*

stupid man so that he will marry her!"

Then the laughter between them erupted again. I laughed along with them, but I was entirely too tired to tickle them into another wrestling match. Eventually, the laughter disappeared and we all fell asleep. I could not see in the darkness, but I know in my heart that we must have all had smiles on our faces as we slept.

The next morning, on the third day after I had returned from Fort Saint Joseph, Kwīnahā and I were packing mud around the rocks in our fireplace and chimney. Kwīnahā would mix the mud in a wooden bucket and bring it up a ladder to where I worked on the roof. I would come down the ladder and give him an empty bucket when he handed me a full one. Then, he would go back to the creek to prepare another bucket of mud for me and I would climb back up the ladder to work on the chimney. I had not felt well at all when I got up that morning. I felt as though I was becoming ill, but I was anxious to complete our work on the chimney. There was a strong throbbing inside of my head and I felt terribly weakened. Occasionally, during the chinking of the chimney, my vision became somewhat blurry. I started to climb down the ladder to take a short rest, and only remember passing into unconsciousness. When I awoke, my entire family was rushing to my aid and I was lying on the ground at the base of the ladder.

"Stay back! Stay back! Don't come near me!"

"What is it John!? What is the matter? Are you hurt!?"

"Stay back everyone! Loweja, I want you and Steechánay to go to the storage hut and prepare a bed for me there. Don't let the children come anywhere near the hut!"

"We take you in house and put you in our bed, John!"

"No! Do as I say! I may just be ill from working so hard the last three days. I know that I am still tired from the trip to get supplies, but I don't want to take any chances. I do not have the strength to argue with you! Just do as I say, please! Now!"

Loweja and Steechánay ran to the storage hut to follow my orders. I tried to stand up, but did not have the strength to do so. I crawled on my hands and knees slowly toward the hut. Kwīnahā wanted to help me so badly, but I would not allow him to come near me. Loweja and Steechánay finished preparing a bed for me and came back to help me walk, but I would not allow them to touch me or come near me either. I continued to crawl until I had reached the bed in the storage hut which they had prepared and laid down, exhausted and dizzy. Loweja and Steechánay stood just outside the door, ten feet away, and were beginning to weep profusely. I tried to console them.

"Please do not let this upset you. It is probably nothing to be concerned about. Bring me a pail of water and a cup, please, and set it here beside me."

Steechánay ran to get the water as Loweja stood there weeping, wanting to do something to help me, but at a loss as to what she could do.

"Loweja, open that black box over there in the corner and get me the large bottle with the yellow paper on it and the small bottle of whiskey, please."

"I don't know what '*yellow*' means, John... John... Please don't leave me... I die without you! Please John!"

"I just need to rest, Loweja. I'm not going to leave you. Hold the bottles up one at a time and I will tell you which bottles to bring to me."

By the time Loweja brought the right bottles to me, Steechánay had returned with a pail of water and a wool blanket. It was all that I could do to remain awake, but I managed to give them some final instructions.

"I want you to close the door, and leave me here. Come in the mornings and the evenings to see if I need anything, but do not open the door, and do not allow the children to come anywhere near the storage hut! That's all. I love you both... Now, close the door and go, quickly!"

As soon as they had left, I drank a cup of water, a cup of elixir, and a cup of whiskey, and drifted off into a fitful, nightmarish, sleep. I awakened sometime during the night drenched in sweat and shaking terribly. I drank some more whiskey, covered myself, and returned to the nightmares which had been tormenting my soul. In my hellish dreams, I was attacked by a bear that had the face of *Elizabeth Cunningham*! Her father was there, laughing in the background and I saw the face of the Frenchman, *Francois Brěaux*, as he was cutting my skin with a knife and throwing the pieces into a fire. It was a horrible nightmare, and there was no one to come to my aid.

It was daylight the next morning before I finally escaped the agony of the nightmares. I was awakened by the soft weeping of two angels outside of my door, and the sweet voice of Loweja calling my name. She called my name a dozen or more times, while weeping loudly before I could answer her.

"John? Please say words to me! Please let me hear you speak words, John! My heart die for you, John! Please say words to me! Please!"

"Loweja...."

"John! Please let me come inside!"

"No, Loweja. I think I feel a little better this morning, but I don't want either of you to come in here. I do not want anyone to be exposed to me until this strange sickness passes. Later today, I will come outside and see if I can walk."

Steechánay's voice called out to me, "What can we bring you, John? We kill chicken and bring you soup?"

"No, please don't do that. Every hen is laying eggs for us now, and we only have one rooster. Please don't kill a chicken. Bring me beans and bread tonight, that's all. Tell Kwīnahā that my rifle is loaded and ask him to keep an eye out for bears and wolves. I will go back to sleep now!"

I was gravely ashamed of the misery that my illness was

causing them. I heard their faint sobbing as they walked away, and regretted the mental anguish which my illness was causing them. Closing my eyes again, I drifted away into another sleep... a sleep that was more restful, and without the hellish nightmares. I woke up near mid-afternoon, having an urge to relieve myself, and stood up next to my bed on the floor. Slowly and carefully I walked outside and relieved myself and went right back to my bed. I drank some more whiskey and elixir and continued with my rest. That evening, Loweja brought me a bowl of hot beans and bread. Following my instructions, she opened the door just wide enough to set the meal inside and then shut the door again. I ate part of the meal, but could not finish.

The next day found me gaining more energy and able to walk with a little more confidence. When Loweja and Steechánay would come to my door I managed to make my voice sound more cheery, so as not to increase their concern. In doing so, I began to notice an improvement in their voices. I remained in the small hut for four days and four nights before I finally emerged and walked to the creek. With the morning sun on my chest and face, I sat there on the bank, breathing in the fresh air and thanking God that I was alive, and for all that He had provided for us here in this valley. Sitting at the edge of the creek, I heard a pleasant voice asking, "Father, are you well, now?"

"Good morning, Kwīnahā! Yes, thank you, I am much better now."

"May I hug you, Father?"

"Not just yet, son."

"Can I get anything for you, Father?"

"Yes, son. Please ask your mother and Loweja to send some clean clothes and lay them on the bank here next to the creek. Make a fire behind the house and put the large kettle filled with water, over the fire to boil. Loweja can help you. I am going to bathe here in the creek, so I will need some soap and a cloth. Also, tell your mother and Loweja and the children not to go near the hut. I have opened the door and the two windows to let fresh air in, but I want no one to go near until I know it is safe. Will you do that for me, son?"

"Yes Father!"

I bathed in the creek, washing away days of sweat and sickness. The water felt cold, but wonderful, and seemed to lift my spirits as I washed and cleaned my body. My wives had sent the buckskin shirt and britches which they had made for me. It was the first time that I had worn them, and their softness felt good against my skin. I placed my old clothes, along with the blankets from my bed in the hut, in a basket and carried them to where the kettle was on the fire. I placed them in the steaming water for a few minutes, and then hung them out to dry in the warm sunshine. Once my chores had been completed, I walked into the house to join my wives and family for the first time in five days. Everyone sat there, looking at me with wide eyes and smiles upon their faces – glad to see me up and about. I stood in the doorway speechless for a minute or two and finally, I proudly announced, "*Necu-ta-say-ha* everyone! *Necu-ta-say-ha!*"

"May we come to you, John?"

"Yes, Steechánay! You may all come to me!"

It was as though I had returned home from the dead. We all embraced warmly and tenderly. There was some quiet weeping as we embraced, but the tears which were shed were joyous tears, tears of relief and reprieve. They were tears of thankfulness to the Great Holy Father for sparing my life. We joked with each other and I played with the children as Loweja put some tea on the stove to boil. She looked at me with loving eyes as she stoked the fire in the stove to get the tea to boil. I paid particular attention to everyone there, enjoying their smiles, basking in the glory of their love, and studying their facial features. For some reason, my eyes were drawn to Steechánay for a minute or two. It was as if her eyes were speaking to me. Her eyes sparkled as she looked at me, but I was not sure of what were they saying to me. Her face glowed with happiness, most likely due to my recovery. But there was something else which I had seen in her eyes. I was being sent a message, yet struggled to read it. All at once, I seemed to be able to clearly receive her message.

I was so happy to be alive and so happy to be with my wonderful family again. I was regretful of the concern that my sickness had caused them. Even though my wives were happy now, I could see tiredness in their eyes, and felt as though they had gotten little sleep while I was recovering from my illness.

"Where are the two chairs that I brought back from Fort Saint Joseph?" Steechánay quickly spoke, "Kwīnahā, go down to the storage hut and bring the two chairs back here."

"Why are our chairs down at the storage hut?"

"Loweja and me sit down there at night and pray to Great Holy Father while you are sick."

"My goodness… I have good wives! I really do. And I am truly sorry that my sickness has caused you to worry so much about me."

"We worried plenty… but we did not worry about you so much," Steechánay said.

"Oh? Well then, what did you worry about then, if you did not worry about me?"

"We worry about where we get sugar and tea if you don't get better soon."

Once again, I found myself wrestling Loweja and Steechánay to our bed and tickling them repeatedly. The children all joined in to be a part of the fun. The marvelous way that Steechánay and Loweja joked with me added greatly to my life, and greatly to our marriage. After we scuffled and played with each other for a short time, we returned to the table to finish our tea, and I turned our conversation in the direction of a more serious theme. We sat there at the table enjoying our tea together, and when we had finished, I asked Kwīnahā to take the children to the henhouse, that I wanted to speak with my wives alone. I asked him to take my rifle with him and to keep a close watch for any bears or wolves he might see. Kwesha carried Little Bear on her hip and they all went to the henhouse. I also asked Kwīnahā to keep a vigilant eye out for eagles, because of Little Bear. Eagles had been known to swoop in and take babies or small children. I told them that I would call for them when they could return. When they had left, and the door was closed and latched, I spoke to Steechánay.

"Steechánay, will you take off your dress and come here to me, please?"

"You want me to be naked, John? Now?"

"Yes, Steechánay, please do this for me."

"You make love with Steechánay now, John?"

"No, Loweja. Not right now, anyway. I want to see something, that's all."

Steechánay removed her dress and came to stand before me. I gently turned her around, to face away from me, and with my hands, I reached around and softly felt of her breasts and her belly, rubbing gently and lovingly. Loweja watched with curious eyes, unsure of what was happening, and perhaps still thinking that I was going to make love to Steechánay. Steechánay stood there with eyes that were closed at the delight of my touch, and breathed heavily. I felt her heart beating strongly beneath the touch of my hand. I turned her back around to face me and looked deeply into her eyes, and holding her hands in mine, I quietly asked, "Steechánay, is there something you wish to tell me?"

"I love you very much, John... and I love Loweja. That is all I know to tell you."

"There's something else, isn't there, Steechánay?"

"Yes, John... I do not like to be naked when you and Loweja are not naked. It make me feel *different*. I like to be naked only when we are all naked together."

"There is still something else you want to tell me, isn't there?"

"Maybe yes… there is one thing, maybe."

"What is it, Steechánay? What do you have to tell me?"

"*Ni and-jioko* come one day, You put a baby in me, John. We will have a baby, you and me."

Loweja screamed with joy and ran to Steechánay, kissing her on the cheek and neck! And as they hugged each other, Steechánay looked over Loweja's shoulder at me and asked, "How did you know this, John? How did you know that you put baby in me?"

"I can clearly see the baby, Steechánay, that's how."

"I don't think that is so, John! I can't see anything yet. It is too soon to see anything! *Agu-chin my-sat*. See this? My belly is flat, look!"

"I did not see the baby when I looked at your belly or felt of your belly. I saw the baby when I looked into your eyes, Steechánay."

"I love you, John! And I love Loweja, too! You both make me happy so much!"

"How about putting your pretty dress back on? I would like for you and Loweja to come with me. I would like to go for a walk on this wonderful day with my beautiful wives and our beautiful children. I would like for us to go to the top of the hill together as a family, and thank the Great Holy Father for all that He has done for us. *Necu-ta-say-ha*! Both of you, more than anything on this earth!"

And so, in the wondrous splendor of another beautiful day, on the hilltop behind our house… we knelt as a family, held hands, and each of us thanked God for His mercy and His blessings. I prayed aloud in English, the rest of my family prayed aloud also, but in their native tongues.

Late that afternoon I napped on the ground, near the house, trying to take advantage of the opportunity to build my strength back up. I had attended no work for a week, and I had many chores to do when my strength returned. Many of my errant chores had been attended by my family while I was ill, but there remained many tasks which could only be addressed by me. I ate well that evening, and with the children now speaking better English every day, I started a ritual of telling them a bedtime story at night. I had to keep the stories very light-hearted and happy so the children would not be visited by nightmares, so I dwelt on stories such as the story of the hare and the tortoise. I used *Ecclesiastes 9:11* as the basis for this story. They were captivated by my stories, and I always enjoyed telling them so much that there was scarcely an evening that passed in which I was not summoned to their bed for a story. At the time, what I didn't fully realize, was that Steechánay and Loweja sat behind me, equally as engrossed in my stories as the children. They enjoyed them so much that they would often ask me to repeat them as we lay in our bed at night. At their insistence, some nights I succumbed and retold the stories. But on this night, after a week of absence from our bed, I wasted no time telling stories. My wives and I celebrated my return to our bed with much affection and joy. When our appetite for pleasure had been appeased, I lay there between them thinking of the baby that Steechánay now carried inside of her. I thought about how the Great Holy Father had blessed our lives by sending us Little Bear. I thought about my wonderful family and our wonderful life here together. I could tell by their heavy breathing that both wives had fallen asleep. Perhaps my late afternoon nap had caused me to remain awake, for I was usually the first to fall asleep. I laid there in the darkness, listening to the pleasant sounds of my wives' breathing and feeling their breath in my ears, thinking of all which had happened and how much my life had changed in just two, short years. I was proud of the happiness which my being had brought into the lives of Loweja and Steechánay and thankful for the happiness which they had brought to me in return. If my acquaintances in Baltimore could see me now, I would be the recipient of endless ridicule and slander. I would be accused of decadence, immorality, polygamy, and all kinds of sinfulness. But here, in the wilderness, with my wonderful wives and family, I was free to live my life as naturally and unashamedly as I wished. I was, after all, far away from the watchful eyes of the hypocrites and the self-righteous. I was viewed naught by the eyes of mankind. Only my creator looked upon me and my family, and I could not help but feel that He was pleased with what He saw. I was at peace with myself, here, in the arms of the women and the family that I loved.

The Weasel in the Henhouse

Modifying and improving our meager living conditions in the valley was an ongoing and never ending project. There were always maintenance issues cropping up which required my attention, and each winter had to be approached with much preparation and meticulous detail. Careful planning would assure us that there would be sufficient food to eat during the course of the winter. Precious commodities, such as sugar, tea, cornmeal, molasses, salt, and meat provisions had to be monitored, and occasionally… rationed. With my family's lust for sugar, we could easily find ourselves depleted in stock if we did not carefully superintend its dispersal. Sugar was a difficult commodity to preserve and keep safe from ants. The bags of sugar which were brought all the way here from Ft. Saint Joseph had to be transferred to clay urns, and sealed tightly with paraffin wax in order to prevent an infestation of ants.

Among our most prized food sources, was that of our chickens. Their eggs helped to sustain us, especially during the winter months when there was little food to be gathered from the surrounding forest or the creeks. Therefore, we kept a close guard over our chickens. There were so many predators of chickens about the valley that we often had to save many eggs to be hatched, so that we could maintain a reasonable number of laying hens. The older hens would be killed for our cooking pot when they stopped laying eggs, and we never kept more than four or five roosters on hand at any given time..

Among the worst and most persistent of the chicken predators, were the eagles. Kwīnahā, being quite the marksman with either a gun, bow, or slingshot, had killed many eagles as they swooped in to attack the chickens. His efforts were eventually successful in keeping most of the eagles at bay, and allowing our chickens to feed in peace as they foraged about the valley. Kwīnahā used the many eagle feathers which he gathered to trade with the Pawnee when they came to visit. Eagle feathers were highly prized by the braves of the Pawnee village, and the Arikara as well. Wolves, coyotes, weasels, and badgers also made frequent attempts to predate upon our chickens, as did the skunks and martens. Even our dogs required our protection at night, when they would be brought inside of the house for the evening and night to protect them from the wolves. Only on rare occasions did a panther enter our valley during the daylight hours. At night, our chickens were safe within the henhouse, and the door was always latched securely from the outside. I was confident that our chickens were safe from all predators once they were contained in the secure walls of the henhouse. When we noticed that a chicken or two were missing, Kwīnahā would scout the area to determine which predator was responsible, so that we could take the necessary steps to eliminate the culprit. The manner in which the chicken had been killed and eaten could almost always tell us which predator was responsible. A hunting strategy was then employed to deal with the situation by eliminating the guilty varmint altogether. Once a predator had tasted a chicken, it was likely that they would return, time and time again, as long as the food source was there.

  As spring and summer approached that year, we began to take notice of the fact that we were occasionally missing chickens. There was a puzzling set of circumstances which accompanied this mysterious succession of missing chickens. For over a week, we had come up missing one or two chickens each night, with never a clue as to the identity of the predator. I was convinced that a weasel was responsible, yet Kwīnahā and I had checked every inch of the henhouse and the surrounding area and discovered no possible means of nighttime entrance. Adding to this great puzzlement, we could find no area which appeared to have been the location at which the chicken had been eaten. Weasels are capable of squeezing their bodies through very small openings, yet Kwīnahā and I had found no such place where a weasel could possibly gain entrance to the henhouse. We would count chickens in the evenings after they had roosted, and be confident in their safety. Yet, the following morning our count would indicate a missing chicken or two. We could ill afford the loss of very many more chickens, so it was incumbent upon us to solve this great puzzle as quickly as possible and take appropriate action. Consequently, we became steadfastly resolved to put an end to our chicken thief's career. Kwīnahā and I would accomplish this by posting an all-night vigil from the nearby storage hut. We would do so, under the beneficial light of a near full moon, where we could see the responsible creature when it arrived to do its dirty work, take careful aim, and eliminate the nuisance. Being overly anxious to prove himself a man, Kwīnahā urged me to let him wait for the predator and shoot it by himself. Knowing that he was a much better marksman than me, I agreed to his proposal but cautioned him to remain awake during his vigil. I stressed that I was sending him to do a man's job, and asked that he not let the family down by falling asleep. He assured me that he would remain vigilant, and thus our plan was put into action on that very night.

      Lying in bed that night with my wives, I fully expected to hear a gunshot outside at any moment, but as the hour grew later and no such gunshot was heard, I faded off to sleep. Very late that night I was awakened by Kwīnahā's soft voice through the closed door of my bedchamber.

      "Father?"
      "Yes, Kwīnahā?"
      "May I talk to you, Father?"
      "Yes, son. I will be right out."

I struck a match to light a candle and put my britches on. Loweja and Steechánay were awakened by this time, but remained in bed to await my return. I carried the candle out of the room with me and placed it on the table. There, Kwīnahā and I sat down to talk.

"I did not hear a shot, son. Did you not see the chicken varmint?"

"Yes, Father, I did see the chicken varmint, but I did not shoot it."

"Why not, Kwīnahā?"

"The varmint is a man, I think... so I did not shoot. I wanted to speak with you before I shoot a man because I did not know if you want me to do that."

"A man!? My Lord! You did the right thing, son. No, I would not want you to shoot a man for stealing a few chickens. A man, you say? That would explain everything. Thank you for what you did, Kwīnahā. Go to your bed now, and in the morning we will think about what to do. A man! My goodness!"

Once we were all back in our beds, I assured Loweja and Steechánay that everything was alright, and they soon returned to their slumber. I lay there for an hour or more until I had derived a plan to deal with this intrusive chicken thief. The moon phase was progressing downward, and we would have only the light of half-moon in a day or two, so I knew that I had to take action the very next night... while there was still enough light outside cast by the moon. I would hide myself nearby and wait for the thief to enter the henhouse. Once he was inside, I would quickly close the door and latch it securely from the outside. Then, I could wait until dawn, and deal with the thief appropriately in broad daylight. An ingenious plan, if I do say so! The henhouse had been constructed to be bear-proof. The door was strong, and the latch and hinges were made from heavy metal. A thief could be contained securely inside, and disarmed safely the next morning if he had a weapon on his person. At our morning meal, I asked Kwīnahā,

"So, our thief is a man, huh?"

"Yes, Father."

"Is he a very large man?"

"I could not see well, Father, but he looked like a very small man to me."

"Good! I will deal with this fellow myself, when he arrives tonight. The chicken that he stole from us last night will be the last one he will ever steal from us."

"We have been missing a few melons from our garden, too, John." Steechánay said.

"Melons? Really?"

"Yes. I did not know until now that they were taken by a man. I thought maybe a bear had carried them off... like that bear you shot last year. But the bear you shot last year ate many of our melons, and this thief only takes one or two when he comes, and he always takes the best ones."

"Well, his stealing days are over now. I'll put a stop to this tonight."

Confident in my plan, we went about our usual duties that day, and as evening approached, I stationed myself in a pile of hay situated only five feet from the henhouse door. After darkness had arrived, I was somewhat ashamed of myself for having told Kwīnahā not to fall asleep, for I felt myself drifting in and out of sleep as I waited for the thief. It was agonizing for me to try to keep my eyes open. My position in the pile of hay was very comfortable, and remaining awake was proving to be extremely difficult for me. Soon, however, I was fully awakened by the sight of the culprit's dark shadow as he opened the door-latch and entered the henhouse. Once he was inside, I quickly sprang to my feet and slammed the door closed and secured the latch. The chickens made much noise inside the henhouse. I was sure that in the total darkness inside, the thief was feeling around the walls, probably desperate to find some means of egress. Soon, all was quiet inside, as the thief most likely came to realize that there was no possible way of escaping their confinement. When things inside had quieted down, I spoke to the thief through the closed door.

"I'll deal with you tomorrow! *Es-cona-ta!*" I said, as I turned and walked back to the house. I tried to be quiet when I entered the house, but everyone had remained awake and was anxious to hear if the thief had been caught. I told them he was locked tightly in the henhouse at that very moment, and I would be dealing with him appropriately in the morning. The household settled down somewhat, and after a few restless minutes we all fell fast asleep.

The hour of reckoning approached, as we ate our morning meal somewhat earlier than we usually did, in anticipation of the impending confrontation with the chicken thief. After finishing my tea, I yielded to the pleas of my family and allowed them to accompany Kwīnahā and me as we went down to the henhouse to expose and confront the thief. However, I cautioned them to keep a safe distance, because I was unsure of exactly what to expect when I opened the henhouse door. The family stood thirty yards away, waiting to see the face of the culprit. Holding my pistol in one hand, I unlatched the door and quickly swung it open. After many of the chickens fluttered through the open doorway, I was finally standing there face-to-face with the thief who was huddled pathetically in the far corner.

"My dear God!" I said, as I looked upon the face of the thief! A terrified, perhaps middle-aged, Indian woman looked back at me with frightened eyes and a horrified look upon her face. She immediately began to chant some sort of strange song as she crouched there in the henhouse and cowered feebly in the corner. With me standing in the doorway with my pistol, her escape was completely blocked. She appeared to be weeping as she sang, and wringing her hands as if she was awaiting her inevitable execution

"Steechánay! Come here, please! Quickly!" The woman continued with her chanting and singing. She was gaunt, and appeared to be somewhat emaciated and weak. Her clothes were filthy and ragged and her hair was stringy and unkempt. Steechánay came to my side, and we looked upon the woman together.

"Is this woman Arikara?"

"No, she is Pawnee, John."

"Do you know her?"

"No, I have never seen her before."

"Ask her to stop singing, and talk to us, Steechánay."

"She is singing her death song because she thinks you will kill her now."

"Tell her that I will not hurt her, but I want to ask her some questions." The woman did not stop singing immediately, even after Steechánay repeatedly told her to stop, but eventually her singing got weaker and weaker until it finally stopped altogether. Still crouched in the corner, she sat there nervously wringing her hands and awaiting an unknown fate at the hands of this strange white man who held a gun in his hand. Her cheeks bore vertical tattoo markings, which only exaggerated her hideous appearance in my eyes.

"Ask her why she has been stealing our chickens, Steechánay."

The woman did not answer at first, and Steechánay had to repeat the question loudly several times before the woman finally settled down enough to offer an answer.

"She said that she only took chickens because her children are hungry and they will die without food."

"Loweja, you and Steechánay help this woman to our house and give her some porridge and tea. Tell her that I will give her food so that her children will not die, and we will feed her something up at our house now."

"She said that she cannot eat until her children are fed. If she eats food now, while her children are hungry, she will die and not be able to care for them, and then they too, will die very soon."

"Kwīnahā, go to the corral, please, and put saddles on three horses, and we will take this woman back to her children and see that they are all fed. Tell her what we are doing, Steechánay, so that she will not be afraid."

We helped the woman onto a horse, but she was so frightened that she could not handle the horse. She had evidently never ridden a horse before and was currently in no condition to learn. With Steechánay's help, I put the woman on my horse with me, and Kwīnahā led the third horse as we followed the woman's directions to take her back to her camp. It took nearly an hour to get there, but we arrived to find three small children who were very glad to see their mother. They were living in very dire conditions in a hastily constructed shelter of limbs and leaves, thrown together in the form of a dome. With their few belongings gathered and wrapped in blankets, we carried them all back to our house where we could see to their needs and nurse them all back to health. The odor from their bodies was horribly putrescent. They smelled as though they had not bathed in a very long time... perhaps not since the last fall. The woman smelled much worse than her children. When she had been on my horse, I was forced to breathe through my mouth. The stench was both horrific and nauseating.

After they were all fed a hot meal, I suggested that Kwīnahā and Kwesha take the children to the creek and see that they were properly bathed and their clothes were washed. Loweja gave them soap and washing rags. They were lovely little children, but quite odorous and filthy. The smallest of the children was naked, and appeared to have no clothes to wear. Steechánay managed to find a garment for the child among her belongings. While they were gone to attend to the task of bathing, my wives and I sat with the woman and tried to gather some facts. Her name was *Pĕllā-tomā*, and she was from a very distant Pawnee village. Her husband had been exiled from the tribe for the commission of some grave offense, and was traveling with his family to return to live in the village of his origin. She did not know where this village was, as she had never been there before. When her husband had disappeared while crossing a deep creek, she was left stranded with her children. The man had evidently drowned while crossing the creek. She said that the creek had '*eaten*' her husband, and would not give him back to her. She could not go back to the village from which they had just been exiled, and she did not know where her husband was taking her. She had been trying to find ways of feeding her children for almost two months. I told her that we would take care of her until such time as we could find a permanent home for her and her children. I would seek the advice and council of my good friend, Lectūschemă when he came for his next visit. Until then, we would sleep under very crowded conditions in our house. Steechánay prepared a bed for the woman and her children in the loft. Lectūschemă usually visited about twice a month or so, and his next visit was long overdue. If Pĕllā-tomā and her children would be staying with us, I somehow had to convince her to bathe first. She smelled so badly, that it was very difficult to be in the same house with her. I was hopeful that Steechánay could find a way to politely suggest that the woman bathe without hurting her feelings.

"Steechánay, I do not want you to hurt Pĕllā-tomā's feelings, but could you somehow tell her that she needs to bathe at the creek, as her children are doing, before we can allow her to stay here with us. Tell her this as nicely as you possibly can, so that it does not upset her, please."

"*Eta-soo-takna-gesha-tõ. Enda-sprē-tek Merde-etela!*"

With that, Pĕllā-tomā rose from the table immediately and walked directly to the creek to bathe with her children. When I looked toward the creek, I could see that they were all in the creek bathing, and washing their garments as well. With Kwīnahā standing at the creek bank, a scant ten feet from the woman, it appeared to me that he was paying entirely too much attention to the woman's nakedness, so I summoned him to return to the house, so that they could be allowed to continue their bathing in private. Kwesha stayed there to superintend the bathing of the children. Curious as to what Steechánay had told the woman to get her to voluntarily attend to bathing so quickly, I asked, "Exactly what did you say to Pĕllā-tomā, Steechánay?"

"I told her that her children and her smelled bad like shit, and she needed to go bathe in the creek if she wanted to eat in our house, and I would be nice to her when she smelled more better... that's all."

"Steechánay! My Lord, woman! You certainly have a sweet way with words! I am glad that I did not tell you to be harsh with the poor woman!"

"I do not understand. Did I not say right thing?"

"Yes, you said the right thing, Steechánay. You said it very well, I suppose... just a little less tactful than I would have said it, that's all."

"I do not understand that word, 'tactful,' John."

"Evidently, you do not, Steechánay! But that's fine. You did well, and I thank you. You are a good wife, and a fine spokeswoman."

"I think I know English pretty good sometimes until I hear you speak it. Then I know that I do not know English pretty good. I only know it pretty bad."

Thereafter, the woman and her family bathed every four days. She was quite opposed to the idea, but did so at Steechánay's insistence. I was quite blessed with the fact that my wives placed a high priority on personal hygiene. I cannot imagine a husband being able to muster amorous feelings toward a woman who smelled as badly as Pĕllā-tomā. I'm quite sure that Steechánay was both diplomatic and tactful each time she told the woman to bathe. As far as Kwīnahā's interest in the naked woman was concerned, he was not permitted to superintend the woman's bathing after that. He had seen quite enough the first time.

Steechánay and Loweja were quite generous with the woman after she had bathed. They provided her with much better clothes to wear, yet had to keep a close eye her at all times because she was very prone to thievery. Knowing this, they kept a watchful eye on the woman whenever she was inside of our house.

When Lectūschemă arrived two weeks later, I invited him to sit with the woman while she told her story. They talked for several minutes and surprisingly, the woman's husband had been a distant relative of Lectūschemă, and he remembered the man well from years earlier. The woman and her children left with Lectūschemă to go back to the Pawnee village, and I later learned that she had been taken as a wife by one of Lectūschemă's uncles. I could only hope that for his sake, she had become accustomed to bathing regularly, and would continue keep her children bathed as well. Before leaving, the woman expressed her gratitude for my family's hospitality, and swore an oath that she would never steal another chicken again, unless her children were hungry. I appreciated both her gratitude and her honesty, but perhaps more than anything, I appreciated something which Lectūschemă had told me before he left.

"You are not just white man, John Welch... you are good white man who help people. And you are the friend of me and my people. We will always remember that you have been good to us."

During the early fall of that year, Kwīnahā and I rode to the Pawnee village for the first time and visited with our many friends there. My good friend, Lectūschemă and I had spent a great deal of time together over the previous six months and our friendship had grown into a very sovereign relationship, filled with mutual admiration and trust. I met his two wives and their five children, as well as his aged mother and some other relatives whom I cannot remember. Lectūschemă seemed to take great pride as he introduced me as his friend, *John Welch*. Kwīnahā was speaking very good English by this time and he had always been well versed in the language of the Pawnee as well. I could understand the most basic words of the Pawnee or Arikara, but had sporadic difficulty understanding even with the most basic of words when the person I was speaking to talked quickly or did not pronounce the words distinctly. Kwīnahā acted as my interpreter whenever I found myself struggling to communicate, but the more I spoke the language on my own, the more confidence I gained. Even with the occasional language difficulties, Kwīnahā and I had a wonderful time visiting with our friends and sharing information with each other. I would often look around for him and see him in the distance, talking with other boys who appeared to be about his same age. We spent one night in their village as guests of Lectūschemă, and left very early the next morning to go home. I was greatly relieved that Lectūschemă did not offer one of his wives to lay with me. In previous conversations, I had shared my disdain of such immoral behavior with him and he was respectful of my stance on the matter, without taking any offense. If the sharing of a wife had been offered, I would have dismissed the offer summarily, even though it would have been an insult to my host for me to have refused such hospitality. Knowing this, and in respect of our friendship, Lectūschemă reverently withheld the offer so that our friendship and trust could endure. I felt as though a great deal of Lectūschemă's tolerance of my beliefs was based upon the fact that I was married to his sister, Steechánay. He knew that his sister had found unimaginable happiness in our marriage, and her happiness and welfare had brought great peace of mind to Lectūschemă as well. I suppose that every brother wishes for his sister to be healthy and happy. In respect of my marriage to his sister, he made concessions to me and my strange beliefs which he may not have offered to anyone else.

After sharing a warm breakfast with Lectŭschemă, Kwīnahā and I left the village near mid-morning to return home. I took advantage of the opportunity to have a '*man-to-man*' conversation with Kwīnahā as we rode along the trail together.

"Thank you for coming along with me on this trip, Kwīnahā."

"Thank you for taking me with you, Father."

"You are welcome, Kwīnahā. I like being able to spend some time with you when it's just you and me like this, and I am glad we did this thing together. Did you have a good time with the other young men while we were there, son?"

"Yes, Father. I like Lectŭschemă and his family, and I saw many wonderful things while we were there in the village."

"Oh? What kind of wonderful things did you see, son?"

"People, mostly… many of them, but only one that was so wonderful."

"What is the name of this one wonderful person you saw?"

"I do not know her name, Father. I just saw her there. We did not speak, we just looked at each other."

"*Her*? Oh… I see. Well, I'm glad you had such a good time. Hopefully, we can do this again soon. Hopefully you can to talk to this wonderful person the next time we come here."

"I hope so, Father!"

Could my young Kwīnahā possibly be of an age now that he had experienced some sort of attraction to a young girl? I did not think so. He was still a child, I thought. Yet the sincerity in his comments left me puzzled. One of my biggest frustrations in Indian cultures resided in the fact that no one seemed to know their true age in years. As Mrs. Parker had told me once, '*you are either young, or you are old.*' As far as Kwīnahā was concerned, I would have guessed his age to be fourteen years now, perhaps fifteen at the most. He was strong, intelligent and handsome, but he was still a child, I thought. Too young to be showing an interest in someone of the opposite sex, I was sure. Or was he? I was mindful of the obvious attention which he had given to the nakedness of the Indian woman, *Pĕllā-tomā*, as she bathed in our creek, and felt certain that his boyish curiosity had been evoked. I would mention this to Steechánay, his mother, and see what she had to say about it. I remembered when I had once mistakenly looked upon Loweja as a young child, when she was actually a woman. Could I be making the same mistake with my son, Kwīnahā? Is it possible that Indian children develop into maturity sooner in life than whites? I did not think so, but in the future I would pay closer attention to Kwīnahā. Perhaps this was just a temporary phase that he was going through… one that would soon pass. Perhaps I would soon find it necessary to sit down with him to explain the details pertaining to the miraculous differences between a man and a woman, and why the Great Holy Father had created them as he did. It would be a *'father-son'* discussion such as I had never had the benefit of receiving when I was an adolescent. I gave the matter some more consideration as we rode, and started to address the subject of a father-son talk about the opposite sex, but could not seem to get the words to come forth. I would put some thought into what I would say and address the subject at a later date.

We had harvested many vegetables and melons from our garden during the summer, and were able to stock one of the earthen huts with great quantities of dried beans, potatoes, and corn. Our orchard had produced a bountiful crop of apples and pears which were stored inside one of the earthen huts where they could be kept without fear of freezing when winter arrived. Some of the great herds of wapiti and antelope were beginning to return to the valley and Kwīnahā and I had already killed and butchered two wapiti. I would like to have had some pigs to raise for meat, but realized very quickly that the resident wolves would make that an impossibility. For the time being, I would have to remain content to buy my salted pork in kegs from the merchants in Fort Saint Joseph. In the very early fall, Kwīnahā, Joseph, and I would travel a half-day's ride to the south, where we would harvest great bags of cedar shavings to bring home. These shavings would be placed around the floor of our home and in the corner near the fireplace where the dogs slept. The shavings prevented fleas, bedbugs, and many other such insects from taking residency in our otherwise, clean home. They also presented a pleasant aroma about the house which I enjoyed.

The lean-to behind the house was filled with firewood for the coming winter, and we had cured and softened the hides of the bears and wolves we had killed and taken them into our house to be used for rugs and sleeping mats for the children. These hides would prevent dampness from rising from the floor in the winter, and provide us with added warmth inside the house. The wolf hides would be used for making winter coats for me and Kwīnahā. Our moccasins and boots would be made from buffalo hides which I had purchased in the Pawnee village. Loweja and Steechánay worked together in the light of our two lanterns one night, making winter boots for me, and as they worked, I took the opportunity to speak with them within the privacy of our room.

"Tell me something, Steechánay, when do you think that Kwīnahā will become a man and not a boy anymore?"

"I do not know, John. Maybe when the next winter comes, or maybe two winters. He grows big like man now. He stands almost as tall as you, now. Why do you ask this?"

"He was looking very closely at *Pĕllā-tomā's cūmă*, and other private parts when she bathed in our creek that day, and then last week when we were at the Pawnee village he showed a lot of interest in a certain girl there."

"I do not know this word, '*interest*,' John. What does it mean?"

"It means, to desire or want something... or want to know more about something."

"He is old enough maybe to show this '*interest*' to girls, but I do not think he is old enough to marry yet. You are his father now, and it is for you to decide when he is a man."

"I don't think he's old enough to marry, either, and I am surprised that he is even old enough to show any kind of *interest* in a girl."

"That is not so, John. Kwīnahā is old enough to show his *interest* to girl! I know this to be truth!" Loweja emphatically said.

"Why do you say that, Loweja? How do you know he is old enough to show an interest in a girl?"

"Because... in mornings, when he get up from his bed, you can see his *interest* under his breechcloth when he leave bed. He tries to hide this *interest*, but his cloth he cannot hide it. It is too much *interest* to hide."

"Loweja speaks truth, John. I have seen Kwīnahā try to hide this interest on many mornings, but I did not know until now that it was called, '*interest*.' I did not know what it was called. He goes out quickly to do his chores and this interest soon goes away and is gone when he comes back in."

"You don't say anything to him that will embarrass him when you see that, do you?"

"No. I think maybe he cannot help it. I think maybe this *interest* comes to him in his sleep... maybe when he dreams about girl. Anyway, it is there, under his cloth every morning and he cannot hide it, just like Loweja say. I don't say anything to him, but I can see it."

"It is good that you don't say anything. I don't want anyone to say anything that might hurt his feelings. Kwīnahā is a good boy, and I love him dearly. It would make my heart hurt if anyone said something about this to him. It is a very private thing, and many young men just like Kwīnahā, cannot help this. It just happens to them when they sleep. I think he is too big to only wear a breechcloth now. You and Loweja need to make him britches, like I wear."

"We will, John, but I do not think he is ready to be husband yet, though."

"I agree with you, Steechánay. I think I will open the rifle box and give him a rifle as a present. He has already shot mine many times, and I think he is ready for his own. Maybe that will give him something to think about instead of girls."

"He needs good father now, and you are good father for him, John. He has much love in his heart for you."

"I have much love in my heart for him, too. I think I will also talk to him about girls and boys, and why the Great Holy Father made them as He did. I think Kwīnahā is old enough that he should know these things. He has seen Pĕllā-tomā when she bathed in the creek, and he sees us when we bathe in the creek, and he knows that girls are different from boys. He has probably wondered why this is so. Perhaps it is time that his father told him why girls are made different. I also think it may be a good idea in the future, if Kwīnahā, Joseph, and I bathed by ourselves, and allowed you and Loweja to bathe in private with the girls."

After I poured us all another cup of tea, Steechánay walked over to Loweja and whispered something into her ear and they both burst out with laughter, almost to the point that they were unable to control their laughing hysterics. They laughed so loudly and so happily that they soon had me laughing. They laughed until their faces turned red and tears came from their eyes.

"What is it that you two laugh at? Can you please tell me, so that I can laugh with you?"

"If we tell you, then you will tickle us!"

"If you don't tell me, I will tickle you even more! Now what is it? Tell me!"

"Steechánay….. Steechánay say that….."

"Loweja, will you please stop laughing long enough to tell me what it is? I want to laugh, too!"

"Steechánay say that you have much *interest*

sometimes, too! Maybe Steechánay and me need to tell you why boys are different from girls!"

Then, Steechánay spoke sporadically as she continued to laugh hysterically, "Maybe Loweja and me... make you bigger britches for your interest to have plenty of room! Maybe then, me and Loweja will tell you why boys are different from girls!"

They laughed so hard that I thought they would become ill. And thus began another session of friendly, lovable tickling, for both of them! I always delighted in seeing them laugh, for it always brought such great joy to my heart. They both had such wonderful fun when they laughed!

Through the door came a sweet little voice, "Father, why is everyone laughing so loud in there?"

"It's nothing, Joseph. Please go back to your bed, son. We will be quieter. I'm sorry if we woke you."

I sympathized with what young Kwīnahā was going through, however, and wanted to be there for him as a father. The adolescent years are difficult and confusing years for a young man. Kwīnahā was no longer a child, yet he was not yet a man. He would need help and love from his family as he struggled through the next two years, and I would try my best to help him as much as I could. I remembered how difficult those years had been for me. I did not have a father to guide and comfort me through my adolescence, but Kwīnahā had me now. I would be the father for him that I never had as a child. I would help him. After that evening conversation with my wives, I would pay greater attention to Kwīnahā. A week or two later I gave him a rifle for his very own. He treasured it above any possession he owned. With my help, he had already become an expert marksman with my rifle, and now he had one of his own. He always took great care in cleaning and maintaining his new rifle.

The simple and innocuous word, *'interest'* would

become a private joke between my terribly mischievous wives and me. One or the other of them would often ask me at night, when I came to bed in the darkness, if I would be willing to show them my '*interest*,' and of course, when the question was asked, then the laughter would begin. When the laughter began, then the tickling would begin. Ours was a happy and joyous bed, and a happy and joyous marriage as well. While the subject was often a laughing between my wives and me, I knew in my heart that to Kwīnahā, it was nothing to joke about.

Fall soon came and Kwīnahā and I spent much time together hunting and tending to the animals that we killed. We had to cut additional firewood for the family, as Steechánay and Loweja used our cook stove more and more. I had showed them how to make a bread by using a yeast powder along with the flour. With a little salt, and some renderings from pork fat, after much trial and error their bread turned out perfectly each time. In fact, it was the finest bread that I had ever tasted in my life. Every one of us enjoyed it. However, baking so much bread took additional firewood, firewood which Kwīnahā and I would be glad to provide as long as my wives kept making the delicious bread. Little Bear was now eating some solid foods and continuing to grow before our very eyes. Loweja often wore a type of basket on her back when she was working outside in which she carried Little Bear. Kwīnahā and I talked frequently as we worked, and the more we talked, the more we got to know each other. I always delighted in talking with him. He had not voluntarily mentioned the opposite sex as a topic of conversation, so I assumed that his initial infatuation over the girl in the Pawnee village had subsided somewhat. However, the more we talked, the more I saw him as a young man, instead of a boy. He was maturing rapidly into a young man that I was proud to call my son. Even though he was actually my younger half-brother, to me, he was my son... and to him, I was his father. I took notice one morning that Loweja and Steechánay were correct when they had reported that Kwīnahā showed a lot of '*interest*' in the mornings. He was wearing britches now, but they did little to hide the source of his embarrassment. I always acted as though I had seen nothing, but I could tell that he was gravely shamed by his '*condition*' as he quickly rushed outside. Loweja and Steechánay looked at me to see if I had noticed Kwīnahā's condition, but I just shrugged my shoulders and said good morning to the other children. My heart, however, sympathized greatly with Kwīnahā. When the children had all gone outside, I told Steechanay and Loweja, "I am going to speak with Kwīnahā today, and tell him why boys are made different from girls. He needs to know this."

Later that afternoon, as Kwīnahā and I oiled our saddles and bridles at the storage hut, I took the opportunity to approach the subject of girls and boys. Even though I had rehearsed the words over and over in my mind, it was not as easy as I had thought it would be, and initially, I stumbled to find the right words.

"Kwīnahā, can I talk with you about something, my son?"

"Yes, Father... what is it? You look worried."

"No, son, I'm not worried about anything. I just want to talk to you about something important. I'm sure that you have noticed that boys are made much different than girls... I mean, down here, between their legs... you have noticed that haven't you, son?"

"Yes, Father. Everyone knows that, I think."

"Do you know why the Great Holy Father made boys different than girls?"

"Yes, Father... I do."

"You do? Really? You already know this?"

"Yes, Father. It is so that a boy and a girl can have *ohgā-sá-ho* with each other and have babies when they are married."

"Uhhh... Well... yes... that is right. How do you

know this? Who told you about this, son? And who taught you that *ohgā-sá-ho* word?"

"I talk to Pawnee boys when they come here, and I talk to them at Pawnee village when I go there with you that day, and they teach me about this. We talk about it much there."

"I see. Are there any questions that you would like to ask me? I mean... is there anything about it that you don't understand that I could tell you about?"

"No, Father. I understand everything about it, I think. Thank you, Father."

"Well, if you ever have any questions... uhhh... just ask me."

I should have known. Adolescent boys were the very source of my own feminine anatomical education when I was a boy. I knew full well that Kwīnahā did not know everything about the subject... no boy ever knows quite as much as they think they do about women, and perhaps no grown man ever knows quite as much as they think they do, either. Nevertheless, I had taken a bold step forward and discussed the issue with Kwīnahā and brought it out into the open. If he did have questions in the future, perhaps he would now be more relaxed in asking, and I would be glad to answer his questions as best I could. I felt as though I had just reached an important milestone in being a father, yet I also felt that I had been robbed of the privilege of explaining the subject to him myself. In two or three years, when he was old enough to marry, perhaps I could again offer him an opportunity to ask questions. That night, in our bed, my wives and I had our usual nightly conversation.

"John, did you speak with Kwīnahā today and tell him why boys are different from girls?"

"Yes, I spoke with him, but he already knew why boys were different than girls. He even knew how to make a baby."

"How did he learn this, John?"

"From boys at the Pawnee village... they told him all about it."

"Do you think he really understands all about it?"

"No. But I think if he has any questions about the subject he will come to me now and ask them. I would rather he asked these questions of me, than the boys at the Pawnee village... and I think he will now."

After a pleasant fall that year, winter soon fell upon us and arrived one night in the form of a hallmark blizzard which lasted for three days and left thirty-six inches of snow in its wake. Our horses were gathered, and we stabled them under the large lean-to at the corral, where we brought hay to them which had been stored under one of the other lean-tos. The grasses that Kwīnahā and I had cut for hay during the summer and fall would be used to feed the horses during the cold winter. Kwīnahā and I had to use shovels to make paths in order to get our firewood, and also in order for us to have a pathway to the storage hut. We also had to dig paths to the creek where we got our water. It was Kwīnahā's responsibility to use an axe to keep the ice cut away from the creek and fetch water when it was needed. When working outside, Kwīnahā and I took frequent breaks to come inside and warm ourselves by the fire. Winters, and bitter-cold weather, found Loweja and Steechánay continuously busy inside. There was hardly an idle moment for any of us. Loweja and Steechánay were always occupied with sewing, preparing meals, or cleaning our house. The buffalo hides which we slept upon were shaken each day to keep them clean, and free from insects. There was always work to be done, and my wives seemed to always be in attendance of their chores. They never tired of being around each other. Quite the contrary was true. Their love and respect for each other was evident in all they said and did. They were always engaged in conversation as they went about their tasks. Sometimes I would walk by the house and hear them inside speaking in Arikara or Pawnee. It always worried me when they spoke to each other in Arikara, for I assumed they were talking about me. However, I never made an issue out of their speaking Arikara, unless I was present. If they were talking about me, I only hoped that what they were saying was complementary. Yet, many times when they spoke of me I would hear them giggle or laugh. Each time I heard it, however, it only brought a smile to my face and joy to my heart.

After receiving thirty-six inches of snow, a subsequent storm battered us within four days of the first storm, and deposited another four inches of snow. With our outdoor activities severely limited, our family had been driven into the confines of our warm home, where we spent many wonderful hours together. It was a time of year to be thankful for the many hours of preparation which we had performed over the course of the summer and fall. To have exhausted our precious supply of firewood at such a critical time of year could have been the prelude for a disaster. We had made adequate preparations, however, and were enjoying the benefits of our labors. Still, every family member yearned for the approach of spring, which was several months forthcoming. When I had been in Fort Saint Joseph, I had purchased a checker board and checkers. One-by-one, I taught my family how to play the game. I delighted in beating them at the game regularly during the first two weeks or so that we played. Little-by-little I began losing games occasionally, until it seemed that I could never win even a single game. They had advanced quickly, and beat me fancily in every match. Still, during the winter months, the checker board came out each night after our meal, and I tried desperately to improve my playing skills, but it seemed as though my efforts were in vain. I was no match for any of them... even little Pokeem could beat me with very little effort.

It was in the dead of winter that year, late in the afternoon of one bitter cold, windy day, that Kwīnahā had walked to the creek to fetch water. When he returned, he sat the pail of water on the porch and shouted to me, "Father! People come! Get your rifle!"

Quickly, I grabbed my rifle from above the fireplace and joined Kwīnahā on the porch. I handed Kwīnahā my rifle and went back inside, where I got my revolver. Rejoining Kwīnahā on the porch, I could see the dark figures of two people approaching in the distant snow. The intensity of the bitter-cold wind was horrendous. We closed the door to our house tightly, in order to prevent snow from blowing inside. Kwīnahā and I continued to watch the approach of the two dark figures, trying to identify them and discern any indication of their intent. Why are they here? Why have they chosen such brutal weather to travel in? They came slowly, for the depth of the snow made for difficult walking. As they drew closer, I could tell from their attire that they were Indians, but I could not see their faces. I could see that they bore no obvious weapons and were having a great deal of difficulty walking in the deep snow. As we watched them come closer, the larger of the two people suddenly dropped in the snow. The smaller of the two struggled to help the one who had fallen to their knees, but seemed to be unable to do so. I told Kwīnahā to stay there on the porch, as I put my revolver under my belt and rushed to see if I could render any assistance. When I got to them, I found an Indian man, probably Arikara, lying in the snow with a young Indian girl trying to help him rise to his feet. I picked up the cold, weakened man into my arms and trudged back to the house through the deep snow. The Indian girl trailed behind me, stepping into the tracks which I had made. No words were spoken as we walked. From the distressed look on her face I doubt if she could have exchanged words with me at that time anyway. The wind blew with such force as to take our breath away when we opened our mouths to speak. I noticed that the young girl was almost too exhausted to walk by herself, but we finally managed to walk through the door of the house and escape the wind. Both of them were nearly frozen to death. The young girl collapsed on the floor, and Steechánay helped her back to her feet. The man appeared to be in much worse condition than the girl. Loweja put extra wood on the fire and I sat the man down at the hearth. The girl sat there next to him, and shivered from the cold, while trying to absorb the life-sustaining heat which emitted from the fireplace. Both of them were wet and their clothes were practically frozen to their flesh in places.

"Steechánay, will you help both of these people out of their wet clothes, please? Loweja, get some blankets! Kwīnahā, take the children into the other room and close the door! Stay there with them until you are called!"

Loweja and Steechánay worked together to get the wet clothes off of the young girl and then wrapped her in a blanket. All three of us had to work together to undress the man as he seemed unresponsive and stiff. His buffalo-hide boots were frozen to his feet, and we had to hold them near the fire before they finally slipped off of his frozen feet. Once he was stripped of his wet clothes we wrapped him in a blanket, but he slumped to the floor and lost all signs of consciousness. We made a bed for him next to the hearth and the young girl sat beside him in the warmth of the fire. Steechánay boiled tea on the stove as Loweja and I massaged the man's wrists. His hands were frozen and greyish in color, and ice-cold to the touch. I knew that if he lived, he would lose both of his feet, and possibly both of his hands as well. In my medical kit, I had the surgeon's tools which would be required to perform amputations, but I had reservations within my mind as to my capabilities to perform such drastic and gruesome procedures. Furthermore, I had serious concerns as to how a person would react to such permanent disfigurement, and how they would possibly go through the rest of their life after the removal of both hands and both feet. Loweja and I continued to try to bring signs of life back into the man.

"Steechánay, these people are Pawnee, aren't they?"

"Yes, John. They are Pawnee."

"Ask the girl where her village is."

"She try to speak to me but she cannot speak yet."

"There's no hurry… we'll wait. Just tell her that we will help her and this man who is with her. Tell her not to worry, we will take care of them."

I did not want to alarm the young girl who was with this man, but I felt as though the man was very near death, despite our efforts to warm his cold body. His hands were frozen to the point that they were rigid and starting to turn very dark, his feet were even darker in color and his toes could not be bent. His cheeks, nose, and ears were equally blackened. The girl was wearing two layers of clothing, and the man, only one. I could only assume that with an over-sized coat on her body, that the man must have shed his own coat in order to keep the little girl alive. He had obviously made the ultimate sacrifice for this young girl. Loweja and I continued to massage his wrists in an effort to get life back into his hands. Steechánay managed to get the young girl to drink some hot tea but her condition did not seem to improve at all. The man's condition however, became much worse. Within half an hour, he died while Loweja and I worked to save him. I did not want to alarm the girl, so I asked Steechánay, "Steechánay, tell this girl that I am going to take this man into another house where he can rest next to a warm fire."

"What other house do you speak of, John?"

"Just tell her what I said! I'll explain later."

Loweja opened the door, and I carried the dead man to the lean-to at the rear of our house and laid his body down upon the firewood there. I covered his head with the blanket and walked back into the house. Loweja was well-aware that the man had died, but Steechánay was not. Loweja whispered the news into Steechánay's ear as I poured myself a cup of tea and sat down to examine the girl. I felt of her head, neck, and thighs, and thought that her body was still dangerously cold. Her feet were also very cold, but not discolored.

"Steechánay, I would like for you and Loweja to

undress and take this girl into our bed, naked like she is, and warm her up with your bodies under some blankets. Call the dogs onto the top of the bed, too. There is much warmth in their bodies also. Do you understand?"

"Yes, John. We do this quickly!"

Under the blankets, Loweja and Steechánay massaged the girl's calves and upper legs, aiding the circulation of warm blood. I put my hands under the blanket and massaged the girl's feet and legs. They felt as though they were ice-cold in my hands. The finger nail of one of her small fingers was turning black from the bite of the cold, and I had Loweja tuck that hand between her breasts and massage her fingers.

"Steechánay, ask this girl if she is able to talk to us now."

"She says, *yes*, she can talk to us now."

"Ask her where her village is."

"She says she does not know where her village is. They have come a very long way from her village and she does not know where she is."

"Ask her if the man that sleeps in the other house is her husband."

"She says that the man is not her husband, he is her father. She does not have a husband because she is too young. She says that her mother die in snow, then two horses die also when great snow comes."

"Steechánay, do you have any dry clothes to dress this young girl with? Her body feels warmer now."

"Yes, John. I get them."

Once she was dressed, and Loweja and Steechánay redressed, I carried the young girl to the bottom tier of the children's bed and laid her down. Her body was much warmer now, and I felt as though her life was no longer at risk. I covered her with a dry blanket and watched over her until I saw her eyes close for sleep. She must have been wrought with exhaustion, because it only took a few moments for her to fall asleep. The intense snow had stopped sometime during the previous night, but a strong northeast wind had caused the snow on the ground to drift into deep mounds in places. We made a bed for the children up in the loft, where they had slept before, so that our young guest could continue to sleep undisturbed. Kwīnahā and I dressed warm and carried the body of the dead man to the storage hut, where we wrapped it in deer skins and bound it with twine. His body had frozen solid in the short time that it had been under the firewood lean-to.

"Who is the girl in our bed, Father?"

"I don't know, Kwīnahā. We'll find out tomorrow when she awakes from her sleep."

The morning broke clear and crisp, and although the temperature outside remained bitter cold, the strong northeast wind had subsided and it was pleasantly warm inside of the house. Kwīnahā worked tediously at the creek, cutting through the ice with an axe before he was able to draw a pail of water for our breakfast tea and porridge. He also brought back another pail filled with ice that Loweja placed on the back of the stove to melt. The young girl had awakened by this time, dressed in my warmest wolf-skin coat, and had gone outside to tend to her morning business, then she returned to join us at the table. She ate well, as it was probably the first food that she had eaten in days. Loweja made a pot of tea and sweetened it with a generous portion of sugar for the girl to drink. I studied over the young Pawnee girl for some time before I spoke to her through Steechánay.

"Ask her if she feels better today, Steechánay."

"She says, yes. She is asking about her father, and wants to know if he is feeling better today."

"Say this as gently as you can, Steechánay. Tell her that her father has died and gone to be with her mother. He dressed her in a second coat so that she might live, and then he went to be with her mother."

The girl looked down and closed her eyes momentarily, but showed no terrible signs of stressful emotion or extreme sadness. It looked as though she simply accepted the news. Perhaps she even knew that her father was not going to survive. Perhaps she even knew that he had sacrificed his own life so that she would live. Then, a concerned look came over her face and she spoke to Steechánay.

"She wants to know what will become of her now. She says that she has no family to watch over her."

"Tell her that she will stay here with us until spring. Then, I will take her back to her people. I promise. Tell her not to be afraid. Tell her we will take good care of her, and we will be her family until she returns to her people."

"She says that she thanks us, and she is not afraid."

"Ask her what she is called by her people."

"She says that she is called, *Nõvimimĕsch*."

"Tell her that I cannot speak that name with my tongue. Ask her if we may call her, *November*."

"She says that she likes that name."

"Very well, I want each of us to come here before November and speak our names to her, so that she may soon come to know us."

There were too many names for November to comprehend at one time, but we each introduced ourselves one-by-one as she sat there at our table with her tea. I was proud of the way that my family treated her so warmly and compassionately, even though she was a total stranger. I knew that there were some tribes who would have shunned the girl because she would have been one more mouth to feed. My family had much greater compassion than that, and we would do everything we could to make this child feel at home. I knew that it would take some time for her to memorize all of our names, but I strongly sensed that there was one name among us that she would not easily forget. When Kwīnahā and she had looked upon one another, I was not the only member of our family who noticed an immediate connection between them. It was as if both of them had been struck by lightning. I attempted to dismiss the thought from my mind, but could not help but give some fleeting consideration to the situation because I felt uneasy with the way that they had looked at each other. They were most likely very close to the same age, which was still far too young to consider marriage, or even a casual boy-girl relationship I thought. I still felt like Kwīnahā was entirely too young to even show any type of serious interest in girls. I would have to keep a close eye on this situation and hope that my instincts were misleading me. I did not want to see Kwīnahā or November have their feelings hurt in any way.

In the meantime, we had the body of a dead man in our storage hut which would remain in state for days or weeks. I would eventually have to dispose of it by giving the Indian a proper burial which would somehow be in accordance with the customs of his people. I did not want to offend the Pawnee people by doing something contrary to their customs and beliefs. We lived in complete harmony with one another, and had thus far been respectful of each other's feelings and beliefs. When the snow melted, and we could travel, I would seek the counsel of my good friend, Lectūschemă, at the Pawnee village. In addition to being my friend, he was a man of great wisdom, who would tell me what I must do in this situation.

We made a proper bed in the loft for November and hung her wet clothes from the rafters to dry in the warmth of our home. Loweja and Steechánay shared their hair brushes with her and constantly made efforts to make her feel as if she was among caring people. They doted over her as if she was a little adopted sister. November received these gestures quite well, and during the coming weeks she settled in and adjusted to our family's routine until she felt just like another family member to us, regardless of the fact that she did not seem to be learning very many English words. I noticed that Kwīnahā had changed his usual seating location at our table with Pokeem so that he could sit directly across from November at each meal. Everyone else noticed this also, but no one said anything for fear of hurting Kwīnahā's feelings. At night, November would climb the ladder to the loft, and Kwīnahā would never miss an evening watching her climb the ladder. Once she was in the loft, and ready to draw the privacy curtain, Kwīnahā and her always had their eyes locked together when the curtains were drawn. After November would retire to the loft, the children went to their bed, and my wives and I soon retired to our room. Kwīnahā was so innocently obvious in his adoration of November that my wives and I often chuckled about it in private. This evening routine continued every evening for several weeks, as spring drew closer. November had lost the fingernail of the finger which had frozen so bad, and she did not regain feeling in that finger. Other than that, she made a full recovery and was very happy to be living with us. She actively helped Steechánay and Loweja throughout the day with their chores. When Kwīnahā went outside of the house to tend to his chores, November would often open the door slightly and peek out to see if she could see him. Their adolescent love-sickness amused my wives and me, and although we chuckled about it frequently to ourselves, we never said anything which we thought might hurt their feelings. I was worried somewhat, though, that their amorous musings may lead to more serious consequences, and they were both entirely too young for me to permit that to happen. I would intervene, if necessary, as any father would.

    One night, after November had been in our home for more than seven weeks, when everyone was in their beds, in the privacy of our bedchamber I quietly spoke to Loweja and Steechánay about the ever-developing amorous infatuation between November and Kwīnahā. This was the first time which had I discussed my serious apprehensions with my wives in any detail. I felt that their youthful attraction to each other was becoming much too serious, and I wanted to know what Loweja and Steechánay thought. I wanted to know if they thought that I was over-reacting to an otherwise harmless enchantment between youths.

"Have either of you noticed the way that Kwīnahā and November are looking at each other nowadays?" Loweja was the first to answer.

"How could such looks go unnoticed here in our home? They have looked upon each other that way for many weeks now, John."

"I think Kwīnahā has been smitten!"

"Why do you always use words that Loweja and me don't understand?"

"Because, that is the only way for you and Loweja to learn new words, Steechánay."

"I think we know enough English words already, but what does this new word, '*smitten*' mean? Does it mean the same thing as, interest?"

"In an odd sort of way, yes, it does, Steechánay. '*Smitten*' means to be completely in love, so much, that you walk around in a daze, like you are dreaming."

"And then when he dreams, his *interest* comes up?"

"Loweja, I'm being serious now! Stop laughing! I'm afraid this could hurt Kwīnahā's heart if this gets out of hand! If it will hurt his heart, then it will hurt mine, as well."

"I don't think that Kwīnahā is in love with her yet, John."

"Oh? Why do you say that, Steechánay?"

"Because he has not seen her fishing naked, yet!"

"Stop laughing! Both of you! The children will hear you! I am being serious! I think they are both too young to be smitten with each other. In another year or two they will be old enough for that sort of thing, but not now. Neither one of them are any older than fifteen... sixteen at the most. That is far too young for them to be serious with each other!"

"Do you think they are too young to have *ohgā-sá-ho*

with each other, John?"

"Steechánay! I am surprised at you for asking that! Of course they are too young for something like that! *Ohgā-sá-ho* is something that is only for adults, it's out of the question for them at their young age! I'm surprised that you should even ask such a question! November is just a young girl!"

"She is old enough to make her blood."

"How do you know this?"

"Because I see her at the creek when she wash her rag."

"Well... Still... They are much too young for *ohgā-sá-ho*. Much too young!"

"I hope that you don't tell them that they are too young to do it, John."

"If I thought their young lovesickness could lead them to something like that so soon in life, then I would have to try to prevent it, and I would have to tell them so. Why shouldn't I talk to them?"

"Because there is only a ladder that separates them at night, and Kwīnahā has been climbing that ladder each night after we go to bed... then climbing back down each dawn before we get up."

"What! Kwīnahā? My little Kwīnahā is sleeping with November? Up in the loft? Under my own roof? I don't believe you! That can't be!"

"I don't think they are doing much sleeping while Kwīnahā is up there... I think they have been doing much *ohgā-sá-ho* up there instead of sleeping. November is always very sleepy during the day, and so is Kwīnahā."

"This can't be! I still don't believe it!"

"Peek out at his bed to see if he is in it, but do not make any noise. It may disturb them if they know you are walking around and I think they are in the loft, together now, doing it. Just like they do every night."

I slowly and quietly opened our bedroom door and looked into the top tier of the children's bed to see Joseph, sleeping... with Kwīnahā's side of the bed empty. I sneaked back into our bedroom and quietly closed the door and returned to my bed.

"My Lord! He's up there with her right now! How long has Kwīnahā been climbing the ladder at night?"

"Many days now."

"And everyone knew that they have been up there in the loft at night, doing... whatever they're doing... but me?"

"The children don't know, but Loweja and me know this, and we thought maybe you know this, too, and just not say anything."

"Why am I always the last to know what goes on in my own house?"

"Loweja and me talk about this and we just think that you know... Kwīnahā is boy... November is girl... a ladder will not keep them apart."

"Well, I didn't know. I had no idea. My goodness... What should we do now?"

"As his father, maybe you can talk to him. As your wives, Loweja and me will do whatever you say. We love you, John, and we also love Kwīnahā and November, too. Just remember that their hearts have made them do this thing. If you pull them apart, you will hurt their hearts very bad, and they might not love you as much if you separate them. I know this is true. I was in that loft many nights before you take me for your wife, so I know maybe how November feels too, when she is up there alone."

"Loweja, what do you think I should do?"

"I think you should talk to Kwīnahā, just like Steechánay say. I think you should talk to Kwīnahā as man, not boy, and I think Great Holy Father will put words in your heart and you will say right thing. I know this is true. You always say right thing... that is why Steechánay and me love you so much."

As was usually the case, my wives were right. I should

speak to Kwīnahā, and when I do, I will talk to him as one man to another. He was a fine young man, with a tender, lovable heart. I wanted to do nothing, or say nothing that would hurt him in any way. As for him yielding to his adolescent passions, I understood perfectly. I was once his age, and could clearly recall the awesome force of the driving urges that were so common in my youth. I could also recall that many of the things which I had done as a youth that were much worse than climbing a ladder to exchange nightly sexual favors. Despicably worse! I thought about the situation for a few minutes, then spoke to my wives.

"This is what we will do. I will speak to Kwīnahā... when the time is right. In the meantime, we will say nothing to him about this. We will allow him to continue to climb the ladder at night, and we will continue to act as if we know nothing. If November is not pregnant now, she soon will be, so I need to figure something out quickly. I will find some way to talk to him when we are together."

"You are good father, John... and good husband, too. Your heart has much love in it for your family, and your family has much love in their hearts for you. Loweja and me know that you will do right thing."

There was still a matter of having the body of a dead Indian in my storage hut. The body was still frozen solid, but as the days of spring approached, I knew that I would have to do something with it within a couple of weeks. With most of the winter snows gone, it was time for Kwīnahā and me to visit my friend, Lectūschemă at his village and seek his wisdom and advice on how to properly bury the body in accordance with Pawnee customs. I did not want to do anything that could be considered a violation of sacred tribal rites. Kwīnahā and I left early one morning for our trip to Lectūschemă's village. This would be Kwīnahā's second such trip with me. As we rode alongside one another, I took the opportunity to speak earnestly with him.

"I am very glad that you are here and traveling with me this morning, Kwīnahā."

"I am very glad too, Father. Maybe we will learn what to do with the body of November's father."

"I hope so, son, but that is not the only reason that we go to the Pawnee village this morning."

"What other reason do we go for, Father?"

"I have a surprise for you. I have noticed that you are not a child any longer, son. You are a man, now. I thought maybe while we were at the Pawnee village we could look to see if maybe we could find a wife for you there."

"Father! No! Please do not do this!"

"What's the matter, son? Don't you want a wife?"

"Father, I do want a wife. More than anything I want a wife, but not from Pawnee village. Please, Father!"

"Oh, I understand. Maybe we can go to the Missouri trading post and buy you a wife down there from the Arikara."

"Father! No! Please!"

"Kwīnahā! Let's stop here for a minute and talk, son. Is there something you want to tell me?"

"Yes, Father, but I am afraid. I don't know how to talk to you about this."

"Go ahead, son. Don't be afraid. You can tell me anything. I love you, and I will listen from my heart at what you have to say."

"Father, I know that you don't know this… I have wanted to tell you for many days now… but I have been afraid to… I love November, Father, and I want her for my wife. Our hearts hurt to be together. Our hearts hurt bad."

"November? November? I would never have guessed that! Why didn't you tell me this sooner, son?"

"I was afraid, Father. I was afraid that you would tell me that I could not have her because you promised to take her back to her people. If I could not have her for my wife my heart would die. I know this."

"Does November also love you, son?"

"We have much love in our hearts for each other, Father."

"Do you think November wants to be your wife?"

"Yes, Father. She has told me so... many times she has told me this. She has asked me to talk to you, but I was afraid."

"Well then, I think we should finish our business in the Pawnee village quickly, so that we can hurry home and tell the family! They have much love in their hearts for you and November, and I know they will be happy and surprised to hear this! If you want November for a wife, and she wants you for a husband, then you will have my blessing, son. But we must talk about this with her when we get home. It would be wrong if we made her stay with us unless she wanted to. We will talk when we get home, and we will see what happens."

"Thank you, Father!"

"I'm sorry I got things mixed up. I didn't know that you were in love with November. I remembered that you told me that there was a girl at the Pawnee village that you thought was wonderful."

"That was before my eyes saw November, Father. I love no other girl... just November."

"Oh, I understand now. Thank you for making this clear in my mind. You are a good son, Kwīnahā! I am very proud of you, and I never want you to be afraid to talk to me... about anything."

"You are a good father! You have made me very happy!"

On our arrival at the Pawnee village, Lectūschemă came to greet us. Kwīnahā helped me as an interpreter, and after much discussion, the matter of the man's body was settled. Lectūschemă thought that the man in question was from a faraway Pawnee village, for they were missing no people from his village. Even though the man was not from his village, he agreed to send two of his braves back with us and have the body placed on a traditional raised platform near their burial ground. He was very impressed with the man's bravery when I told him of the sacrifice the man had made when he gave his coat to his daughter. Lectūschemă felt that such bravery warranted a proper burial, and he assured me that his people would be told of this man's bravery.

As we sat and talked, I noticed that Lectūschemă had a revolver on his person. I had seen it before, but never paid a great deal of attention to it. Now, I looked at it closely, and saw that it was exactly the same as the one which I had once carried. I thought back, and remembered leaving a revolver such as that with Oscar and Octeenchaha at the creek camp when Loweja and I had gone to the canyon for gold. My curiosity finally got the best of me and I told Lectūschemă that I admired his revolver, and asked him how he had obtained it. He told me that he and four of his braves had approached a man and his wife to talk to them, and that the man had raised the revolver and killed one of his braves with the gun. They killed the man, and brought his woman to their village, where she was given to the family of the brave who was killed. I asked him if the man they had killed was of dark skin, and he answered, "yes, very dark." I asked him if the woman had been killed, and he said that she had not. She had been taken as a wife by the father of the son who had been killed by Oscar. Thusly, the mystery of the disappearance of Oscar and Octeenchaha had been solved. I imagined that Oscar had panicked and shot out of extreme terror. The Pawnee simply did what they had to do in order to protect themselves. I asked Lectūschemă if the woman was happy to be a wife there and he said that she was very happy now, and would soon produce a child. He was curious as to why I had such an interest in her happiness, but I discussed the issue with him no more, out of sovereign respect for our friendship.

That evening, back at our home, Kwīnahā and I watched the two Pawnee braves ride away with the body of November's father as we stood there at the storage hut. Kwīnahā's eyes constantly looked toward the house as we closed the door to the hut and latched it shut. I looked at him and asked, "Well, son, is there anything else we need to do down here?"

"No, Father, we can go to the house now."

"Do you think we should check the shingles on the roof of the hut while we are here?"

"No, Father, they are fine, and no rain comes through."

"Maybe we should go into the woods and gather some more firewood."

"Father! Please! Can we go to the house now?"

"I suppose we can, but let's see which one of us can run the fastest to the house!"

As I expected, Kwīnahā won our little footrace. He had already been in the house for a few moments when I got there. The family greeted us warmly, but November and Kwīnahā did not embrace. Instead, they looked at each other with shy, fleeting glances, and remained on opposite sides of the room. November was unaware that I was about to give my blessing to their marriage and formally declare them husband and wife. Steechánay and Loweja were also unaware of what I had decided and looked at me with great apprehension, for they knew that I was about to make an announcement. I asked the family to be seated around the table, and November sat quietly off to herself. Everyone looked intently at me to hear what I had to say.

"I want everyone to gather around me and listen very closely to what I've got to say. What I am about to say is very important. *November*, will you come over here and join us at the table, please."

She did not move, and I suddenly remembered that she only spoke Pawnee, so I motioned her over with my hand. She seemed terribly frightened, and looked as though she thought that I may have discovered the secret of the nightly ladder climbing. She looked as though she expected to be beaten at any moment as punishment for her adolescent indiscretions.

Nervously, she walked to the table and sat down.

"Steechánay, I would like for you to repeat everything that I say in Pawnee, so that November will understand what I say. Kwīnahā, why don't you move over there and sit down beside November. I think you will be more comfortable there, son. Kwīnahā and I have been talking today. I think that he is a man now. I took him to the Pawnee village today to find him a wife, but he said that he didn't want me to buy him a wife there. So I offered to take him to the trading post, and buy him an Arikara wife there. He did not want to do that either. When I asked him why, he told me that he only loved November, and wants her for his wife. Isn't that right, Kwīnahā?"

"Yes, Father, that is right."

"Steechánay, ask November if she understands everything that you have said to her."

"She says yes, she understands good."

"Good. November, do you want Kwīnahā for a husband or do you want to go back to your people? We will not keep you here if you do not want to stay with us. It is spring now, and we will take you where you want to go. We love you, but we will not force you to stay with us. We will try to find your people, if that is what you want you us to do. Do you understand that?"

"She says that she understands, but she wants only to be with Kwīnahā, and she wants to be his wife. She has great love for him."

"Let's see now... that may present a great problem... if you were husband and wife, I wonder where you could sleep at night?"

"The loft is good, Father! We can sleep up there!" Kwīnahā eagerly offered.

"That is good, son, if you do not mind climbing a ladder each night."

"We don't mind at all, Father! We like the loft... I mean the loft would be a good place for us to sleep."

"Kwīnahā, do you promise to love November forever, to watch over her and protect her? And to always love her until the day you die?"

"Yes, Father!"

"November, do you promise to love Kwīnahā forever, and always be a good wife for him, until the day that you die?"

"She says, yes, Mr. Welch."

"November, will you try to learn to speak some English words so that I may speak with you at times?"

"She says, yes, Mr. Welch. She says that she will try very hard."

"Let's all hold hands and ask the Great Holy Father to bless this marriage. Father, we come humbly before you and ask that you bless the lives of Kwīnahā and November as they begin the rest of their lives as husband and wife. Please watch over them, Father, and guide them to many happy years together. We ask this in the name of your precious son, Jesus. Amen." When I had finished the prayer, there were only the younger children in the room that did not have a tear on their cheek.

"As of this moment, and forever more, you are husband and wife. Kwīnahā, you may kiss November. She is your wife now."

"Can we go somewhere else and kiss there, Father?"

"You must kiss her once here with us to watch, then, if you want, I suppose you could take her up to the loft and kiss her some more up there. But please pull the curtains closed when you go to the loft... there are children down here. We will call you tonight when your dinner is ready."

With blushing faces, they kissed very quickly, then, fled to the loft. I had never seen a ladder climbed as quickly by two people. I turned to look at Loweja and Steechánay and I could tell by the ecstatic looks and smiles upon their faces that I had done the right thing. They both gave me a kiss and a broad smile and went about their evening chores. Before it got too dark to see outside, I finished my outside chores and tended to the horses. Tending to the horses was usually Kwīnahā's job, but I felt as though he was probably busy doing other things that evening, so I did it myself. Loweja yelled at me that they needed water, which was another of Kwīnahā's chores, so I tended to that as well and closed the henhouse door. I didn't mind. My heart was happy for Kwīnahā and November. Again, I asked the Great Holy Father to bless their marriage. Many times that evening I saw Loweja and Steechánay look up toward the drawn privacy curtains and smile. I knew that their hearts felt good inside, and mine felt good as well. Despite their young age, I had done the right thing. Steechánay was right; their hearts had drawn them together. Who was I, to interfere with sincere passions of their young hearts? Steechánay called up to them for dinner that evening and Kwīnahā answered, "We are not hungry, Mother. Thank you."

Kwīnahā and November did not come down to join us for dinner. In fact, they did not come down until breakfast the next morning. In private conversation, I asked Steechánay and Loweja, "Did you see how quickly Kwīnahā climbed up that ladder with November?" Steechánay thought about it for a moment, then a warm, motherly smile crossed her face, and she said, "He is very young, and he has had a lot of practice climbing ladders for many days now while we sleep!"

When Loweja and I had first returned to our home in the valley, Steechánay lived in our house there with her four children. When Loweja and I moved in, the family grew to seven. When Loweja had Little Bear, the family grew to eight. When Kwīnahā married, the family grew to nine. Steechánay would soon deliver, which would make ten, and I felt certain that with all of the 'interest' that Kwīnahā was showing November, she would bear Kwīnahā a child in the near future. The little house was growing smaller for all of us, and I knew that I would have to make some changes soon. The rider that Captain McBride would send could arrive any day now, and I was busy making a list of the items we would need for the upcoming year.

I thought about building a larger house for my wives and children on the hillside above the garden, and giving this house where we now lived to Kwīnahā and November. Steechánay's belly was now fat with child, and a larger house would give us ample room for our expanding family. I planned for the new house to have a separate bedchamber for our children, and a larger bedchamber for my wives and me. Kwīnahā and November would be pleased to have the privacy that they needed, and the rest of us would have increased living space and ample room for growth. Kwīnahā, Joseph, and I began cutting logs and pulling them to our new house site with the horses. The logs would be close at hand when we were ready to begin building. The children and Loweja brought rocks up from the creek to be used for the foundation and the large fireplace that I wanted to build. I felt certain that if November had not conceived by this time that she would soon, and so there was a sense of urgency in the construction of the new house. I knew that our construction would be interrupted when it came time to plant our spring crops, so the family worked diligently to get the new house under way. I often started work at the first sign of dawn, and stopped at night only when it became too dark to see.

By the first of May, Kwīnahā, Joseph, and I had the walls of the new house set in place, and were starting to set the rafters of the roof. We were working very hard one day, when at mid-afternoon Loweja approached us. She was not carrying food as she usually did at that time of day, and she had a very distressed look upon her face. As she drew closer, I could see that she had been crying, and she looked bewildered.

"Loweja! What's the matter?"

"Steechánay need you! Steechánay need you hurry!"

I jumped down from the ladder and ran toward the

house as fast as I could. When I got there, I found Steechánay sitting on a chair near the kitchen stove, naked. She was holding a small bundle of bloody cloth, and staring blindly into space. There were small splatters of blood about the floor and in the chair where she sat.

"Steechánay! What's wrong, darling!?"

"Our baby die, John. I am sorry to tell you this."

While I had been working on the construction of our new home, Steechánay had apparently gone into labor, and our baby was still-born. I ran to her and hugged her gently, and we wept together. Loweja joined us and the three of us embraced for several minutes while I said a prayer. Loweja wept the loudest. Little Bear was on the children's bed looking at us with curious little eyes and November sat over to the side. She appeared horrified by what she had witnessed. My heart was broken over the loss of our baby, but mostly, my heart was broken over the emptiness that Steechánay must have felt. I wasn't sure of what to say to offer her comfort, so I simply said, "Necu-ta-say-ha, Steechánay. I love you."

"I want to bear you a child, John, but she is dead. I am sorry."

"Loweja and I love you, Steechánay. This bad time that our hearts hurt will pass. But our love for you will never pass."

"John say truth, Steechánay. We love you."

Steechánay was still bleeding somewhat from her ordeal, and as Loweja gently cleaned her, I took the tiny bundle from her arms and walked to the storage hut. The children walked over from the henhouse, and together we placed the tiny bundle in a small wooden box. Back at the house, I helped Loweja move Steechánay into our bed where she was made comfortable, and Loweja and November began preparing our evening meal. The family was somber and respectfully quiet as I walked back to Steechánay's bedside and quietly talked with her.

"Steechánay, do you need anything?"

"No, John. I will soon be better. I will just sleep now."

"Steechánay, I am going now to bury our child. I will be back soon. I'm sorry this happened. My heart hurts for you now. You rest, and I will be back soon. Necu-ta-say-ha, Steechánay."

"Necu-ta-say-ha, John. You talk to Great Holy Father again when you bury child?"

"Yes, Steechánay... of course I will."

I walked alone back to the storage hut and stood there for some time, looking at the wooden box that had become our baby's coffin. I wanted to open it, and remove the cloth from the tiny child so that I could look upon her face, but I did not have the courage. The image would have haunted me for the rest of my life, I'm sure. Instead, I took three nails and nailed the lid shut. With the box in one hand, and a shovel in the other, I walked alone to a hillside overlooking the creek and dug a grave there. In solitude, my tears flowed freely with each shovel-full of dirt that I dropped on the small coffin. From the creek, I carried stones to cover the dirt and to prevent animals from digging in the soil of the grave. And as I had promised Steechánay, I spoke to the Great Holy Father. I asked him to bless the soul of our baby and to restore Steechánay in body and spirit.

The days following the death of our child were agonizingly melancholy, but, as life went on, our hearts slowly healed. The rider sent by Captain McBride arrived as he had promised, and left promptly the same day, bearing the list of supplies that I wanted. It was an extensive list, indeed, and I was sure that the delivery would take nearly twice as many pack horses as I had used to bring in the last supplies. Slowly, the attitudes of our family began to enlighten, and laughter could once again be heard about the house. Spring was upon us, and the entire family worked together planting our crops and finishing the construction of our new home. When I had made my last trip to Fort Saint Joseph for supplies, I had brought back window glass for our new home, and I was using this glass to make two windows on the front of our home. The boards used to frame the windows had to be sawn from logs. This was a tedious task that required more than two days of hard labor for each of the windows. Steechánay was now fully recovered, and often assisted me by handling one end of the saw when Kwīnahā would be tending to other chores. One day while we were sawing lumber, Steechánay and I talked.

"Are you happy, Steechánay?"

"I am very much happy, John! Are you happy?"

"I am worried about Loweja, that's all."

"Why do you worry about Loweja? What is wrong with her?"

"She hasn't been tickled for a long, long time. I think she needs to be tickled tonight. I think she has been very naughty the last few days, and needs to be tickled. Will you help me?"

"Every time I help you tickle Loweja then you start to tickle me too. But I will help you tonight anyway... even if you tickle me too. We will have great fun tonight. I love you, John!"

"I love you, too, Steechánay!"

"May I tell you something, John?"

"Of course, you can tell me anything, Steechánay."

"I tell you one time that I love William Welch. When I tell you that, I did not know what love was. I only think I love William Welch. I know much about love now, because you teach me what love is. William Welch did not kiss me. He did not tell me much that he love me, and when he did tell me that, he did not say it with good heart. He did not touch me in good ways like you touch me. He did not laugh and tickle with me. He did not look at me with his eyes like you look at me. He put babies in me... that is all. And I think that I love him then because he did that. But it was not love. I have real love in my heart now for you, and I have real love in my heart now for Loweja. Now I know that Great Holy Father sent William Welch to me, not for love, but so that you would come to me someday with real love. I know that, and I thank Great Holy Father for that. I am happy to be your wife. I think you know this already, but my heart wants me to tell you this again, so I did."

"Steechánay, there is hardly a moment that passes during each day, that I don't thank our Great Holy Father that I have you and Loweja in my life. I love you, Steechánay, and I would do anything for you... anything!"

"Will you just tickle Loweja tonight, and not me?"

"I would do anything for you, Steechánay... but that!"

Visitors

Life in our beautiful valley continued on for us. For the next two years we lived in sublime contentment and happiness. As I had predicted, November bore a beautiful baby daughter for Kwīnahā and they were both still deeply in love with each other. Watching them grow together as young adults brought much happiness to our family. As she had promised, November had learned to speak some English and we were able to speak to each other finally, in very basic conversation. I continued to encourage my family to speak English as much as possible, yet found myself prone to use more and more Arikara and Pawnee words. Even the occasional use of French words was employed, and I feared that the language we now spoke to each other was an odd, yet uniquely effective, language of our own. Kwesha and Pokeem were old enough to assist with many of the chores that they were previously too young to perform, and Steechánay and Loweja had taught them to mend clothing and to make simple garments for themselves. Kwīnahā, Joseph, and I completed the construction of the large house, and Kwīnahā, November, and their daughter took over the smaller home. Most of our meals were taken together as a family in the larger home that was only forty yards away from the smaller home. Steechánay and Loweja remained as close as Siamese twins. There was never a trace of dissent in their relationship, and we really had become three hearts as one. I had always felt as though Loweja would have eternally been first and foremost in my heart, but after two years it would have been impossible for me to choose one over the other. I loved them both dearly, and would gladly sacrifice my life for either one of them. I was always susceptible to Loweja's charms from the first time we met, but soon found myself equally as susceptible to Steechánay's beauty and her gentleness. They often conspired together in order to play little jokes on me. Yet their jokes never riled me in any way, they only brought laughter and happiness into our home.

    Our crops grew well there in our valley, the fruit trees were yielding a good harvest each year, and we had ordered jars and equipment from Captain McBride that would allow us to preserve some our harvest for the winter months. This was a new concept for me, and I looked forward to learning the principles and putting it to use. Steechánay had become pregnant with child again, and presented me with a healthy son at the beginning of the second year, without complications. We named our newest son, *Hūhyĕh*... a Pawnee name, meaning, *"happiness in the morning."* Loweja had not conceived again as yet. This seemed a strange puzzlement to us all, although no one in our family grieved over the matter, including Loweja. If the Great Holy Father chose to give us no more children, we still had plenty of them to love and care for. There was an abundance of love abiding within our house, and we all felt that Loweja would bear another child someday, and if and when it happened, it would happen. She was a wonderful, caring mother for Little Bear, and helped Steechánay by giving a lot of attention to Kwesha and Pokeem and occasionally helping with Himasay and Hūhyĕh. I began to pay particular attention to Kwesha as she was growing into a fine young girl. In the warm weather, at the creek where we bathed as a family, I noticed that Kwesha's breasts were beginning to develop and she was starting to grow pubic hair. Loweja and Steechánay had told me that she was starting to ask many questions about her body. She wanted to know why blood had appeared in her bed one morning. This concerned me, for she would probably be ready for a husband in a few years and I would be faced with a father's agony in seeing that she met and married someone who would be good and kind to her. For now, however, it was not necessary for me to give the matter very much much thought. I guessed her age now to be thirteen. I would do everything in my power to see that she had a happy and safe future. I knew that her only option for eventual romance would be a possible suitor from the Pawnee village. I was at peace with that, for I knew that there were many fine young men in Lectŭschemă's village. I knew that she could be far happier here in the mountains than in a boarding school in some far away city. When the time came, I would find her a suitable, kind and loving, husband, and I would not offer her up for sale to do so! She was a sweet child with a tender heart, and I would do everything in my power to see that she was not hurt.

As accustomed as I had become to the Indian way of life, my friends, the Pawnee, had many customs and superstitions which I did not agree with, nor approve of. I often expressed my points of view with Lectŭschemă when we spoke in private. Yet when I did express my opinion, I was always very careful not to offend him in any way, nor did I criticize him for his beliefs. I simply told him what my beliefs were, and we were each respectful of the other's customs and beliefs. In his village, obtaining a wife was a process which was handled altogether different than in the Arikara village. A young man would approach the mother of the girl whom he wanted to marry and inform her of his desires. The woman would discuss the issue with her husband, and if the husband was in agreement he would recommend a price; such as two horses, a number of buffalo hides or beaver pelts, etc., but the mother made the ultimate decision regarding an appropriate dowry. In two weeks, the suitor would visit the mother again and she would inform him of the dowry which needed to be paid, or inform him that he was not worthy. If the suitor could meet the dowry demanded, a ceremony was eventually performed and the couple were married. The groom was then required to consummate the marriage in the lodge of his bride's father… under the watchful eyes of her father, his wives, and any brothers or sisters who wished to attend. After the marriage was appropriately consummated, the groom had to abide there in the lodge of his father-in-law for a full year, during which time he was not allowed to converse with the father at all. All conversation with the family had to go through the mother. When a child was born, the couple was free to go and live their own life and the groom was free to talk directly to the father. I could not imagine a man being able to maintain the ability to consummate a marriage while the entire family looked on. It is truly the most miserable excuse of a honeymoon that I have ever heard of, as well as the most embarrassing and even '*unromantic*' demands of a groom imaginable.

    A warrior who sought a wife could expect to pay a much reduced dowry requirement for a wife if he had performed extreme acts of bravery in battle. Bravery was a highly revered quality in a man – a quality which was widely believed to be passed down from father to son, therefore assuring the family of strong, courageous offspring. Some braves, having taken four scalps or more from their enemy, could possibly be given a wife for no dowry at all.

    Lectūschemă's village had many other strange rituals and beliefs that were equally as difficult for me to embrace, yet I was always respectful of their beliefs. I knew that my continued happiness there in my valley depended greatly on my ability not to offend them. The friendly commerce which I had with these people enabled my family and I to live joyfully and peacefully among a tribe of people who were feared by most outsiders. And I was no longer viewed as an outsider. I had never tried to exploit their friendship in any way, nor would I have permitted anyone else to. With Lectūschemă being one of the leaders of his people, provided me with further assurance that my presence in the valley was accepted, and my family's future was sovereign.

People from the Pawnee village still came to gather at our home every month or two, but now they came in much greater numbers and camped for a day or two when they came. The occasion had turned into much more than a simple friendly visit. We traded together, shared knowledge together, and enjoyed much food and merriment together. They began bringing their wives and children to the festivities with them. It was a grand opportunity for our children to have other children to play with, and the event enabled me speak the Pawnee language better and better. My good friend, Lectūschemă, had become the leader of his people, and the bond that held us together only strengthened with each passing season. His wisdom, kindness, and generosity served as an inspiration to me. His village had not been contaminated with the horrible small pox, diphtheria, or the venereal diseases of the Europeans, and I had taken great pains in forewarning him and his people of the dangers of copulating with outsiders. I gave them a vivid account of what had happened in Hidessa's village, and the Mandan villages as well. They knew that I spoke the truth, and Lectūschemă had taken my warnings to heart. Someday, the Europeans would come in greater numbers, but Lectūschemă had assured me that the strangers would not be offered carnal favors, in fact, they would not be permitted to go near his village. Lectūschemă knew that I spoke the truth, and that my forewarnings were offered only for their protection.

Loweja, Steechánay, and November used these occasional get-togethers to do some trading of their own with the Pawnee women. They made garments and moccasins for our own family, but they also made items for the specific purpose of trading. These friendly get-togethers also provided me with an opportunity to serve as an unofficial physician of sorts. People with ailments would come to see me and I would assess their injury or sickness at the storage hut. If their ailment was of a nature that I could give them some relief, I would gladly do so. There were some pitiful cases that I could do nothing about, but most of the time I was able to provide some type of relief. There was a little girl, whose shoulder and arm had been badly chewed by a wolf before her father could kill the animal. The wound had become septic, and was causing the child great pain. I gave her a small dose of whiskey and cleaned and dressed her wounds, applying hot saltwater compresses for two days. I took great comfort in the fact that the child made a full recovery from a wound that would have undoubtedly killed her in a matter of a few days had it gone untreated. Even with successes such as this, I still felt heart-sickened when confronted with a situation where I could do nothing. I had been successful in treating a serious ear infection for one of Lectūschemā's own children… further solidifying the bond that existed between us. I was well liked by the Ree, primarily because I often gave them much, and seldom asked for anything in return. In return for the attention that I gave to their sick and injured, my presence when I visited their village was welcome. They would look upon me with smiles and admiration as I walked among them. I felt honored to have their friendship.

Each spring, when the supply caravan arrived, I would receive any mail that had come for me at Fort Saint Joseph. I eventually sold my house and belongings in Baltimore and slowly stopped receiving correspondence of any kind from the east. I arranged through my bank in Fort Saint Joseph, to invest some of my money into the railroad industry and was receiving substantial returns on my investment. With each order that I placed with Captain McBride, I always included orders for several of the newest rifles and revolvers. My stockpile of weaponry grew each year, as I seemed to sense that one day they might be needed. I prayed that there would never be such a need, but felt comfort in preparing for the worst eventuality. Times were changing, and they were changing rapidly. We had seen the first white men in our valley, and talked to them briefly as they traveled westward. I cautioned them to travel well south of the Pawnee village that lay to our northwest, in hopes that the Rees would not be bothered by the encroachment of whites. There had been fighting between the Arikara and the Ree, and between the Arikara and whites. People had been killed, and the news saddened me. There had always been fighting between the Arikara and other tribes, such as the Pawnee and the Mandan, but I knew that with the coming of the white man, dissention between the different tribes would only increase. As badly as I had wanted to remain neutral, I felt that someday I would have some important decisions to make.

As my wives were preparing our mid-day meal on one late summer afternoon, Kwīnahā came inside and announced,

"Father! Many men with horses come! I think it is our supplies!"

I looked to the southeast to see that Kwīnahā was correct, it was our summer supplies from Fort Saint Joseph, and we were very much in need of some of the items they were bringing. As the men drew closer, I was astonished to see two very familiar faces approaching. I had to wipe my eyes and look again! I could not believe my eyes! In the lead was Hidessa, and right behind him was Captain McBride, on a horse, no less! I was beside myself with joy! I greeted each of them with a hug and invited them into my home. Once inside, everyone was properly introduced, although Loweja remembered both Hidessa and Captain McBride. She was extremely glad to see them both. We sat at the table and I sent Kwīnahā to the storage hut for two bottles of wine.

"I cannot tell you how good it is for my heart to see you both again. Captain McBride, sir, I must tell you that you are a peculiar looking sight when you are on a horse, and not at the wheel of your boat!"

"I'm getting older, John. I wanted to see you again, and I am unsure of whether I would ever be able to travel this far on a horse again... so I thought that I would come along on this delivery."

"I am very pleased that you did! Who is attending to the care of your vessel while you are gone, Captain?"

"My vessel's engine is being reconstructed, John. It will be out of commission for the next two months, so I traveled by pirogue, and then by horseback."

"Hidessa, whatever possessed you to travel this far away from your village and your three wives!?"

"I am getting older, too. I have not traveled this far in ten years... maybe more. My wives are tormenting me badly, so I thought I would leave them for a while. Maybe they will be glad to see me when I go home, but I don't think so." Captain McBride had been looking about the house with great admiration in his eyes. As I opened a bottle of wine and poured us a glass, he looked at me and spoke.

"For more than three years now, I have been dreadfully curious about the source of your happiness. Looking about me, and looking into the eyes of your wonderful family... seeing the beauty of your valley and your home here... my curiosity has been satisfied. I can feel the love that is here in this house, and I can see it with my own eyes. I am envious, my friend, but I am also very happy for you. May I present a toast?"

"Please do, Captain. Your words are always eloquent. Allow me to pour a glass for my wonderful wives and my oldest son and his wife, first." I was somewhat hesitant to give wine to Loweja, Steechánay, and November, as they had never tasted spirits before, but felt as though this was an unusually joyous occasion that warranted celebration. As the seven of us raised our glasses, the Captain uttered appropriate words, befitting of the occasion.

"May your current health and happiness be merely a small sampling of that which you and your family will receive during the years to come. God bless you all!"

"Thank you, Captain, and may God bless you as well!

I trust that you and Hidessa are both hungry?"

"Hidessa and I are both terrible cooks. The food that we have eaten on the trail was not fit for man or beast. Sitting here like this, and smelling the wonderful aroma of your wives' cooking has really aroused my interest!" Upon hearing the word, '*interest*,' Loweja and Steechánay quickly raised their eyebrows and turned to look at the Captain and immediately started whispering and giggling between themselves. Then the giggles quickly escalated into outright laughter. Soon, the laughter became very loud!

"Did I say something amusing, John?"

"No, Captain. It's just that my mischievous wives can sometimes become unruly. It's their way of expressing their true happiness, that's all. I'm sure that they will settle down now and finish preparing our meal. **Won't you, ladies**?!"

"Yes, John. We are sorry."

As we sat and talked, Indian workmen were unloading our supplies from the pack horses. Kwīnahā excused himself to go to the storage hut and supervise the proper storage of our items. The three of us talked exuberantly for an hour while the women continued to prepare a meal for us. I noticed that Steechánay, November, and Loweja giggled softly between themselves. This was the first time that they had tasted wine, and even though I only poured them each a very small cupful, I suppose that it was enough to put them in a giddy mood. From Captain McBride, I learned that Martin Van Buren had been elected President of the United States, and that there were great conflicts with various Indian tribes taking place throughout the nation. This news that he presented was hurtful to me, but not surprising.

We had all walked down to the storage hut after the last of our goods were unloaded and stacked inside. We attended to the release of the workmen from their duty, and Captain McBride paid their wages. I had turned to walk back up to the house, when the Captain put his hand on my shoulder and spoke.

"John, before we return to your wives and children, there is something I must tell you." I saw urgency in the Captain's eyes which I had never seen before. I saw that same sense of urgency in Hidessa's eyes as well, as they both looked at me with deep concern.

"May Hidessa and I speak with you at will, in front of your son?"

"Kwīnahā is my son, but he is also a man. I sense that what you are about to tell me is meant for the ears of men. You may feel free to speak in front of my son. I know that you and Hidessa did not make this long and tedious journey here because of your curiosity. What do you wish to tell me, Captain?"

"You have your father's wisdom, as well as his intuition. John, listen closely to what I am about to say. There are men coming here with the intention of doing you harm. They are being led by a person known as, *Edmond Flanagan*... a wealthy and malevolent man who lives in St. Louis. He has always been an adversary of your father's, and he has been in pursuit of your father's wealth for many years now. He has unscrupulous connections within the banking industry, and he was informed of a large deposit of gold which your father made nearly sixteen years ago, and he knows about the large deposit of gold which you made four years ago in the bank of Fort Saint Joseph. He knows of the vast wealth that you and your father have discovered, and he is intent on learning the precise location from whence this large amount of gold comes from."

"How could you possibly know about all of this... about the gold that I deposited, and this so-called evil man? I don't understand, Captain."

"There is very little that goes on in St. Louis or Fort Saint Joseph of which I don't know about. I also have sources of information... many of them. Flanagan and his thugs have chartered a pirogue to bring them to the trading post. The pirogue is piloted by a dear friend of mine... a close confidante, so I arranged for a delay in its departure so that I could bring word to you before this threat arrived here to catch you unprepared. When they arrive at the trading post they will buy horses from the Frenchman. These thugs are well-armed, and they will be at the trading post soon. They have probably arrived there already, and are now on the trail to come here. They should have had very little difficulty tracking down some of the Indian workmen which have been delivering your goods. Once they've done that, they will know exactly where to come and find you."

"I have told all of the workmen not to mention my name or my location to anyone."

"Your reputation as a generous employer is on the lips of every young man in Hidessa's village. There are many ways to loosen a man's tongue. Flanagan probably knows all of them. He will stop at nothing, John. He's a ruthless madman! And he is a remorseless killer as well!"

"How many men will be coming with him, Captain?"

"I don't know for sure. I had to leave Fort Saint Joseph quickly, so I could arrive here ahead of him. But I do know that Flanagan himself will be among them, and it is likely that he will have five or six men with him, perhaps even more."

"So you've known all along about the gold that Father and I have found?"

"Yes, I have, John. Your father established an abundant fund in St. Louis for me to draw upon before he died... to be used by me in order to safeguard your welfare. He did not want you to know about it, so I withheld this and other information from you as long as I possibly could. I did not mean to deceive you, John. I was merely complying with your father's request that I remain an anonymous guardian, of sorts. Now that there is an eminent threat to your life, I have no choice but to intercede, and superintend you and your family's escape to safety. It's what your father would have expected of me."

"And exactly how would you propose to do that, Captain?"

"That is why Hidessa is with me. He knows of a trail about twenty miles to the southwest of here where we can escape through the great grassland to the south and back to my pirogue without Flanagan and his men knowing. They are most likely already traveling on the main trail to the northwest and will be here any day now. As I said, Flanagan and his cutthroats are most likely less than a day or two behind me..."

"I see..."

"You and your family must come with me. Once you are all in a location where I can see to your protection, I can hire people of my own, and devise some sort of plan to deal appropriately with Flanagan and his men... permanently, once and for all. The most important thing before us now, is to get you and your family to safety, and we must do it as quickly as possible... there is no time to lose."

"You are asking me to take my family away from the valley where we have found such great happiness? The valley of my father? To flee as scared rabbits from this Flanagan fellow?"

"For the safety of you and your family... yes, John. That is exactly what I am asking, and if you care for your family's welfare, you will comply with my request."

"And what about the next group of thugs to come along? Am I to flee from them as well? And the ones who come after them?"

"It is unlikely that there will ever be others who come after Flanagan."

"Captain, I am greatly touched and honored that you and Hidessa would come to my aid at such a time as this... especially at the great distance which you had to travel to get here. I value the friendship I have with both of you... immensely. But, I cannot and will not leave my valley. This was my father's valley, and now it is mine. I will live here with my family until I die and I will defend it with my last breath!"

"If these men come and find the location of your gold, there will be an unending wave of others who will come behind them. Your valley will never be the same as it is today, John."

"Then I'll have to deal with each of them, as they come."

"But John, think about what you are saying! These men who come are murderers! Flanagan does not negotiate, he does not bargain, and he has no compassion, John, he is a killer of men! In St. Louis, Flanagan owns the police and the politicians. He will stop at nothing! He will come here and kill your children and your wives in front of your own eyes, one by one, until you tell him what he wants to know… then he will kill you! He sent a thief to your home in Baltimore to search for your father's manuscripts. When the man was unsuccessful, Flanagan had him killed! He sent another thief to rob you on the train. When that man returned with a satchel full of worthless newspapers, Flanagan himself shot the man in the face and had his body thrown in the river! Then he sent three men to the trading post. They were supposed to find you and bring you to him in Fort Saint Joseph. But he never heard from them again. No one knows what happened to those scoundrels. Then he lost track of you, and did not know where to look until one of his scouts spoke with a Frenchman at the trading post. This time he is coming here himself! He will not leave until you are dead and he knows the location of your father's gold!"

"You knew about the attempted robbery of my home? The thief on the train… all of that?"

"Yes, John."

"How do you know all of this, Captain? How did you get all of this information?"

"I told you that I have many sources of information, John. Not all of my acquaintances are good, honest people. I am sometimes forced to deal with less scrupulous people in order to achieve an end. Please trust me John, and let me oversee the safety of you and your family as I swore to your father that I would... Please!"

"Kwīnahā, my son, do you understand everything that has been said here?"

"Yes, Father... almost everything."

"Good. It will be dark in three or four hours. I want you to take a horse and ride to the Pawnee village. Tell Lectūschemă that I need for him to come here as quickly as possible in the morning. Tell him that it is urgent, but don't tell him anything else. I am counting on you to do this for me. This is a job for a man, and I am sending a man to do this. Do you understand?"

"Yes, Father!"

"Good. Go quickly!"

Captain McBride and Hidessa looked confused over the fact that I was sending for an Indian friend. I remained as calm as possible, but in my mind, I was formulating my own plan to deal with this Flanagan fellow. I had always sensed that I had not heard the last of the evilness which followed me from Baltimore, and somehow I wanted to rid my life of any such future threat. I felt that it was now necessary for me to confront this vile and evil person... face-to-face if need be. Strangely, even with the threat that this confrontation posed, I felt somewhat relieved in knowing that it was finally going to happen. I should have been expecting it, and I should have been better prepared. I regretted not having a plan in place, ready to be implemented. At the same time, I realized that dealing with this threat would be much more difficult and dangerous than dealing with a chicken thief. As Kwīnahā quickly rode into the distant woods and out of sight, I turned the Captain McBride and Hidessa, saying, "Gentlemen, let's go to the house and have the meal which my wives have prepared for us and we can talk some more afterwards."

Hidessa and Captain McBride accompanied me back to the house where we ate a grand meal, suppressed only by the knowledge that an impending threat was in the immediate forecast. Steechánay and Loweja both knew that something important was going on. They were often successful at keeping little household secrets from me, but I was rarely successful in keeping any secrets at all from them. I saw them each paying me frequent glances, while attempting to read my face and occasionally looking at each other as they whispered between themselves. As wonderful as our meal was, there was very little conversation shared as we ate. The Captain and Hidessa expressed their delight with the food to Loweja and Steechánay, but little else was said, until I broke the silence after our meal was eaten. I called Steechánay, Loweja, and November before me and addressed them directly. I spoke softly, but sternly, so that there could be no misunderstand of the serious nature of my words.

"I want each of you to pack a few of the items you will need to go on a journey for a few days… perhaps as much as a week. Pack the things which you will need for you and the children. I want you all to be ready to leave by first light in the morning. November, I want you and the baby to sleep here in our house tonight. Captain McBride and Hidessa will sleep in your home. Steechánay, if there is anything I have said that November does not understand, please tell her in Pawnee. And tell her that Kwīnahā has gone on an errand for me and he won't be back until tomorrow morning."

"Where we go tomorrow, John?"

"Just do as I say, Loweja! I'm sorry that I raised my voice, but this is not a good time to ask questions. Please just do this thing that I ask, Loweja."

"Yes, John."

I regretted the harshness in my voice when I had spoken so gruffly to Loweja, for I had never raised my voice in anger at her before. It did serve to send a message to the entire family, however, that there was urgency in the issue at hand. Captain McBride and Hidessa seemed relieved, because they were now of the opinion that it was my intention to comply with their wishes and flee the valley alongside my family. My plan, however, if it could be carried out, did not include my leaving the valley. I would not do that. I could not bring myself to do that! In my bed that night, my wives greeted me with extended hands as I lay down, but the only words which were spoken between us that night, were simply and sincerely, "*Necu-ta-say-ha.* I love you." Our general light-hearted mood was solemnly repressed that night, and they both knew that there was indeed, something serious going on. There was no frolic or laughter, nor pleasures of the flesh. Our world was about to be invaded, and I was being forced to defend our valley, our family, and our simple way of life there... all because of another man's greed for gold.

After a very fitful night, and precious little sleep for my wives and me, daylight slowly arrived. The wives prepared tea and a meal, and soon Captain McBride and Hidessa arrived from the small house as the first glimmers of dawn began to arise in the east. After hastily eating, we busied ourselves making arrangements for my family to leave. We prepared the horses, and saw to the task of packing some of the family's clothes and smaller belongings on two of our pack horses. Hidessa and the Captain then attended to the readiness of their own horses. We had barely made the horses ready for travel when I saw Kwīnahā approaching from the west with Lectūschemă and four of his braves. I called to the house for Steechánay to come to the corral hut. I could speak some of the Pawnee language with relative ease now, but the issue which I was about to discuss was so important, that I did not want to lose anything in translation. After welcoming Lectūschemă and introducing him to my guests, I asked Steechánay to repeat everything that I was about to say in the Pawnee language.

"Lectūschemă, you are my brother, and I love you as such. I ask great thing of you now. I ask that you take my family to your village and keep them safe from harm until I come for them. Kwīnahā will come with you to help watch over them. I would only ask this thing of someone who I loved as a brother. Will you do this thing for me?"

"He says, *yes*, he will do this thing, but he wants to know why you ask this of him, John."

"It is because there are evil white men who would come here to hurt my family... men who would even kill them. I must fight them, and defend our home here. I must stay here and kill them, all of them, or there will never be peace for me and my family here." The Captain looked perplexed, and interrupted, "John, are you saying..."

"Captain, I'm sorry, but please wait until I have finished speaking with Lectūschemă, sir."

Captain McBride looked distraught. He was puzzled, and somewhat taken aback to learn that my plans were to remain in the valley.

"Steechánay, please tell Lectūschemă that I cannot fight my enemy and protect my family at the same time. I will depend on him to take my family and protect them until there is no danger here."

Lectūschemă and I finished speaking, and shortly he rode away with my tearful family. Steechánay and Loweja wept openly and looked at me with pitiful eyes as they rode away... as if they were being taken away against their will... and I suppose they were. This could possibly be the last time that I would ever see my family, I thought. Kwīnahā looked back at me with pitiful eyes as well, yet rode away with our family as I had instructed him to do. I watched until they had disappeared into the woods beyond the valley. Then I turned to address Captain McBride and Hidessa.

"Captain McBride, I want to thank you from the bottom of my heart for everything that you have done for me and my family. Hidessa, I am equally as thankful for everything that you have done as well, my friend. At this time, I would like to say goodbye to you both, and wish you Godspeed on your journey."

"Our journey where, John?"

"Your journey home, sir. I have much work to do here before I can prepare myself to meet my enemies."

Captain McBride was mightily frustrated with my determination to stay and fight, taking me by the arm and asking, "Even after all that I have told you about these men; the pure evilness that Flanagan is capable of, you are planning to meet them here, by yourself? Have you lost your mind, son!?"

"I have little choice in the matter, sir. I will not leave my valley. I will not allow a stranger to ransack my home here as they did in Baltimore. I only ask that you go quickly. You can take the same trail that Hidessa told you about and avoid this bastard, Flanagan. Once you are back at the trading post you can board your vessel and be on your way without harm… but you must hurry. If I understand you correctly, they could arrive here at any time after today. If they are determined men, they might possibly arrive here tonight. Now please, be gone with you, so I might attend to my defense."

"Hidessa can go, if he wishes. I am staying here with you, John. I swore an oath to your father that I would watch over your wellbeing, and I take my oaths very serious, my son. I should not have been surprised that you have inherited your father's stubbornness… but it seems as though you have. I will not go! I can be just as stubborn as you, my friend!" Just as quickly, Hidessa spoke, "I will not go either. You have been good to me, John Welch. Would you have me repay your goodness by running away when you need my help?"

"I don't know what to say… to either of you…"

"Then say nothing, John. If you are so foolhardy that you really want to do this, then how would you suggest that we stage a proper defense here?"

"Follow me."

We went to the storage hut and moved all of the rifle

boxes up to the small house, along with all the lead bullets, powder, and percussion caps. The small house where Kwīnahā and November lived offered a much more commanding view of approaching threats, and the windows were at a proper height to allow for shooting. We arranged four rifles at each window so that each of us had the capability of discharging four shots before the rifles needed to be reloaded and primed. Captain McBride had his own revolver, and I equipped Hidessa with my extra revolver. As we busied ourselves making preparations, Hidessa called out to me.

"John! There is someone coming this way on a horse, from the west!"

I looked in the direction which he was pointing and saw that it was Kwīnahā. Why was he not with our family, watching over them as I had instructed? My heart sank as I watched his approach. Had something gone wrong on their trip to the Pawnee village? Has one of my family been hurt, or injured? I quickly stepped outside to greet him as he rode up.

"Kwīnahā! Is something wrong, son?"
"Yes, Father. Something is very wrong!"
"What is it, son?"
"I am a man, Father! I am not a woman or a child! I will stay here and fight with you like a man! I cannot leave you here! My heart will not let me do that! I would rather die here beside you than to leave you here to die alone."

I nearly choked on my words when Kwīnahā told me this, but finally, holding my tears back, I mustered up the courage to say, "I am greatly touched, Kwīnahā... that you would do this thing, but you have a wife and a child now, and you need to watch over them."

"I also have a father, and I will not leave him here to fight without me!"

"Alright, my son. I understand. Put your horse in the corral with the others and help us get all of these rifles loaded and primed. Draw some extra water from the creek and bring it into the house."

I should have known that sending Kwīnahā with the women and children would cause him torment and humiliation. I should have given the matter more thought before mandating that he leave with the women and children. That he would ride back to me, as he did, and demand to stay at my side only served to reaffirm the fact that he truly was a man now... and he truly did love his father. I had to muster all of my strength in order to hide my emotions and keep my mind on the task at hand. My heart was swollen with the pride, and enriched by the love that I felt for my son.

Now, there were four of us who were poised to receive our enemies, with four rifles each and three revolvers between us. I knew that Kwīnahā was an incredibly accurate shooter, but I was unsure of Captain McBride or Hidessa. The table in the center of the house was cleared and set up to be a station for reloading our weapons. Our powder, bullets, and percussion caps were neatly arranged on top. In a little over two hours, we had made all of our preparations and were ready to confront an unknown number of assailants – assailants who would also have guns. Perhaps there would just be six of them to deal with. But there was also a possibility that Flanagan had hired additional help at the French outpost. We did not know, and all that we could do at this particular point in time was to sit and wait. We nervously asked questions between ourselves as we waited.

"Suppose they circle us before they come in? We need to open the portal at the rear of the house, and post someone there to be on watch," I said.

"What if they go to the main house and burn it, Father?"

"They will have to cross in the open meadow, and will be easily seen from the west portal, where you are, Kwīnahā. Just take your time and shoot as though you were shooting a wapiti or a deer, son. Hidessa, have you ever shot a rifle before?"

"I have seen it done. I think I know what to do."

"Captain McBride, have you been in battle before, sir?"

"I served under Andrew Jackson during the Battle of New Orleans in 1814. I was about Kwīnahā's age at the time. I saw many men die, and sent many an Englishmen to their maker. I took many lives during those two years that I served... yes, John... I have been in battle before. Nowadays, I prefer to avoid fighting and killing when possible, but it would seem that I am about to engage the enemy once more. It's a pity, though... Flanagan himself is an Irishman. Right now, I rather wish that he was French, instead."

We waited for hours and hours until darkness came to the valley. We took turns watching at night while the others slept, and still there was no sign of our aggressors. Coyotes, wolves, and assorted other animals of the night were all that was seen or heard. The next day came and went with the same result. Still, no one came. Captain McBride cited the possibility that Flanagan and his men could have encountered an unforeseen delay, and it could perhaps be a week or more before they would arrive at the valley. But the Captain had no doubt in his mind that they would eventually arrive in force. We remained ever so alert.

Our nervousness and our apprehension did not subside... it only rose commensurately as each hour and each day passed. The third day appeared as though it was going to begin and end the same as the others, until shortly after mid-morning. Captain McBride was watching out of the front portal, and Kwīnahā was watching out of the rear, when the Captain said, "John! Come here and look at this. I think they are coming! I think that is them, over there. Look closely through the trees down there to the east! I can see something moving in the trees."

I looked through the window and soon spotted movement in the deep woods. First, I only saw one figure approaching, then two, then ten, and soon there was more than I could count. My heart sank at the prospects that Flanagan had brought an army of men with him. With his wealth, there was no end to the numbers of evil mercenaries he could employ. I had the sickening feeling that their sheer numbers would be the factor which would seal our fate, and I hated the fact that Kwīnahā would be there to die with us. But as the figures in the woods began to emerge from the trees, I could clearly see that they were all Indians. I saw no white people among them. Had Flanagan solicited the help of mercenary Indians, perhaps the Crow, to do his dirty work? Was he, himself, hiding in the woods nearby? We could never stage a proper defense against this many Indians. Had Flanagan outsmarted me? We were doomed if he had, but we would surely shoot as many of them as we could before we died! We readied our weapons as they drew closer. I felt a strange measure of comfort in knowing that my family was safe at the Pawnee village, and that Lectūschemă would watch over them, should I be killed.

"Do not shoot until they are very close to the house. Aim carefully at the center of their chest. Once you have shot, don't wait until the smoke clears to see if your shot was good, quickly pick up a fresh gun and take careful aim on another enemy... Do not rush any of your shots. Make them all count! God bless you!"

The army of Indians came closer and closer. When it appeared that they had all come out of the woods, I could see that there were thirty or more of them. One-by-one, I could hear Kwīnahā and my friends behind me cocking the hammers of their rifles in readiness to shoot. As the Indians drew closer, they looked more and more like Pawnee Indians to me. Why would Pawnee Indians be approaching from the direction of the main trail, from the east? And why were their faces painted with the paint of war? Had Flanagan somehow managed to conspire with the Pawnee? Had my friends turned against me? Were these Pawnee warriors from a different village than my friends? The large party of warriors stopped, more than a hundred yards from the house, and a lone figure among them rode slowly forward toward the house, to offer us an ultimatum I assumed. Initially, I thought I would go ahead and shoot this first fellow when he drew close enough... that it would be one less Indian that we would have to deal with. Then, I decided to wait. I did not want to rush in to a fight with my friends, the Pawnee. They had always treated me with respect. If they have come here to kill me at the behest of this evil man, Flanagan, there must be a reason they have turned on me, and I would rather see if I can negotiate with them than to jump to conclusions and start shooting.

"Do not shoot at these people! They are Pawnee, and I'm going to go out and see what they want. Do not shoot at them! They have been good to me in the past! This may be some kind of misunderstanding that I can correct by talking with them. Remember, don't shoot unless I say so!"

I tucked my revolver behind my belt at the base of my back, and slowly opened the door. I took slow and careful paces toward the lone Indian who sat atop his horse, and was well aware of the fact that I was now within range for them to shoot me. I could see that nearly half of them were armed with long rifles, but they were not raised and pointed at me. As I drew closer yet to their apparent leader, I was stunned to see that it was none other than my old friend, Lectūschemă. I had not recognized him or his horse as they were dressed in their full war paint. Lectūschemă's attire was different as well. He wore his war bonnet upon his head and had painted streaks of red and black about the sides of his face. I had never seen him or his horse appear as terrifying. In his Pawnee tongue, he spoke down to me from his saddle, proudly saying, "Hello, my brother. *Chin-conte-say.*"

His cheerful greeting gave me a moment of relief, as I answered, "Hello, Lectūschemă. *Chin-conte-say.* Why are you here, my brother? You must take your people and leave quickly, before any of you or your people are harmed by my enemies! They may be here at any time, and they are sure to have many guns with them when they come!"

"I bring you gift, John Welch." With that, he handed me a bloody buckskin bag, and said, "It is safe to come and bring your family back to your home."

"*Safe*? I don't understand." I struggled to comprehend why he was saying such things, for I did not have the benefit of an interpreter this time. Even so, I understood his words quite well, but they failed to make sense to me. How could Lectūschemă possibly consider my circumstances to be safe here? I opened the rawhide bag enough to look inside and found it filled with bloody scalps... probably ten or twelve altogether, undoubtedly taken from white men, and undoubtedly taken very recently, as the blood was still wet and oozing from the bottom of the bag. Lectūschemă and his braves had obviously taken it upon themselves to intercept and eliminate my antagonists well before they entered my valley. The battle must have happened at a great distance from my home, for we never heard as much as a single gunshot.

I had been too proud to ask Lectūschemă for his help, other than providing for the temporary safety of my family, and would never have asked my brother or his people to put themselves at risk on my behalf. But Lectūschemă had taken our vows of '*brothership*' very serious, and had somehow felt obligated to come to my rescue. He also knew that his sister, Steechánay was happy in our marriage, and she and her children were loved and well cared for here with me. Perhaps he had done so because of the strong friendship we shared. Perhaps he had done so for the sake of his sister, Steechánay, and did not wish to see her widowed again. I was deeply touched. I looked up at him and asked, "Why would you do this thing for me, Lectūschemă?"

"As you told me, we are brothers. If someone comes to harm you, they come to harm me. You are a good man, John Welch, but you are not a good warrior. You make very foolish plan here... like plan a stupid woman would make. A wise man does not wait for his enemy to come to him... he goes to his enemy, and he finds his enemy, and he kills his enemy, so that when he goes home, he can sleep well with his family. Please come and get your family, John Welch. My ears grow tired of their weeping."

"I will, my brother. I will. Tell me, Lectūschemă, were any of your braves hurt in battle?"

"I did not go there to do battle with these men. I went there to kill them, and that is what I did. No, none of my braves were killed. Please send Kwīnahā with me to get your family so that their crying will stop. They have wept so much that my wives now cry with them and my lodge is not a happy place."

With that, Lectūschemă and close to forty of his braves rode off westward toward their village, holding their newly obtained rifles high above their heads and shouting the accolades of victory. Kwīnahā was right behind them, hurrying to bring our family back home. Captain McBride and Hidessa came out to join me, and Captain McBride looked curiously at the bloody bag which I was holding, but said nothing at first. He had heard everything which had been said, but he did not understand the Pawnee language. I told him and Hidessa what Lectūschemă and his people had done, and we all breathed a collective sigh of relief... except for Captain McBride. He remained somewhat reserved and even skeptical.

"Are you not relieved that our enemies have been destroyed, Captain?" I asked.

"I am assuming that those are the scalps of our enemies which you are holding in that bag? Am I correct in assuming so, John?"

"Yes, Captain, this bag does indeed contain the scalps of our enemies."

"I do not care to look into the bag, John, but would you

please do so, and tell me if one of the scalps is from a man with very long and curly red hair? Very long, curly red hair." I opened the bag at his beckoning and looked through the mess of bloody scalps.

"Yes, Captain, one of the scalps is from a man with very long and curly red hair. How did you know?"

"Then, I can breathe a sigh of relief along with you, for Flanagan himself was a man with curly, long, red hair! His hair came to his shoulders."

Hidessa looked at me and asked, "What are you going to do with all of the scalps, John?"

"I don't know. Burn them, perhaps. Why do you ask?"

"If you are going to burn them, may I have them?"

"Certainly. I have no use for them. What will you do with them, Hidessa?"

"The French pay money for scalps. I will sell them to the French."

My friend in Baltimore, Marcus Attenborough, had told me that Europeans were buying human scalps as curiosity pieces to be displayed in their homes. That the Europeans would do something like this came as no surprise to me. I gave the bloody bag of scalps to Hidessa, for him to dispose of any way he saw fit, and wiped the blood from my hands on the dew of the grass at my feet. I felt that I would never be able to repay the debt which I now owed to Lectūschemă. However, if such an occasion were to arise, I would gladly run to his aid. Lectūschemă was a much better war strategist than I could ever hope to be. He was correct; those who wait patiently for their enemy to come to them, wait patiently for their own doom. I should have known as much and acted accordingly. Either way, Lectūschemă and his braves had saved the lives of me, my son, and my two dear friends.

We discharged and cleaned all of the weapons and returned them to the rifle boxes in the storage hut. One box of four rifles was set aside, so that I could personally present them to Lectūschemă as a gesture of my gratitude. Once we had finished, we sat on the porch and had pleasant conversation in the warm afternoon sunshine while we awaited the return of my family. The Captain looked at me and asked, "Do you ever find yourself longing for the conveniences of living in a city, John?"

"The conveniences of the city would command a much higher price than I or my family would be willing to pay. Besides, what are the conveniences of living in the city, really? Hypocrisy? Hatred? Greed? The only convenience of the city that I find myself missing sometimes is the library. Do you need for me to explain why I feel that way, Captain?"

"No, John. There is no explanation necessary. I know precisely why you feel as you do. There is wisdom in your words, and I understand perfectly, my son. I have never told you this, John, but your father would have been mighty proud of you if he could see the way that you have chosen to live your life... and he would have been mighty pleased that you did not stay in Baltimore to marry Elizabeth Cunningham."

"Elizabeth? You knew about my betrothal to Elizabeth Cunningham also? I hope that you will someday tell me how it is that you seem to know so much about me, Captain."

"Perhaps someday I will, John. I will tell you this much, however, in order to bring you up to date on a few things. Mr. Cunningham married a woman half his age, and died within six months thereafter. On the day he died, he died in his bed in the company of a mistress while his wife was away. His young widow inherited all of his wealth. Elizabeth married a man from Cambridge, a schoolteacher I believe, and now lives a modest life there with him. I am told they have a child now... and another on the way..."

"Your home is in St. Louis, Captain. How could you possibly know all of this which has taken place all the way back in Baltimore? How?"

"I have my sources... sources which I am compelled by

oath to keep to myself. I will ask you this, though; are you familiar with an organization known as the *Ancient Free And Accepted Masons*?"

"Of course I am… My father was a… wait a minute! Are you saying that…"

"I've told you all that I am at liberty to say. Perhaps someday I will tell you everything. For now, I must simply ask that you abolish your curiosity and trust me, John."

"I will always trust you, Captain. I swear it."

Kwīnahā returned before dark with our family. Captain McBride and Hidessa were both amazed and amused by our joyous greeting. Neither of them had ever seen an entire family wallowing on the ground, tickling and kissing as we were. Our laughter and our joy were infectious, and soon Hidessa and the Captain were both laughing loudly as well. I had never seen Hidessa laugh that hard before… I don't even remember even seeing him smile before. During much jubilance, at a late dinner that night, I overheard Hidessa telling Captain McBride, "I have never tickled my wives. Maybe that is why they never laugh. When I go back to my lodge I think I will tickle all of them and see what happens."

"Well I certainly hope it works as well for you as it seems to work here for John and his family. You deserve all the happiness you could find, Hidessa."

"When we get back to my village will you stay with me at my lodge to rest before you leave for Fort Saint Joseph?"

"I would be greatly honored to spend a night at your lodge, Hidessa. I enjoy the conversations that we have, and I enjoy both your company and your friendship."

"Do you know what *ohgā-sá-ho* is, Captain?"

"No, Hidessa. I don't believe that I've ever heard of that before. What is it, pray tell?"

"I will get one of my wives to show you what it is when we get back to my lodge, Captain. She can show you better than I can explain…"

"That would be fine, my friend. I shall be looking forward to it."

Hidessa visited me again that same year just as the fall leaves were beginning to fall, and well before winter's arrival. He told me that the Frenchman, François Brěaux had been murdered by Arikara warriors, along with three other Frenchmen, and that the operation of the trading post had been taken over by another Frenchman who had thus far proven himself to be an honest and forthright man. I supposed that the Arikara had tired of being cheated by François Brěaux. Hidessa told me that when he and the Captain had returned to his village, that Captain McBride did spend a night at his lodge, in fact, he spent nine days and nights at his lodge instead of just one, as he had planned. I did not query him for any unnecessary details regarding the Captain's extended stay, but imagined that the good Captain, as a lifetime bachelor, had indeed learned the meaning of the word, *ohgā-sá-ho*. Hidessa did volunteer to tell me that all three of his wives had wept openly when the good Captain finally did depart, and that on his departure, the Captain vowed to return soon. This came as a great bewilderment to Hidessa, because he said that his wives never wept when he left to go somewhere. Hidessa also told me that he had discovered that his wives did not like to be tickled. He said that tickling them only made them angrier and much more difficult to live with. Even though the journey from his village to my valley took more than three weeks, he visited me once or twice a year after that, and I always enjoyed his friendship and his company.

We began to see more travelers as they passed near our valley, not in great numbers at first, but generally three or four small families or groups a year. In conversation, I would usually ask them for information concerning what was going on back in the United States. Generally, any news which I received was bad in nature, and only left me saddened to hear it. Eventually, I ceased asking for information. My world was here in the valley, with my family now, and it was a happy and contented world. Hearing the latest discouraging words from civilization distracted me momentarily from my happiness here, so I stopped listening to this distressing dribble.

A Valley Rendezvous

In the late summer that same year, my Pawnee friends visited again for another social event. Word of these social events and trading sessions must have spread like wildfire through the mountains. There were six white trappers and their wives who came to visit us that summer. They brought with them many fine hides and pelts and an assortment of small contrivances for trading. I was particularly fond of the woolen items of clothing which were brought there, and other woolen items such as blankets and coats. One of the wives there was a white woman, about the same age as Loweja. Loweja and Steechánay seemed fascinated as they talked with this woman and looked closely and curiously at her bright golden hair. Loweja had seen many white women in Fort Saint Joseph, but I don't think she had ever looked upon one with golden hair. She was undoubtedly the first white woman whom Steechánay had ever seen, and they were both in sheer awe of the woman's golden hair. The white woman was reluctant to speak much with them at first, but shortly after being exposed to Loweja and Steechánay's friendly nature, and discovering that my wives spoke some English, the white woman couldn't seem to stop talking. The three of them talked continuously for over an hour. The Lord only knows what they had found to talk about for over an hour, but there was a good deal of laughter involved in whatever they were saying between themselves.

There must have been close to seventy-five people camped in our valley for the five days that the festivities lasted. Aside from two or three incidents of harmless drunkenness, there had been no discord among my visitors, and all was in peace and harmony. The Pawnee Indians did not partake of spirits. It was strictly forbidden for them to drink alcohol spirits of any kind. Drunkenness on the part of a Pawnee could have commanded a stiff penalty, and under certain circumstances, tribal censure or death. If a Pawnee was discovered to have brought spirits into his village, he would be put to death with little or no compunction. Pawnee visitors to our trade gatherings never indulged in spiritous drink. In fact, they shied away from any location within the gathering where spirits were being consumed. Shooting matches were a common event at these gatherings, and took place in the far northwest corner of the valley. I would not permit the discharge of weapons in the general area of the trading for the sake of everyone's safety. My rules of conduct were generally well observed. Most of the attendees were very eager to trade, and even more eager to have friendly conversation. In the solitude of the mountains, one could often find themselves lusting for human companionship and the simple pleasure of having someone to talk to. I enjoyed the festivities, yet the only meaningful companionship that I yearned for was that which my family already provided me.

A missionary from Fort Jefferson also attended the event quite frequently. He was accompanied by his wife, who was white, and their three children. He was a good man at heart, and a good Minister of the Gospel. My wives and I always attended his morning sermons and enjoyed hearing his spiritual messages. Out of respect, I suppose, he never condemned me for having two wives, and was always courteous to the extreme whenever he spoke to me. He and his family had taken more than one meal at our home with us, and he was good company in addition to being a good man of God. There were always several of the Pawnee people in attendance of his sermons there in the valley, and Steechánay often translated his messages for the Pawnee attendees who did not understand the English language. The good pastor had asked me to use my influence to convince Lectūschemă to give him permission to enter the Pawnee village for the purpose of establishing a church there. I offered him the use of my valley if he wished to establish a church, but would not attempt to influence Lectūschemă into permitting white encroachment. When I had refused to do that, the pastor had packed his horses and left very early one morning without so much as a farewell. I was regretful that he had left, but I was determined to live in peace with the Indians and not interfere with their way of life. I wished that he had chosen to establish his church in my valley, or somewhere near the village, rather than inside the village. If that had been the case, I would have been a regular attendee and a generous benefactor as well. Many of the Pawnee Indians were Christians already, and had been for several years. They often came to me with spiritual questions and I would use my Bible to try to answer their questions to the best of my ability. I would continue to serve in that capacity as I felt called upon, but I would not attempt to endorse any white visitors to Lectūschemă's village. That I could serve in some meager capacity to answer their spiritual questions pleased me greatly, and I never attempted to establish myself as some type of ecclesiastical leader. I was simply a consultant, and offered my opinions both from my heart and my interpretation of the Holy Scripture. I had come to realize that since I had lived in the wilderness among the Indians, that I was not a Catholic by faith, as I had always thought myself to be. Nor was I a necessarily a Protestant. By my faith in God, I had come to recognize myself as a believer and follower of God's word. My faith was entirely too strong and devout to need the support of a denominational affiliation as recognized by the standards of civilized humanity. The simple truth of the matter, was that my faith in God had been influenced and inspired greatly by Loweja and Steechánay, and their daily prayers.

After the first day of the trading event in our valley, I lay in bed with my wives that night, and we spoke about the sights we had seen during the day. It was the most exciting time of the year for them, even with all of the confusion that fell upon our valley. In bed with my wives, after the first day of the event, Loweja asked, "Can we buy new cooking pot and water pail from the man with many pots?"

"As long as you and Steechánay promise to keep cooking good food, I will gladly buy you a new pot and water pail tomorrow. I want to buy a new axe and some chickens for us as well."

"Did you see man with all of the buffalo hides?"

"*Tonka-peaux*? Yes, I saw all of his hides. He had some good ones, but we don't need any just yet. We still have three packed away in the storage shed."

"Did you see white woman with yellow hair?"

"Yes, I saw her. Her husband is from the east, very near to where I used to live, when I lived in Baltimore... He's from a place called, Philadelphia, if I remember right."

"Do you think woman with yellow hair is pretty, John?"

"Who?"

"The woman with the yellow hair?"

"Oh! Her! Yes, I think she is very pretty, indeed." Being quite familiar with the way that Steechánay and Loweja's minds worked, I knew what was coming next, and waited patiently for the inevitable question. After a long silence, Steechánay finally asked,

"Do you think she is more pretty than Loweja and me?"

I thought that it was time for me to have a little fun with my wives, so I waited for a while, and then answered, "Well, yes, as a matter of fact, I do. I talked with her husband about selling her to me, and he said that he would gladly sell her to me tomorrow... so we will need a bigger bed here... or maybe I could just take her up to the loft and sleep with her up there. That way, there will be plenty of room in this bed for you and Loweja. I think I can still climb a ladder very quickly at night... Kwīnahā taught me how to do it. I'm sure you two would not mind sleeping here by yourself while I'm up in the loft tickling her. You and Loweja would not mind if I did that, would you?"

Steechánay made a fist and struck me firmly and painfully on my right arm. Then they both started to pummel me with their fists. Loweja gave me a pretty good lick on my other arm as Steechánay drew back to punch me again on my right arm. I attempted to block her punch, but in the darkness, I was only successful in diverting it, and it caught me squarely in the nose. Stars filled my eyes, as I tried to regain my senses. My nose immediately started to bleed profusely, depositing a great deal of blood about the area of my chest before I could tilt my head backward and slow the flow of blood. Loweja ran to the table to light the lamp and get a damp cloth and Steechánay just sat there in horrified disbelief that she had done such a thing. Over and over again, she wailed, "I am sorry, John! Please forgive me! I did not mean to do that! I am so sorry! Please forgive me, John!"

"Please do not make tears over this, Steechánay! I got exactly what I deserved! I should not have made a joke about a thing such as that," I said, as I stuffed small strips of cloth into my nostrils and Loweja washed blood from my face and chest. When I had boxed while I was in college in Washington, I had successfully won 27 matches as well as a university championship, and none of my opponents had ever been successful in causing my nose to bleed. I could only surmise that Steechánay was a much better boxer than any of my opponents! I loved to tease and joke with my wives, just as they loved to tease and joke with me. Playful joking brought a lot of joy into our lives. But I learned a painful lesson that night; joking with them about bringing another woman into the house was not a laughing matter for either of them, and with the painful bruises that adorned my arms the next morning, I wasn't doing much laughing over the matter either. It took several minutes that night for me to convince them that I was only joking, and several more minutes for my nose to stop bleeding. Steechánay summed up their feelings best, once she stopped sobbing, when she made a simple statement that would become the guiding light in all of my future jokes with them.

"Joke not funny when they hurt our hearts bad, John."

"What you say is true, Steechánay. I am very sorry. I truly am. I will not do that again. That was cruel of me to joke about something like that. And just so that you and Loweja will know how I really feel... there are no other women on this earth that are prettier than Steechánay and Loweja! None! Anywhere! Does everyone understand that?" I was truthful when I told them that they were the most beautiful women in the world, because I honestly felt that way.

On the second day of the event, I was speaking to two Pawnee Indians about locations where serviceberries could be harvested in great abundance in the fall. As they told me about a particular location, they also warned me of the great bears that came there to eat berries in the early fall. In the very middle of our conversation, Loweja impolitely interrupted by grabbing me by the arm and pulling me away. I apologized to the two Pawnee men and told them I would be back shortly. Loweja was obviously very excited about something and wanted to show me the object of her excitement as she pulled me through the crowd of people. When she stopped and pointed, I looked ahead and saw the familiar faces of Mr. and Mrs. Earl Parker! I was held dumbfound! It had been several years since we had shared a camp together! I could not even recall how many years, but certainly it had been more than three or four! They looked as though they had not changed much at all! In fact, it looked as though they were still wearing the same clothes which they had worn years earlier! We were equally happy to see one another again. There was far too much confusion for us to talk in peace there amongst all of the festivities and trading, so we invited them to our house that night for a quiet meal. From the porch of our house that evening, we could see the glow of more than thirty or forty campfires in the valley below as we walked into the house to talk and eat our meal. Once we had finished our dinner, and the children had gone to their room, Kwīnahā and November walked back to their house with their baby, and my wives and I sat down to have pleasant conversation with the Parkers. Mr. Parker was the first to speak, when he asked, "Did you ever find any beaver in that area you was goin to, John?"

"No, sir! You were right all the time! I never saw one single beaver up there... not a one."

"Ya can't say I didn't warn ya."

"Did you ever take on a second wife, Earl?"

"Yessir! *Eètnă-ĕsh* and me picked out a real dandy of a wife last year, her name is *Lēmăssē*. She's fixing to have a baby in another month or so, so she couldn't come along with us, but she's a fine woman. She loves Eètnă-ĕsh and me both, and she's gonna make a fine mother, too!"

"I'm very happy for you and Eètnă-ĕsh, Earl, and Lēmăssē, too!"

Mrs. Parker had been studying the faces of my wives and me for some time, and could not resist the opportunity to comment.

"I am pleased to see that you have not yet burst from holding your wind inside of you, John Welch." This statement had put an immediate look of bafflement on the faces of my wives. They had no idea what Mrs. Parker was talking about, but I surely did. I knew exactly what she was referring to.

"No, Eètnă-ĕsh, I haven't... but I could have easily burst from my own arrogance and stupidity several times. I have learned much about the ways of the Indian, and I have learned much about the wisdom which was in the words you spoke to me when we met on the trail that year. You may not know it, but your words in that camp that evening helped me through a very difficult time in my life. I thank you for sharing your wisdom with me. You are a very wise and good woman, Eètnă-ĕsh, and we are very happy to see you and Earl again."

"What has happened to your nose? It is very red and bruised on the side, and even swollen."

"I just had a little accident here at home, and it will mend quickly, Mrs. Parker." Steechánay blushed, and lowered her head in shame.

"I see that you have children now, John Welch. There must not have been anything wrong with your *pēneă* after all, and you must have finally learned how to be a husband for Loweja." Mrs. Parker quipped.

"Yes, Eètnă-ěsh, I finally learned. I was very slow in learning, but I learned."

Loweja immediately spoke up with unsolicited candor, saying, "It just took him long, long time, till he see me fishing naked... and when he see me fishing naked, then he soon get naked too and we lay on *tonka-peaux* and....."

"**Loweja! Please say no more!** Please stop laughing, Steechánay! Both of you stop laughing! Mrs. Parker, please don't laugh along with them, it only encourages them to be even naughtier! I'm sorry, Mrs. Parker... but my wives can become a bit unruly at times. I think it is because I never beat them... I only kiss them and tickle them! But if they continue to misbehave, **maybe I will stop showing them *interest*!**" With my loud words, Steechánay and Loweja stifled their laughter into mere muffled giggles.

"It is good for my heart to see you all laughing like this! It makes me want to laugh, too! I cannot help it! The three of you seem to be very happy here with your children, and it brings happiness to my heart to see it with my own eyes."

"We are very happy here, Mrs. Parker. John is best husband in whole earth for Loweja and me. We have much love here, and we have much fun, too!" Steechánay said.

"Yes," Loweja added, "We have very much love here! John is reason we are happy, too."

Mrs. Parker cleared her throat, and said, "Let me tell you all something about love... Love is like a campfire. You can see it from a great distance, but you cannot feel its warmth until you get close to it. The closer you get to it, the more you can feel it. Here, inside of your house, I can see it with my eyes, but I can also feel the warmth that is here, too, and I know that there is much love here."

"I did not know that you were such a fine philosopher, Eètnă-ĕsh." I said, after being both inspired and surprised by the wisdom in the analogy I had just heard from Mrs. Parker.

"I do not know that word, '*fill-a-s-oper*,' John, and I do not think I could speak it with my tongue. What does it mean?"

"It means that you have the supreme wisdom of a great *Shaman*, a foreseer, and as I have told you before, I believe your words are always very true."

Turning her head toward Loweja, Mrs. Parker said, "You have learned to speak English well, Loweja."

"Thank you, Eètnă-ĕsh. John teach me, and Steechánay teach me, but you were the first to teach me."

Mrs. Parker continued to study me intently, almost to the point of making me feel uncomfortable. She stared deeply into my eyes, and asked, "And who is this strange man who sits here before me now?"

"I don't understand what you are getting at, Mrs. Parker."

"This man I am looking at is not the same man that Earl and me shared a camp with just a few years ago. This man is not foolish man, and this man is not afraid of his wives. This man is different man."

"I *am* a different man, Mrs. Parker, much different. I wouldn't even recognize the man that I used to be if he were to walk in the door right now. I am at peace with who I am now. Everything that I love in this life is right here with me in this valley… my wonderful wives… my children. There is nothing else that I long for in life… nothing!"

"May I ask you a question, John?"

"Yes, please do."

"You came from many miles away to be here in this place, all the way from where there are big cities of people. What made you come here, and how did you meet your second beautiful wife, Steechánay?"

And so, for the next half-hour or more, I started at the beginning, and told the story of how I had come to be where I was today. I omitted very little, and only excluded mention of the gold which I had found. I told them about the manuscripts which Father had entrusted me with, and how they had led me to a valley somewhere north of there, and when I was returning home, how Loweja and I had accidently found Steechánay, and the place which had once been my father's home. I told the Parkers that once Loweja and I had lived with Steechánay for a short time, the three of us had fallen deeply in love. I told them that the biggest question in my mind, was why my father's maps had not guided me directly to Steechánay and this beautiful valley. Mrs. Parker smiled, and replied, "I think I know why your father did not direct you all of the way here to Steechánay, John."

"Really, Eètnă-ĕsh? What do you think his reasons were?"

"It is because a man prizes that which he finds for himself, much more than that which has been given to him. I think that your father wanted you to prize your precious family and the valley here above all things. I think that your father led you just close enough so that you could find these things for yourself. That is what I think."

"As I said earlier, you truly are a wise and wonderful woman, Eètnă-ĕsh. I think you have possibly answered my biggest question for me. I am grateful to you, and I am truly amazed at what you just said!"

"May I ask you another question, John?"

"Yes, Mrs. Parker?"

"How old are you now, John?"

"Me? How old am I? Well, let's see, I am….."

"Yes John?"

"Well, let me see, now….. Wait just a moment, please. I am…… I was twenty-three years old when I left Baltimore…

so that would make me….. No, wait just a moment, I was twenty-two years old when I left Baltimore, I think…"

Mrs. Parker smiled broadly at me and chuckled softly as she awaited my reply.

"Mrs. Parker, It shames me to say, but I am not really sure how old I am in years. No one has asked me how old I was since before I left Baltimore. I would have to take the time to think about it for a moment… I'm sure I could eventually figure it out… but… I'm kind of puzzled right now, and I am having much difficulty in answering your question."

"It seems ridiculous to me that a person would not know how old they are, in years, John. I cannot imagine a person going through life, not knowing how old they are!"

"You are using my very own foolish words against me, are you not, Mrs. Parker?"

"Yes… But it doesn't really matter anyway. I already know how old you are, John. And I also know how old Loweja and Steechánay are, too."

"Really, Mrs. Parker? How old are we then?"

"You… Loweja... Steechánay… and your wonderful family here… You are all young, John Welch!"

Made in the USA
Charleston, SC
20 April 2016